PITTWATER

First published in paperback in 2024 by Sixth Element Publishing.
Previously published in 2022 by Austin Macauley Publishers.

Sixth Element Publishing
Arthur Robinson House
13-14 The Green
Billingham
Stockton on Tees
TS23 1EU
www.6epublishing.net

ISBN 978-1-914170-55-3

British Library Cataloguing in Publication Data.
A catalogue record for this book is available from the British Library.

Printed in Great Britain.

PITTWATER

KEVIN E M CLARK

Dedicated to
my late parents
Doreen and Harold
God bless

My wife Beverley Clark
and Keith Campbell
Love forever

Eleri Denham
*Thanks for her writing patience
and helping me through The Dark Times*

Thanks to
Gillie Hatton and Jonathan Barder
Editing and printing

ABOUT KEVIN E M CLARK

Originally from Middlesbrough, Kevin E M Clark spent many years in London and travelling the world, before returning to North Yorkshire, where he now lives with his wife.

At fourteen years old, Kevin left school without a formal education, struggling with dyslexia and learning difficulties. He went on to have a career as an electrician and control engineer, never having any interest in writing until, at a low point in his life, creative writing was recommended to him as a form of therapy.

He is the Executive Producer of the short film 'As Time Goes By' (2018). He is now writing two more novels: SEVEN, an epic story that follows the lives of seven young Americans as they navigate the cultural turmoil of the 1960s, and also, a horror story that is a new twist on a famous and legendary cult figure. He also writes song lyrics for recorded musicians and short stories for TV dramas.

PROLOGUE

Robert was wide awake. His parents had sent him to bed hours ago, but their voices, too muffled to be heard clearly except for the acidic tone, still wafted through the house's vents like poisonous vapour.

Robert glanced across the room to the bed against the opposite wall. His sister Suzie lay there, fast asleep. At least she didn't have to hear any of this.

Her arms cradled Wally, a stuffed toy koala. Wally had been a present for her fourth birthday. As his parents continued to argue, their voices growing more vicious with each passing minute, Robert let his mind drift back to that sun-drenched day: the four of them – Robert, Suzie, their mother and father – were at the Rocks Market on Sydney Harbour. A passerby had knocked into Suzie and she'd fallen to the ground, scraping her knee on the cobblestones. Their parents had pulled her aside and attempted to soothe her crying, but tears continued to drip down her face. While their parents tried to console her, Robert had slipped away to a nearby market stall.

Holding the $20 bill his parents had given him that morning, Robert had looked over a small army of fuzzy, round-eyed creatures: seals, pandas, elephants. They'd been at the Taronga Zoo that morning and Robert recalled how Suzie's face lit up with delight as koalas nibbled leaves from the branch in her outstretched hand. He spotted a koala among the plushie ranks, pointed to it, and handed over his $20. He returned to his family, ignoring his mother's scowl and her mutter of "She already has a mother, you know," and handed the toy over to Suzie.

Her sniffles stopped instantly, and her round face broke into a wide smile. It had made Robert so happy, seeing her smile return. He felt joy shine off her like light from a beacon.

She grabbed the toy and buried her face in its soft fur. "Wally," she dubbed it, stroking the toy's ears. Wally had hardly left her side ever since.

Robert was brought back to the present by the distant sound of glass shattering. He heard his mother's voice sharply berating his father in response. Intermittently, Robert caught fragments of their argument when their voices climbed to an audible pitch. He discerned the name Wayne Brewster, whom he knew from a school project was the governor of Sydney. He heard words like contracts, and inquiry, and scandal. His father's voice built to a scream as he said, "If this ever gets out, we will lose everything."

"And what if you don't do it?" his mother snapped. They had moved and now, Robert could tell, they stood near the staircase that led to the children's room. "How exactly do you plan to continue paying for our yacht? My God, have you thought about what it would do to me if we had to end our membership at the yacht club? I couldn't face our neighbours ever again. And what about our son's boarding school? Do you expect me to raise him here, by myself?"

Robert's father pleaded, "Janet, please, you're not being rational…"

"And you are being a coward." The coldness in his mother's voice made Robert instinctively press into the blankets. She wasn't even speaking to him and yet it still felt as if her words could pierce him. "There is no proof. They've got nothing but hearsay. So get it together, David. For God's sake. You're embarrassing yourself."

His father answered, much more quietly, and Robert caught only the words "married you." A door slammed. Another glass broke… this one hurled against a wall, by the sound of it.

Robert pulled a pillow over his head, closed his eyes, and willed himself to fall asleep.

•

Robert woke the next morning and the first thought through his brain immediately eclipsed all memory of the previous night: today was his twelfth birthday.

He raced downstairs. Suzie was already at the breakfast table, along with their father.

"Hey, kid," his father said, reaching across the table to ruffle Robert's hair. His father, David, was bespectacled and had a widow's peak that made him look professorial, distinguished beyond his thirty-something years. The look suited him. He was an up-and-coming architect who spent weekdays in the city and only came home on the weekends. "Happy birthday."

"Happy birthday, Robbie!" Suzie said, and let go of Wally (who was joining them for breakfast) long enough to give him a fierce hug. Robert kissed the top of her head.

He glanced around, but his mother was nowhere to be seen. His father was already reading the paper. Suzie looked up at Robert and asked hopefully, "Breakfast?"

A few minutes later, Robert was setting down two plates of pancakes on the table, one for himself and one for his sister. As they started to eat, Suzie chattered happily about their plans for the day; their father had told them they would take the yacht out to a secluded cove on the bay. They'd go fishing, have a picnic on the beach. It struck Robert as the design for a perfect day.

Then their mother appeared, arranging herself in the one remaining chair at the breakfast table. Janet was a severe woman, beautiful in a statuesque, near-lifeless way. Suzie, with her warmth and her bubbly laughter, had inherited her blonde curls from Janet but nothing else.

"Nice of you to finally join us," Janet simpered to Robert.

The mood of the room frosted over. Robert asked, "Are you still coming with us today?"

"Oh, you won't miss me if I stay home, will you?" she said. "I'm sure you'll all have a fine time without me."

Robert dropped his eyes to his plate, trying to hide his disappointment. "You promised," he whispered.

"What was that?" she said sharply.

Robert was startled by his father's hand on his shoulder. "That's all right, son," his father said. "We'll still go. The three of us."

•

Robert walked toward the dock behind the house, his arms laden with supplies. Suzie trotted beside him, a tiny life jacket dragging from one hand and Wally held more carefully in the other. Their father had sent them down to load up the yacht, promising that he'd join them in a minute. Robert's pace slowed as the sound of raised voices floated over to them from the house. It was like a nightmare that had followed him into the daylight.

"Come on, Suze," he said, doing his best to shepherd her out of earshot.

Moments later, their father appeared at the back door. He joined them at the dock and made an effort at a breezy smile. "Everything ready to go?"

Robert looked up at him. "She didn't change her mind?" he asked quietly.

"I'm afraid not, kid," his father answered. "She, ah... she has some things to take care of here at the house."

Robert was silent for some time. "But she promised."

"I know she did, Rob. But when we get back..."

"I hate her," Robert said. "She never keeps her promises. I *hate her!*"

Suzie looked between Robert and their father with wide, uncertain eyes.

Robert's father was silent for what seemed like a long time. Then he set one hand on each of his children's shoulders and steered them toward the boat. "Come on. Let's get those life jackets on, now."

They cast off. As the yacht began to manoeuvre away from its slip, Robert caught sight of his mother on the back deck of the house, a martini glass in hand.

She watched the yacht's departure for a few moments. Then she knocked back her drink, turned and walked into the house without a backward glance. Robert stared after her until his father told him to come help with the sails.

By the time they'd reached open water, Robert had forgotten his anger at his mother. In fact, when he remembered to think of her at all, he was quite pleased she hadn't come with them. Without her, everything seemed as it should be.

They set up a fishing line to trail along behind the boat. At his father's instruction, Robert made studious adjustments to the sails. He took deep breaths of the salt-laced air, enjoying the satisfying snap of the sailcloth as the wind caught it. Suzie was in the cockpit, deep in conversation with Wally.

"Think you can handle things up here for a few minutes while I go make us some tea?" Robert's father asked.

Robert nodded dutifully, and his father cracked a smile at the seriousness on Robert's face. "All right. Hold her steady." He stepped aside and offered the helm to Robert.

He took up his new post as his father disappeared down into the cabin. Robert heard the clatter of cupboards being opened as his father extracted a tea kettle and filled it with water.

"Turn on the gas, would you?" his father called up.

Robert opened the locker beside the helm so he could get at the gas canister within it. As he had been taught in the safety lessons that his father insisted upon at the beginning of each season, Robert shouted, "Gas on!" as he twisted the valve on the canister.

A few minutes later, Robert heard the whistle of the tea kettle, accompanied by his father's voice telling him to shut off the gas. At the same moment, the fishing line at the back of the boat snapped taut.

"Dad, come quick! We've got something on the line!" he shouted down.

Suzie, overhearing him, let out a squeal of delight and bounded up to the deck to watch the excitement. Their father was right behind her, rushing to grab hold of the reel.

His father let out a whoop as the line jerked in the water, the catch resisting his efforts to bring it to the surface. "We've got a whopper here, kids!"

At last, he managed to haul the writhing fish into the boat. It landed on the deck with a *thud*. "Look at that. Beautiful Australian salmon," his father observed. He neatly dispatched the fish with a winch handle to the head, splashing the deck with blood and scales.

Suzie gave a disgusted shriek and raced back to the safety of the cabin. But Robert, never squeamish, watched as his father opened the cooler they'd brought and started to pack the fish in ice.

"We'll have a barbecue on the beach. How's that sound for a birthday lunch?" his father grinned.

From the cabin came Suzie's impatient voice. "Daddy! I need the toilet!" she called.

"Be right there, sweetie!" He quickly towelled the blood off his hands and went to help his daughter.

Robert remained on the deck. He leaned on the railing, contentedly watching the sparkle of the sun off the water. This was, he decided impulsively, his favourite birthday ever.

His father helped Suzie into the head and closed the door behind her. Then he picked up a pack of cigarettes and a lighter from the table in the cabin. From his vantage point up on the deck, Robert saw his father place a cigarette between his lips, raise the lighter, and press his thumb on the trigger.

•

When Robert's eyes finally cracked open, it seemed to take ages for him to make sense of what he was looking at. Finally, he understood: there were phantoms of thick black smoke drifting across the sky.

He was floating on his back in the water. With a groan, he lifted his head and found himself surrounded by wreckage – wood and cloth and shards of fiberglass. And all at once, he remembered. There had been a burst of light so intense it had blinded him, and an earth-shattering sound that was still ringing in his ears, as if some part of the explosion had been trapped in his skull and lodged there.

He flailed, searching for some sign of movement in the water. In desperation, he cried out to his father, over and over again. He called for his sister, too, "Suzie, where are you? Can you hear me?" his voice almost lost in the ringing in his own ears. He yelled until it felt like his throat would bleed. But no response came. Just a deep, awful silence.

Something was floating toward him. Compulsively, he reached out and grabbed it. Its waterlogged shape wasn't recognisable until he turned it over and saw its kind, cheerful eyes staring out of a charred face.

Wally.

There was no other sign of his sister. Robert was alone.

CHAPTER 1:
TWELVE YEARS LATER

In a glimmering haze of pink and gold, the sun was just beginning to set over Pittwater.

Wayne Brewster was backstroking the length of his pool. His villa, set high in the hills above the bay, was perfectly quiet, the kind of luxurious quiet that can be obtained only either deep in nature or with a great deal of wealth.

As he reached the end of a lap, he draped an arm on the edge of the pool and checked the watch on his opposite wrist. Nearly time, now. The Prime Minister would be arriving in less than an hour.

Brewster got out of the pool. He showered, shaved and applied a cologne that a young woman at an upscale boutique had assured him was very in-season. Then he poured himself a gin and tonic, and, with his drink in hand, made one last round through his study, where the meeting with PM Johnson would take place. In a meticulous procession, he checked the flower vase, the small figurine of a man on horseback, and the base of the antique brass lamp on the desk, ensuring that the tiny microphone and pinhole camera in each location was in place and fully functional.

He'd been surprised, and almost a little disappointed, at how easy it had all been to set up. When he first came up with this plan, it had seemed clever and dangerous, like he was taking part in a heist or an international espionage mission. But it turned out that most anyone could walk into a hardware store and purchase these sorts of contraptions. It all felt a bit unceremonious, and put something of a damper on his excitement, but at least he hadn't had to waste any time learning newfangled technology. These recording devices were synced with his laptop, which would capture and encrypt every word that the Prime Minister spoke in this room.

He had been Johnson's scapegoat exactly once, and his career had never fully recovered. He had no intention of making the same mistake again.

Brewster opened the study's French doors and stepped onto the veranda. Far below him, the bay sparkled in the late evening sun. As he watched, Johnson's official helicopter came into view, flying low over the water.

Brewster drained the rest of his G&T and returned to the study. Then, making the assumption that his maid was somewhere within earshot, he called out, "Make sure everything is ready. The Prime Minister will be here shortly."

•

Brewster met Johnson in the foyer. The PM strode in, predictably tanned and well-groomed in a bespoke Armani suit. He wore a broad and somehow unmistakably politician-like smile as he walked up to Brewster with his arm outstretched.

"Too long, my friend," he said, clasping Brewster's hand in a strong grip. "It's been too long. I've been worried about you, you know. Wasting away up here in these backwaters."

Brewster finally extracted his hand from Johnson's grip. "Time enough to reinvent myself." He beckoned Johnson into the high-ceilinged corridor. "Come on, then. I've got some brandy that I think you'll like."

Johnson followed him to the study. The doors had been thrown open, letting the sweet perfume of the warm evening breeze waft into the room. A decanter and a set of tumblers sat on the table between two large leather armchairs. Once each of them had a drink in hand, they settled in, and Brewster listened with what he hoped appeared to be rapt attention as Johnson prattled on. He knew where this conversation was headed, eventually. But there was no rushing Johnson. He'd get there in his own time and until then, Brewster had to endure Johnson's complaints about how the state of his yacht club had been going downhill ever since a new raft of foreigners had been allowed to join.

Finally, after a long pull on his brandy, Johnson said, "Well, Wayne."

Brewster tried to maintain an air of nonchalance, although he couldn't help straightening in his seat.

"Have you given any more thought to our last telephone conversation? What I said about you running for governor again?"

Brewster turned the glass tumbler in his hand in contemplation, as if he had not been contemplating this for the past week. "I'm not sure, Howard," he said. "When that last story broke, about all our old action – the bribes, the dodgy contracts – it pretty well sank my image, I'm afraid."

Johnson scoffed. "Oh, you give the public too much credit. They've got the memories of goldfish. Anyway, you know what they say… we are a nation of convicts. Australians love to give a man a second chance." He raised his glass to Brewster as if in a toast.

"Could be you're right," Brewster answered. After a few moments, he added, "And the campaign? Who would pay for that?"

"You're so quick to get stuck in the details, my friend," Johnson said expansively. "You ought to let yourself dream a little before you get bogged down in practicalities. But if you insist." Johnson took another swig. "Let us say… you pay half and the party pays half."

"And the party has a lot to spare, does it?"

"As it happens, we've a set of new investors that would love to support your campaign." Johnson gave him a glossy smile.

Brewster sensed there was more to that story than Johnson was letting on, but he'd have to return to that later.

When Brewster didn't answer, Johnson pressed on, "Think about it, Wayne.

We'll go after *the people's* vote. You know, the slums in the outlying suburbs, the poor workers in the city. Refurbishing the government housing projects to win the Aborigine vote. New transportation infrastructure for the commuters in the urban centre. We'll even toss something in for those tree-hugging eco-nuts up in Lavender Hills. It'll be…" He snapped his fingers breezily, indicating, Brewster assumed, how fast the election would be over.

Finally, and with a crafted amount of caution in his tone, Brewster asked, "And what about you? What's your angle in this, Howard?"

Johnson let out a bark of laughter. "Quite the cynic, you are!" He shook his head. "All right, since you've got such little faith in me. If you become governor, that's a mutually beneficial arrangement, isn't it? I happened to check and see that you still own those building supplies companies. You could stand to gain from some new construction projects. And it'd be, you could say… advantageous for me to have someone in my corner taking charge of this part of the country."

Ah. Brewster topped off both of their brandies before he said, "This is about your policies that have stalled in the House of Representatives. Lifting the gambling restrictions. The new highways bill, and the denationalisation of parks and reservations that you need to go through with it."

He could have been imagining it, but it seemed that Johnson's eyes sharpened on him. When he spoke, though, it was with the same easy affability that he'd had all evening.

"Wayne, my friend, you must look at the big picture," he said warmly. "With the support of my investors…"

"I'll run for governor," Brewster said. "And I think you're right. It will be easy for me to win. But if I'm going to go back into business with you, I want to know the truth. *Before* we start. Not like last time."

Johnson studied him in silence. When he went on, his voice had dropped to a murmur. Brewster said a silent prayer that the hidden mics were properly calibrated. "All right. Here's the truth. The world is in freefall. Financial crises everywhere you look. Banks going under. The growth in our economy is slowing and our natural disasters are increasing. And who is going to pay for it all? Our tourism is taking a nosedive. Our exports are failing by the day. Less coal is being shipped out from Newcastle, and all the while coal prices are falling. So it's up to me, up to us, to find new ways to boost our economy and to bring in new investments. Let's face facts, Wayne… China is the one holding all the cards now. They've got power. They've got money. They are the second biggest economy in the world, and their billionaires are looking for ways to invest their newfound wealth. So…" Johnson leaned forward, his eyes reflecting lamplight. "I have been negotiating trade deals with China, building up stronger ties between our countries. With that investment, we'll be able to construct a brand-new Pacific Highway running from north to south, the length of the Gold Coast, as soon as we denationalise the parks and reservations that are in the way. We'll build international hotels, brand-new leisure facilities, the best in the world. Once the gambling laws are relaxed, we'll have super-casinos like we've never had before." He described it with the ardour of someone explaining a vision of utopia. Brewster was reminded why Johnson had risen through the political ranks so quickly.

"That way, in five years," Johnson went on, "when the world's finances are stable again, we will have an unmatched tourism infrastructure. We'll be a destination for the world's rich and famous. And that's how we save this country."

Brewster was quiet for some time. When he finally spoke, he managed to keep his voice level, although his heart was beating harder at the possibility of it all. Talking to Johnson was like that. He could sweep you away if you weren't careful.

He said, "Well, Howard, I'm impressed. You've come a long way since we used to take a little money off the top building condominiums and beach homes for old folks." He thought for a moment. "All right. So you need help getting people on board with these policies of yours. Keeping the opposition in line."

A grin overtook Johnson's face. "Yes. Exactly. You see it. I knew you'd see it. You never lost your talent for politics, Wayne." He stared into Brewster's eyes intently. "You're going to make all the difference."

And, Brewster reflected silently, he could also make a killing. There were opportunities here… not like the grubby little deals they'd made before. Big opportunities. The kind of opportunities he'd be able to retire on after a couple years.

He'd have to negotiate with Johnson, of course. The Prime Minister wouldn't tolerate anything unless he got a cut of it. In the past, that would have proven tricky… without leverage, there was little negotiating to be done with Johnson.

Brewster's eyes slid to the brass lamp, where the nearest microphone was capturing every word that left Johnson's mouth. Brewster let himself smile. This time, when he went in to negotiate with Johnson, he wouldn't have to worry about leverage.

CHAPTER 2:
SYDNEY CONCERT

Strobe lights bathed the crowd in pulsing waves of red and blue.

Paula and Lindsay edged toward the stage until they were close enough to feel the thump of the bass vibrating in their ribcages. They were some of the youngest people there. The headliner, a band called ABC, had been the radio heartthrobs of their parents' generation, which was why Paula and Lindsay had grown up listening to their records and knew the words to every song they played. The band might not have been their first pick to see at the Sydney SuperDome, but it was as good an excuse as any to get out of the house and get drunk.

The song ended in a cascade of guitar power chords and synthesizer sustains. The frontman announced an intermission, and Paula saw that Lindsay's drink was empty.

"Come on," she said, taking Lindsay's wrist. "Let's grab another."

They waded through the crowd and made their way to the beer tent. Lindsay leaned up on the counter until she caught the eye of a bartender. She waved him over and ordered a couple of beers. When he returned, foam spilling over the lip of the plastic cups in each hand, Lindsay squinted at him.

"Hey," she said. "You look really familiar. Have we met before?"

He gave her a smile and handed over the drinks. "You've probably seen me around. I've worked at a lot of different bars."

She nodded, still studying his face as she fished some cash out of her wallet and set it on the bar. "Right. That must be it. Cheers."

They each finished their beers in a few quick swallows. Then they squeezed through the groups of milling concert-goers into the washrooms.

Lindsay hopped up on the sink counter in front of the mirrors. Past her, a row of women reapplied lipstick and adjusted their hair. Paula was rolling a joint with practiced precision. She finished it with a final twist and handed it to Lindsay, who was waiting with lighter in hand. They passed it back and forth until it had burned down to the roach, then stumbled back out to the main concourse, holding each other up and giggling.

The band had just taken the stage again. The girls made their way back up to the barricades at the very front of the crowd. They reclaimed a patch of trampled ground, where they gleefully belted along to the songs they'd grown up hearing on their parents' scratchy stereo.

After a while, Paula caught Lindsay's shoulder. "Hey," she yelled over the blaring speakers, "we should get going."

"The concert's not over yet!" Lindsay protested, trying to wiggle out of Paula's grip.

"We're going to miss the last bus to Pittwater. Come on!" She tried to pull Lindsay along by the strap of her purse, but Lindsay dug her heels in.

"One more song," she said stubbornly.

"Ah…" Paula checked the time on her phone, then glanced back to the stage. "Fuck it. One more song."

One song turned into three, plus an encore, and Paula realised suddenly how late it had gotten just as the spotlights on stage went dark. She grabbed Lindsay and together they weaved through the throngs of people emptying out of the arena, nearly losing one another in the chaos.

Finally, they managed to reach the street. The bus stop was only a block ahead of them.

"Oh, thank God," Paula muttered, hurrying toward it and dragging Lindsay along behind her. She glanced back to see how her friend was keeping up, and happened to catch sight of a bus, flashing PITTWATER in white letters on its marquee, come around the corner.

The bus roared past them. It pulled up to the stop and slowed, then halted.

"Come on, Lindsay," she yelled, "that's the last one! *Run!*"

The two girls broke into a sprint toward the bus. Just when Paula felt certain they would make it, she heard a short yelp and then a crash.

She turned. Lindsay had slipped in a puddle of someone's discarded drink and lay sprawled on the concrete.

"*Shit!*" Paula cried, scrambling back to try and pull Lindsay to her feet.

Too late. She looked up at the squeak of the bus's door closing, just in time to see the bus pulling off and disappearing around the next corner.

Lindsay, now sporting a bloody scrape on one knee, began to cry. "Aw, no, Paula, I'm so sorry…" she slurred. Then she turned, retched and threw up over the curb.

Paula sat back on her heels and let out a long sigh. "Christ, Lindsay, it was just beer and pot…"

She was interrupted by Lindsay throwing up a second time.

Around them, the street was rapidly emptying as people dispersed from the arena and made their way home. The area would be deserted in a few minutes. Before she got a chance to ask Lindsay how the hell they were going to get home now, a car pulled up alongside them.

The window rolled down and a young man leaned out. "Hey," he said, with a concerned glance at Lindsay, "do you need a ride?"

Somewhat guardedly, Paula answered, "Where are you going?"

"Pittwater."

Paula, whose own head was starting to swim from the combination of drugs, alcohol and sprinting, managed to feel a flicker of relief. "That's where we're going, too."

The man gestured to invite them into the car. "Hop in."

Paula rose unsteadily and opened the car's back door. She hauled Lindsay to her feet and helped her stretch out in the back. "Where're we going?" Lindsay mumbled, as Paula prevented her from hitting her head on the car's frame.

"We're getting a ride home. Just lay down."

Lindsay obliged. By the time Paula had climbed into the passenger's seat, her friend had fallen fast asleep.

That left Paula on her own to try and keep up with the driver's attempts at small talk.

"Did you enjoy the concert?" he asked, putting the car in gear and pulling back onto the street.

"Yeah," she answered, and when he seemed to expect more of a response, she added, "It was great."

"You look a little young to remember the eighties."

"ABC is a favourite band of our parents. We both heard their albums all the time as kids. Thought it would be fun to see them in person," Paula said, wishing he would stop talking.

"Really? I thought ABC never got too popular here in Australia."

"Both our parents are from England. They only know British bands, really." She reclined her head against the headrest and closed her eyes, fighting a wave of dizziness. "Do you know Irrubel Road?"

"Sure."

"Could you drop us off at the end of Irrubel, near the Prince Albert Yacht Club?"

"No problem."

"Thanks. We really appreciate it." She allowed a slight pause. The hum of the car's interior was making her nauseous. The forty-some minutes until they reached home suddenly seemed agonising. "You don't mind if I put my headphones in, do you?" She had already pulled them out of her bag and started untangling the wires.

Paula didn't bother to turn her head toward the driver (any time she moved, the dizziness came back), but she thought she saw him smile out of the corner of her eye. "Not at all," he replied.

She plugged the earbuds into her ears and set her favourite playlist to shuffle. Within moments, she'd drifted off to sleep.

CHAPTER 3:
THE PERFECT PLACE

The car raced through the darkness along the dual carriageway of Pittwater Road. Its driver glanced in the rear view mirror at the girl in the backseat. He'd seen her vomit at the side of the road and hoped she wouldn't be sick again in his car. She wasn't as good-looking as the one in the front seat. Still, he couldn't help but notice her large breasts and wondered, idly, what it would be like to massage them, to suck on her nipples.

A car horn blared. Jolted back to his senses, he yanked the wheel, pulling the car back into his own lane. The car he'd inadvertently cut off was now roaring past him with the window rolled down so that the driver could yell obscenities at him. He shook his head to clear it and forced himself to focus on the road.

Eventually, though, his eyes drifted to the passenger's seat, where the prettier girl was still asleep. She was wearing a crop top that exposed her midriff, revealing a small pink gem in her belly button piercing. Her breasts were smaller than the girl in the back, but her nipples showed through the thin material. He could feel himself getting aroused and shifted in his seat to make it more comfortable.

He turned off the motorway onto the dark streets of suburban Pittwater. After changing gears, he let his hand graze the thigh of the girl beside him. She didn't react. He rested his hand on her leg and, slowly, began moving it up.

The girl woke with a start. "What the fuck do you think you're doing?" she snapped, jerking away from him.

"Nothing," he said, putting his hand back on the steering wheel. "My hand just slipped when I was changing gears."

"Yeah. Sure." The girl pulled at the hem of her skirt to cover more of her legs and looked out the window, pressing her face to the glass to read the street signs. "This is close enough. Let us out here."

"We're still two kilometres from the yacht club. I can take you the rest of the way."

"No. Stop the car and let us out."

The driver didn't respond, his hands tightening on the steering wheel.

"Hey, asshole. I said *stop the fucking car!*"

"Fine," the driver said smoothly, and pulled the car to the kerb. "Suit yourself."

The girl in the front seat twisted around. She grabbed her friend's arm and shook it. "Hey, Lindsay. Wake up. Come on, we're going."

The one named Lindsay pulled her arm free with a groan. "Leave me alone," she mumbled, trying to turn away. "I'm sleeping."

While the girl in the passenger's seat fumbled with the earbud wires, trying to stash them back into her bag, the driver reached into the door well. He felt around until his hand closed on the slim handle of a stiletto knife.

She turned her back to him as she reached for the door handle. With one quick thrust, he plunged the knife deep into the exposed skin of her lower back. Her scream crashed over him like a wave and he ejaculated.

Fucking bitch, he thought, watching her struggle to claw her way out of the car with her last few breaths. *What had she expected? She was asking for it.*

She managed to get the door open, although she never made it out of the car. He extracted the knife from her limp body and carefully wiped the blood away on her white shirt. Then he reached across her chest and shut the door.

He put the car in drive, his eyes flicking up to the rear view mirror and the girl in the backseat. She'd stirred slightly when the other girl had given her last choked scream, but now she slept peacefully as the car sped on.

Pittwater was quiet this time of night. The car's headlights skimmed past silent, dark houses on deserted streets. Eventually, by the glow of the streetlamps, he caught sight of a narrow track leading off into the brush of an undeveloped lot. He swung the car onto the dirt road and followed it until he was safely out of view of the neighbourhood's watching windows.

The dense tangle of brush opened into a clearing. In the middle of it loomed the skeleton of a half-built house. He stopped the car behind the shoulder-high beginnings of a brick wall, checking when he got out to make sure that the vehicle wouldn't be visible from the road.

The spark of his lighter broke the darkness. He lit his cigarette and inhaled deeply, enjoying the quiet of the evening. The only sound was the rhythmic chirp of crickets, a steady thrum marking time in the moonlit world.

He walked forward, coming to the edge of the lot. It was on a steep rise of land, providing a clear view of the bay's dark waters below.

The perfect place, he thought, and threw the stub of his cigarette to the ground. He crushed it under his heel, and began to walk back to the car.

CHAPTER 4:
NEW ASSIGNMENT

Aglow with mid-morning sunlight, Lisa Gordon's home was peaceful and perfectly still.

Then her mobile rang, shattering the silence.

Lisa said, "Oh, *shit*," before she'd even opened her eyes.

She fumbled for the phone on her bedside table. Once she managed to get it in her hand and accept the call, her editor did not wait for a greeting.

"Where the *hell* are you?" he quipped, and then, while Lisa was still rubbing the sleep from her eyes, he added, "And while we're on the subject, where the hell is your article?"

"Ah… I'm so sorry, Brian." In a sudden flash, Lisa remembered that her lodger, Paul, had knocked on the door of her room earlier that morning. Paul was a 26-year-old photographer for the same paper where Lisa worked, the *Sydney Telegraph*. With a coffee in hand, Paul had told her that he was heading out and that she'd better get a move on if she didn't want to miss the ferry across the harbour. She'd sleepily told him she'd be up in a few minutes, and he had shrugged and left the coffee sitting on the dresser for her.

Glancing at the clock, she saw that it was past ten. So much for a few minutes. "I'm running a little late today," she told Brian. "I'll be right in."

"No, don't come into the office. Just email me your article. I've just got a tip in and I want you to follow up on it straightaway."

Lisa sat up in bed. "What's the tip?"

"Two high school girls went missing up in Pittwater last night. This morning, the police found something at an abandoned building site in that same neighbourhood. They're still setting up the crime scene now, but it's definitely something big."

"Do you think they found the girls?"

"No one's said for sure yet. But you're going to find out."

Lisa took a deep breath. "All right. I'll head out now."

"Grab a camera, too. It'll take Paul ages to get across the city and by then the place will be swarming with other newshounds. So don't wait for him. Once you're on the road, I'll call you back and give you the rest of the details."

"Got it. Thanks, Brian."

"My pleasure. Now get going."

Brian hung up. Lisa shoved off the blankets and rose to her feet, determinedly ignoring the headache that was already setting in at her temples. She found her laptop on the kitchen table, where the article she'd been working on was still up on the screen. With one last glance over the text, she sent it off in an email to Brian.

She sat back in her chair and caught sight of the empty bottles of red wine on the counter. Right. That was why she'd slept in so late. And why her head was pounding now.

Lisa showered quickly and threw on some clothes, a pair of black slacks and a green blouse. She gave herself a few minutes to blow-dry her dark curls and apply a layer of mascara to her lashes. Straightening up, she blinked at herself in the mirror, touching a stray dot of mascara away from the corner of her bright blue eyes. Then she went back to her bedroom, hurriedly downed the now ice-cold coffee Paul had left for her, and crossed from her room into Paul's.

Standing in the doorway, she surveyed the utter mess he'd managed to create in the second bedroom of her house. He was a bit of a pain really, often falling behind on the rent and leaving his room in a shocking state of disarray. But after her divorce, with bills coming due, she'd needed a lodger sooner rather than later. And at least he brought her coffee sometimes.

She spotted a spare camera among the piles of clothes and stacks of photography magazines. After a quick check to confirm that it had a charged battery and a memory card in the slot, she packed it up and headed out.

While she climbed into the driver's seat of her Saab convertible, she mentally calculated how long it would take to get to Pittwater. Luckily, she lived north of the city, so it wouldn't be long. In any case, it was a beautiful day for a drive. She put down the car's top, listening to the whir of the mechanics while the sun warmed her face.

As Lisa navigated the streets that led to Pittwater, she heard the buzz of a chopper above her. She glanced up and spotted a police helicopter slicing through the sky, going the same direction as her Saab. A few moments later, several squad cars overtook her. They were heading north too, their sirens blaring.

A frown pulled at Lisa's mouth as her convertible sped on. Brian was right… whatever she was headed into, it was definitely something big.

CHAPTER 5:
CRIME SCENE

It was easy to tell when she was getting close… the road became increasingly clogged with police cars and people in uniforms. As Lisa slowed the Saab to a crawl, she noticed a Fox News van at the side of the street. A TV crew was already setting up in front of it.

She parked about twenty yards from a turn-off to a dirt track. Here the street was crowded with onlookers, many of them probably neighbours who had come to nose around when they saw the cops. As she approached, the police were unspooling their blue-and-white tape to cordon off a large swath of land down the dirt road.

Lisa made her way through the clumps of people until she reached the Fox News crew. She spotted the anchor, a man named Bob Whelan, at the same moment he spotted her.

"Well, you are quick off the mark," he said, turning towards her with raised brows. "I didn't think this was your sort of thing." He hooked a thumb towards the police tape.

"A one-off, I hope," she said with a thin smile. "So, Bob. What do you know?"

"Not much," he shrugged. "A report went in late last night to the local police about two missing schoolgirls. But you know what teenagers are like these days. No one thought there was much of a story there at first. Then, next thing you know, somebody's out walking their dog this morning and they find… something. But the police are staying tight-lipped. Haven't heard anything from them yet."

"I see," she murmured, eyeing a group of police officers as they ducked under the cordon. "Thanks, Bob."

With that, she turned back to her car and retrieved the camera from the bag on the passenger seat.

She wandered a short distance from her car, keeping an eye on the news crews in case she missed any big developments. Before long, she spotted a footpath leading through the brush and looked over at the long line of police tape stretching away into the scrub. The officers were still putting it up, but they hadn't reached this side path yet.

With one quick glance around to make sure she hadn't attracted any attention, she ducked into the undergrowth and followed the path into the undeveloped lot. She walked about a hundred yards, with branches and thorny shrubs scratching at her with every step, until she found herself peering through a screen of branches at a clearing. In it, she could make out the unfinished framework of a large house.

The clearing was crowded with more police officers and forensic technicians.

Several of them were in the process of erecting a white tent. She could see several people near it, kneeling over a dark shape on the ground.

Lisa dropped to a crouch, doing her best to ensure that she was hidden by the bushes if anyone should look her way. She tweaked the camera's unwieldy zoom lens as Paul had taught her and raised the viewfinder to her eye. With a start, she saw that the technicians were examining a body. She adjusted the focus and clicked the shutter a few times in quick succession. Her shots certainly wouldn't be as good as any Paul would have gotten, but she hoped they'd at least be salvageable.

She was still watching through the viewfinder when a branch snapped behind her. Startled, she whipped around and found herself looking up at a police officer.

His look of surprise turned immediately to annoyance as he spotted the camera. "I'm going to need you to come with me, please," he said.

It didn't seem worth an argument. Lisa rose to her feet, brushing off the twigs that had gotten stuck to her blouse, and followed him into the clearing.

"Wait here," he told her once they were out in the open, "while I report to my commanding officer."

She watched as he crossed over to a plainclothes officer standing near the body. They exchanged a few words, and the one who'd found her turned to point her out. When he walked back, he informed her that she'd need to wait in a car until Detective Campbell was finished at the scene.

"Wait in a car?" she repeated incredulously.

"That's right."

"Look, I'm a journalist. I work for the *Sydney Telegraph*, and I need to get back to my office. I haven't got time to sit around waiting for someone called Detective Campbell."

"Miss," the officer said wearily, "you've just been found trespassing on an active crime scene. You are very close to being arrested. Please wait in the squad car." He eyed the camera in her hand. "May I take that from you?"

She pulled the camera away from him, as if shielding a child. "Absolutely not," she retorted.

The policeman's mouth thinned. "Suit yourself," he said, and gestured her toward a squad car at the edge of the clearing. "This way, please."

With an irritated glance back at the plainclothes officer, she followed the other policeman to the car. He opened the back door for her and she slid into the seat. Before shutting the door behind her, he paused.

"Just so you know," he said, "Detective Campbell won't be as polite as I am."

The frame of the car rattled as he closed the door and started to walk away. She watched as he hit a button on his key fob, and the doors locked with a muted click.

"Oh, for *God's* sake," she huffed, and manoeuvred to the other side of the car so that she had a better view of the crime scene.

From here, she could see forensic team members in crisp white paper suits making slow, methodical progress in a wide radius around the forensic tent. She set the camera aside, pulled a steno notebook out of her bag and began to take down notes, craning her neck to try and see around the barrier separating her from the car's front seat. She paused a few times and called into her office, but the line was always busy.

There was a sudden sound as the doors of an ambulance banged shut. She turned in time to see a medic and another police officer walking slowly toward the crime scene, passing by the car as they did. The window was cracked open just far enough for Lisa to hear the officer's words.

"So where is our dog walker now?"

"He's been sedated," the medic answered, nodding back toward the ambulance. "He's in bloody shock, and I don't blame him. Not exactly the first thing you expect to see in the morning, is it? I still can't believe that some sick bastard could do that. Cutting up that poor girl and carving a letter 'A' on her stomach…" She shook her head and tutted. "I hope they catch him, and quick."

The medic and officer continued walking away. Lisa was too preoccupied with straining to catch the next words of the conversation to notice Detective Campbell approaching the car. When the doors unlocked, her head snapped toward the driver's side window, where Campbell was peering in at her.

"Would you step out of the car, please?"

Lisa gathered up the camera and opened the door. When she met the detective at the front of the squad car, he was looking at her with a scowl. He had a sharp jawline with a shadow of scruff, and a neat swoop of dark blond hair.

"Walk with me," he said.

She fell into step beside him. After a few yards, he told her gruffly, "My name is Detective Ryan Campbell. And I'd like to know what you were doing wandering around the woods."

"I'm Lisa Gordon and I'm a political journalist for the *Sydney Telegraph*. My editor called me this morning and said he'd gotten a tip about something going on in Pittwater. He sent me up to take some photos and find out what was happening. So that's what I was doing."

He was quiet for a few moments. "A political journalist," he said finally. "This isn't exactly your area. Where did the tip come from?"

"Concerned local resident maybe," she answered evasively. "The woods weren't cordoned off when I got here. I was walking on what looked like a public footpath. I haven't committed any crime that I can think of. So, Detective Campbell…" Lisa stopped walking and turned toward him. "Can I go now?"

"Actually, Miss Gordon, this is private land. So you were trespassing." Before Lisa could respond, he added, "May I see your camera?"

"Look, I've got rights. You can't go round confiscating people's private belongings…"

"Who said anything about confiscating?"

Lisa regarded him for a few moments, then handed over the camera. He took it and she watched as he flipped through the images on the memory card. His mouth twitched into a smirk.

"I'm guessing this isn't yours," he said.

"No," she said warily. "I'm borrowing it from a friend."

He returned the camera to her, his expression sobering. "Now, Miss Gordon, here's what I don't like. I don't like having to face a mother and tell her that her daughter has been killed, and that I can't release her body, and that I don't know how she died or under what circumstances. But that's what I'm going to have to do. Now, imagine how it would feel to hear all that from me, and on top of it, you have to see all this on the front page of tomorrow's newspaper."

Lisa felt a sting of remorse. But she shook it off and replied, "We both know that if it wasn't me, there are a dozen other newshounds over there who would have gotten the same shot."

Campbell started back toward the police cordon at the edge of the lot, and Lisa followed in step. "Tell your editor there will be a press conference later today." He motioned to another officer standing nearby. When he was within earshot, Campbell told him, "Please escort Miss Gordon off the site and back to the main road." To Lisa, he added, "Next time, pay more attention to whose land you're trespassing on."

With that, Campbell turned and began to walk to the forensic tent.

The officer gestured Lisa toward the police tape, clearly intending to supervise her exit, but she shot him an impatient look and began to walk without waiting for him. She reached the barrier and ducked underneath it, drawing stares from the group of onlookers. Bob caught sight of her from his post near the Fox News van, and he quickly stepped past his crew to speak to her.

"Find anything out, Lisa?" he called.

"Nothing much," she answered, slowing to let him catch up. "The investigating officer is someone called Campbell. He said there'll be a press conference later today."

He nodded and said thanks, dropping back and returning to his camera crew. Lisa continued on toward her car. Once she got there, she leaned on the door and pulled out her mobile. While she listened to Paul's phone ring, she turned the camera on and flipped back to the images Campbell had been looking at. Immediately past the photos she'd taken of the crime scene, there was a series of slightly blurry photos of some negligee-wearing ex-girlfriend of Paul's. She suppressed a sigh.

"Hello?"

"Hey, Paul," she said, hurriedly scrolling back to the crime scene photos. "I managed to get a couple shots here, but I didn't have the auto exposure on. Some of them are pretty dark. Think you can work your magic?"

"Sure, I'll see what I can do. Get home and send them over to me before midday, and we'll try to get them into the evening edition."

"Perfect. Thanks, Paul."

Lisa got in her car and guided it past the small knot of neighbours, who had begun to disperse as the police waved people off. She navigated the quiet streets of Pittwater until she rejoined the main artery of the highway that connected the northern suburbs to Sydney.

Driving south, she saw that the traffic was starting to back up going the opposite direction toward Pittwater. With another small pang of guilt, Lisa wondered if the dead girl's mother was in one of those cars.

As soon as she got back home, she put on a pot of coffee and threw together something resembling a sandwich. Then she carried her mug and her plate to the kitchen table, where her laptop was open and waiting.

Between bites of food, Lisa copied the pictures from the camera's memory card to her computer and sent them off to Paul. She paused long enough to get up and turn on the TV, switching it to Fox News so she could listen over her shoulder in case any new details came in. Then she started on her articles: one for tonight's edition (if she could get it in on time, she thought, glancing nervously at the clock in the corner of her laptop screen), and another more in-depth piece for the morning edition.

For the first article, she typed out the headline: TWO TEENAGE GIRLS GO MISSING IN PITTWATER.

Below it, she explained that a missing persons report had been filed for two high schoolers named Lindsay Brook and Paula Thorn by their parents after they hadn't returned home last night. She noted in the final paragraph that a body had been discovered in Pittwater this morning, but that there had been no confirmation about the person's identity so far. She finished her second cup of coffee, gave the article a last once-over, and emailed it to the office.

Lisa wrote what she could of the next article, but she'd have to wait for the press conference to finish it up. In the meanwhile, she started to chip away at her other work. Most pressingly, she had an article coming due about the impending Sydney governor's election. She planned to profile each of the candidates. While she was still putting together notes on the various parties, she got a phone call. She was expecting it to be Brian, her Editor, again, but it turned out to be an old friend.

"Sophie!" she said, leaning back in her chair. "God, it's been ages. How are you?"

"Oh, you know, same old," Sophie laughed. "Listen, I'm in town for the next few days. Do you want to meet up and have a few drinks? I was thinking the Oaks in Neutral Bay."

"Yeah, I'd love to. How's Saturday evening?"

"Perfect. Oh, it'll be good to see you. It's been years, hasn't it? I think since last time…"

On the television, the anchor was announcing breaking news. A press conference was just starting from the crime scene in Pittwater.

"Oh, shit, Sophie, I'm so sorry…" Lisa fumbled with the television remote as she spoke, trying to get the volume up before she missed anything. "I've got to run. Thanks for calling, okay? Talk soon."

Lisa grabbed her steno pad from her bag and dropped onto the couch in front of the TV. Detective Ryan Campbell was on screen, in front of a backdrop festooned with criss-crossing police tape. He was, she mused to herself, rather more attractive when she wasn't looking at him from the backseat of a cop car.

The Fox News anchor, Bob, was asking Ryan a question. "Detective, have you identified the body?"

Ryan's expression was drawn as he replied, "We have, and we're very sorry to say that the body has been identified as Paula Thorn, one of the two teenagers reported missing last night. It appears that Ms Thorn's death was caused by stab wounds from some kind of blade, although we have not found the weapon yet. There is evidence of rape, and the body has been mutilated. This is, of course, an unspeakably horrible situation for the parents of the victim. We ask that members of the press please respect the family's privacy as they grieve."

The crowd erupted into a flurry of questions, with reporters doing their best to yell over each other, jostling one another to position microphones closer to the podium. One journalist could be heard shouting, "What about the other girl?"

Ryan's booming voice sounded clearly over the din. "*This — is — a murder enquiry.*"

The crowd abruptly went quiet.

"*Not* a circus," he went on in a growl. "And I will answer the questions one at a time."

Ryan let the silence ring for a few seconds. Then he continued in a more reserved voice, "As for the whereabouts of Lindsay Brook, we are operating on the assumption that she has been abducted. All possible efforts are being made to find her and bring her home safe." His eyes lifted from the group of reporters in front of him to stare straight down the lens of the camera. "I'd like to remind everyone that this remains an active crime scene, and that no person is to trespass in the area or hinder the police in any way." Maybe she was imagining it, but Lisa couldn't help but feel that this last comment was aimed at her.

The first article she'd drafted made it into the evening edition. By then, though, the news was out. Ryan's press conference had been widely watched, which unfortunately made Lisa's piece irrelevant. But the second article, with the latest details from the conference, would hopefully make the front page, alongside a photo of the forensic tent at the crime scene. Paul had done a good job fixing up the lighting. Underneath Lisa's photo was a school picture of Lindsay Brook that had been released by the girl's parents.

The police were pouring every resource they had into finding her, and a twenty-four-hour sweep of Pittwater was already underway. They were talking to security guards, vendors, bar staff… anyone who had been working at the concert that night. They were checking the social media of the girls' friends for any hints of what might have gone on after the show and combing through CCTV footage of the arena and the surrounding streets. It was a massive undertaking, and Lisa was impressed they'd coordinated it all so quickly.

The last lines of her article read: *Anyone who has any information about what may have happened to the two girls is being asked to call the emergency line as soon as possible. With the community's help, the Sydney police are confident that they will be able to find the perpetrator of these heinous crimes.*

CHAPTER 6:
POST-MORTEM

Ryan Campbell had been awake for close to twenty four hours.

He'd spent a good portion of that time setting up an incident room at the Sydney police headquarters. The once bare room had been transformed, and it was now filled with the clutter and chaos of an ongoing investigation. A huge whiteboard on one wall was steadily filling with the black marker handwriting of the officers working on the case. On the opposite wall, a bulletin board had been thickly plastered with diagrams and crime scene photos. At the centre of the board was the school picture of Lindsay Brook, the same one that had been circulated through the papers. She smiled warmly out over the room.

The deputy commissioner had made it extremely clear that he wanted results on this case as fast as possible, and Ryan was determined to deliver. In truth, ever since the body in Pittwater had been ID'd as Paula Thorn, he'd had a nagging fear in the back of his mind that it was already too late for the other girl. But for now, there was still hope.

As he reclined in a desk chair, gazing absently at the board papered in details from the crime scene. Something was niggling, something he couldn't quite put his finger on…

He sat up straight in his chair.

The crime scene.

His first case as a detective… A young architect, whose career had become mired in corruption, was killed in an explosion on his yacht. Foul play was suspected and Ryan had been part of an extensive investigation, but it hadn't turned up anything. He recalled that at the time of his death, the architect had won a major contract for the planning rights to a land lot, but things had fallen apart before the property was developed. Where had that building site been?

He opened his computer to the Sydney planning commission and quickly tracked down the plot of land that was now a crime scene – it was registered with the city as Lot #30512B – and pulled up the property details.

The 'Last Updated' date was twelve years ago. The development rights were assigned to David Leadman. Of course… Ryan remembered all of it now. Leadman was the victim of the yachting accident. It was this lot that the architect had been awarded just before his death. Ryan leaned in closer to his screen, scrolling through the drab government website until he came across the name of the lot's owner: Wayne Brewster.

Ryan's mobile rang, startling him back to the present. He answered and heard the familiar voice of Dr Pearl Tabard, the head forensic scientist, asking him to come down to the lab as soon as he could.

He thanked her and hung up, then looked across the room. He spotted Ann Nguyen, a ten-year veteran of the detective squad who was serving as Ryan's second-in-command on the current Pittwater case, filling a mug from the coffee pot in the corner. Her long black hair was tied neatly into a bun at the nape of her neck, as usual.

Ryan joined her at the coffee stand. "Hey, Campbell," she said, glancing up at him. "How's it going?"

He started to pour a cup for himself and told her, "Forensics is ready for us. Walk down with me?"

They made their way down to the morgue. As they walked, Ryan did his best to steel himself. He'd seen a lot of dead bodies in his time as a detective, but the young girls were always the hardest to deal with. His own daughter, Madison, was in New Zealand, where his ex-wife had taken her to live after the divorce. She was only a little younger than the missing teenagers from Pittwater.

Dr Tabard, a sharp-eyed, silver-haired woman in her fifties, was standing at an examination table. When she saw them crossing the room toward her, she pulled back a sheet and revealed the starkly pale face of Paula Thorn.

Ryan had seen the body at the crime scene, so he was braced for it. But even so, the sight of the wide, glassy orbs of her eyes with no lids to conceal them sent a jolt of horror through him. He took a sip of his coffee, struggling to keep it down. It was hard to imagine that barely forty-eight hours ago, she'd been walking the hallways at her school and laughing with her friends.

"What've you got for us, Pearl?" Ryan asked.

"Cause of death was severe internal bleeding," she answered. "The blade cut into the spleen and liver causing near-instantaneous death."

Ryan nodded. "Defensive wounds?"

"None. She would have been facing away from the killer to sustain those injuries, so she may not have seen him coming. Or she could've been unconscious due to drugs or alcohol. Tox reports are still out, so we'll know more when we get those back."

"What about the sexual assault?" Ann prompted.

"There was evidence of rape – vaginal trauma and bruising to the upper thighs – but no semen, suggesting the killer used a condom. No viable fingerprints, but there were smudged hand marks in the blood on her back. Likely the killer was wearing gloves. As far as the mutilation…" Pearl shook her head. "Well, you can see it clear enough. The right nipple and both eyelids are missing. Cut off with an instrument that was sharper than the blade used for the stab wounds. I'd guess maybe a scalpel. Based on the rest of the evidence, I'd say they were probably taken as trophies. And that leaves… this." Pearl lightly touched two blue-gloved fingers to the girl's stomach, beside the deep gashes carved into her navel. "The letter A."

"Any idea what that could mean?" Ann asked.

Pearl gave her a sideways look. "Isn't that more your guys' department?"

Ann let out a sigh. "It is," she admitted. "But at the moment, we're open to suggestions."

"No big breaks yet, then?" Pearl asked.

"Not yet," Ryan told her. "But we'll keep looking. Thanks, Pearl."

Pearl gave them a wan smile. "Good luck. We're all pulling for you to catch this guy."

•

In the incident room, Ryan and Ann stood in front of the pinboard. Both of them had their arms folded across their chests in mirror image of each other. Surrounding them were three other officers working on the case.

"What did we find at the crime scene?" Ryan asked.

"Plenty, but not too much that's turned out to be useful so far," Vaughn, the supervisor of the field team, answered. "Far as we can tell, the place is used on a regular basis by local teens to drink and smoke dope. The whole lot is littered with empty beer cans, cigarette butts, broken glass. Place is a minefield for potential evidence."

"Well, get back out there," Ryan said. "I want the whole place gone over with a fine-tooth comb if you have to."

"Boss, we've been there all night already," Vaughn protested. "We bagged everything we could."

"Go over it again," Ryan returned sharply, "and do not miss a thing. What about tyre tracks? Footprints? Have we done house-to-house interviews in the neighbourhood? And you…" He turned to the other two, Officers Everly and Tran. "Check the records for sexual offenses in recent years. Rapists, flashers, old wankers, whatever you can find. Then look into where they are now and what they've been doing over the past couple days. Check into any ex-boyfriends of either of the victims. See if any of their classmates have a record."

They nodded, exchanging brief glances among themselves. Ryan fixed the three of them with a cold look. "I'm sure I don't need to remind you that there's a girl down in the lab right now, and another girl missing. Unless you want her to end up in the lab next to her friend, I suggest you all get moving."

The other officers gathered up their jackets and dispersed. After they left, Ann turned to Ryan. "And what's our plan?"

His eyes were on the board, specifically, on a blown-up map of Pittwater, where a red flag was planted at the spot where Paula's body had been found. "I need you to find out where Wayne Brewster lives," he said, "and then get us a squad car. We're going to pay him a visit."

•

On the way up to Pittwater, Ann pulled into a deli. "Just grabbing some more coffee," she said as she got out of the car.

Ryan watched through the window as she walked up to the small shop, then stared vacantly out at the street. He tried to keep himself focused on the upcoming meeting with Brewster, but his thoughts kept drifting back to the mutilated face of Paula Thorn.

New Zealand felt a world away. He tried to count back the months… how long had it been since he'd seen his daughter?

The driver's side door opened, breaking his reverie. He turned as Ann slid into the seat and held out a pastry to him.

"Eat," she said, gesturing for him to take it.

"I don't want…"

"Listen, Campbell. I don't know when you last had a meal, but I know it wasn't today. Eat."

He accepted the pastry with a gruff word of thanks. Ann ate her own croissant one-handed, the other hand on the steering wheel as she drove them up into the hills of Pittwater.

They wove through the quiet streets, the land gradually rising above the bay. Before long, they turned onto a side road that led into the grounds of Brewster's villa. Ann parked under an imposing covered entryway at the front of the house.

She killed the engine. "Seems like a bit much," she mused, nodding to the marble statues that flanked the door.

"Brewster's not really one for subtlety," Ryan agreed. They stepped out of the car and walked up to the front doors.

Ryan knocked. After a few moments, a housekeeper in a neat navy sweater and khakis answered the door. "Can I help you?" she asked.

"We're here to speak to Wayne Brewster," Ryan said, flashing his badge. "Is he in?"

The housekeeper gestured them inside. "Please wait here," she told them as they stepped over the threshold. "I'll see if Mr Brewster is available."

The housekeeper vanished around a corner. Ryan glanced around the foyer, which was trimmed with expensive wall hangings and vases that looked like they'd been heisted out of a museum display. He and Ann exchanged a bemused look just as the housekeeper reappeared.

"Mr Brewster would be happy to see you. Follow me, please."

Her low heels clicked on the flagstone floor as she led Ann and Ryan out to the pool deck, where a small crew looked like they were just wrapping up a photoshoot. A few assistants were in the process of taking down a lighting setup as Wayne Brewster caught sight of them.

"Welcome, welcome," he called, and beckoned them over to where he was standing beside the pool. "Hello, detectives," he said as they approached. "I've been expecting you."

Ryan arched a brow. "Is that so?"

"Can I get you anything? Some drinks or refreshments?"

"Something cold to drink would be lovely," Ann answered.

"Gin and tonic?"

"As nice as that sounds, we'll stick to something non-alcoholic."

"Of course." Brewster waved over the housekeeper, who had lingered near the doors to the deck. "Would you bring our guests some lemonade, please?"

"Certainly," she said, and turned crisply back into the house.

Brewster led them to a poolside table with a few wrought iron chairs around it. He motioned for them to sit before pulling out his own chair and reclining on it, taking in the view of his pool and the calm, sailboat-dotted waters of the inlet beyond. "Sorry about all this." He gestured to the photography crew, busy packing away tripods and light stands into hard-sided black boxes. "We were just taking a few promotion shots. Lot of upcoming events for the governor's race and all. But at any rate, you came at a good time. We were just finishing up."

The housekeeper reappeared, carrying a serving tray with a carafe of fresh lemonade and three glasses. She laid it on the table between them. Brewster thanked her and told her that would be everything for now, and she retreated back into the house. The photographers finished packing away their gear and headed out the back gate toward the driveway, leaving the three of them alone on the pool deck.

"Can I ask," Ryan said, as Brewster poured each of the three glasses, "how you knew we were coming to see you?"

"Ah, well, there's not too much that happens around here that I don't know," Brewster replied. "It is my job to keep an eye out and know what's going on in the city. And of course, everyone is talking about the Pittwater case."

If he noticed how closely Ryan was watching him, he gave no sign. "Care to share your source of information?" Ryan prompted.

"The local police sergeant is an old friend of mine. He came by to give me an update on things and said that you might be paying a visit sooner or later."

"An old friend? Who might that be?"

"Sergeant Jack MacDonald."

"Well, maybe you should remind MacDonald," Ryan said, with a scowl deepening on his face, "that I'm running this case. If he has any new information about it, he should relay it directly to me. Not his drinking buddies."

"Of course, Inspector," Brewster said mildly. "I meant no offense. And MacDonald meant no harm. I only wanted to know if there was any news. Awful, isn't it? What happened to that girl. And now the other one is still missing. So tell me, Inspector. Do you have any leads on the case? Anything look promising?"

"We're following up on a few leads," Ryan answered. "Since you seem to have all the details, Mr Brewster, I'm assuming you already know that the crime was committed on land that you own."

"Of course," Brewster answered. "I own quite a bit of land in this area. That particular plot has been in the family for ages."

"And the planning permissions for that plot?"

"What about them?"

"They're in the name of a dead architect. David Leadman. I was wondering if you remembered anything about him."

Brewster looked hard at Ryan. "I believe you're aware of the story about Leadman. I recall you were a young detective on that case before you became Detective Chief Inspector."

"I was. And you were accused of offering the contract to him as a bribe."

"Nothing was ever proven," Brewster said sharply. "I had employed him to design and build a new villa on that lot. And then, after the tragic accident that killed him, I decided to call off the whole thing. That's why the land is still sitting empty now." The edge left Brewster's voice as he continued, but his eyes remained fixed on Ryan. "I'm not sure what this has to do with anything, Inspector. The rest of the world has moved on. I don't know why you haven't."

"As I said, we're following up on every lead we can find. Are you aware of any illegal activity on that land?"

"Well, MacDonald did mention a few times that the place was being used by local teenagers for parties. Violating noise ordinances, underage drinking, causing a nuisance. There had been a couple of calls from the neighbours to complain about it, apparently. I already had a demolition order in for the property when all this happened. It had been delayed, as usual, and of course now it's all on hold while the investigation is ongoing. Soon as this crime is solved, maybe I'll be able to get on with the demolition."

Ryan studied him for several moments. "Would you mind telling us where you were two nights ago?"

"Two nights ago? I was right here," Brewster said, gesturing to the house behind them. "Matter of fact, you can ask the Prime Minister himself. He was here to discuss his endorsement of my nomination."

Ryan didn't offer a response. Eventually, Brewster shifted in his chair with a hint of discomfort. "Look, I want this crime solved as much as anyone," he said, glancing between Ryan and Ann. "It's terrible, what that madman did. Now if you've got any more questions for me, I'd be happy to assist your investigation in any way I can."

"Happy to hear that, Mr Brewster." Ryan rose to his feet and Ann mirrored him. "But I think that's all we need for now. We appreciate your cooperation."

They left out the back gate. Ryan felt Brewster's eyes on them with every step.

Back in the car with the engine idling, Ann glanced at Ryan. "What do you think? Anything he's not telling us?"

He didn't reply right away. "I don't like him," he said reluctantly, "but I can't figure out a way to tie him up directly with this case. At least not yet."

"Well, the day's still young," Ann said breezily. "Where to next?"

Ryan considered his answer for a few moments before he replied, "The crime scene."

The lot was only about fifteen minutes away from Brewster's villa. They arrived to find a forensic team on the site, combing over the area just as Ryan had directed.

Ann got out and looked over the clearing. "There's Vaughn," she said, nodding toward the officer in charge of collecting evidence. "I'll go see how it's going."

While Ann jogged over to Vaughn, Ryan took a slow lap around the half-built house in the clearing's centre. He reached a brick wall that had only been constructed up to shoulder-height. From this vantage point, he let his gaze scan methodically over the lot. It was significantly cleaner than when Ryan had first laid eyes on it, scrubbed of cigarette butts, condom wrappers, bottle caps and crushed cans. And, of course, the body of Paula Thorn was no longer sprawled out on the ground.

Ryan's eyes found the exact spot where she'd been lying. There was nothing there now but a slightly flattened patch of weeds and a small yellow evidence flag.

He turned away from the house, looking out to where the land dropped off. Slowly, he paced forward to the edge of the lot, trying to imagine this place two nights ago when a killer had stood where Ryan was now. Trying to imagine what he would have been thinking. Where he would have gone from here.

Far below him, the calm waters of the inlet sparkled in the midday sun. There was something about this place… about Pittwater, about this undeveloped lot overlooking the bay. The feeling at the back of his head was still tugging him toward that case with the architect. That had been twelve years ago now. But somehow it was connected to this crime that had happened on Wayne Brewster's property – he could sense that much, even if he couldn't see it yet.

Ann joined him at the lip of land jutting out over the water. "Nothing much new," she reported. "They bagged a few more fibres and took photos of some tyre tracks. Forensics will start working on those this afternoon. But none of it looks likely to have been from the killer."

"All right. Let's get back to the office. We still need to find Lindsay Brook."

•

Just before they walked back into the incident room, Ryan caught Ann's shoulder. "Listen. I've got something in particular I need you to do."

"Sure," Ann said, caught off guard. But her expression of surprise faded as she studied Ryan's face. "You want me to take another look at the Leadman case?"

It was Ryan's turn to be taken aback. "How do you know?"

She nudged him with her elbow. "I can tell when you've got a hunch. You get a look in your eyes."

He cracked a smile. There was no getting anything past Ann. "I don't know exactly what you're looking for," he said, "but just have a poke around and see if anything stands out to you. And check into the architect's wife and son. They both survived the accident, if I remember correctly. Find out what they're up to these days."

"I'll get on it."

"Thanks, Ann."

She gave him a nod and headed for the staircase, which would lead her down to the archives in the lowest floor of the building. Ryan watched her go for a few moments before he stepped into the incident room.

Immediately, Officer Morris, their technical liaison, spotted him. "Hey, boss," he said, waving Ryan over. "Got a second?"

Ryan followed him to a computer and looked on over his shoulder as Morris sat heavily in his office chair. "What have you got?" Ryan asked.

"Some new clips from the SuperDome. Just came in." He hit play on a video file and a grainy image of the arena's entryway, packed with concertgoers, began to move.

"That's them?" Ryan said, leaning toward the screen and pointing to two young women in the crowd. Paula and Lindsay. Walking around. Happy. Safe. Alive.

"That's them," Morris confirmed. The two walked through the turnstiles at the front entrance and disappeared off the bottom of the frame.

Morris played the other clips in quick succession: the girls making their way down the main concourse into the beer tent, then ducking into the washrooms; at the end of the concert, pushing their way to the exits as if in a hurry. Then, as they finally broke free from the press of the crowd, making a dash out of the arena before they turned a corner and vanished from sight.

"Nothing after that, huh?" Ryan asked, straightening up.

"Nope," Morris said. "Looked to us like they were probably trying to get to the bus stop on the next street. But there aren't any CCTV cameras with a clear view of it, and the driver doesn't remember seeing them get on. So it seems like they never made it to the bus."

Ryan nodded, chewing the corner of his mouth. "And the house-to-house inquiries?"

"Still ongoing," Morris answered. "Inquiries at the school, too. But so far, we haven't found anything to go on. The girls were well liked. They didn't get in any more trouble than you'd expect from a couple of teenagers. No current boyfriends, no exes with histories of violence. Nothing out of the ordinary in either of their family backgrounds, either." He shrugged. "Both of them seemed about as normal as you can get, really."

"And the interviews with known sex offenders?"

"Tran and Everly are coordinating the contacts right now."

Ryan let out a short breath through his nose. "Good work. Keep me posted if you hear anything."

"Of course, boss."

CHAPTER 7:
WEEKEND PLANS

It was finally Saturday, thank God. It felt to Lisa as though this week had lasted about a month and a half. But she'd arrived at the weekend, after finishing a follow-up piece on Paula Thorn's life plus all the research for her big feature on the candidates for the governor's election. It was coming together quite nicely, she thought, and her editor was pleased with her progress.

Last night, a group of people from the office had gone out to celebrate a young copy editor who was going on leave to have a baby. Lisa had spent a couple hours out at the pub with them, then came home to find Paul on the sofa, chatting with some new girlfriend. She'd turned out to be nice enough and Lisa had a few more drinks with them before turning in.

Next morning lying in bed and watching the shadows of tree branches move on the opposite wall, Lisa was pleased to note that she didn't have any headache despite drinking the night before. Still, she reflected to herself as she rose from the bed and gathered up some clean clothes, she really ought to start drinking less and exercising more. Right after this governor's election, she thought, stifling a yawn.

She had a quick shower and decided to go out for breakfast. She'd booked an appointment at the hair salon, but that wasn't until three o'clock, so there was plenty of time to kill before then. As she was leaving, she caught sight of the mess Paul had left – the detritus of a takeout meal and empty bottles of wine scattered through the living room. Honestly, the state of this place. She fought an urge to neaten up, telling herself she wasn't his mother and if he'd made the mess on his own he could damn well clean it on his own.

Pulling on a pair of sunglasses, she left the house and stepped out into the pleasantly warm, cloudless morning. She decided to leave the Saab at the curb and walk a few blocks up the road to Dovetail Cafe.

Lisa ordered at the register and meandered over to the news stand in the corner, grabbing a copy of the free local paper. When her latte and warm pastries appeared on the pickup counter, she gathered them up and took a seat by the window, where she had an ideal vantage point to idly watch the pedestrians on the busy street outside.

She sipped at her coffee and skimmed over the paper. '*WHERE IS LINDSAY BROOK?*' demanded the headline on the front page. It had been three days since the girls had first disappeared, and, as Lisa discovered from a cursory glance down the text, there had been no new leads or promising breaks in the case. The article didn't say it outright, but Lisa could sense from the recent police statements that hope was dwindling for Lindsay to be found alive.

From the depths of her purse, Lisa's mobile began to ring. She dug it out and hit accept just before it rolled to voicemail. It was Sophie, making sure they were still on for tonight.

"Absolutely," Lisa promised her. "Believe me, after the week I've had, I need the chance to relax."

"Eight o'clock at the Oaks all right with you?"

"That'll be perfect. See you then."

She finished up her pastry and stuck the paper in her purse, intending to finish reading it later. Then she strolled back out into the sunshine, perusing the shop windows. She held a brief internal debate about whether she ought to buy something new for her dinner, but in the end she decided against it. Paul hadn't paid the rent for a second month in a row, and her bank account balance was rather dismal. She made a mental note to talk to him as soon as she got the chance.

No sooner had the thought crossed her mind than her phone rang a second time. She answered it without checking the ID, figuring it would be Sophie with some last-minute change of plans. But it was Paul.

She listened for several seconds, then stopped walking dead in her tracks.

CHAPTER 8:
DINGHY CLASS

The juniors at Bayview Yacht Club met every Saturday morning. The group of pre-teens was tolerating the weekly life jacket check and safety lecture from Henry, their fastidious instructor. With everything in order, Henry gave them the go-ahead to sail out into the bay.

"All right, everyone line up at the red markers," his voice barked out over the loudspeaker. "On my whistle, it'll be three times round the course. Remember, *no* cutting across each other's bows."

Each in their own dinghies, Ron, Jennifer, Sarah and Johnny were ready and waiting for the whistle. Out of the ten students in the class, the four of them were easily the best, and spent every Saturday trying to shoulder each other out of the top slot.

The whistle sounded across the water. Johnny got an early lead, and he held it all the way until the third lap. He tried to take a marker too tight, with too much wind in the sail, and his boat capsized. Jennifer swung out to avoid hitting him, allowing Sarah to sail past her with Ron just behind. The two of them were neck and neck coming up on the finish line, until, abruptly, Sarah's sail sagged. Ron had taken her wind and used it to eke out a narrow lead. He was already shouting and punching his fist in the air, a celebration that turned out to be premature.

BANG. The bow of his dinghy hit something in the water. The boat capsized, and Ron went tumbling into the water.

He broke the surface just in time to see Sarah crossing the finish line, with Jennifer trailing a short distance behind her. "Shit!" he gasped, laughing, as he searched through the water for the sail line to pull his dinghy upright. He managed to find it and gave it a pull, but to his surprise, the boat wouldn't budge. When he tried again, he felt a weight shift on the other end. He looked closer and saw that something had gotten caught up in his sail.

He gave a final tug. The line went slack as something gave way. The object that had been weighing down the sail suddenly rolled toward him, and Ron found himself staring into the blue, bloated face of a dead girl.

Ron's screams pierced the air. Moments later, Henry's boat pulled up alongside him.

"What's wrong? Are you hurt?" Henry called, but Ron didn't answer. "Swim over to the boat! I'll pull you up!"

Ron stared fixedly at the girl's face as if she held him in a trance.

Henry followed his gaze. "Fucking hell," he blurted, before he could stop himself.

Finally Henry managed to snag Ron's life jacket with the rescue hook.

He brought him in toward the boat and hauled him up over the side. "You're all right," Henry assured him, although Ron's white-faced expression of terror made him look anything but. "Everything will be all right, son."

"What's going on?" Johnny called over to him.

"Go back to shore!" Henry shouted back. "All of you! *Now!*"

The students obeyed, casting uncertain glances back toward Henry's boat. When Henry was sure Ron could sit on the bench without falling back over the side, he got on the shortwave radio and called into the yacht club.

"Henry, we hear you," came the operator's voice through a crackle of static. "What's your situation?"

"Call the police. Call emergency services."

"Emergency services? What's going on?"

"There's a body in the water."

Henry tossed a marker over the side of the boat so that they'd be able to find the spot again. Then he quickly guided the boat back to shore.

Several members of the yacht club staff met them at the beach. Ron was still unsteady as he stepped off the boat, and it took two of them to make sure he made it safely to solid ground. The first aid officer put a towel around Ron's shaking shoulders and led him away as Henry told the rest of the students to get their dinghies out of the water and head back up to the clubhouse, where their parents would pick them up.

By then, the police had arrived. They met Henry on the front steps of the clubhouse. A tall man with a crop of red hair named Sergeant MacDonald introduced himself and asked Henry to describe what had happened. Henry recounted the incident as best as he could, distracted by the crowds of onlookers who were starting to gather on the beach as police officers strung up blue-and-white tape along the sand. Once he'd given his report, MacDonald thanked Henry and asked if he could guide his officers to the spot where the discovery was made. "Of course," Henry answered, and gestured for MacDonald to follow him to the water.

The marker had stayed in place, but the body had moved with the currents. Even with multiple vessels searching, it was almost an hour before they found it again.

A few minutes after that, the body of Lindsay Brook was being brought to shore.

CHAPTER 9:
A NEW DEVELOPMENT

Ryan picked up the phone before it had even finished its first ring.

"Hello?"

"Ryan, it's me, Ann." Ryan sat up straighter in his armchair. "Just got a call that they found a body in Pittwater."

So much for his quiet day at home. Ryan switched off the TV and stood. "When was this?"

"Just a couple minutes ago. Are you at home? I'll come pick you up now."

Ryan was already snatching clean clothes off the hangers in his closet. "I'll be ready by the time you get here. Have you told Dr Tabard yet?"

"I'll call her next."

Ryan had just enough time to take a few bites of leftover takeout from the night before, As Ann pulled up in front of his house. He slid into the passenger's seat and accepted a cup of coffee Ann was holding out to him. "Pearl's already on the way with her forensics team," she said by way of greeting.

"Who called it in?" he asked as they sped off toward Pittwater.

"Sergeant MacDonald, apparently."

Him again. "And who found the body?"

"Local yacht instructor named Henry Adams. He and his junior class were out on the water doing a practice race. One of the students' boats hit the body and capsized. Instructor said the body floated up right next to the kid while he was trying to get the dinghy upright."

"Jesus," Ryan said. He was quiet for a few moments, watching the residential streets roll by. "Has the body been identified yet?"

"Not conclusively. But the report is a young female, late teens or early twenties."

As they neared the Bayview Yacht Club, Ann slowed down to edge through the groups of curious pedestrians who were bottlenecking the road. Ryan could see from the car that the police had set up a cordon around a long section of the beach. Standing directly up against the plastic barrier was someone with long, dark curls. He did a double take and saw that it was Lisa Gordon.

"Hell," he muttered. "News travels faster than a bushfire around here."

They parked and crossed quickly to the clubhouse. Inside, a low, anxious burble of conversation reverberated off the high wood-beam ceiling. There were several frazzled-looking staff members interspersed with a handful of MacDonald's officers, conversing in tight groups under the glaring fluorescent lights. With Ann at his side, Ryan headed straight for MacDonald.

"Ah, Detective Ryan," MacDonald said in his characteristic slow drawl. He nodded a greeting to each of them and asked, "Have you been brought up to speed?"

"Just about," Ryan said. "Where's the body?"

"Still down on the beach. A forensics team is on site."

"Has the victim been identified?"

"Not officially. But we're positive it's Lindsay Brook. I had one of my guys notify her parents. They're on their way here now."

"You notified them already?"

MacDonald raised his brows at Ryan's tone. "Yes."

Ryan rolled his tongue along the inside of his cheek. "I'll want a word with you later. Don't go far."

Ann and Ryan set off for the back of the clubhouse, which opened out toward the water, and ducked under the police tape. The white screen that had been set up around the body was the only landmark on the beach, which had been cleared of its usual cheerful weekend crowds. The only people there now were in white forensic suits or black police uniforms.

Ryan braced himself as he stepped around the screen. Even so, the sight of the girl's naked, mutilated body sprawled out on the wet sand felt like a punch to the gut. One technician was snapping close-up photos of the bruising and lacerations that marred the blue-tinged skin. Dr Tabard, crouched on the ground, was taking notes on a clipboard propped on one knee.

She glanced up as Ryan's shadow fell across her. "Not a nice thing for a kid to find out on the water," she said grimly, straightening up.

"Where is he now?" Ann asked.

"With the medics. Poor thing's still in shock. He'll have nightmares for weeks, I'm sure."

Ryan studied the dead girl's face. "Does it look like the same killer?"

"If I had to guess right now, I'd say it must be. We've got some of the same mutilation that we saw on Paula Thorn. The left nipple is missing, although both eyelids are intact here. There's similar carving with a sharp instrument…" She pointed out a heart with an arrow through it that had been etched into the girl's skin, just above the left breast. "…and, of course, the letter." Her fingertips hovered above a painstakingly precise 'B' carved into the girl's abdomen. "Then there's the bruising around the upper thighs, suggesting sexual assault. Just like Paula Thorn."

"Cause of death?"

"Right now, it's looking like blood loss from multiple stab wounds."

"Do you have any idea how long she was in the water?" Ann inquired.

"I'm guessing about twenty-four hours, give or take," Pearl answered. "But I'll know more once we do the post-mortem."

Ryan turned to look out over the water, where a few police boats were still out searching for any other evidence that might be caught on the tide. "If she's only been in the water for a day, that means the killer was holding her captive for some time," he murmured.

"Or her body, at least," Ann pointed out.

Pearl nodded. "I should be able to get you a closer guess on the time of death once we get back to the lab."

Ryan let his eyes trace the shoreline. Beyond this beach, Pittwater branched into a labyrinth of backwaters, a dense network of coves and creeks. Somewhere, out of all those places to hide, there was a killer who needed to be found.

They thanked Pearl and headed back up to the clubhouse. As they walked, Ryan asked Ann to arrange a press conference for that afternoon, and charged her with making sure that all of the witness statements and local police reports ended up on his desk as soon as possible. She assured him they would be there, then glanced at him curiously. "Where are you going now?"

He nodded up ahead, where MacDonald was talking to one of his deputies. "Just going to have a quick word with the sergeant."

Ann chuckled. "Good luck with that one," she said.

Ryan waited until he caught MacDonald's eye, then gestured him over. "Any chance there's somewhere around here we can talk in private?"

MacDonald shrugged. "The office should be empty. Follow me."

He led Ryan into the yacht club's administrative office, a small room with a row of dented metal file cabinets and a desk against one wall. Ryan shut the door behind them and then turned to MacDonald. "First things first," he said, squaring up with him. "Why did you call Lindsay's parents so soon?"

MacDonald looked surprised. "What do you mean? I had to inform them…"

"The initial investigation isn't finished yet. What if it wasn't her? We have a formal process for this and it needs to be followed, always. The last thing that family needs is to get dragged into the middle of this circus. And second of all," he pressed on, holding up a hand as MacDonald made to interrupt him, "how in God's name did the press get here so soon?"

"I don't know, Inspector," MacDonald said, growing annoyed. "I was just here doing my job and they showed up."

"Well, while you're *doing your job,*" Ryan growled, "keep in mind that we have a maniac out there who's more than likely getting off on all this publicity. So try a bit harder to keep things under wraps next time." He waited until he got a sullen nod from MacDonald before he continued. "Now listen. I expect your boats to do a full sweep of the area. I want a search party on land, too, combing the whole place for anything that might be evidence. Get in contact with the other nearby yacht clubs and ask them if they've come across anything unusual in the past few days. And you make sure that if anything turns up, you report it to me directly."

There was a knock, and both men turned toward the sound as Ann appeared at the door. "Sorry to interrupt," she said, her eyes bouncing between them before landing on Ryan, "but Lindsay's parents are here. And so is Wayne Brewster."

Ryan spun back toward MacDonald. "Did you call Brewster?"

"It seemed appropriate," he answered, with a trace of unease.

"Listen to me, MacDonald," Ryan said, taking a step toward him. "From here on out, before you call *anyone*, you talk to me first. Understand?" When he didn't reply immediately, Ryan snapped, "*MacDonald*. Do you understand?"

"Yes," MacDonald answered, in something approaching a sneer.

"Good. Now get out there and find me something." With that, Ryan swept out of the room. Ann walked at his side. "Where are the parents now?" he asked her.

"Waiting out front."

Ryan nodded. "Pull them aside and bring them into that office. Tell them I'll be in to speak with them as soon as I deal with Brewster."

He threw open the front doors and found himself staring into a large group of reporters. At his appearance, the entryway lit up with the rapidfire white flash of cameras.

Brewster was standing in front of the journalists, in the midst of offering a placating remark: "…doing everything possible to find this fiend. Rest assured, folks, we will catch him."

"Detective!" one of the reporters yelled in Ryan's direction. "Do you have any details about the body that was just found?"

"There will be a press conference later," Ryan answered shortly. "In the meantime, I'll need all of you to clear out. Now. And Mr Brewster, I'd like to talk to you."

He jerked his head, indicating that Brewster should come with him. After waving off some persistent journalists, Brewster followed Ryan to a quiet spot under a tree on the yacht club's grounds.

"What exactly," Ryan asked, "gave you the right to be a spokesperson for the police?"

"Inspector Campbell, the public needs to be reassured," Brewster said, in the same ingratiating tone he'd used to speak to the press. "People are frightened. Pittwater isn't like the city. Our community's not used to hearing about violent crimes like this happening in their own neighbourhoods. We don't want anyone to panic."

"No," Ryan shot back. "We don't. But as far as I'm concerned, what you did back there wasn't reassuring people so much as it was a publicity stunt for your own campaign."

"Come on, Ryan. There's no need to be so cynical," Brewster replied evenly. "I know these people. Some of them are my friends."

"Be that as it may, you have no authority to speak on behalf of the police. You don't even have any authority to be here. So clear out."

"I'm only here to give my condolences to Lindsay Brook's family," Brewster protested, holding up his hands in a gesture of surrender.

Ryan's scowl deepened. "Not until I've spoken to them first," he said, then turned on his heel and strode back toward the clubhouse.

Ann was standing guard outside the administrative office, holding a number of nosy clubhouse staff members at bay with her cold glare. As Ryan approached, he nodded to the door. "Are they in there?"

"Yes. They're waiting for you," she said, and opened the door for him. Ryan paused for a moment to collect himself before he walked inside.

He found the couple standing, awkwardly, in the centre of the cramped room. "Mr and Mrs Brook, I'm Inspector Ryan Campbell," he said, shutting the door behind him. "I want to apologise for the way you've been treated today. We didn't intend to have the press here, but… word got out, apparently." He strained to keep the annoyance out of his voice as the image of Lisa Gordon leaning over the police tape on the beach flashed through his mind.

"Where's our daughter?" Mrs Brook asked softly.

Ryan took a deep breath. "I understand you want to see her," he said. "Unfortunately, there are some procedures to follow here. We will need to have you formally identify the body, but there are some time sensitive elements to our investigation that we'll have to complete first. And in any case…" He trailed off, glancing behind him, where he knew the press was still lurking just outside the clubhouse's doors. "We want to be able to offer you some privacy when you do see her. You don't need a bunch of cameras going off in your face at the moment. So we'll bring you into the lab as soon as we can. My office will be in touch with you shortly."

They nodded back at him, mutely. The silence felt oppressive.

Ryan cleared his throat. He offered, gruffly, "My sincere condolences to you both."

Lindsay's mother met Ryan's eyes as she spoke, her voice flat and cold. "Just find the person who did this."

Ryan held her gaze and nodded. "I swear, I will do everything I can to find him."

At the press conference a few hours later, Ryan answered the journalists' questions seriously and sternly. There wasn't much to tell them, anyway. He'd wanted to wait to give a press conference until he had more leads to go on, but he knew the local media would only get more aggressive the longer he put them off. So he stood in front of them and used a lot of phrases like "yet to be determined" and "still being investigated," and tried not to see Mrs Brook's heartbroken eyes every time he blinked.

Ann took over for the last few questions. While she spoke, Ryan scanned over the crowd. He spotted a number of faces that had quickly become familiar, thanks to the unprecedented press coverage this case had drawn. Among them, seated next to a young male photographer, was Lisa Gordon.

CHAPTER 10:
THE OAKS

The moment the press conference ended, the reporters immediately began to buzz in animated discussion among themselves. Many of them lingered, milling around and making calls to editors, but Lisa and Paul headed off as soon as Officer Ann Nguyen stepped away from the microphone. They cut through the crowd as quickly as they could, making their way back to Paul's car a few blocks up the street.

"You'd have to send something in the next few hours if you want to get it into the Sunday edition," Paul said, as they dodged past a group of tourists on the sidewalk. "Think you're going to make it?"

"Damn well going to try," Lisa said, already mentally working on the copy. "What time is it now?"

"Just past five."

"Ah… shit." As they got into the car, Lisa pulled out her phone to call Sophie. After three rings, she answered.

"Hello?"

"Hey, Sophie, it's me," Lisa said, cradling the phone between her ear and her shoulder while she paged through her steno notebook. "Listen, I'm so sorry, I'm going to be a little late for dinner tonight."

"No worries, then. Is this about the body they found on the beach?"

"Yes," Lisa said, surprised. "You've heard already?"

"I watched the press conference at that yacht club. They were running it on every news channel. God, it's awful, isn't it? That poor girl."

"It is awful." Lisa trailed off briefly, remembering how the detectives had described the mutilation on the girl's body. From what they'd said, she was rather grateful she hadn't needed to see it in person. "Anyway, I've got to get this article in to my editor. But I'll catch up with you at the Oaks around nine o'clock or so. How's that?"

"Sounds good. I'll grab us a table if I get there first."

"Thanks, Sophie. See you later."

When they got home, Paul and Lisa both made a break for their laptops. Paul paused long enough to make them a pot of coffee while Lisa got to work on her piece. She managed to put something together within a couple of hours, and by then, Paul had polished up enough photos for their editor to choose from. Lisa sent the images and her article into the office, then ducked into the shower.

Minutes later, wrapped in a towel, she stood in front of her open closet with the phone to her ear while she arranged for a cab to come pick her up in thirty minutes. She selected a lilac dress, confirmed the cab's arrival time with the woman on the other end of the phone, and went to finish getting ready.

Slipping on a pair of heeled sandals at the front door, she called to Paul, "Are you going out tonight?"

"Yeah, out to Manly," came the response from the direction of his room. "With my girlfriend."

Lisa resisted the temptation to ask which one and answered, "I won't be back 'til late, so make sure you lock everything up."

"All right. Have fun."

The cab sped through the streets of Neutral Bay, plunging into a neighbourhood of bustling restaurants and bars. It pulled up in front of the Oaks Hotel and Lisa paid with a generous tip, then hurried inside.

The hotel's interior was pleasantly cool after the heat of the evening. A huge, curved window looked out into a shaded courtyard, sparkling with white string lights. Lisa spotted Sophie at the bar, sipping a glass of Chardonnay with a bottle and a second glass in front of her.

She hurried over and slung her purse across the back of the chair next to Sophie.

"Lisa!" she exclaimed. "So good to see you!" They exchanged a hug and Lisa settled into her seat as Sophie poured her a glass.

"I'm sorry I'm late," Lisa said, accepting the wineglass gratefully. "Didn't exactly plan to have to work today."

"Oh, no, don't apologise," Sophie said. "I don't envy having your job at the moment. It must be so hard, having to write about such a horrible crime. Those poor parents, can you imagine?" She shook her head. "Anyway, I've only just got here a few minutes ago. So you haven't kept me waiting." She slipped Lisa a menu from a pile at the end of the bar. "Should we order?"

After a few minutes of consideration, they placed their orders with the waitress. Then, each with a glass of wine in hand, they were led outside to a table in the courtyard.

CHAPTER 11:
AT ANOTHER TABLE

Dinner had been Ann's idea. After the press conference, Ryan had insisted that he wasn't really hungry and would just as soon go home and microwave a frozen meal. But she'd been persistent.

"Come on," she declared, already turning the car away from Ryan's neighbourhood. "It's probably been ages since you've had a decent meal. And God knows I'm not going to cook for you."

"The Oaks Hotel?" Ryan read the sign dubiously as the car pulled up to the curb.

"Yes. It's good. You'll like it."

They got a table in the courtyard, under the massive oak tree at its centre. Its sprawling canopy of branches was draped in twinkling white lights.

For the whole length of the dinner, they managed to make lighthearted, pleasant conversation. Then, with an empty bottle of wine and two cleaned plates on the table between them, Ann asked, "So… how've you been?"

"You know how I've been," he said, somewhat nettled. "I've been losing sleep over this damn case."

In truth, Ann had been entirely right about one thing – he could hardly remember the last time he'd been out to dinner at a decent restaurant. He'd gotten used to his dark, quiet apartment. The lively courtyard, filled with the relaxed chatter of other diners, felt unfamiliar, and it was putting him off.

"How's your daughter?"

Although he knew Ann didn't intend it, the question stung. "Fine," he said stiffly, and then, relenting a bit, he added, "She's doing well. Seems happy in New Zealand. Made new friends at school." He paused. "I miss her, of course."

"Of course," Ann agreed softly. She was quiet for a few moments. "I know you're blaming yourself for what happened to Lindsay Brook. But you shouldn't. You know that."

Ryan looked away, uncomfortable. She could be so aggravatingly perceptive sometimes. "I was hoping we would be able to catch him before…" He fell silent, remembering Lindsay's lifeless face. She had looked a lot like her mother.

"We will catch him," Ann said, with a certainty that Ryan tried to find reassuring. "You're good at your job, Ryan." She offered a smile. "And, for what it's worth, I'm not so bad at my job, either. With us two, the guy doesn't stand a chance. I'm sure of it."

He nodded, though he was still uneasy. "There's just… something about it. I mean…" He grappled for words. "Why Pittwater?"

Ann tilted her head. "What do you mean?"

"I don't know, exactly. I just keep thinking about that old case. The one I told you to look into."

"You still think this has something to do with David Leadman?" Her scepticism was obvious.

"I can't say for sure. I just think the two events might be connected, somehow."

"That explosion was twelve years ago. And it was ruled accidental after a full investigation… that you were part of."

"I know." Ryan gave a shrug. "Like I said. I just can't seem to shake it. Maybe you're right, though. Maybe it's nothing." He took the last remaining sip of his wine. "Anyway. How are your wedding plans coming along, then? Have you found a venue big enough yet?"

"No," she sighed. "Katie and I are still looking."

Ryan laughed. "You're inviting half of Sydney to this thing."

"You're lucky I'm inviting you, Mr Judgement," Ann shot back, before her face broke into a grin. She picked up her napkin from her lap and set it on the table. "All right. You about ready to get home?"

They left cash on the table and stood up to leave. Ryan took his jacket off the back of the chair and began to pull it on, but was surprised to feel his arm collide with something quite solid.

"Shit!" said a sharp female voice. "Don't you look before flinging your arms around in a crowded restaurant?"

He spun around and found himself staring into the Chardonnay-drenched face of Lisa Gordon.

Her mouth had dropped open in shock, but as she recognised him, her expression morphed from surprise to indignation. "Of bloody course," she snapped. "It had to be you."

"Excuse me," Ryan protested, "but I'm sure it was *you* who walked into *me.*"

"I don't think so," Lisa retorted, glancing down at herself. "God, look at my dress. I'm soaked."

"Look, I don't have time to stand around and argue about who walked into who," Ryan said exasperatedly.

"I don't want to argue," Lisa returned. "What I would like is an apology for spilling wine all over me."

Ryan scowled. "I'll pay to have your dress cleaned," he said, "since you're so certain it was my fault. Here…" He dug a business card out of his pocket and handed it over. "Give my office a call on Monday morning. It'll be taken care of."

Lisa took the business card without a word and stared after him as he shouldered past her and her stunned friend. Ryan thought he heard Ann exchange a few murmured words with her before she followed after him.

As they walked back to the car, Ryan was still fuming. "What is it with that woman?" he muttered. "Somehow she's been in my face for days."

"Maybe she's stalking you," Ann suggested, deadpan.

"Bloody hope not. That's the last thing I need. God help me."

"Well, since you keep running into her, why not take her out to apologise?"

Ryan looked at Ann in alarm to see if she was joking. "I am not," he said, "taking that woman out on a date."

"Why not? She's not bad-looking."

"I haven't noticed how she looks."

Ann laughed. "Yeah," she said, opening her car door. "Pull the other one."

They got in, Ryan still grumbling under his breath. Ann put the car in gear and started the drive back into Sydney.

CHAPTER 12:
DR BRANNAN

"All right," Ryan said, leaning back against his desk, "who's got updates?"

He was standing at the front of the incident room for the Monday morning briefing. Ann was beside him.

Officer Tran spoke up first. "We talked to all the kids and staff from Bayview Yacht Club. No one saw anything out of the ordinary in the last few days. We asked around at some other yacht clubs in Pittwater, too, but didn't turn anything up. So that looks like a dead end."

Ryan nodded tersely. Not surprising, but still disappointing. "Anything new from forensics?"

"My guys finished up at the scene late Saturday night and worked through the weekend. Full report should be on your desk in a couple hours," Vaughn replied. "We've got the parents coming in to identify the body this morning. Post-mortem is scheduled for this afternoon."

"Good. I'll check in with Dr Tabard later." Ryan looked toward Detective Ross, a woman with a halo of short blonde hair. She'd taken the lead on the girls' initial disappearance. "What've you got, Julie?"

"Just got done going over the reports from the staff at the Sydney SuperDome," Ross told him. As she spoke, she thumbed through a thick manila folder in her lap. "Turns out they use an employment agency for big events, so it took a while to chase everyone down. But we found eight agency employees who worked the concert. Mostly backpackers. Let's see…" She ran her finger down the page. "Two from the Netherlands, one from Germany, two from Sweden. Three Aussie blokes, one of them quite a bit older than the others."

"Well done," Ryan said. "Follow up with the agency and see if you can't get any more information on those employees. Especially the older one."

There was a sharp knock on the door frame. All eyes turned toward Dr Brannan, the police psychologist, who was standing at the threshold of the room. He was a tall, wiry man with browline glasses and a mop of unruly black hair. "Sorry I'm late, Detective Campbell," Brannan said. He looked around, taking in the room full of faces staring back at him. "Am I interrupting?"

Wonderful, thought Ryan with a twinge of annoyance. Exactly what we need.

"I was just finishing up," Ryan said. He gestured for Brannan to come in. "Floor's all yours."

They'd worked together on other cases, and Ryan had never been especially enthusiastic about it. As far as he was concerned, fingerprints and blood samples had solved a lot more murders than psychology theories. But Brannan had been useful once or twice in the past. And truth be told, Ryan needed all the help he could get right now.

Brannan strode forward to stand beside Ryan and pushed his glasses up on his nose. "Right. I spent the weekend reading through the case file, and I've started to form a profile of the killer. Of course, I'll have to make adjustments as you gather new information. But here's what I'm thinking so far. We're likely looking at a male suspect, age range twenty to thirty. Average IQ or higher. Good chance that he's well educated. He's probably a bit of a loner, lacking in family bonds. Emotionally underdeveloped, has trouble connecting with other people. Unable to form romantic or sexual relationships. Considering the pattern of mutilation, I would guess we're dealing with someone who can't tell fantasy from reality. He's living in a fictional world that he created for himself… might be suffering from hallucinations that are part of that fiction. He experiences episodes of extreme violence when his delusions are triggered in some way. But outside of that, he's generally able to function in the real world, and if you saw him, you probably wouldn't think there was anything out of the ordinary about him." He paused, glancing at the bulletin board on the far wall, where photographs of Bayview Yacht Club had recently joined the images of the first crime scene. "That, frankly, is what will make him so hard to catch. Until something sets off one of those violent episodes, it would be very difficult to know that he was any different from you or me."

"Well," Ryan said, into the sombre quiet that followed Brannan's words, "have you got any theories about the carving on the bodies? The letters and shapes?"

Brannan nodded. "The most obvious explanation," he said, carefully adjusting his glasses again, "is that the 'A' and 'B' are connected to the group that performed at the concert. A-B-C. I took a quick look through the band's discography. There's a song called 'The Look of Love,' which could relate to the cutting of the eyelids. Another song is called 'Poison Arrow'…"

"Which could explain the heart with the arrow on Lindsay Brook," Vaughn jumped in.

Brannan shot him an impatient glance. "Precisely. And, following that logic… we can expect that there will be at least one more victim. We've got an 'A' and 'B,' so we're missing a 'C'. As I said, it's likely that this person is experiencing hallucinations or delusions. He may even believe that he's a part of the band. Assuming that's the case, the band members themselves may be in danger as well."

"Bloody hell," Ann murmured. For a few moments, a stunned silence blanketed the room as they all had the same realisation: these two grisly murders could be only the beginning of even more bloodshed.

"Right," Ryan said briskly, straightening. "Time to step this up. We'll need more staff. I'll talk to management about getting additional officers on the case. All leave is hereby cancelled. I need someone to contact ABC's manager and tour organiser. We'll want to set up interviews with the band members and their PR people, and ask if they're aware of any mad fans who might be behind this. And for God's sake, *no* leaks to the press. Got it?" He looked around the room and waited until he got a nod from everyone before he said tersely, "Good. Go."

The room broke into a flurry of movement. Ryan felt Ann's hand on his elbow and turned toward her.

"Could I have a word?" she asked, holding up a slim black binder.

They walked out of the incident room and down the hall to Ryan's office. He pulled the door closed behind them, muting the ambient buzz of the office. "You looked into the Leadman case?" Ryan prompted before she could speak.

Ann rolled her eyes good naturedly. "You just have to cut in on my spotlight, don't you?"

Ryan cracked a small smile. "Sorry. Go ahead."

She set the binder on Ryan's desk and flipped it open to a stack of photocopied pages. "Yes, for your information, I did look into the Leadman case. Unfortunately, there wasn't all that much to see. The documents were all hard copies, and a lot of them didn't make it over when we switched to digital. But," she said, cutting off Ryan as he opened his mouth, "here's what I did find. I looked into the wife, Janet, and the son, Robert, who survived the explosion. Apparently, afterward, Janet couldn't cope with the press. She more or less vanished from the public eye. The son was twelve at the time. Then, six months on from the accident, Janet and Robert picked up sticks and moved to Brisbane to live with Janet's older sister. She rented out the place in Pittwater and hasn't lived there since."

Ryan nodded slowly. "And the older sister?"

"I think she might still be in Brisbane, but I'll have to track her down."

"That'd be great."

She gave him a crooked smile. "You're lucky I happen to trust your instincts. Most people wouldn't go to this much trouble for your crazy hunches."

"I know. Thanks, Ann."

A soft knock sounded at the door to Ryan's office. It was Detective Ross. Ryan waved her inside.

"Hey, boss," Ross said, "we've just got in touch with ABC's tour manager. The band is in Brisbane now. They've got a performance scheduled there on Thursday night."

"Brisbane?" Ryan said. He and Ann exchanged a glance. "Looks like we can kill two birds with one stone." He turned to Julie. "Contact the Brisbane HO and tell them we'll send up a team from Sydney. We can help with extra surveillance at the concert and interview the band while we're up there."

"On it," Ross affirmed, then turned on her heel and disappeared down the hall.

Ryan looked back to Ann. "Try and set up a meeting with Janet Leadman's older sister, if you can?"

"Sure," she said, "right after I have a cleaning voucher sent to Lisa Gordon."

Ryan groaned. "Strewth, you're not still on about that. I'd forgotten all about it."

"I know. That's why I'm handling it for you."

He huffed. "Fine. Just the cleaning voucher. Nothing flash."

Ann hummed noncommittally, picking up her binder from Ryan's desk and tucking it under her arm.

"Ann."

"What?"

"Did you hear me? Just the voucher."

"Of course, Detective Campbell."

When she used both his rank and surname, Ryan knew it was hopeless. "Just let me know what you find out about the sister," he sighed. "We'll head to Brisbane on Thursday morning."

CHAPTER 13:
LISA'S INVITATION

Lisa was at her desk, sipping a coffee as she scrolled through the latest notes from her editor on her laptop. She was interrupted by a soft knock on the wall of her cubicle, followed by a chorus of giggles.

She looked up. An intern, flanked by the receptionist and Lisa's friend Rachel from administrative, stood there, holding a large bouquet wrapped in a red satin ribbon. Lisa stared at the three of them blankly until the intern held out the flowers and said, "They're for you."

She rose from her chair and took the bouquet, perplexed. "You've certainly been keeping things quiet," Rachel teased. "Who's the new boyfriend?"

Lisa felt a blush stealing across her face. "I'm not seeing anyone," she muttered. "When would I have time to go on dates?"

"Ah, so you've got a secret admirer then," Rachel surmised. "Even better."

"Go on, read the card!" the receptionist said.

"All right, enough," Lisa said, shooing them on their way. "It's probably just a joke."

Ignoring their protests, she managed to shepherd them out of her cubicle. Once she was alone, she picked up the small card nestled among the lily blossoms. Her eyebrows climbed steadily higher as she read it.

Dear Lisa,
Sorry again about the other night at The Oaks. Here's a voucher for the dry cleaners.
I've booked us a table at Brambilla in Darling Harbour. Eight o'clock next Tuesday. Hope to see you there.
Sincerely,
Ryan Campbell

"Well," she murmured to the card. "Never expected that from Detective Ryan Campbell."

He may be human after all.

Lisa tucked the note back in among the flowers, shaking her head with a disbelieving laugh.

She set the bouquet to the side of her desk and returned to her work. With the campaign for the governor's election in full swing, she had plenty to keep her busy. There were four major candidates... first was Peter Duncan, an up-and-comer for the Eco and Environment Party who was expected to win a good portion of the youth vote. Then, for the Liberal Party, there was Susan Harrison, a current member of the House of Representatives and a mainstay of Sydney politics for decades; she'd first made headlines as a recovering alcoholic who'd gone on to win massive support from the progressive community. Colin Jenkins represented the Democrat Party, and his platform was essentially to oppose anything that the national government wanted to do. And then there was Wayne Brewster, running as a Republican, who had already won the public endorsement of the Prime Minister.

All of them had press events and promotional parties happening that weekend. Lisa would try to attend a few to get interviews and new details for her feature, although she figured she could safely skip the Brewster events. She'd seen quite enough of him over the last few days. Besides, she doubted there would be much point. It was already clear that Brewster would be toeing the Prime Minister's line on just about everything. No breaking news there.

Every once in a while as she worked, she would catch the faint scent of lilies and glance over at the flowers on the corner of her desk. The whole idea – sending a bouquet, asking her on a date after spilling wine on her dress – made her roll her eyes each time she remembered it. But it made her smile, too, against her better judgment.

CHAPTER 14: BRISBANE

The blazing floodlights over the stage went dark.

ABC had just finished their last song of the night. The crowd roared, rattling the windows of the security station near the entrance, where Ryan and Ann had made a point to stay on-site for the event. He'd wanted to personally oversee the extra security measures that had been put in place to protect the band and monitor the audience and staff. They'd interviewed the tour organisers earlier that day, but not much had come of it. Apparently the band hadn't received anything other than the usual fan letters and requests for autographs. No deranged threats or cryptic messages. Still, Ryan was on edge the night of the concert. If Brannan was right, the killer could be there, somewhere in the crowd.

All his worry came to nothing, though. There had been a grand total of five arrests: one for pickpocketing, two for a fistfight, two more for drunk and disorderly conduct. A quiet night, really. After the arena emptied out, Ryan headed back to the hotel, half relieved that nothing had happened and half disappointed that he was no closer to catching the murderer.

They spent Friday and Saturday with the Brisbane team, cross-referencing their data with what the Sydney officers had found. For hours, they pored over the details of the case, but made little headway. Then, on Sunday morning, Ryan made his way from his room down to the hotel lobby, where Ann was already waiting for him.

"What's this person's name, again?" he asked sleepily.

Ann arched an eyebrow. "Good morning to you too."

"Sorry. Good morning. What's the name?"

"Melanie Dean. Janet Leadman's niece. And hurry up. We're late."

The taxi ride from the hotel to Melanie's home on the outskirts of Brisbane was short, giving them just enough time to rehash the details Ann had uncovered in her research: it turned out that Linda, Janet's older sister, had died two years ago. But her daughter Melanie was alive, and she had agreed to meet with them and answer their questions. She'd sounded happy enough to do so, if somewhat puzzled.

The cab dropped them off in front of a neat, well-kept suburban house. Melanie opened the door before they'd even had a chance to knock. She was a small woman with mousy brown curls and a warm, kind smile. Ann and Ryan introduced themselves, and she gestured them into her living room, which was decorated with artificial flowers and macrame.

"Would you like a cuppa?" Melanie asked, already halfway to the kitchen.

"No, thank you," Ryan said. "We won't bother you for long. We just have a few questions."

"Sure," Melanie replied, perching on an armchair across from the sofa where Ryan and Ann sat. "What can I help you with?"

"We were wondering if you could tell us anything about your aunt, Janet Leadman," Ryan said, as Ann pulled a small notebook from her jacket pocket and flipped it open to a blank page. "She came to stay with your mother, is that right?"

"She did, yes. But that was years ago. I was a teenager then."

"Can you tell us anything about that time?"

"Well…" Melanie seemed to search her memory, her eyes drifting through the window over Ryan and Ann's heads. "She came with her son, my cousin, Robert. He was maybe ten or twelve at the time. It was after that terrible accident that killed Suzie and my Uncle David. I remember my mum and Aunt Janet didn't get along, I can tell you that. I didn't like her much, either, to be honest. She was always shopping for new clothes and going out to restaurants she couldn't afford, leaving Robert all by himself. I felt sorry for the kid. I'd loan him books to read. Play him my records sometimes. He was really smart, once you got to know him. Quiet, though. Quiet and sensitive." She shrugged. "I knew he and his mum didn't get on, either. He blamed her for their deaths. Suzie's and David's, I mean. That's common, I guess, for kids to blame the one surviving family member after a tragedy like that. He had some counselling while he was here, but I'm not sure if that changed much. Considering what he'd been through, though, it seemed like he was doing all right."

Ann's pen scratched across the paper. "And how long did they stay with you?" she asked.

"Oh, I dunno, maybe… three or four months? Then Aunt Janet came in one day, announced she'd met a rich American surgeon, and that she and Robert were going to live with him in the States. So they left, and that was that. My mum got a letter a few years later, saying that Janet was off living in a mansion with her rich surgeon husband. She got exactly what she'd always wanted, I suppose."

"Any idea what part of America they went to?" Ryan said.

Melanie shook her head regretfully. "Sorry, not a clue. I'm sure it said in the letter. But when Mum died I cleaned out her house and chucked all her old papers. Place was in such a state, it took us three weeks to get it clean enough to sell. Anyway, if I had it, I'd give it to you. But it's long gone now." She paused. "What's your interest in Janet, anyway? Did something happen?"

"No, we're just… gathering information on a potentially related case."

"I see." She clearly didn't, but didn't seem troubled enough by the mystery to ask more questions. "Well, good luck with gathering your information."

"Thanks, Ms Dean."

"I'll walk you out."

The taxi, waiting at the curb, started its engine as they climbed into the back. "The hotel, please, for our bags," Ann told the driver. "Then the airport."

As the car set off along the suburban street, Ann gave Ryan a long look. "Well?" she prompted, when he remained silent. "What do you think?"

He sighed, watching the trees flicker by outside the window. "I think that was probably all a massive waste of time."

"You know, you never actually told me. What do you think this accident has to do with Lindsay Brook or Paula Thorn? The case has been closed for years."

"It was closed, but it was never really resolved. Something didn't add up. I was sure of it then. And I just had this strange feeling…"

She frowned at him. "What?"

He realised he'd trailed off in the middle of his sentence and tried to collect himself. "That the missing piece in that case would help us solve this new one. But it hasn't gotten us anywhere." He shrugged. "I guess I was wrong. But at least I was just as wrong as Brannan. So much for his psychology theories. We didn't get anything from the concert, either."

"That's true," Ann agreed, turning to look out her own window. "Guess it's time to head back home."

•

They got their suitcases from the hotel and made their way to the airport. On the flight, Ann read the paper while Ryan stared blankly at his case notes, hoping to somehow spot something he hadn't already seen.

"By the way," Ann said, without raising her eyes, "I sent that cleaning voucher to Lisa Gordon."

"Oh. Good. Thanks."

"I also booked you two a table at Brambilla, that Italian place in Darling Harbour. Tuesday. Eight o'clock."

Ryan's head snapped towards Ann, who idly thumbed to the next page. "You did what?"

"It'll be good for you, Campbell. You've done nothing but work for months. Trust me. You need this."

He let out a long sigh and pinched the bridge of his nose. After a few moments of internal struggle, he said, "Fine. Yes. Brambilla on Tuesday. Until then, can I focus on the case, please?"

"By all means." A slight knowing smile tugged at Ann's mouth, which Ryan pretended not to see.

He tried to refocus on the notes in front of him, but, annoyingly, it was even harder now that Lisa had been invoked in his mind; he was surprised at how clearly he recalled her keen blue eyes, the messy tumble of her dark curls.

Maybe one dinner wouldn't be so bad.

CHAPTER 15:
BARRENJOEY HOUSE HOTEL

The Barrenjoey House Hotel's waterfront restaurant was sparsely occupied at nine o'clock on a Saturday night. There were a handful of businesspeople having a late dinner. A few vacationing families were finishing their desserts before they headed up to their rooms. At the bar, a young couple spoke in hushed, angry tones, the tones used when one would prefer to yell but the company of others compels quiet.

And at the other end of the bar, the killer sat alone, listening idly to them.

He'd been there for a couple of hours, and from snatches of their conversation he'd gotten the gist of the argument. The man had been caught having an affair with some girl at his office. The woman had found out and was furious, but had acceded to the man's suggestion that they book a weekend away to try and rekindle their relationship. It was clearly a pointless effort, the killer thought, watching the ice melt in his drink as the woman hissed, *"She was my best friend and you slept with her for five months."*

They'd been having the same conversation for some forty minutes now, and while the sordid details of their misery had entertained him for a while, the killer was growing tired of hearing it. He was just about to leave when the woman's voice finally climbed above the stage whisper she'd been using all night.

"Forget it. It's over," she snapped. "Go home, pack your things and move out. It's my apartment anyway."

Some of the restaurant staff began to cast nervous sidelong glances at the couple.

"God, I can't *believe* you," she went on, unaware of the attention she was drawing, her voice starting to crack. "After all these years, how could you betray me like this?"

"'All these years? You mean all the years you've spent ignoring me so you could scheme your way into high society, pretending to be something you're not. You're *obsessed*.'"

Typical, the killer thought, watching them from the corner of his eye. A snarl began to curl his lip. He'd seen it a million times. Women were always chasing something… wanting to be more beautiful, more rich, more perfect, and to hell with anyone who loved them. It was enough to make him sick.

"Just leave, Alex," the woman said.

"Fine," the man replied, rising to his feet. "I'll leave. At least I have Amanda. She cares about me. She cares about who I *am*, not just what she wants me to be."

"Great. Go find Amanda then."

The man called Alex hesitated, suddenly uncertain. But it was too late to go back on his bluff now. He snatched up his jacket and said, "I'll go get my things out of our room."

"Hurry up," the woman said sullenly. "I'm staying the weekend."

"And I'm taking my car. At least I won't have to be your damn chauffeur anymore."

"Fine. I'll get a taxi."

Her cold eyes followed him all the way out of the restaurant. When he had gone, she let out a long breath, carefully gathered up her purse and sweater, and walked out to the deck adjoining the restaurant. The killer watched the spark and flare of her cigarette lighter, a burning point of orange in the dark. His eyes traced the glow, moving in an arc as she took the lit cigarette from between her lips.

The killer stood up, smoothed a crease in his shirt, and followed her onto the deck.

By the time he got outside, the woman had taken the stairs and was crossing the road toward the hotel car park. He trailed along behind her at an inconspicuous distance as she walked through the aisles of cars. She stopped at a black Lexus, new and obviously well cared for. Then she dug through her purse and pulled out a set of keys, set the tip of one against the front headlight, and strolled the length of the car, scratching a deep gouge along its side.

Spiteful bitch, the killer thought as he watched her from a distance.

The woman gave a self-satisfied chuckle and tucked the keys back into her bag. She carried on walking across a grassy area and onto the strip of sand. She ambled slowly along the beach, away from the lights of the hotel, enjoying the last few pulls of her cigarette.

The killer followed. He glanced back over his shoulder; by now, they were out of view of the restaurant's windows, and the last few patrons on the deck were preparing to leave. The beach here was dark, out of reach of the streetlamps, and in a few moments they would be alone.

He stayed back and walked along the side of the grassy area, where he found a storm-damaged tree and picked up a branch that had fallen from it. Then he lengthened his stride to catch up to the woman.

When he got close enough, he snapped the branch in half. She started to spin around at the sudden noise. Before she had finished turning, one swift blow to the temple knocked her unconscious, and she dropped to the sand without a sound.

He glanced up at the road and then at the empty stretch of beach between them and the hotel. No one had seen them. He'd struck with precision, waiting until they were near a thicket of trees that grew down to the waterline, where his dinghy was tied up out of sight.

He dragged her body into the waiting shelter of the undergrowth, leaving a trail in the sand like a snake's. Soon enough, that wouldn't matter. All trace of them would be gone with the tide.

He rolled her into the dinghy and pushed the boat out into the water, then climbed in after her, dropped the outboard motor over the back, and pulled the cord. The engine came to life with a soft growl, and the boat skimmed away across the black waters.

CHAPTER 16:
BACK IN THE OFFICE

The weekend trip to Brisbane had taken more out of Ryan than he thought. On Monday morning he got into the office a little later than usual. He was pouring his first cup of coffee when Ann tracked him down.

"So," she said, sidling up to him. "I just talked to Julie. Looks like we *might* have a lead. Finally."

Ryan turned to her in surprise. "What is it?"

"Don't get too excited," she warned. "It's not much to go on. But it's more than we've had so far." She poured herself a mug, topped off Ryan's to empty the pot, and started to brew a new one. "Remember that one agency employee who was older than the others?"

"What about him?"

"Turns out he wasn't Australian like we thought. He's English, just arrived a couple weeks ago as an exchange student. Name's John McCann. Except Julie went to talk to McCann this morning, and according to him, he wasn't working at the arena that night."

Ryan's brow furrowed in confusion. "Then why was he on the agency's list?"

"That's the interesting part. McCann says that when he first arrived in Sydney, he had his passport stolen while he was still at the airport. He's been waiting on a new one from the consulate but hasn't gotten it yet."

Ryan swirled his coffee pensively. "So someone used the stolen passport to book a job at the staffing agency."

"That's what it looks like."

He gave a decisive nod. "Have we put a notice out for that name?"

"Already done. Julie reported it to the federal police. Anyone attempting to use that passport should be apprehended immediately, and their information sent to our office."

"Good." Ryan let out a slow breath, turning over this new information in his mind. Someone using a stolen identity was definitely suspicious. It might not be anything to do with their case. But then again, it might.

The brief improvement to his mood faded quickly as he caught sight of Brannan on the other side of the incident room. Brannan caught sight of him too and waved him over.

"How did it go at the concert?" Brannan asked.

"Fool's errand, I'm afraid," Ryan said, testily. "Didn't get anything out of it. And now I have a stack of expense reports to explain to my boss."

"Oh," Brannan said. "Well, sorry it didn't turn anything up."

"Yes. Maybe take another look at that psychological profile of yours before you send us on another wild goose chase."

Without waiting for a response, Ryan returned to his desk. He immediately dived into the new reports that had rolled in over the course of the morning. He was tempted, briefly, to take one more look at the details of the Leadman case, but he pushed the thought from his mind. Ann was right. It wasn't worth the distraction.

Just look at Wayne Brewster running for governor again, Ryan thought grimly. It was clear that it was time for all of them to move on.

By that afternoon, Ryan had finally slogged through all of the new information that had arrived on his desk. Just as he finished up, he got a phone call from Dr Tabard, asking him to come to the lab. Ryan told her he would meet her there in a few minutes.

Pearl was standing outside the entrance to the lab, frowning down at a clipboard in her hand. She looked up as Ryan approached.

"Good to have you back from your weekend in Brisbane," she said, and quirked an eyebrow. "Heard you got to see ABC. I didn't realise you were such a fan of eighties pop. Did you enjoy your concert?"

"No, not really," Ryan admitted. "I didn't have anyone to dance with, you know. Ann's not exactly the dancing queen."

Pearl chuckled and gave him a wink. "Next time you'll have to invite me. If it's an eighties concert, I'll be your date any day," she said, married and easily twenty years Ryan's senior.

"I'll be sure to let you know," he laughed.

A few moments of silence followed as the smiles faded from their faces.

"Well," Ryan said. "I'm hoping you have something to tell me."

"Ah. Yes." Pearl flipped back to the first sheet of her clipboard. "I'll have the full report sent up to your desk, but basically… we finished the autopsy on Lindsay Brook and we didn't find anything that's a surefire connection to the killer. We did get a partial fingerprint, but it's badly smudged. We swabbed the print and it looks like he was probably wearing medical gloves, took them off and touched the body. The cornstarch residue from inside the gloves left a very weak print on the girl's shoulder."

"Any chance the residue can be traced to something specific? A brand or a manufacturer, maybe?"

"Unfortunately, there are dozens of brands of those disposable gloves, and many of them are similar. If you had the exact glove that the killer used, you might be able to make a positive match. Otherwise, it's not much use to us."

Ryan nodded, disappointed but not surprised. "Any other evidence?"

"Well, there were some fibres of clothing stuck to her skin. A few different types of them. Some clearly came from her own clothing, but some of it was likely from the killer's. But again, you'd need the exact clothes to make a definite match."

"Tox report back yet?"

"Yes, just got it in. Relatively low levels of alcohol, and high levels of an opioid. She's never been prescribed painkillers, so it was either recreational…"

"…or the killer drugged her," Ryan finished.

Pearl nodded. "All of the injection sites looked very recent, a day or so antemortem, meaning she wasn't a regular user. So my money's on the latter," she said. "But you're the detective."

"And the incisions?"

"Just like Paula Thorn. Clean and precise. Surgical, almost. Weapon was probably a scalpel or something like it."

"I see," Ryan said slowly. "All right. Thanks for your help, Doctor Tabard. You said you'll have the full report sent up to me?"

"It'll probably beat you back to your desk."

He nodded. "Give me an update if you find anything new."

"I always do." She glanced up from her clipboard and caught his eye. "Chin up, Detective. I'm sure you'll catch him," she said, with a small, encouraging smile.

Ryan hadn't meant to make his worry so obvious. "You're right. I'm sure we will." He lapsed into a brief silence. When he spoke again, it was in a quieter tone. "I just hope we manage to do it before he hurts anyone else."

CHAPTER 17:
ANOTHER VICTIM

Somewhere in Pittwater, in a windowless room, a woman was crying softly. She was tied down to an old bed, her hands bound above her head, one foot secured to each of the lower corners of the mattress.

The killer stood over her, gently tapping the air bubbles out of a syringe full of morphine. He ignored her whimpers as he placed the needle against a blue vein in the crook of her arm. In went the needle. Down went the plunger. The woman's whimpers subsided. She was still conscious, but only just.

He walked over to a record player in the corner of the room and put the needle to vinyl. Scratchy music filled the thick air. It was an old song, one that rhapsodised about how sweet it was to love a woman, how tender they were, how beautiful and perfect and good.

He hated these songs. He hated them so much it made the blood build to a pounding roar in his ears. To think that there were people who actually believed this, who believed that women could offer anything except deceit and shame and pain. What fools they were. He knew better.

Someone had to pay for this overwhelming rage that engulfed him. *She* had to pay. He watched her face as he carefully and methodically slipped the latex gloves onto his hands, pulled a condom over his erect penis, and picked up a scalpel. The woman, in her opiate haze, didn't scream when he climbed onto her, nor when he climaxed. She never screamed… not when he drew the scalpel along her skin, not when the blood ran in little rivulets and pooled into a stain of sticky red beneath her.

Tempting though it was, he restrained himself from cutting too deeply. He wasn't done with this one yet.

CHAPTER 18:
DATE NIGHT

Tuesday seemed to move at a snail's pace. Ryan's team was still busy chasing down the shadows of leads in old arrest records and long-buried case reports. Ryan himself spent the morning writing up a full account of their weekend excursion for his boss, who had made clear in no uncertain terms that he expected the report to justify the time and money spent in Brisbane. He still thought that it should have been Brannan who had to write a tedious report to explain the mistakes in his so-called psychological profile, but apparently Ryan's boss disagreed.

Just after lunch, he spotted Ann in the hallway and tapped her shoulder before she reached the incident room. In a murmur, he asked if she would mind looking up the address of the old Leadman house in Pittwater.

"I thought we were through with all that business," she said, peering at him dubiously over the rim of her coffee mug as she took a sip.

"I know. But Melanie didn't mention anything about who owned the property now. I just want to see if it was ever sold."

"What difference does that make?"

"If it wasn't sold, I thought I'd go over and have a look."

Ann's eyebrows raised higher into her fringe.

No one seemed to be paying them any attention, but Ryan dropped his voice anyway, knowing that his theory wasn't wildly popular around the office. "Paula Thorn was found at that old plot that belonged to Brewster, where Leadman was building a new property. I don't think that's a coincidence."

"You want to hear what I think?"

Ryan swallowed a sigh, knowing it wasn't actually a question, and gestured for her to go on.

"I think you're letting yourself get distracted. This Leadman lark isn't going to help you solve the Paula Thorn case. All it's going to do is get the brass breathing down your neck as soon as they find out how much time you're putting into this."

"Then let's just hope they don't find out any time soon," Ryan muttered under his breath.

"What was that?"

"Nothing. Forget about the address. I'll track it down myself."

"No, I'll find the address," Ann said, scrutinising him. "Because I don't want you to cut me out of this. Who knows what shit you'll get into if I'm not around to keep you in line."

Unwillingly, Ryan cracked a smile.

He'd all but forgotten about his plans for the evening until he sat back down in his office and caught sight of the calendar on the wall. It was Tuesday, which meant the reservation at Brambilla was at eight o'clock tonight. He felt a renewed surge of annoyance at the prospect. He should have told Ann to cancel the bloody date as soon as he found out about it.

At ten to five, the monotony of his afternoon was broken by a phone call.

"MacDonald?" Ryan said, straightening up in his chair. "What have you got? Anything on Paula Thorn or Lindsay Brook?"

"No, nothing on them," MacDonald answered, and a twinge of disappointment went through Ryan. "Nothing new over here at all, really. Except for a bit of an oddity from the Barrenjoey House Hotel."

Ryan frowned. "What about it?"

"Staff contacted us this morning. Apparently a young couple booked a room for the weekend. They checked in on Friday, had dinner at the hotel restaurant on Saturday, and drinks at the bar later that night. But no one's seen them since. Housekeeping found all the girl's stuff still stashed in the room Sunday night."

"So did anyone contact her?"

"The hotel has been trying to reach her by phone and email so they could ask her what to do with all her things. But they haven't heard anything back for two days. They got nervy and finally called us."

Ryan gave a dismissive shrug, as if MacDonald could see him. "Sounds like they had an argument and the girl took off. She'll probably ring them any minute once she realises all her stuff's still there. Anyway, thanks for the update. If you hear anything new, call me right away, all right?"

MacDonald agreed and hung up. As soon as Ryan set his phone back down on the desk, Ann appeared at the door to his office.

"Just came to remind you, you've got a date tonight," she said. "In case you forgot."

"I didn't," he replied gruffly.

"Good. I just emailed you her phone number in case you need to call her."

"Thanks."

"Get there early." She glanced him over critically. "And wear something smart."

Before he could respond, she withdrew from his office and disappeared down the hall.

He looked down at himself, realising with a sinking feeling that he'd forgotten to bring a change of clothes. He checked the clock and decided that if he left right now, he'd have just enough time to get to his place in Paddington and back into town again.

After a quick shower and shave at home, he pulled a suit and dress shirt out from the depths of his closet, trying not to think about how long since he'd needed to wear this stuff, and went over it all with an iron. He put on the aftershave that had been a gift from his daughter for his most recent birthday, looked himself over in the mirror one last time, and smoothed back his hair. Then, with a deep breath, he pulled out his phone to order a cab.

The taxi dropped him off a half block from Brambilla. As he headed towards the entrance, he spotted a woman walking ahead of him. She was in a form-fitting, navy blue dress and Ryan took a moment to appreciate how stunning she was before she disappeared through the door to the restaurant. A few moments later, he stepped inside and gave the maître d' his name.

"Ah, yes," the man smiled. "Reservation for two. I believe your date is already here."

He turned to gesture and Ryan followed his gaze to Lisa Gordon, sitting at the bar in a striking navy blue dress.

That was *her?*

"Thank you," he said, and crossed to the bar.

"Hi," he said, rather awkwardly, to get Lisa's attention. She turned towards him with a blank look. "Erm… it's me. Ryan Campbell."

A coy smile formed on her lips and she arched a brow. "Haven't we met before?" she asked with wide innocent eyes, before laughing at his mildly panicked expression. He was surprised at how quickly her laughter put him at ease. "Come on then, I've just ordered a drink. What would you like?"

"A schooner of light beer," he said to the bartender as he sat on the stool next to hers. The bartender returned a moment later with his beer and her glass of chardonnay. Ryan started to say, "Listen, I wanted to apologise for the other day."

But just as he began to speak, so did Lisa. "I should say sorry about last time we ran into each other."

They both cut off, shared a moment of brief silence, and then broke into mutual, embarrassed laughter.

"Well," said Ryan, "I think our table's ready. Shall we sit down?"

They chatted as a waitress showed them to their seats. Lisa mentioned that she'd been here only once before and the food had been lovely, so she'd been looking forward to coming back. Ryan told her he'd been here a number of times for retirement parties.

"That's probably why Ann picked this place," he said, realising it as he spoke while a look of dawning comprehension came onto his face, which made Lisa laugh.

He pulled out her chair for her and they settled in.

Ryan never would've guessed it from their first few interactions, but it turned out that when neither of them was on the job or spilling drinks on the other, they actually got on quite well. Ryan asked her how she'd gotten into her line of work, and she told him that she'd always wanted to be a journalist.

"Even when I was a kid," she said, taking a sip of her chardonnay. "My dad ran a little community paper in Parramatta, right up until he died. I grew up loving the newsroom."

"So that's what you went to uni for," Ryan prompted.

"Yes. Studied journalism at Canberra. Then got married after leaving University to an advertising exec. Didn't last too long. Obviously." She gave a self-conscious laugh.

"What happened, if you don't mind my asking?"

"Oh, he had an affair with one of his secretaries," she said, disinterestedly. "One day he informed me that he was madly in love with her, and also that she was pregnant. We got a divorce and they moved up to Perth to raise the kid near her parents." She shrugged. "Anyway, that's me. Tell me about you. How'd you wind up being a detective?"

So Ryan told her. It didn't take long, because his story wasn't too far off from hers. He'd always known what he wanted to do, ever since he was a kid watching old police shows on TV. He'd also got married in his twenties "Much too young," he admitted to a barmaid from New Zealand. At the wedding she was already pregnant with their daughter Madison. After she was born, it hadn't taken more than a few years for the two of them to admit that they were completely incompatible. They split, and his now ex-wife went back to New Zealand with Madison.

"She's twelve now," Ryan said. "I try to get over there and see her whenever I can, although it's not as often as I'd like. We Skype all the time. But it's not the same. I miss her like crazy."

Lisa gave him a small smile. Ryan quickly dropped his gaze back down to the menu. "Should we order?"

When the check came, Lisa grabbed for it, saying they could split it, but Ryan was faster. He insisted on paying for the whole thing, and Lisa conceded with a flicker of amusement in her sharp blue eyes.

With their meal paid for, they lingered for a few moments in uncertain silence. Finally, Ryan screwed up his nerve. "If you wanted to pay me back," he said, "we could go down to Harbour Bar, just down the street, and you could get the first round."

A smile split Lisa's face. "Well," she said, pretending to consider it, "that sounds more than fair to me."

They left Brambilla and walked down the road, admiring the lights glittering on the water as the boats bobbed with the gentle swell. Once they reached Harbour Bar, they found that it was packed. They had to push their way to the bar, managing to snag the last two empty stools.

The two of them kept up a lively banter for hours, pausing often to laugh at the antics of a group of girls in the bar who, they deduced, were at a hen party. Ryan altogether lost track of the time, and before he knew it, the bartender was cupping his hands around his mouth to announce last orders. Someone shouldered up to the bar to order his final drink for the evening, and as he did so, he pushed Ryan closer to Lisa. Ryan narrowly stopped his head from colliding with hers, and she laughingly put a hand on his shoulder to steady him, and then neither of them pulled away.

Ryan had time to think, *I know I'm going to regret this*, before he kissed her. Maybe she thought the same thing, but she kissed him back anyway.

As the bar staff shooed everyone out, they made their way to the street. It took ages to hail a taxi with so many people wanting them, but when Ryan finally managed to get one, he held the door open for Lisa and she slid into the back.

"Paddington for me, and then Mosman for her," Ryan told the driver as he climbed in after her.

"Actually…" Lisa said.

Ryan closed the door behind him and turned to her, finding her eyes on his and a smile on her face.

"…I think Paddington will do just fine."

CHAPTER 19:
PALM BEACH

Mrs Shanna Jones was running late. This was not uncommon, with two young children who seemed allergic to doing anything on schedule. She managed to drop off her eight-year-old son Harry at Maria Regina Primary School with three minutes to spare before the bell rang. Then she set off to take her four-year-old Mary to a birthday party at Palm Beach.

She pulled into the parking lot, where she spotted a few other parents who were there for the same event, most of them unloading folding chairs and bags full of plastic beach toys from their cars. She parked just in front of the public toilets, and Mary, seeing this, announced that she needed a wee.

"The toilets aren't open yet, love," she started to say, but she hadn't even finished her sentence before Mary had unlatched her seatbelt, thrown open her door, and skipped off towards the building.

"Mary, wait!" her mother called after her. She jumped out of the car and followed her, noticing as she approached that the door to the ladies' toilets *was* open, which was puzzling, as she was certain that it was not normally unlocked until ten am. "Mary, come back here."

But before she could set foot inside, her daughter's piercing screams sent a horrifying chill through her body.

•

Ryan was staring into his coffee like he was trying to see the future in it. He was doing his best to ignore the throbbing headache he'd had all morning. If he was honest, though, he'd admit that his date with Lisa had been worth every bit of the eminently bad hangover he was now suffering because of it.

The ache in his temples twinged as the phone rang. "Detective Campbell," he said in a tired voice.

"Campbell, it's me... MacDonald."

Ryan rubbed his face. "This isn't about the girl who forgot to pick up her things from the Barrenjoey Hotel again, is it?"

"Actually, it is," MacDonald said. "We may have found her. And it's not pretty."

Ryan, Ann, Pearl and several other officers from their unit arrived at Palm Beach less than thirty minutes later. As soon as they got there, Ryan was pleased to note that MacDonald had done a much better job this time around. The whole area had been efficiently cordoned off, with the public held at bay a good distance away from the crime scene.

A group of white-suited forensic technicians was already hard at work.

Pearl split off to join them while Ann followed Ryan. Together they ducked under a line of police tape and found MacDonald in front of the North Palm Beach Surf Lifesaving Club building, which had been commandeered for use as the police's base of operations.

"Three major crime scenes in as many weeks," he said grimly as Ryan and Ann approached.

"Not exactly our usual routine," Ryan acknowledged.

"No kidding. Guess this is the way the world's going now."

Ryan nodded to the tiled building that seemed to be at the epicentre of the activity. "What have we got?"

MacDonald sighed heavily before answering. "A kid found her," he said. "Four years old. She walked in to use the toilet and the body was… well, you'll see."

"Is the girl okay now?" Ann asked.

"Yes, she and her mum are with the medics. They were here for a birthday party. Had to have all the families cleared out of the area, of course."

"Do we know anything else yet?" Ryan asked.

"Just that it looks like the building was broken into during the night. Usually, the cleaning attendant comes to unlock it at ten every morning, but the padlock had been forced open sometime before the girl and her mother got here, around nine."

Pearl rejoined, wearing an unnerved expression that Ryan had rarely seen on her.

"The techs have already done their first sweep," she told them. "If you put on a bunny suit, you can come in and have a look."

MacDonald shook his head, looking slightly queasy. "I've seen all I want to, thanks," he said.

Ann and Ryan exchanged an uneasy glance and took the white forensic suits that Pearl held out to them. They put the suits on over their plainclothes and followed her to the building at the edge of the sand.

Between the flash of the photographer's bulb and the technicians going over the space inch by inch, the already small interior felt claustrophobic. The tiled floor and walls seemed to capture and magnify every noise. When Ann gasped, the sound echoed in Ryan's ears, which had begun to ring unpleasantly.

The woman's body was marble white and grotesquely contorted. She'd been pushed up against the back of the shower wall. Her eyes appeared preternaturally huge. Both lids had been removed and she looked out at them with a glassy blank stare. Wide slits had been carved on either side of her mouth, giving her a gruesome frown. There were other injuries – bruising on her neck, lacerations around her sides – but it was hard to tell the full extent of the mutilation with her limbs twisted up around her like a broken doll's.

There was another injury that was clearly discernible, though, starkly red against the startling white of her skin. The letter 'I' had been carved into her stomach.

Ryan glanced at Ann, who'd gone pale. She swallowed and turned away to ask one of the technicians a question, although it was obvious that she was just trying to get the girl's body out of her line of sight. Ryan didn't blame her. He wished he could do the same, but he couldn't seem to tear his eyes away.

"Same killer?" he asked Pearl quietly.

"Same killer," she said. "I'd bet anything on it."

"Do you have a cause of death?"

"From the bruising I can see, I would guess strangulation. But I'll know more once we get the body back to the lab."

Ryan nodded tersely. "Well… keep me posted."

He finally managed to look away and caught Ann's eye, beckoning her outside.

As soon as they were out of the building, they both unconsciously drew a deep, long breath of fresh air. MacDonald met them at the edge of the parking lot. "I've just phoned the council to get the beach closed off," he said. "They'll have a notice out to the public shortly."

Ryan nodded. "Press'll be here any minute."

"Reckon so. I'll post some officers at the cordon to keep everyone in line."

Maybe his last talking-to really had gotten through to MacDonald.

Ryan felt a pang of guilt in his gut. MacDonald had been the one who was concerned about the woman who'd gone missing from The Barrenjoey House Hotel, and Ryan had all but written it off. Was he losing his touch?

He pushed the thought from his mind. "We'll head up to the hotel to see if we can get any details on the missing person," Ryan said to MacDonald, a little gruffly. "Keep an eye on things here and stay in touch."

"Will do."

CHAPTER 20:
EARLIER THAT MORNING

Lisa woke up with Ryan still sleeping soundly beside her.

She rose from the bed and padded quietly to the washroom. She wiped the smudged mascara from under her eyes and then called for a taxi to take her down to Circular Quay, all without waking him. After catching a ferry across the bay to Taronga, she'd planned to grab another taxi, but decided impulsively to walk instead. It was a beautiful day, with bucketfuls of sunshine and a pleasant, cooling breeze off the water.

When Lisa unlocked her front door, she found the house empty. Paul must have left for work already. Truth be told, she was glad he wasn't around. This way she didn't have to answer any questions about the contented smile that wouldn't budge from her face. She hadn't dated much since her divorce. Last night had been a more than welcome change of pace.

It seemed a little strange, actually, that a man like Ryan would still be single. But then again, her first impression of him – rude, standoffish, abrasive – hadn't exactly won her over. She chuckled a little at the memory. Nothing could have been further away from the version of Ryan she had seen last night.

She'd already told the office she was taking the morning off, and with a glance at the microwave clock, she saw that she had enough time for an hour-long nap before she headed into work. She slipped out of her navy blue dress, draped it over a chair in her room, and crawled into her bed.

It felt like only a few moments later that she was startled awake by the sound of her mobile ringing. She picked it up and squinted blearily at the screen, which flashed the name BRIAN PALMER. Her editor.

"Hello?" she said into the phone.

"Lisa. Good, I got hold of you. Something's happened up in Pittwater."

Haven't we done this before? Lisa thought as she pushed herself upright and rubbed sleep from her eyes. "What's 'something'?"

"They found another body."

"Jesus."

"It was Palm Beach this time. I've already sent Paul and Nikki out there, but I want you to get on this too. How soon can you get there?"

Nikki? She was a junior reporter, a recent addition to the staff. Lisa would've been happy enough to hand off the whole story to her—as a political reporter, the last few weeks had been more dead bodies than she felt especially equipped to handle. But now didn't seem like the time to argue with her editor.

"I'll be there in ninety minutes."

Brian tutted.

She suppressed a yawn. "Okay, Forty minutes."

"That's better. Cheers."

Lisa dressed quickly, made a muffin with jam to eat on the way, and started the drive up to Pittwater. As she drew closer, she spotted a number of police helicopters circling in the sky like vultures.

Traffic snarled as she neared Palm Beach. Peering ahead, she could see police stopping cars and diverting them.

"Damn it," she muttered. She cast a glance around, and spotted a turn-off to Barrenjoey Road. She drummed her fingers on the steering wheel. She was almost certain that if she took that road past the jetties, she could come round the other side of the beach access, where there was no police block. Maybe she'd have a clearer vantage point of the action from there?

While she was still deciding, her mobile rang. She glanced at the screen before she answered. It was Paul.

"Where are you?" she asked.

"I'm with Nikki at the police tape line down by the beach," he said. She could hear the muted, collective jabber of a crowd around him.

"Any idea what's going on?"

"Not really. The police aren't saying anything. Are you coming down here?"

At that moment, Lisa spotted two figures as she was driving down the Barrenjoey Road as she passed the Barrenjoey House Hotel.

She did a double take. Was that…?

Detective Ryan Campbell and his assistant Ann? her eyes traced the trajectory of their path. They were headed straight towards the entrance of the hotel.

"Barrenjoey House Hotel," she murmured under her breath.

"What was that?" Paul asked.

"Ah… listen, it's impossible to get through to the beach at the moment, traffic's all backed up," she told him. "But I might have a lead. Tell Nikki to stay at the beach in case anything breaks. Meanwhile, you come meet me in the lobby of the Barrenjoey House Hotel. It's on the back road to Palm Beach."

"Got it. Be there in a few minutes." The line went dead.

Lisa swung her car around and pulled into the hotel carpark.

CHAPTER 21:
INVESTIGATION AT THE
BARRENJOEY HOTEL

The young receptionist of the Barrenjoey House Hotel greeted Ann and Ryan with a nervous smile. The police swarm that had descended on the neighbourhood clearly had everyone on edge. He flashed his badge and said, "Detective Ryan Campbell. Is there a manager here I can talk to?"

"Of course," the woman said, and stepped out from behind the desk. "Come with me."

Under his breath, Ryan told Ann, "I've got this. Can you go talk to the bar staff and start asking around for details? Check for CCTV cameras, too."

Ann nodded. "Catch up with you later," she said, and set off towards the hotel restaurant.

The receptionist led Ryan through a door off the lobby and down a corridor. "This is where all the admin stuff is," she said. "Breakroom there, security office there, and the managers' office... right here." She knocked before opening a nondescript grey door and introduced the two people inside as Mr and Mrs Pearson. Both appeared to be in their late fifties, Mrs Pearson with curly, henna-red hair and Mr Pearson with no hair at all. When Ryan told them he was here to find out more information about the woman who'd left her belongings in one of their rooms, the couple exchanged grim looks.

"I knew something had happened to her," Mrs Pearson said darkly. "I just knew it."

"What was that woman's name?" Ryan asked.

"Amy Shelton. No... Amy Shepherd. Just a moment. I'll check the logs." Mr Pearson wheeled around to punch a few keys on a laptop computer on the desk.

"So the room was under her name?" Ryan said.

"Yes, she made the reservation," he confirmed. "Here it is. Amy Shepherd."

"Did either of you talk to her personally?"

"I did," said Mrs Pearson. "Spoke with her on the phone when she booked."

"Anything unusual about the call?"

"Not at all. Mentioned that it was a reservation for herself and her boyfriend. We get a lot of professional couples coming up for the weekends from the city."

"And do you remember anything about their stay?"

Mrs Pearson shook her head slowly, her brow furrowed. "They checked in around three thirty Friday afternoon. I showed them to their room, like I do with all our guests. Gave them the usual rundown... hours for the hotel breakfast, when the restaurant was open, all that. But as far as I know, nothing particularly eventful happened the whole time they were here." Mrs Pearson shrugged. "Neither of them came down for breakfast Sunday morning and no one ever came to turn in a key."

"But the boyfriend's things were gone from the room."

"Yes. The room was quite a mess, actually. Like somebody had packed up in a big hurry. But all of her stuff – clothes in the closet, makeup on the counter, that sort of thing – that was all left behind."

Ryan nodded slowly. "And you tried to contact her?"

"Well, yes. After the maid found all her stuff still piled up, we rang her and tried emailing, too. But I never got an answer."

"I see," Ryan murmured. "Do you still have the belongings from that room?"

"Sure. We've set them aside here, in the back office." Mrs Pearson gestured to a suitcase in the corner of the room.

"We'll need to collect that as evidence. I'll send someone from my department to pick it up shortly." He glanced over at the tense expressions on Mr and Mrs Pearson's face. "I'm sorry to say that with all this going on, your hotel is officially now part of an ongoing crime investigation. I'll have to get a forensic team in here and need to check your CCTV cameras."

"Did they find her?" Mr Pearson piped up. He'd been listening silently from the computer desk for so long that Ryan had almost forgotten he was there. "Is that what all this fuss is about down at the beach?"

"We're not sure just yet," Ryan admitted. "But we'll keep the public informed as we learn more."

"Will we have to cancel any reservations?" Mrs Pearson asked with concern.

"No, that shouldn't be necessary. Just keep everyone out of Ms Shepherd's room, please. I'll send forensics up there shortly."

"It's all been cleaned already, I'm afraid."

"I know. But my team is pretty good. We'll see if they can find something." The two of them nodded solemnly. "Well, you've both been very helpful, Mr and Mrs Pearson. Thank you very much. We'll be in touch if we need any more information from you."

Ryan left quickly, stepping out of their office and retracing Ann's path across the lobby to the bar. He caught up with her just as she was finishing up an interview with one of the restaurant staff, a woman with a long braid of jet-black hair. He hung back a few steps while Ann thanked the woman and scribbled something down in her notepad. When she headed off, Ryan stepped up next to Ann.

"Who was that, then?" he asked her.

"That," she said, flipping to a fresh page in her notebook before looking up at him, "was Mandy Wong. She's a bartender here. Worked Friday and Saturday night."

He nodded to the notebook in her hand. "What'd you get?"

"Well, she definitely remembered seeing them. Sounds like they came down to eat dinner here on both Friday and Saturday night. On Saturday, they stayed late in the bar. Mandy says they had an argument, a big one. The whole staff heard it." She leaned against the bar. "It sounded like the girlfriend was ending things. The boyfriend wasn't taking it too well, by all accounts."

"And according to the management, neither of them came down for breakfast the next morning. So it seems like that argument is the last anyone saw of Amy."

"Boyfriend seems like the obvious suspect."

Ryan hedged. "But Pearl was pretty certain that this was done by the same person who killed Paula Thorn and Lindsay Brook. You think it was all this one bloke?"

"Hard to say. I'll have to look into him when we get back to the office. But so far, he doesn't seem much like the profile Brannan gave us."

"Yes, well. Not sure how much faith we can put into that profile."

"Ah, yes. I heard you gave Brannan a scolding," Ann said. "Anyway, I got a list from Mandy of the other people who were working that night. I'll follow up with them in case they saw anything she didn't."

"What about the CCTV cameras?"

"According to Mandy, there are a handful here around the bar, a few overlooking the car park, one in the lobby. Pretty good coverage, by the sound of it. I was just going to the security office to see what we can find."

"I'll go with you."

They left the bar and navigated through the area off the main lobby. There was a middle-aged, very sunburnt guard in the security office, reclining in his chair in front of an array of monitors. Each one displayed grids of grainy security footage feeds. He looked up from his magazine when they walked in and hurriedly took his feet off the desk.

"Can I help you?" he asked.

"We hope so," said Ann, who had raised an eyebrow at the many overlapping coffee cup rings he'd left all over the white surface of the desk. "We're detectives with the Sydney police, investigating a disappearance."

The man straightened noticeably in his seat.

"Would you happen to have security footage from this past weekend? Specifically, Friday afternoon around three thirty pm?"

"Well... let's see. Sure. Yes, I have tapes from then." The guard continued to look up at the two detectives with a somewhat vapid expression.

"Could you bring it up, please?" Ann said, with more patience than Ryan would have managed.

"Oh... sure." He leaned forward, took up a computer mouse on the desk and began clicking around on the monitors, rearranging the screens so that he could comb through a directory of video files. "Why I ask about the day is," he said, his face lit blue by the screens, "we erase the disks every week. Friday morning, usually. Clear out everything from the preceding week. But as it's only Wednesday today..." He clicked on a file and a display of six moving thumbnails sprouted up on the largest monitor. "I've got Friday afternoon for you right there."

Ryan and Ann both leaned over him to peer more closely at the screen. "That one," Ryan said, pointing at the upper left thumbnail, which he recognised as a view of the reception desk. "Put that one in full screen."

The image ballooned to fill the monitor. The guard scrubbed quickly through the frames until Ann said, sharply, to freeze it.

A man and a woman stood at the reception desk, pulling suitcases behind them. There was no audio, but it was evident that they were just checking in.

"Can you zoom in on the woman?" Ryan asked.

"Er… a little, but not a lot. These things aren't exactly state of the art." He used the mouse to draw a box around the woman and her image was magnified, her features made hazy by pixelation. Still, it was clear enough to be recognisable. Over the security guard's head, Ryan and Ann exchanged a significant glance. That was the woman in the shower stalls, Ryan was all but certain of it.

"Save that image," Ryan instructed, "and I'll send someone from my tech department to get a copy of all the footage from this weekend, Friday through Sunday. Understood?"

"You got it, boss."

"And by the way, you should really keep the footage for at least a month before you wipe it. Just in case there's ever an incident where something comes up later."

"Sure, yes. I'll run that by the managers." It sounded very much like he would not.

Ryan suppressed a roll of his eyes and thanked the guard for his time. As they walked out of the office, Ann asked where they were headed next.

He chewed it over for a moment. "Let's check the restaurant. Might as well see if we can talk to any of the staff while we're here."

Ann nodded her agreement and followed him to the restaurant overlooking the water. Behind the bar, a waitress they hadn't seen before was engaged in lively conversation with someone. Two someones, in fact. A man with a professional camera on a strap around his neck, and a woman with her back to Ryan, whose dark curls were decidedly familiar.

He approached the bar, disbelieving. But as he drew closer, he saw her face in profile and his hunch was confirmed… the woman talking earnestly with the waitress was Lisa Gordon.

CHAPTER 22:
LISA INVESTIGATES

"Lisa?"

She turned at the sound of her name and found the stunned face of Ryan Campbell looking back at her.

"Oh, hello," Lisa said. She smiled and nodded a greeting at Officer Nguyen, hoping that she didn't look as uncomfortable as she felt.

She'd had her fair share of awkward run-ins with boyfriends at uni. But leaving someone asleep in their bed and then running into them at the scene of a murder… that was a new one for her.

"What are you doing here?" Ryan asked. He seemed to have recovered from his shock and now looked annoyed.

"Well, there was a commotion down at the beach. My editor sent me to see what's happening. Maybe you can tell me."

"No, I'm afraid I can't," he said, rather more sternly than Lisa thought was necessary.

"All right," she said coolly. "In that case, I'll be getting on with my conversation with Jenna, then." She tilted her head towards the waitress, whose eyes were bouncing between the two of them.

"Actually, I'll need you and your photographer to leave. Now."

Lisa frowned. "This is a public space, *Detective*," she said, with a snide emphasis on the word. "Isn't it?"

"No, it isn't. It's a crime scene."

"As of when?"

"As of right now," Ryan answered sharply.

She gave him an impatient look. "Come on. I'm only doing my job here, the same as you. If you're going to throw me out, you can at least tell me what's going on."

"There'll be a press meeting later. You can find out with everyone else." Ryan leaned towards her and dropped his voice. "We're talking about privileged information, Lisa, and if you think I'll give it to you just because we went out last night—"

She leaned away from him in equal proportion, indignant. "That's *not* what's going on here, so don't kid yourself." She straightened up. "Fine. We'll go." She glanced at the waitress across the bar. "Thanks again, Jenna. You were a wonderful help." She beckoned to Paul and stalked off. Paul followed, after snapping a few more photos of the restaurant and earning a sharp reprimand from Ryan.

"Blimey, who does he think he is?" she huffed to Paul. "He's like Jekyll and Hyde, that one."

"Ah, well, he has a job to do too, I suppose," Paul said, framing a shot of the lobby and clicking the shutter as they walked out.

"Oh, don't you take his side."

"I'm not!" Paul said, laughing a little at the fierceness of her scowl. "I'm just saying… the press and the cops, they argue like cats and dogs, don't they? It's practically part of the job description for you two not to get along."

He had a point there.

"Besides," he went on, "we got some good shots of the hotel, so we'll be out ahead of everybody else whenever the press conference happens." They stepped out the front doors of the hotel, back into the warm sunshine. "Where to next?"

"Let's go back to the beach," Lisa said begrudgingly. "Maybe Nikki's found something out."

When they reached the police barrier, they separated, Paul heading south to find Nikki and Lisa heading north to see if she could track down someone who would talk to her. She walked alongside the blue and white checkered tape, parallel to the water's edge, until she came upon a small building with a sign outside it that said 'North Palm Beach Surf Lifesaving Club'. A number of police officers were clustered outside. To her surprise, she spotted two people she recognised… Wayne Brewster and Sergeant MacDonald.

She caught the last half of MacDonald's sentence. "…still don't know how long the beach will be closed. As I said, I'm waiting for Detective Campbell to get back."

"Listen, MacDonald," Brewster said. "The election is next week. I need to be able to tell my voters that the situation is well in hand, and show them that I'm working with the police. Now the press is going to want to talk to me, and it will not look good if they start asking questions I can't answer."

Stubbornly, MacDonald told him, "You'll have to wait to talk to Campbell."

With that, MacDonald walked away and disappeared into the surf club building, to the visible aggravation of Brewster.

"Mr Brewster!" Lisa called.

He turned towards her, his expression of annoyance vanishing as he spotted the steno pad in her hand. It was instantly replaced with his usual, photo-op approved smile.

"Hi there. Lisa Gordon, *Sydney Telegraph*. How do you feel your campaign for governor is going? Are you worried what the press will say about these high profile crimes…" She gestured with her pen to the crowds and police vehicles surrounding them. "…will negatively impact your chances?"

"No, not at all," he said smoothly, as if he'd rehearsed his answer beforehand, which he almost certainly had. "I think it's important for people to see how their leaders will respond in a crisis. As for myself, I'm meeting with the Chief Commissioner of Sydney later today. Once I have all the facts, I'll be making a statement to the public to keep them informed of the situation. Of course, I have every confidence that our police department is doing their utmost to catch the killer." He flashed a smile that was clearly meant to be reassuring, although there were no cameras pointed at him.

"It seems that the election is shaping up to be quite close between you and Colin Jenkins. Peter Duncan is gaining in the polls, too."

"Ah, well." He waved his hand dismissively. "We'll just have to wait and see, won't we? There are still a few more days of canvassing left. You can never rely on the polls, anyway."

"I suppose not," Lisa said pleasantly, while silently wishing hard for someone, anyone, other than Brewster to win the election. "Thanks for your time."

She flipped her steno pad closed and started to walk back towards the spot where she'd split up with Paul. She'd only taken a few steps before she saw both him and Nikki coming her way.

"All right, Nikki?" she greeted the younger journalist.

"Oh, about as all right as you can be at the scene of a murder, I suppose," Nikki answered.

"Fair enough. So what did you find out?"

"Come on. Let's get out of this mob first."

Nikki led them down Ocean Road, through the gaggle of curious onlookers and past the TV crews from the local networks who were setting up their equipment. Lisa paused to say hello to Bob from Fox News, then hurried to catch up with Nikki and Paul.

They crossed the street and ducked into a café. It was crowded inside, and Paul went to put in an order at the counter while Nikki and Lisa searched for a table, finally finding one all the way at the back.

"So," Lisa said as they sat down, "did you find anything out?"

"Some," Nikki said. "Apparently, the body was discovered by a four-year-old girl and her mum. I didn't talk to them, but I found one of the staff members at the Palm Beach Surf Club. The girl's mother reported it to him and he's the one who actually called the police. It sounds like the body was mutilated quite badly."

"My god," Lisa said. No wonder Ryan had been so angry at the hotel. "That's horrific."

"To say the least," Nikki agreed.

Paul reappeared, artfully balancing three coffees and two danishes. He handed Nikki one of the coffees, which she accepted with a murmur of thanks. He slid a danish and another coffee to Lisa, keeping the rest for himself, and took the last remaining seat.

"Awful, isn't it?" he said heavily. "Three dead bodies in three weeks. What the hell is going on in Pittwater?"

"You picked a busy time to join the *Telegraph*," Lisa said to Nikki.

She smiled grimly back at Lisa. "Not exactly the kind of busy I would choose." She took a sip of her latte. "What did you two find out at the hotel, by the way?"

Lisa filled her in on what she'd managed to learn from the waitress, that a woman and her boyfriend had been overheard fighting, and the next day all her clothes were found abandoned in her room after she was meant to have checked out.

"It sounded like rumours had already been going round the hotel. One of the managers has been convinced since Sunday that something happened to her."

"And do we know for certain that the body was the missing woman?" Nikki asked.

Lisa shrugged. "That's as much as I found out before I got chased off by a police officer. *Very* rudely, I might add."

Nikki raised her eyebrows and looked ready to ask questions, but before she could, Lisa's phone rang. "Oh, it's Brian," she said, tapping the screen to accept the call. "Hello?"

"How's it going up there?"

"Not bad. Between the three of us, I think we have a decent start here. More than the other papers have got, anyway."

"Glad to hear it. In that case, can you jump back on your politics beat sooner rather than later? We want to fit in at least one more big piece before the election."

"Sure. I can come into the office this afternoon and get back to it."

"You sound exhausted."

"Erm… I suppose I'm a bit tired." She stifled a yawn, still feeling the effects of last night's lack of sleep and overindulgence in wine.

"You go home and rest for a bit. Then come into the office. Let Nikki cover this Pittwater story."

"Roger that."

She hung up and looked to Nikki. "Well, looks like it's your lucky day," she said. "Brian wants me back on the governor's election, so I'm going to turn this one over to you."

"Really? But this is a huge story," she said, looking a little nervous.

Lisa smiled encouragingly. "Brian will work with you on it, don't worry. If you're looking for your next step, I'd head back to the Barrenjoey Hotel if I were you. I don't think the other outlets have put it all together about the missing woman yet, so you'll have a chance to get ahead of the pack."

"I'll do that. Thanks, Lisa."

"No worries. Good luck."

Paul and Nikki waved her off as she left the café and made her way back to her car. As she got in and started the drive back home, she felt a renewed twinge of annoyance at Ryan for the way he'd spoken to her at the hotel. It was probably for the best that Brian had asked Nikki to cover this one. Lisa was in no mood to cover the heroic antics of Detective Campbell at the moment.

She got home, took an ibuprofen for the headache that had been plaguing her since she left Ryan's house this morning, and crawled into bed. Before she fell asleep, she resolved to put him out of her mind. Men were just an annoying distraction, anyway. With everything else going on in Sydney at the moment, she had plenty to keep her occupied.

CHAPTER 23:
A ROAD TRIP

In his den, the killer cultivated a very precise level of cleanliness. Every stray footprint, every speck of blood… all of that had to be wiped away. And yet the place could not appear *clean*. It had to look unlived in, abandoned to the elements, as if no one had been here for many years. As if the girl who'd cried and bled here had never existed at all.

His tools, though… these were scrubbed to a shine. They were made immaculate and then concealed away, primed and ready for the next time he would need them. The killer was good at this, this attention to detail, this unyielding standard of precision. He'd been told so, many times. He would have been better than any of the others. He knew that.

On the just-grimy-enough floor lay a map. The killer leaned over it and considered the little black dots that represented all of his potential destinations. Where to go, where to go.

Finally, he settled on Melbourne. It would be crowded there, easy to become as invisible as he needed to be.

He packed his car and within hours, he was speeding down the M31.

Long before he neared Melbourne, he decided to stop in a small town to pick up a few things. Lunch at a Greek café. Some snacks for the road. A newspaper. A baseball hat that he could pull low over his eyes. A whole set of new clothes, nothing flashy or distinctive. The sort of thing that if you saw someone wearing it, you'd forget who they were before they even walked away. He capped it off with a new haircut, and, as a spur-of-the-moment finishing touch, a pair of reading glasses. He didn't need them, and only bought them because he thought that this person into which he'd transformed – the one wearing these clothes, with this haircut – looked like the sort who might wear glasses.

He took his time with it all, strolling along the sidewalk, peering into shop windows. He liked looking at things the way this new person would see them. It felt good. Relaxing. There was no hurry. He planned to arrive in Melbourne around midnight, get a motel, sleep in late the next morning. Then he'd go out and see what the new city had to offer.

Once he'd fully assembled his latest identity, he changed into his new clothes, gathered up the old ones and shoved them into a shopping bag. He drove around town for a few minutes until he spotted what he was looking for: a near-overflowing dumpster behind a chain restaurant. It looked like it was bound to be emptied in the next day or two. This would do nicely.

He got out of the car with the bag and glanced around, imitating casualness, and saw that there was no one nearby. Then he walked over, shoved the bag into the dumpster, and covered it with rubbish until it had disappeared under the ketchup-encrusted husks of fast food wrappers.

This done, he returned to his car and navigated back to the freeway.

By the time he finally arrived in Melbourne, it was well after dark. He found a motel eight kilometres out of the city centre, its neon 'VACANCY' sign blazing through the dark. He went in and asked for a room for one night. The lanky teenager at the reception desk advised him.

"We've got a special on," he said, pointing at an advert on the wall behind him. "Book three nights and get the fourth free."

The killer – or, rather, the person the killer had now become – regarded the boy from under his baseball cap. "Yes," he said. "That'd be fine."

He paid in cash. The boy slid a room key across the desk and cheerfully wished him a good night.

The room was suitable. Sometimes, he knew, these motels could be so dirty. He couldn't stand that, sleeping in a room that was dirty. He liked things neat, orderly, well-managed. This one would be all right, for now.

In the morning, he woke up, had breakfast at the motel and caught a bus into the city centre. He was wearing more of the clothes he'd bought yesterday and feeling quite pleased about it. It was fun, existing as someone else. He wondered why he hadn't done it sooner.

Melbourne felt different from Sydney. More vibrant, more metropolitan, more alive. Someone bumped into him and smiled when they apologised. People, he noted, were polite to this new person.

He wandered the bustling streets, eventually finding his way into a bookshop where he bought a local magazine and a map of the city. She would have loved it here. They would have gone to all the galleries and museums, and she would have pointed and laughed at the funny statues, and it would have made him laugh, too.

It was a hot day. Around lunchtime, he sought refuge from the sun in a place called Bar Americano. He ordered a drink, found a table and sat down to peruse the magazine, flipping through the glossy pages of people who were unremarkable and forgettable, just like the person he'd become.

That reminded him. He cast a glance around to make sure no one was looking his way – they weren't – and then dug his documents out of his backpack. He thumbed through them, one after the other: four passports and two driving licenses in total. He'd have to be strategic about which one he used while he was here.

After settling on an alias, he tucked all of the documents back into his backpack, zipped it up and set it on the floor at his feet. He looked through the window towards the busy street and settled in, deciding he could spend a few hours here. Why not? He was on vacation, after all.

CHAPTER 24:
GOVERNOR'S ELECTION

The week of the governor's election was every bit as chaotic as Lisa had expected it to be. She was working overtime getting interviews and writing up pieces on the ever-evolving race. If she was being honest, the timing of it was perfect. The busier she was with work, the less time she had to think about Ryan. That suited her just fine.

She caught a replay of the press conference where Officer Ann Nguyen confirmed that the body found at Palm Beach belonged to Amy Shepherd, the woman who'd gone missing from Barrenjoey House Hotel a few days before. Nikki had done a good job on the article. When Lisa read it, she was pleased to see that her initial investigation at the hotel had helped Nikki fill in some details that none of the other papers had included. Still, she'd been clear with Brian in her last meeting with him. She'd had quite enough of being a crime reporter and from here on out, she'd much prefer to stick with her first love: politics.

In the midst of writing daily overviews of where the candidates stood in the polls, she also covered a last-minute visit to Sydney by PM Johnson. He flew in to help Wayne Brewster – whose numbers had begun to slip – with his campaign. Brewster had one stroke of good luck. Just a day before Johnson's arrival, news leaked that Colin Jenkins, the Democrat candidate and clear frontrunner, was having an affair with one of his aides. Considering his wife had just given birth to their third child, things did not look good for his image as a devoted family man. Lisa fully expected that the scandal would damage Jenkins' chances beyond repair.

Peter Duncan of the Eco and Environment Party, on the other hand, was putting up a better fight than she had predicted. He'd been steadily gaining ground on Brewster for several days. It was his advances in the polls, Lisa guessed, that had prompted Johnson to come to Sydney in the first place. By this time next week, they would know if Johnson's final push was enough to save Brewster's chances. Personally, Lisa had her doubts, but that was one of the things she loved about politics: nobody ever quite knew what would happen next.

CHAPTER 25:
THE SYDNEY
HARBOUR HOTEL

Brewster had to admit that the view from the penthouse suite was rather spectacular. He stood at the window and looked out over the white sails of the Sydney Opera House, framed by the sparkling waters of the harbour.

"Here you go."

Brewster turned and found the Prime Minister proffering a tumbler of brandy. He was here at the Sydney Harbour Hotel at Johnson's invitation, and although Johnson had sounded genial enough on their last phone call, Brewster could not entirely shake the feeling that he'd been summoned to the headmaster's office for a telling off.

He accepted the tumbler with a word of thanks. He started to take a sip and then paused as he made uncomfortable eye contact with the third man in the room, who'd been there ever since Brewster arrived.

This was unusual. Johnson always had a sizable security team with him, but typically he kept them posted outside during closed-door meetings. Those guards wore sunglasses, stood inconspicuously in corners, and generally made themselves unobtrusive. But this stranger was standing in the middle of the room, seemingly taking up the whole suite with his presence. He wore an expensive, tailored suit and had his jet-black hair slicked back from his face. Brewster wasn't sure why, but the man made him uneasy.

He finally took a sip of his drink and then said, "I don't believe we've been properly introduced."

"Ah, yes. Of course. Wayne, this is Chan Jianjun. Chan, this is Wayne Brewster, the one I was telling you about."

Chan stepped forward and held out a hand. Brewster shook it, surprised by the strength of the other man's grip.

"Well, have a seat." Johnson gestured broadly to the armchairs ringed around a low table, on which sat the bottle of brandy. He sank into one of the chairs and Chan took the one beside him.

Slowly, Brewster sat down across from them.

"I'm pleased the two of you are finally getting the chance to meet," Johnson went on. "Very pleased. Chan has been an invaluable resource for me, you know."

"Is that so?" Brewster said, with an effort to sound polite, although he was still privately puzzling about why Chan had been allowed into what was meant to be a private meeting between him and Johnson.

The PM nodded as he took a sip of his own brandy. "Oh, absolutely. Chan is employed by the governments of both Australia and China… on a freelance basis, of course. He looks out for our, let's say, mutual interests. And he's been very helpful to both parties in the past. So, Wayne, if you ever need help sorting anything out, you have Chan at your disposal."

He said this offhandedly, as if he were recommending Chan's services as a tax accountant. Brewster was so disconcerted by Johnson's nonchalance that he couldn't immediately come up with a response. It turned out not to matter, though, because Johnson turned to Chan and said, "That'll be all, Chan. Brewster and I are going to have a little chat on our own now."

Chan rose to his feet, and Brewster was struck by how intimidatingly tall he was. He smiled down at Brewster. "It was a pleasure to meet you," Chan said, in a polished British accent. "I hope we can work together in the future."

With that, he turned and left the room. Brewster waited until the door closed behind him before knocking back his brandy in one. Then he held out the glass to Johnson, who refilled it after topping off his own.

"And what the hell," Brewster said, "does Chan do for our government?"

"Relax, Wayne," Johnson said smoothly. "Let me worry about that."

He shook his head. "I don't ever recall working with people employed as agents of other governments in my previous term…"

"This isn't your previous term," Johnson replied, a slight edge rising in his voice. "Times have changed. You've got to collaborate. There's just too much scrutiny these days to try and make it on your own, with all the social media posts from ages ago being dug up into the light, all the digital paper trails getting people into trouble. Just like that old Colin Jenkins, eh? His political career is over. Vanished like…" Johnson snapped his fingers together. "…that. Someone like Chan, he can make sure that if someone's reputation is going to take a hit, it'll happen in our favour. What's so wrong with that, hmm? That's how the game is played, isn't it, Wayne?"

Not quite sure whether he wanted to know the answer, Brewster asked slowly, "Was he responsible for that? Did he leak the information about Jenkins' affair?"

"Chan believes in a very, shall we say, proactive approach to reaching our goals. That's why I introduced you two. If you're going to be governor, it'll be up to you to ensure that our policies stay on track. And if you need some assistance in doing that – if you need help getting past the roadblocks, so to speak – Chan is here to help you clear the way." Johnson raised his eyebrows. "Oh, don't look so surprised, Wayne. You're no stranger to Chan's methods. He's helped you out of a bind before, you know. Worked out for you quite nicely, even if you did end up stepping away from politics for a while afterward. The point is, you're back in the game now." Johnson's eyes seemed to spark with eagerness. "And we've so much to accomplish together."

Brewster was staring back at him in disbelief. "The yachting accident that killed the architect," he said numbly. "You arranged that with Chan."

Johnson smiled. "I'm not saying any such thing. I was just reminding you how fortunate you are to have him on your side."

Brewster just shook his head, still struggling to understand it all. Twelve years ago, that accident came shortly after Brewster had agreed to take the fall for Johnson. His political career was torpedoed, and he was condemned to more than a decade of insignificance and anonymity. But Johnson said it all could have been much worse. He had told him that the freak accident was a lucky break, because the architect would've testified against them, undermining their entire plan and sending them both to jail. But that wasn't true… it wasn't a lucky break, or a freak accident. It was by design. Chan had orchestrated it.

Johnson pressed on. "It's harder than ever to get things done nowadays. You've got all these liberals trying to obstruct us at every turn." He waved his hand dismissively, as if he could swat his political opponents away like flies. "They think they're saving the world, but what are they really doing? They're holding up progress. Inevitable progress." He leaned forward, eyes fixed on Brewster as he spoke. "That's why it's so important that you are fully committed to our vision. Once you're elected, these plans of ours are going to bring great benefits to the people. Now, that said, it doesn't do us any good for you to be getting into petty disagreements with the police." He gave Brewster a reprimanding look.

Brewster scowled. "You mean that piece in the *Telegraph?*" he asked. It had been days, but he was still smarting from it. A reporter had written that he'd been spotted *quarrelling with Sergeant MacDonald, in a rare but perhaps zealous conflict between the aspiring governor and the city's police force.*

"Yes," Johnson said, and then took a long contemplative swig of his brandy. "Those murders are taking up too many headlines. Your campaign can't compete with a serial killer on the loose. We need to get it resolved and out of the news cycle as quickly as possible. We'll have to put some pressure on the police commissioner to get this cleared up and out of the public eye."

His words unsettled Brewster. "You are talking about three young women who've been murdered, you know," he muttered.

Johnson looked up at him sharply, his eyes flashing. "Yes? And? Mourning a few dead girls isn't going to bring them back. But they could keep you from winning. We can't lose sight of our goal."

Brewster drew back. "My god, Howard," he said slowly. "What's happened to you? Don't you hear yourself?"

"Enough of this, Wayne. I saved your arse by taking care of that snitch architect. If not for me, you'd be rotting in a penitentiary somewhere." Johnson's usual charming persona had vanished. His voice was harsh, his expression ruthless as he stared Brewster down. "You *owe* me. I got you out of that scrape and now I'm going to help get you into the governorship. In exchange, you're going to help me do so much more. We're moving onto bigger and better things. I'll need your support. And if I don't have it, your career ends right here and now."

Brewster didn't offer a reply. With a pang of regret, he couldn't help but wish that this conversation was happening in his own house, with all his recorders and cameras quietly doing their work. Then it would be Johnson's career that was at its end. If Brewster tried to report him now, he would have nothing but his own word, and that was worth nothing against Johnson. Others had tried. There was a reason Johnson had stayed in power this long.

Johnson seemed to accept Brewster's silence as compliance. The sharpness in his expression was once again replaced by an easy going affability, and he leaned back in his chair. It was unnerving, really, how he could don that public facade as easily as slipping on a mask. "I'm glad we have an understanding, Wayne," he said, his tone now level and calm. "Now just to get this election over with, eh? But not to worry. This weekend we'll be celebrating your victory. And then the real work begins." He raised his tumbler. "To the New Australia," he toasted.

Swallowing his reluctance, Brewster raised his own glass and clinked it against the Prime Minister's. "To the New Australia."

CHAPTER 26:
CHAN

Thirty-some years ago, Chan Jianjun had been one of many thousands of children in Communist Party orphanages in Guangdong, China, where, alongside his peers, he memorised aphorisms from Chairman Mao's Little Red Book. He could still recite them, if someone were ever to ask him. Not that he had much use for those sorts of political certainties now.

He had joined the People's Liberation Army at sixteen, where he quickly displayed an aptitude for strategic thinking paired with excellent combat skills. By eighteen he had been recruited into the Central Military Commission Intelligence Bureau.

From there, it was a rapid ascent through the ranks. He was sent away to get his education in England, then France. By age twenty-five, he spoke six languages – Cantonese, English, French, German, Russian and Japanese – and could pass as a native speaker in any one of them. He had passports and documentation for the corresponding countries and half a dozen more.

Strictly speaking, Chan didn't need to be working. He was already a millionaire a few times over, and owned numerous properties scattered across China, France, England and Australia. Most of these he rented out to other wealthy expats, many of whom needed a discreet place to lay low for a while. He gladly provided them with a safe haven for the right price.

This enterprise earned him a respectable living. But he kept at his first profession for no other reason than he liked the work. It felt like a calling.

He served China for many years. But with the skills he'd gained there, he found himself in an ideal position to go freelance. Once he'd carved out a niche for himself in the world of international assassins, he continued to take jobs that served the interests of his motherland, or, more precisely, served the interests of his motherland's corrupt politicians and billionaires. They were happy to pay a small consideration to ensure that he always acted with their prosperity in mind.

It'd taken him years to establish his network of contacts, and in that time he'd continued to hone his skills. By now he could devise a method of dispatching almost anyone on the planet, no matter how powerful or well-known, without arousing the slightest suspicion about the death. That little yachting accident twelve years ago had been one of his first contracts on the international market. Looking back, it seemed like child's play… a no-name architect who'd been blissfully unaware that anyone might want to kill him and so had taken no precautions to guard his life. These days, his targets were trickier. Like the once and future governor of Sydney.

So far, Johnson's instructions were merely to shadow Brewster, not to cause him any harm. He'd also requested that Chan provide reminders, as needed, of Brewster's part in the plan, which was to get Johnson's policies enacted, by any means and at any cost. It was a simple enough task, and Chan had accepted the assignment readily. Johnson was willing to pay Chan's rates just in case his primary skill set became necessary later.

If he kept on with contracts like this one, Chan reflected to himself as he walked out of the Sydney Harbour Hotel's penthouse suite, he'd be able to retire by the time he was forty. Maybe he'd end up on a tropical private island somewhere. That would be nice.

CHAPTER 27:
THE LEADMAN HOUSE

Ryan and Ann stood side by side, both of them staring at the pinboard in the incident room. By now, it had been divided into three sections: Paula Thorn in Brewster's lot, Lindsay Brook at the Bayview Yacht Club, and Amy Shepherd in Palm Beach.

Three crime scenes. Three victims. And they carried with them the sinister possibility of more to come.

"A, B, I." As Ann spoke, her eyes moved between a trio of photographs on the bulletin board: overexposed closeups of the carved letter on each victim. "What in the hell does that mean?"

Ryan shook his head slowly. "Not a clue. But it blows up our ABC theory. Which was more or less our only theory."

"Do you think it's meant to be a message for us? Something he's trying to tell the police?"

"Wish I knew," he answered tiredly.

Ann walked over to examine the photos tacked to the pinboard. "Pearl thought this was done with a scalpel," she said, tapping two fingers to the image of the grisly letter "A."

"Yes. She said that about all of them, that the blade was so sharp it must've been a medical grade instrument."

Ann turned back to him. "Could it be someone in the medical field? Someone who would have access to those kinds of tools from work?"

He mulled it over for a few moments. Then, slowly, he admitted, "Could be. Can you get in touch with the city hospitals and ask around about stolen equipment? Any incidents with disgruntled staff members, that sort of thing?"

She nodded. "I'll get on it." Her expression remained neutral, but Ryan saw the spark of excitement in her eyes, lit by the slim chance that they might be onto something.

Ann started to return to her desk, but then she paused. "By the way," she said, in a quieter tone, "I tracked down the Leadman place for you."

Ryan tried not to show his own eagerness on his face. "Oh?"

"Yes. Turns out the property is still registered to Janet Leadman. According to the records, she worked with a letting agency and they rented the property out to an English family. The dates seem to correspond with when she went to Brisbane with her kid. Then, after a few years, the English renters moved out. By then Janet would've been in America. She never got a new tenant, and the place was more or less abandoned."

Ryan frowned. "Abandoned? So she just… walked away from it?"

Ann shrugged. "That's what it sounds like. I called the letting agency. They've still got the property on their books, but it's so rundown now that they haven't bothered trying to show it to anyone in years. The only recent note in their records is about some bloke who asked to use the boathouse to store the sails and supplies for his yacht. But they had to tell him no, because the house is still technically private property and they couldn't track down the owner to get permission."

"That's odd," he murmured.

She raised her eyebrows. "Is it?"

"Don't you think? Just letting your house go to ruin like that. Bit strange. At least I think so." He'd been staring into the middle distance as he spoke. He shook himself out of his reverie and glanced up at Ann. "Well, anyway. I'll look into it. Could you get me a copy of your notes from the letting agency?"

"Yes, of course. And I'll start calling the hospitals next."

"You're a gem," he said, absently.

She flashed him a look that was half eye-roll, half smile. "Cheers," she said, and set off to get him a copy of the Leadman address.

CHAPTER 28: ELECTION WEEK

The election was only days away now. Lisa had continued working at a breakneck pace, keeping a pulse on all four major candidates' campaigns. There was the catastrophic implosion of Colin Jenkins' political career, which had been brought to a decisive, scandalous end before it had even really begun, and the unexpected ascent of Peter Duncan, a dark-horse candidate who was now neck and neck with Brewster. Duncan's momentum had been hindered by PM Johnson, who'd embarked on a whirlwind press tour on Brewster's behalf. Just that morning, Lisa attended yet another media event where Johnson stood at a podium near the Grand Post Office and assured Sydney voters that Brewster was the right man for the job.

"He knows how this city works. He knows what its people need," he had told a melee of reporters gathered for the speech. "Wayne Brewster will build up the great city of Sydney and promote the prosperity of all Australians. Once elected, his plans will focus on creating new jobs, rejuvenating infrastructure, bolstering the economy…"

"At what cost?" A heckler's piercing voice rang out from the crowd. Johnson tried to speak over him, but the man persisted. "At what cost to the environment? To our communities? Brewster will let corporations take over our city, he will sell our wellbeing to the highest bidder… get *off* me…"

That was the last Lisa heard from him before a burly security guard escorted him bodily from the scene.

The audience returned its attention to Johnson, who appeared unruffled. "Tough crowd today," he said lightly, to scattered polite laughter. "In any case, as I was saying… Wayne Brewster is the ideal candidate to lead Sydney toward true progress…"

As Lisa recalled the events of that morning, she couldn't help but wish she'd been able to find the protester so she could ask him some questions for her article. But by the time the speech ended, he'd been hauled off by the security guards, presumably to the local police station. It was a shame, he'd raised some good points, after all.

Plenty of people had taken issue with Brewster's policies, and Johnson's enthusiastic endorsement was, frankly, racking up those concerns. There were a whole host of things in Brewster's platform that'd raised eyebrows: support of a proposed Gambling Act that would encourage the establishment of so-called 'super-casinos' on the Gold Coast, new legislation to forge ahead with the construction of conference centres and high-end hotels, and, perhaps most divisive of all, the Pacific Highway bill. The proposed superhighway would run the full length of the continent, demolishing anything in its path… including hundreds of miles of national parks, nature reserves and heritage sites.

Johnson had addressed some of these concerns… in a manner of speaking. "Friends, the economies of the West are in freefall," he'd intoned, looking out over his audience with the sombre expression of a pastor giving a graveside sermon. "We have a responsibility to protect our own interests. The nations of the Far East are flourishing, and we cannot allow ourselves to be left behind. We must forge a path into the future with our sights set on Australian prosperity. With his bold legislative plans, Wayne Brewster is the man to lead Sydney into that bright future."

Lisa had worked around politics for her entire adult life, so it didn't come as a shock to her that many politicians weren't exactly of the highest moral calibre. Still, there was something about Johnson that made her skin crawl. But, being a professional, she did her best to provide an unbiased report of the speech. It was a tiresome effort.

As much as she loved the rush of an upcoming election, this particular campaign season was starting to wear on her. Just a few more days, she thought, before it was all settled, one way or the other. At this rate, no matter what happened, it would be a relief.

CHAPTER 29:
McCARRS CREEK

Ryan arrived at the office Thursday morning in low spirits. He did his usual rounds through the incident room, but no one had anything pressing to report. Staring down another long, frustratingly unproductive day, he made a snap decision: this was as good a time as any to go up to the Leadman house.

A few minutes later, he was sitting in his car with the engine idling while he punched the address into his GPS. He almost trusted his memory to get to the place, but not quite. It had been twelve years ago, and there had been a lot of crime scenes between then and now. At the direction of the sat nav's smooth female voice, he navigated up into the hills of Pittwater, threading his way through quiet residential streets.

Twelve years ago. That felt hard to believe. He'd been young and eager then, excited about taking on his first big investigation. But in the end, he'd been left with more lingering questions than concrete answers.

The road turned and began to wind alongside McCarrs Creek, hugging its bank for miles. Eventually, the voice giving him directions fell silent. He checked the screen and saw that he was now out of the sat nav's range.

He'd anticipated that, though. Glancing over at a paper map he'd propped up on the passenger's seat, he turned off the paved road and onto a rutted dirt track. *No wonder the letting agency couldn't get anybody to live here,* he thought to himself, as his car dipped violently into a divot in the road. *Be lucky just to find the place.*

Some ten minutes later, he was pulling into a small clearing. Under a tangle of vines, the shadowy outline of a house was barely visible. The structure was so overgrown that it was difficult to see any details, except that most of the windows were broken. The sagging roof looked close to collapse.

He parked and stepped out onto the spongy weed-choked ground. The sound of the car door slamming behind him felt incredibly loud in the silence. With an uneasy glance around, he started to approach the abandoned house.

As he drew closer, he had a sudden vivid memory: the last time he'd walked this path, he'd been a few paces behind the senior detective on the Leadman case. They were there to interview Janet Leadman about the accident that had killed her husband and young daughter. Everything had looked so different back then.

In front of him, a broken wooden gate hung off its hinges. Ryan pushed it open and started to make his way up to the door, but he quickly found his progress halted. The brush was so thick that it would take a machete to carve a path to the front of the house. He peered through the heavy shadows of the trees and, to his surprise, spotted a faint trail in the undergrowth. Curious, he followed the track, which led him round the side of the house to the top of a rickety wooden staircase. The handrail was broken and the steps weren't in much better shape. From here, he was able to get the lay of the land: the house was built into the side of a hill, and the stairs would bring him around to the back of the house, which faced out onto the water.

He descended the steps cautiously and found himself on a large moss-spotted deck. At the edge of it was a jetty that reached out into the calm waters of the creek. An old dinghy with a rusted outboard motor was tied to the jetty's far end. Beyond that, three yachts were moored to buoys out on the water. On one of them, an old man with white hair and a beard was attending to his rigging. Ryan stood watching him for a few moments, but the man paid him no attention.

At the water's edge stood an old boathouse, half-hidden by brambles. As Ryan approached it, he saw something glint silver in the dappled sunlight. Frowning, he drew closer, pushing aside the vines in his way. Surprise flickered through him as he saw what had caught the sun; it was a padlock, quite new by the looks of it, at least compared to the rusty hasp it was securing.

He put one eye to the gaps in the boathouse's siding. It was dark inside, but he could make out sails, rigging, a set of tools on an old workbench.

What was it Ann had told him? Someone had contacted the letting agency to ask about using the boathouse for storage, but the agency had turned him down because they couldn't reach the owner to obtain permission.

Ah. Well, from the looks of it, the inquiring yacht-owner had taken matters into his own hands.

Ryan cut across the deck to another staircase, this one rising up to a second, elevated deck that ran the length of the house. Up on that balcony, he found a dilapidated picnic table, strewn with rubbish that looked relatively recent… sweets wrappers, cigarette butts, crushed beer cans. Evidently the place wasn't quite as abandoned as it first appeared.

Ryan scanned the back wall of the house. The door and windows had been covered with plywood, but some of the planks seemed to be coming loose. The board over the door, for example, came off with hardly any force at all. The door itself consisted of a single large pane of glass in a metal frame. He tried the handle but it was, unsurprisingly, locked.

He cast a surreptitious glance around the lot. There was no one in sight except the old man on the yacht, who seemed not to have noticed Ryan at all. Ryan took a step back, squared up, and delivered a sharp kick against the door.

The sound of shattering glass startled a small flock of birds from the nearby trees. Ryan looked again to see if the noise had attracted any attention, but the old man hadn't even turned around. Careful to keep the sharp edges from snagging his jacket, he ducked through the door.

The first thing that hit him was the stench. The air was damp and stale, and so thick with dust that it made him cough. It was pitch dark, and he didn't dare try to walk until he pulled his mobile from his pocket and switched on the flashlight.

He was standing in what had once been the kitchen. The sink was filled with noxious-looking black water and towers of filthy cups spilling over with furry green mildew. The table was layered with rusty tins and overturned food boxes. As he swept the beam across the counter, the light caught a container of what had once been milk, and was now a round clump of yellow mould.

"No tea for me, thanks," he muttered to himself, still cringing from the smell.

He took a few steps forward. As he directed the flashlight to the floor in front of him, he could just make out another set of footprints. They were faint, already under a layer of dust. Someone else had been inside the house, but not very recently.

Ryan picked his way to the living room, which was populated with the vaguely menacing shapes of furniture under bedsheets. He spotted a staircase leading to an upper floor, but before he could reach it, a dark form caught his eye. He spun towards it, just in time for a furiously hissing cat to launch itself at him.

"Shit!" he yelped, and aimed the light at the animal. Eyes flashing green, it streaked past him and vanished under the sheet-covered sofa.

Simultaneously trying to calm his pounding heart and berating himself for his overreaction, he turned back to the staircase.

The musty, unpleasant smell that permeated the house grew steadily worse as he climbed higher. By the time he reached the top landing, it had become so intense that he pulled a handkerchief from his pocket and placed it over his nose and mouth.

In an upstairs hallway, a door stood slightly ajar. Beyond it, Ryan heard the buzzing of flies. He steeled himself and kicked the door open. As it swung inward, several rats bolted out of the room, scampering under his feet and then disappearing into holes above the hallway's baseboard. He paused briefly, listening as their scratching and squealing receded into the walls, then stepped into the room.

Here the smell was overpowering. A black cloud of flies had dispersed slightly when the rats fled, but now they had once again congregated near the sloping corner of a bed with a broken leg. Ryan approached slowly, the blood roaring in his ears.

He shone the flashlight downward and, after a few dizzying seconds, finally understood what he was looking at: the decaying carcass of a wombat, and beside it an equally decomposed cat. The rats had been gnawing at both of them, exposing white patches of bone between the blackish-red sludge that had once been muscle and organ.

"Oh, fuck…" Ryan grimaced and turned away from the putrid odour. He backed out of the room, trying not to trip on the uneven floorboards, and then swept the flashlight's beam down the hallway.

There were a few other rooms on this floor, two more bedrooms and a washroom. He checked all of them, now braced to meet bad-tempered animal inhabitants every time he opened a door. But these rooms were all the same: broken furniture, boarded windows, a decade's worth of dust and nothing more.

Ryan hurried back down the stairs and navigated through the kitchen to the balcony outside. He stood gratefully in the sunshine and gulped down a few lungfuls of fresh air, trying to erase the memory of that godforsaken stink. After he'd caught his breath, he made his way down to the deck and looked out across the water. The old man with the white beard finally seemed to be looking Ryan's way. Ryan waved to him, but the man turned and once again busied himself with the boat's rigging.

Ryan glanced behind him at the weather-beaten house and scrubbed a hand over his face. What had he expected to find here, anyway? Did he think he'd stumble across the killer in this old house, long forgotten by everyone except Ryan?

Time to face facts. He was grasping at straws. He'd only come out here because he had no other leads. And now he'd burned through yet another day, with nothing to show for it.

Listlessly, he retraced his steps around the side of the house, through the wooden gate and over to his car. He climbed inside and braced himself for the rough drive back to the paved road.

By the time Ryan got into Sydney, it was edging on towards evening. He stopped at a convenience store, where he bought a ready-made meal that looked reasonably edible, a bottle of decent wine and a late edition of the *Sydney Telegraph*. It wasn't until he got home and looked at the front page, which declared 'GOVERNOR'S RACE REMAINS NECK AND NECK ON ELECTION DAY', that he realised he'd completely forgotten to vote.

Ryan wasn't much for politics. He was ready to flip to the sports section and not bother with the whole thing, but in the end his sense of civic duty got the better of him. It was a few hours until the polls closed, so he dug out his voting card and dragged himself back to his car, consoling himself with the promise of the bottle of wine waiting for him when he got home.

CHAPTER 30:
THE NEW SYDNEY GOVERNOR

It was approaching two am and Lisa was on her third coffee of the night. She and Paul were in the ballroom of the Sydney Harbour Hotel, which the Brewster campaign had chosen as their election night headquarters. There were murmurs among the press section that the count was nearly finished, and the race would be called within the next few minutes.

"Good," Paul said through a yawn. "Can't wait to get home and go to sleep."

"Lucky you, going home after this," Lisa said as she continued scrawling notes in her steno pad. "I'll be up all night finishing this story for the morning edition."

A huge TV at the front of the room was set to a local news channel. Before Paul could reply to Lisa, the anchorwoman broke into a commercial to announce that the numbers had just come in from the last of the counting sites.

A hush swept the ballroom. After a few tense moments, a graphic flickered up onto the screen:

Spoiled Ballots = 6,462
Spike Davison (Homes for All Party) = 158,906
Alan Jameson (Time for a Change Party) = 251,081
Susan Harrison (Liberal Party) = 884,437
Colin Jenkins (Democrat Party)= 987,112
Peter Duncan (Eco and Environment Party) = 1,156,419
Wayne Brewster (Republican Party) = 1,382,772

Lisa and Paul, along with all of their fellow reporters, leaned forward in their seats as their eyes skimmed over the tangle of numbers. "So that means…" Paul said, squinting at the TV.

"It's Brewster," Lisa pronounced, slouching back in her chair. She wasn't allowed to have a preference when she wrote her article for the paper. But she could still be disappointed as a private citizen.

The news anchor came back on screen to confirm Lisa's proclamation. "With all ballot-counting centres now reporting in," the woman said, "we can project that Wayne Brewster will be the next governor of Sydney."

The ballroom, filled with a combination of journalists and Brewster's benefactors, erupted into chaos.

"We picked lucky, eh?" Paul said, raising the camera's viewfinder to his eye to snap a few shots of Brewster's rejoicing supporters. "Nikki's stuck at Duncan's campaign headquarters. She'll be disappointed she has to cover a concession instead of a victory speech."

"I wish she was the one covering the victory speech," Lisa muttered under her breath.

Moments later, Brewster appeared at the podium on the ballroom's stage to deliver a statement on his win. It was the standard line about how the people of Sydney had made their voices heard, how he was so deeply honoured to serve the city. No mention of the suspiciously timed leak that had tanked his opponent's chances.

Lisa reflected, as she listened to Brewster's predictably dishonest speech, that it was a minor miracle he'd managed to eke out a win. The man had come back from the grave of public opinion to reclaim the city's most powerful position. She had seen a lot in her days as a journalist, but these politicians kept finding new ways to surprise her. Brewster was certainly one of those surprises. And not a welcome one.

CHAPTER 31:
A NEW LIFE

The killer was seated in the apartment of a woman named Barbara Stevenson. He was immaculately groomed and dressed in neat, respectable clothes, the very image of an upstanding young man. This was not an accident.

"Thanks again for answering the ad," Barbara said cheerfully. She was sitting across from him at the kitchen table. She had curly blonde hair cut into a bob, a button nose, and a sheen of lip gloss on her small pink mouth. The killer could smell it. Strawberry. "I'm glad you could meet me on such short notice."

"My pleasure," he replied, smiling back at her.

The ad in question was one she had placed in a trendy local magazine, announcing her search for a tenant for her flat. When he saw the listing, he had just decided that he'd spend at least a few months in Melbourne. Of course there was no way that rundown motel would do for a long-term stay, so he'd need to find another place. It seemed like serendipity. He'd called the phone number listed under 'PLEASE CONTACT' and she'd arranged to meet with him that same evening.

"Right, well, I'll be off to England quite soon to visit my sister and my new baby niece," Barbara said, "so I'll need to fill the apartment very quickly. Would you mind telling me about yourself?"

"Of course," the killer answered smoothly, and gave a rehearsed speech that had served him well in situations like this in the past: he was from an English family and had the good fortune of a monthly allowance that let him travel the world. He explained that he had arrived in Melbourne recently, was impressed by the city, and would love to have this apartment as a home base while he explored southern Australia. He provided an English passport to corroborate this story and offered to provide contact information for his references.

Barbara was suitably impressed. "Well, it sounds like you'd be a good fit for the place. But I should let you know that I'm in touch with a few other potential tenants. I can get back to you in the next couple of days…"

"I am in a bit of a hurry," he interjected. "Of course, I understand you might need some time to consider all the applicants. But if you'd be willing to make a quick decision, I can pay in full. All twelve months, upfront. Plus a non-returnable deposit."

She didn't answer immediately, but her stunned expression made him think he'd miscalculated. He backpedalled with a nonchalant smile. "I know it sounds a bit odd," he told her. "But I've been staying at this hotel downtown, and it's quite expensive. The sooner I can get settled in somewhere, the sooner I can get out of there. So you'd be saving me money, actually."

Barbara gave a noncommittal hum, glancing down at the pad of paper onto which she'd been scratching notes. Then she looked back up at him curiously. "What was it you said you wanted to do here?"

"Oh, the usual adventure stuff," he said. "Diving, rock-climbing, white-water rafting, sailing." He gave her a self-effacing smile. "Bit of an adrenaline junkie."

"I see." She fiddled with her pen.

"You said you were going to England?"

Barbara nodded. "And you're from there, are you? What part?"

"Family home's in Hampshire," he said. "I grew up there, but afterwards I spent most of my time in London. Kensington. I'm sure you'll have a lovely time on your trip. Especially since you'll be visiting with family. Congratulations, by the way, on your new niece. You must be very happy."

A smile flickered on Barbara's face, her wariness fading away. "Well, you seem like a very nice gentleman," she said. "And I really do have to get a move on with this, so… all right. You can have the place. I'll tell the other candidates I've rented it out."

He feigned concern. "Are you certain you wouldn't want to check with my references first?"

"I would, actually, but my flight's in only three days," she said with an embarrassed laugh. "I put all this off a bit longer than I should have, if I'm honest. And I've still got loads to do before I leave. So I'll just have to trust that you'll take good care of the flat while I'm gone."

"You have my word."

Three days later, Barbara Stevenson handed him the keys. She left for the airport and he got himself moved in.

It was a one-bedroom flat, modern and minimalistic, within walking distance of the city centre. He was quite happy with it, all in all. Standing in the living room, where his suitcase and backpack were propped against the sofa, he allowed himself a contented smile.

"Look at this place," he said. "You'll like it here. And I know you'd like for me to be happy here. No more little errands like before. We'll just enjoy this time together." He let his eyes fall shut, finding her, as he always did, in the darkness behind his eyelids. "I know you're here with me."

From his backpack, he pulled out the documentation for his assorted aliases and started to file them away in a drawer. As he shuffled through the papers, a photograph slipped out and fluttered to the floor.

He set the documents aside and knelt to retrieve the picture, handling it with care. "I'll get this framed," he said quietly. "I'll keep it on the bedside table. That way you'll be the first person I see in the morning. You'll keep me safe."

Once he'd gotten his suitcase unpacked, he went out to shop for groceries, then came back and cooked himself dinner. Afterwards, he cleaned up in his usual fastidious way. He scrubbed down the counters, inch by inch. It had to be clean, had to be tidy, how could he expect to be able to sleep in a place that wasn't tidy…

Abruptly, he straightened up from the counter. "Stop it," he told himself sternly. It wouldn't be like that here. *He* wouldn't be like that here. For her sake.

He set himself on the couch and turned on the television, flipping through channels for a while but finding nothing that held his interest. He felt edgy. Unsettled. He opened his laptop and spent maybe an hour reading about the tourist attractions of Melbourne, mentally planning an itinerary for the next few days. That worked to distract him, for a while. But soon enough he ended up where he always did… at his usual line up of pornography websites, the kind that couldn't easily be found or traced, the kind that catered in videos most people would prefer never to see. He finished and showered and fell asleep on the bed, his damp hair leaving a wet mark on the pillow.

About an hour later, he woke to find that darkness had settled over Melbourne. From the bedroom window, he could see lights spilling from the rows of stylish bars and restaurants a few blocks away. On a whim, he decided to go out.

He got dressed and left the apartment building. The night was humid, electrified by the thousands of people caught in the city's glow, talking, laughing, flirting, drinking. They were inside clubs, seated at outdoor booths, clustered in groups on the street while they smoked or waved down a cab or ambled to the next bar. There were so many of them, all smartly dressed, most of them young and attractive. It was like a scene from a movie, he thought to himself, trying not to feel overwhelmed.

From the innumerable options, he picked a bar and made his way inside to order a double vodka and tonic. As he stood sipping his drink, he found it difficult to avoid catching people's eyes. Some of them said hello to him, as if they already knew one another, and a few of the women even offered him brief, flirtatious smiles. The attention made him self-conscious at first, but by the second vodka and tonic he'd started to think that maybe he ought to try and make friends.

No. Her voice rang clearly in his head, catching him off guard. *These aren't the sort of people we make friends with. Just look at them. They love themselves.*

His eyes skated across the throng of faces in front of him, and he saw what she meant. These people were vain, self-absorbed, obsessed with their own image.

"You're right," he muttered. "Awful, aren't they? I don't like them."

He threw back the rest of his drink and slammed the glass down with a bang, making the people nearest him jump. But he paid them no mind. He started to shoulder towards the door, ignoring the annoyed protests of those in his path.

Once he made it outside, he quickly ducked into an alleyway, out of the suddenly invasive gaze of the late-night crowd. He took several deep breaths, trying to calm down, trying to regain control. Then he started walking.

He had no particular destination in mind. After a few minutes, or what felt like a few minutes to him, he found himself at the doorway of another bar. This one was a rough-looking place, its windows lit by flickering neon signs for bottom-shelf whisky. It was on some backstreet, far away from the busy neighbourhood he'd started in.

The killer stepped inside. It smelled like cigarette smoke and cheap beer. A small group of men were huddled under a few TVs in the corner, shouting at a football match. There were only a few other patrons, mostly scruffy backpackers and moody teenagers, their eyes hidden under their fringes. At the far side of the room was a pool table. He vaguely recalled that he used to be good at pool.

He got a bottle of beer from the bartender and walked over to the green-felted table. For a few rounds, he just watched. A number of players came and went, but one person – a tall, broad bloke with a crew cut and a chip in one of his front teeth – stayed game after game. He was easily winning against everyone who played him. Finally the man, who someone had referred to as Al, took notice of the killer watching from the side.

"Come on," he said, with a jerk of his head. "Play a game with me."

The killer gave a cool shrug. He walked over to the table and started to pick up a pool cue, but Al stopped him.

"Money down first," he said in a throaty growl, nodding to the pile of crumpled dollar bills at the corner of the table. "And whoever wins gets the pot."

He pulled a few bills from his wallet and added them to the pile.

Al grinned.

It was a quick game. The killer beat Al soundly, then beat him twice more. He remembered, now, that this was exactly how he'd gotten good at pool, playing barflies for money. He'd made quite a lot of cash off drunk uni students when he was at University.

After the third game, Al gave him a dark sneer and stalked off without a word. But the killer stayed, quite enjoying himself by now. He hung around until the early hours of the morning, alternating between drinks at the bar and rounds of pool, and he didn't hear her voice again.

CHAPTER 32:
A CALL FROM IMMIGRATION

It was eight weeks this Tuesday since Paula Thorn's body was found in the abandoned building site in Pittwater.

Since then Ryan's investigative team had interviewed dozens of people and combed through hundreds of old case files, searching for something, anything, that might provide a promising lead. Ann had called damn near every hospital and medical centre in the city, and none of them had anything unusual to report, no missing medical instruments or disgruntled employees.

In fact, despite their weeks of effort, they had found almost nothing at all. No clues. Nothing that had brought them any closer to stopping the murderer from striking again.

Ryan did his best to hide it from the team, but he was becoming more and more discouraged. The other officers were losing their optimism, too. He'd taken to working in his own office instead of the incident room, avoiding the atmosphere of dwindling hope and growing frustration there.

On that Tuesday afternoon, he was sifting through yet another case file, this one having just been faxed over from Adelaide, when Ann suddenly appeared at his door. She was out of breath.

"Campbell. There you are," she panted, leaning against the door frame.

He frowned. "What is it?"

"The immigration office in Melbourne just called."

Ryan straightened and set the packet of papers down on his desk. "And?"

"They picked up someone who was using John McCann's passport. And it's not John McCann."

"That's the stolen passport that someone used at the temp agency," Ryan said, dredging up the name from his memory of their conversation weeks ago.

"Someone who was at the concert the night of Paula and Lindsay's abduction. Yes, that's right."

"So if it's not McCann, who is it?"

"Someone called Simon. Visa overstayer from England. He tried to get work at a restaurant using McCann's passport. The Restaurant ran a check and found our flag on the name, so they called it in."

"Where is Catterick now?"

"At a detention centre. They're holding him there before sending him on a flight back to England."

Ryan was already out of his seat. "Will they keep him there until we can talk to him?"

"Yes, but we've got to get to Melbourne fast."

Finally. He ventured a slight smile, revitalised by the possibility of some kind of movement in the case. "Then let's get to Melbourne."

•

Ann managed to book them on the next flight out. They arranged to have a squad car take them to the airport. Even after being fast-tracked through security, the timing was tense, but they reached the gate just as the final boarding call was announced. The two of them were the last ones on the plane before the doors closed.

By that afternoon, they were in the immigration detention centre not far from the Melbourne airport. Simon Catterick, a man with red horn-rimmed glasses and an unruly mop of black hair, was sitting opposite them at a bare metal table.

An immigration agent was in the room with them. He stood in the corner with his arms folded while Ryan set a tape recorder on the table and pushed 'REC'. On the face of the device, a red light began to pulse steadily.

"Mr Catterick, this is Detective Inspector Campbell and Officer Nguyen," the agent said, when Ryan nodded at him. "They're here to ask you some questions about a series of murders in Sydney."

"Whoa, hang on. I didn't murder anybody," Catterick protested, his eyes bouncing between the three of them. "All I did was overstay on my visa." He slumped in his chair. "I haven't even been in Sydney. I've been living in Melbourne for the last year and a half."

"Right now, we're mostly interested in how you ended up with John McCann's passport," Ryan said.

The man's expression twisted in confusion. "The passport? I just got it about two weeks ago."

"Where?" Ryan asked.

"At the bar where I worked. This place called The Last Schooner. When me and Jan…"

"Who's Jan?"

"My girlfriend."

Ryan motioned for him to go on.

"When me and Jan got off work, there was this bloke there. Kind of a posh-looking type, for that place. I'd never seen him before. He was playing pool with Big Al…"

"Big Al," Ryan repeated, somewhat incredulously.

"Yes. Big Al. Anyway, Al's a regular at the Schooner, and he's *really* good at pool. He plays for pretty serious money and he almost always wins. But this new guy… we were watching him play and he completely thrashed Al. Al was pretty miffed, so he took off. The bloke played a few more games. After a while, he went to sit at the bar. Meanwhile Jan and I are at the bar too, and we're talking about what I should do. She's Australian, see. She wanted me to stay longer but my visa ran out."

"How tragic for you," the immigration agent observed dryly.

"I'm just telling him what happened," Catterick snapped, before turning back to Ryan. "So we're trying to figure out how I could get work with an expired visa. The guy leans over and tells us he overheard our conversation. Says he might be able to help. Apparently he'd flown to Melbourne from Sydney earlier that day, and while he was getting on his flight, he saw a passport someone'd left behind. He was planning to turn it in to security, but his flight was already boarding and he was afraid to miss it, so he just shoved the passport in his bag. But he hadn't had a chance to give it to the police yet."

"So he offered to give it to you," Ryan prompted.

"Bloody well didn't *give* it to me," Catterick grumbled. "He offered to sell it. Two hundred dollars. Seemed like a lot, but I didn't know what else to do. And Jan told me people do this sort of thing all the time. So I agreed to buy it off him. He said it was back at his hotel room so we arranged to meet the next day for the handover."

Ann was studying him with a frown. "Which happened where?"

"He told me to find him on a bench outside the Melbourne Museum, in Carton Gardens. Five pm. Said not to be late and to bring cash in an envelope." Catterick rolled his eyes. "To be honest, I thought he was getting a bit cloak-and-dagger over a passport. I almost didn't go, but Jan talked me into it."

"Could you describe this guy?" Ann asked.

Catterick shrugged. "Dunno. Nothing too memorable about him, I guess."

"Just give us as much detail as you can. What kind of clothes did he wear? Skin tone, hair colour?"

"Yeah, yeah. Lemme think." Catterick's features bunched up in concentration. "White guy, short black hair. Not real tall. Average, I guess, maybe around… five foot eight? He wore glasses, like mine but black. Kinda muscly, like he worked out."

"And his clothes?"

"Well, I didn't know at the time there was going to be a bloody exam," Catterick said. "But I think he wore… uh… a blue shirt. One of those collared shirts with the three buttons, and light chinos. And boat shoes. He was English. Spoke real soft. Like I said, not the sort we usually get at The Last Schooner."

"Any distinguishing features? Visible scars, piercings, tattoos, that kind of thing?"

Catterick shook his head. "Nah. Pretty average looking bloke."

Ryan and Ann exchanged a glance. Not ideal.

"All right," Ryan said. "So you met him outside the Melbourne Museum. What happened during the exchange?"

"When I saw him on the bench, he was reading a magazine. I waved to him and he pointed to the seat next to him. So I sit down, and he slides the magazine over to me and tells me the passport is in it. I go to take the passport out and he says not to do it in front of the whole city. To pretend I'm reading the magazine, like." Catterick rolled his eyes again. "So I check the date on the visa. It was just like he said, an almost-new three-year student stamp. Then he tells me to take it, put the envelope with the cash inside the magazine, lay it back down and walk away. I asked if he didn't want to count the money and he goes, 'No need, you won't cross me.'" He scoffed. "Like I said, the whole thing seemed over the top. It all felt a bit dodgy, like maybe he'd tipped off the cops or something. So I took the passport and left the money and got out of there. Next day I went in for a job at a restaurant, and, well…" He waved a hand disinterestedly at the immigration agent. "You know the rest."

"I don't suppose you ever got a name."

"Nope."

The immigration agent made a show of checking his watch. "Is that all, Detective Campbell? We still need to arrange a flight back to England for this young man."

Ryan turned to him. "Just one more thing. We'd like to take McCann's passport back with us so we can check it for prints."

The agent grimaced in faux apology. "Unfortunately, we don't have the passport anymore."

"What?" Ann said sharply.

"We checked with the consulate and heard that a new one had been issued to McCann. So we destroyed the one we had."

"You're joking," Ryan said.

"'Fraid not."

Ryan swore under his breath and looked to Catterick. "All right. Then we're through here. Thanks for your help, Mr Catterick. Safe travels."

Catterick rose to his feet and the immigration agent gestured him towards the door. Before he stepped out, he paused. "Oh, I just remembered one more thing," he said, turning back to Ryan and Ann. "Not sure if it matters to you or not. I heard a rumour that Big Al was attacked that same night I met the guy in the Schooner. No idea who it was, but it wasn't exactly hard to find someone who'd like to do him over. Not the nicest guy, Big Al."

Ryan nodded slowly. "That is good to know. Thanks."

As the agent led Catterick away, Ryan and Ann were left alone in the interview room. He reached over and pressed 'STOP' on the tape recorder, and its red light blinked out. Then he looked up at Ann.

"So," she said. "I'm guessing we're not heading back to Sydney straightaway."

"Not yet. First we should check in with the Melbourne police. Then I think we ought to pay a visit to The Last Schooner."

She picked up the tape recorder and handed it to Ryan. "No time to waste, then."

CHAPTER 33:
BIG AL

Muttering curses under his breath, Big Al let the door to The Last Schooner slam shut behind him.

Outside, the street was quiet, except for the muffled shouts that occasionally spilled from the nearby pubs. He struck off to a side alley, positioning himself so that he had a clear view of the bar he'd just left.

Al burned through half a pack of cigarettes while he stood there, waiting. It took hours. But finally, he showed up again. That pom bastard who'd beaten Al at pool and taken his money.

The man began to wander up the street. Al tossed his cigarette to the ground, leaving it smouldering in the gutter, and tailed him.

After a block or two, the man paused and cocked his head, as if he'd heard something. Al ducked out of sight behind the corner of a pawn shop. He watched carefully, but the man never turned around. A few moments later, he set off again. Al followed.

The stranger stepped onto a dark, silent road, one that Al knew to be lined mostly with abandoned buildings. He grinned to himself. This would be easy.

He sped up to reach his target, then came around the corner swinging. But when he turned onto the side street, he was surprised to find the man standing there, waiting for him.

It was too late to change course. As Al threw his first punch, the man dodged, not quite escaping the arc of Al's fist. His knuckles connected with the man's shoulder instead of his face. Al had the briefest sliver of time in which to realise he might've made a mistake before he felt a sudden, all-consuming pain plunge into his gut.

He gasped as the man yanked a switchblade from his stomach. Pressing a palm to the wound, Al looked down to see blood dripping thickly from his fingers to the pavement. He tried to stumble away, back towards the main street, towards the Schooner. But he didn't get far. The man quickly closed the short distance Al had managed to open up between them, and then Al's body lit up with pain: his abdomen, his chest, and then his throat.

Al collapsed to the ground. With a blank expression, the man leaned down and reached into Al's pocket, withdrawing his wallet. Al tried to stop him, but he found that his muscles were now as heavy as stone. His killer straightened up, tucked Al's wallet into his own jacket, and then slowly, methodically cleaned the switchblade with a handkerchief.

He started to walk away, leaving Al in a spreading pool of his own blood. Then he turned the corner and vanished. That was the last Al saw of him.

That was the last Al saw of anything.

CHAPTER 34:
BACK TO NORMAL…
FOR NOW

Lisa was cross-legged on her couch, finishing the last few bites of her salad and pasta. She had the television on, and was absently flipping through channels with the remote in her fork-free hand. Almost unconsciously, she was hoping to happen upon a press conference with Ryan standing behind a podium, announcing that they'd finally solved those terrible murders.

Although the news of the crimes had kept the city on edge for a few weeks, most people seemed to have quickly forgotten about the killer on the loose and moved on with their lives. The story had slipped off the front pages, and any new, minor updates were now buried deep in the local section of the Sydney papers, when they were written up at all. But tonight on the television there was no sign of Ryan, and nothing else on the news that she didn't already know. She shut the TV off with a sigh.

The house was quiet. Paul was out with some new girlfriend, undoubtedly cadging off her for his dinner and drinks, or at least, Lisa assumed so, since he kept insisting that he had no money to pay the rent he owed. He was two months in arrears now, and she was rapidly losing her patience.

She set the empty plate aside and grabbed her laptop, opening it up and balancing it on her knee. Out of habit, she clicked into her bookmarks and checked her usual roster of political news sites, scanning the press releases to see if there was anything she had missed. Somewhere in the back of her mind, she knew she shouldn't be working off the clock like this. But in truth, there wasn't much else going on for her at the moment. Just a few days ago she'd learned that another of her long-time friends was moving away. The few close friends she still had in Sydney were all preoccupied with their jobs and families, and Lisa rarely saw them. Whenever they did find time for her, they always seemed to have loads of exciting news about earning big promotions or getting engaged or buying some gorgeous new home. Her own life felt rather dull by comparison.

While she scrolled through the headlines, her mind drifted, trying to come up with something, anything else she could be doing to fill her time. She'd gone to the gym for a while, although her motivation had flagged quickly without anyone to keep her accountable. A few years ago, she'd learned to sail down at the Middle Harbour Yacht Club. That had been good fun, but the club turned out to be quite expensive, and she'd let her membership lapse after a season.

If she was honest, the only real excitement she'd gotten lately was her night out with Ryan. They'd had such a good time together at dinner. And an even better time together back at Ryan's place. She missed him, suddenly… the sincerity of his smile, the unexpected heat of his touch.

It was just a shame that it had all gone sour so quickly. If she hadn't run into him at the Barrenjoey Hotel the next day, things may have turned out very differently.

On impulse, she reached over to the coffee table and picked up her phone. She scrolled through her contacts until she found Ryan's home phone number, held her breath, and hit 'DIAL'.

After an impossibly drawn-out thirty seconds, the call rolled over to voicemail. Lisa hung up just as the tone sounded, half disappointed and half relieved that she hadn't gotten an answer. What would she have said anyway? There was nothing for them to talk about.

Lisa tossed her phone to the other end of the couch and went back to scrolling idly through articles on her laptop. She supposed she would just have to keep herself busy, as best as she could.

CHAPTER 35:
A NEW TERM

For the first time in twelve years, Wayne Brewster sat down at the desk in Admiralty House reserved for the governor of Sydney.

The office had been redecorated since he was last here. He recognised a few pieces of furniture, but the rest was unfamiliar to him. So, too, was the woman who stepped in to greet him. She had a black leather messenger bag on her shoulder.

"Good morning, Governor Brewster," she said pleasantly. "My name is June Atwell. I'm the assistant to the Governor's Office, and I'm here to help you with the transition into your new role."

The woman had brunette hair, pinned up in a sleek bun at the top of her head, and sharp hazel eyes. She wore a tailored, olive-green pantsuit and a string of pearls.

"Lovely to meet you, June," Brewster said. "It's not exactly a new role for me…"

"Of course, sir. Apologies. A new term, rather."

He eyed the numerous electronic devices she had begun to extract from the messenger bag and laid out on his desk.

"But those are new," he went on, somewhat warily.

"Yes, sir. These are devices that you'll use for governmental business. You've got a mobile, a tablet and a laptop. I've had our IT department set them up with your new security clearance, so you have full access to all the intranets and databases that you'll need."

Brewster picked up the mobile and tapped the power button. The phone came to life, revealing a home screen that displayed the city of Sydney's coat of arms.

"Oh, and I've set up an official Twitter account for you." June offered a glossy smile. "You'll want to be careful what you post on it, though. I've set up a meeting for you with our social media team tomorrow. They can give you some pointers."

He nodded. "Wonderful."

She held up another tablet, this one evidently her own. "Would you like to go over your schedule for the week?"

He gestured for her to take a seat across from him. "Please."

June sat down and began to rattle off a number of appointments with other elected officials. "But the biggest thing this week is the financial meetings," she said, using one finger to scroll rapidly on her tablet. "You've got conferences with… let's see. First up is the city councillors to go over all civil and municipal contracts for Sydney's regional boroughs. Then there's the conference with the transportation department, and another one with the city planning commission."

She glanced up at him. "I think that's enough to be getting on with for the first week. But once you get the reports from those financial meetings, I'm afraid you'll have to go through them and approve the final drafts over the weekend. First thing next week you'll be flying down to Canberra to see Prime Minister Johnson. Don't worry, an expense account has been set up for you, so it'll be ready for your trip."

He thanked her, and she gave him a warm smile. He couldn't tell if it was genuine or not.

"Well, I'll give you a chance to settle in. One last thing… I've compiled some reports from the outgoing administration so you can get caught up on everything." She pulled a thick binder from the messenger bag and held it out to him.

He took it with both hands, startled by how damn heavy it was.

"Happy reading," she said cheerfully.

He set the binder down on his desk. Then he slipped off his suit jacket, draped it over the back of his chair, rolled up his sleeves, and opened to the first page. "All right. I'll start on this right now."

"Is there anything else I can do for you at the moment?"

"Ah… yes, actually, there is one thing. Wherever there's room on the schedule, can you book me a meeting with the Sydney police commissioner?"

"Certainly. I'll have that set up right away." She turned crisply and walked away, closing the door behind her with a decisive *click*.

Brewster stared down at the ream of reports in front of him. Time to get cracking, then.

He pressed an intercom button on his desk. The aide in the reception area outside responded brightly, "Yes, Governor Brewster?"

"Hi, Zachary, could you have some danishes and coffee brought in here, please?"

"Of course, sir. I'll have them sent in now."

Brewster hardly moved from that seat for the rest of the day. He ate lunch at his desk, took a brief break to eat dinner and stretch his legs, then went right back to it.

He started with the budgets and city building contracts, since those would be addressed in his first block of meetings. He thought it'd be pretty dry reading, but he quickly discovered things were not as straightforward as he expected. Some boroughs had outsourced contracts to international companies, one a Ukrainian Company and they had delivered estimates that seemed absurdly high to Brewster. And sure enough, when he checked them against the final itemisations, which were tucked away in a dense spreadsheet, he found that the true costs were much lower than projected. That meant that someone, somewhere along the way, had pocketed the difference.

It was taxpayer money funding these inconsistencies. As Brewster studied the unyielding numbers, he became aware that it would look very poor if it was discovered that he'd allowed all this to continue under his watch. It wasn't the principle of the thing so much as the lack of finesse that bothered him. This was sloppy work. If Brewster could spot it, any journalist sifting through the public records would be able to see it too. He would have to figure out who was accountable for this.

Brewster leaned back in his chair, rubbing his eyes. There was so much to do. He'd need the public on his side before he raised the alarm. He made a mental note to meet with his press officer as soon as he could. They would need to work out a strategy… radio ads, television interviews, articles in the magazines and newspapers. Press conferences with pre-screened questions, photoshoots for promotional material targeted at the most important demographics. A full media blitz.

He'd need opportunities to socialise, too. Galas, official openings, parties with Sydney celebrities. He might as well have some fun while he was in office again. And besides, that would give him a chance to accomplish other, equally important tasks. Those events were where he gleaned critical information: who was having affairs, who was taking drugs, who was struggling to pay back their debts and looking for quick money. That information was crucial to his work, just as much as the spreadsheets and data tables in front of him now.

In that moment, Brewster was more sure than he had been yet that he'd made the right decision by running for office again. He almost felt like he was back to his old self. Folding his hands behind his head, he smiled out over the governor's office. His office.

He was right where he belonged.

CHAPTER 36:
WEDNESDAY IN MELBOURNE

Ann and Ryan spent Tuesday night in Melbourne. Wednesday morning they were up early for coffee and a bite to eat before they set off.

They started at the Melbourne police headquarters. There, they learned that the local team had already done a facial composite of the man who sold the stolen passport, based on Catterick's description of him. As Ryan stared down at the printout of the composited photo, he couldn't help but wonder how true to life it was, and whether it could really bring them any closer to untangling this web of questions that had begun two months ago. Or maybe it was twelve years ago. He still wasn't sure.

Their next stop was The Last Schooner. Ryan had spent a fair amount of time in Melbourne, and he could safely say he'd never found himself in this neighbourhood. They arrived in the early afternoon, not long after the pub had opened up. It was nearly empty, although Ryan got the distinct sense that it was often nearly empty. When they asked the manager whether the building had any CCTV cameras, he gave a long, hoarse laugh that turned into a hacking cough, gestured at the shabby surroundings, and asked, "What d'you think, mate?"

The immigration office had collected contact information for Jan, Catterick's girlfriend. Ann and Ryan had planned to visit her for an interview, but she ended up saving them a trip; she was just clocking in for her shift at the Schooner when they finished speaking with the manager.

They sat with Jan in one of the grimy booths under the Schooner's dim, bare lightbulbs and asked her to tell them about the night that she and Simon met the stranger with the passport. Her account matched Catterick's, down to the last detail. If they were lying, they'd put a lot of work into getting their story straight.

She confirmed that he had been living with her in Melbourne for the last eighteen months, and hadn't so much as visited Sydney in all that time. It seemed Catterick's alibi was about as airtight as it could be, which made the man who sold him the passport all the more intriguing as a potential suspect. They asked her about Big Al, mentioning what Catterick had said about him being attacked. But she didn't know any more about it than he did.

After that, it was onto another police station, this one the office closest to the Schooner. It turned out that the neighbourhood cops did have an open case for the attack on Big Al, but it wasn't especially easy to track down. Ryan went looking for a record of an assault, but what he found was a homicide. Al had been stabbed and left for dead. No identification had been recovered from the body, so the case was listed under John Doe. The Melbourne officers intended to visit The Last Schooner with a photo of the dead man's face so that they could get confirmation of his identity. But Ryan didn't bother waiting for that. Based on the description from Simon and Jan, he was certain that this was the right person.

When Ryan asked about potential forensic evidence, the lead detective shook his head. "A thunderstorm came through before the body was found," he told Ryan, disinterestedly. "Washed the whole place pretty clean. My guys are still doing a full investigation, but don't expect them to find much."

Just their luck. Ryan asked to have the report sent over to his office as soon as it was available, then thanked the other detective and headed out.

When they left the second police station, it was nearly time for their flight back to Sydney. They managed to get boarded in a less dramatic fashion than their outbound flight, with plenty of time for Ryan to settle in and stare out the window at the tarmac before takeoff.

"What are you thinking?"

He turned towards Ann. She was in the seat beside him, wearing a thoughtful expression as she studied him.

"Just that it feels like we're getting closer," Ryan answered.

"You think this is going to lead us to the Pittwater killer?"

"I think it's all connected. The stolen passport used by the bartender at the concert, the killing of Big Al, the mystery man playing pool."

Ann arched an eyebrow at him. "Passports and IDs are bought and sold every day, Campbell. You know that. It could've changed hands loads of times in the past two months. Not to mention, Catterick said himself that there was no shortage of people who had it in for Big Al."

"That's true," Ryan sighed. "I didn't say it would be an obvious connection. But you asked what I was thinking, and what I'm thinking is… somehow, it's all pieces of the same puzzle."

She gave a shrug. "Maybe you're right," she said, leaning her head back and closing her eyes. "I hope you are."

Ryan turned to look out the window. The runway started to roll by as the plane began to taxi. "I hope so too," he murmured.

Ann dozed through the flight. Ryan tried to sleep as well, but his eyes felt like they were wired open. The names and places of the case tumbled over one another in his mind, fragments of a picture that stubbornly refused to crystallise.

Outside the arrivals gate of Sydney Airport, Ryan and Ann promised to review everything once they got into the office tomorrow morning and said their goodbyes. They waved down separate cabs and made their own ways back home.

Ryan was exhausted. It had been a long two days. As he stepped through his front door, he decided he needed a hot shower and a stiff drink, in that order. But before he treated himself to either of those, he caught sight of the light flashing on his phone's answering machine.

Eagerly, he reached over to play it, hoping it was a message from his daughter. But whoever it was, they had hung up before they spoke. Frowning, he glanced at the number from the missed call. It was vaguely familiar, but he couldn't place it.

With a shrug, he erased the message and went to get ready for some well-deserved rest.

CHAPTER 37:
CANBERRA

Johnson arranged for the two of them to have lunch not far from the Parliament buildings in Canberra. The whole restaurant, floor to ceiling, was immaculately white, with a scattering of lamps that cast pools of warm light around the space. Brewster felt a bit like he was being seated in a museum exhibit.

"Hope I haven't kept you waiting," he said as he reached their table.

"No, not at all. I only just got here a few minutes ago," Johnson replied, his face partially obscured by the menu he was holding. "Have you been here before? I hear the Wagyu sirloin is outstanding."

"I haven't been here, no. I…"

Johnson set the menu down abruptly and fixed Brewster with a piercing look. Brewster fell silent.

"How goes the new term?" Johnson asked.

"Oh, you know. I'm settling in." Brewster rapidly weighed whether he ought to mention the profiteering that he'd spotted in the city contracts. He decided to wait. "Only been a week, but so far everything's been smooth."

"Good. Glad to hear it." He picked up the menu again. "The vote on the Gambling Act is today. I assume you've been following all the chatter around it?"

"I have," Brewster said, trying to gauge what response Johnson was looking for. "It looks like it's going to be rather close."

"It's that damn Susan Harrison." Johnson's lip curled in distaste. "She'll be our biggest problem. It's *very* important that this gets passed quickly. We do not want the margins to be tight enough that it goes to a second vote. The whole timeline will get bogged down."

Cautiously, Brewster asked, "Whose timeline?"

"Our Chinese investors. Obviously. They're waiting for this to go through so they can start construction on their new super-casinos. Any delay in the process could mean that they take their money elsewhere." Johnson gave a disparaging shake of his head. "Harrison's still the most popular member of the Liberal party. They'll all back her. If she gets the Democrats behind her as well, that will be enough to force a second vote. And if *that* happens…" Johnson dropped the menu to peer over the top of it at Brewster. "…then I'll need you to drum up support in Sydney. Try to get some of the Democrats to see the error of their ways. Make sure we've got all the Republicans in line."

Brewster nodded. Before he could reply, Johnson changed course.

"And once we've got this taken care of, it'll be on to the Pacific Highway bill. That one's got plenty of widespread support, but it'll be Peter Duncan who gets in our way. Bloody eco-warrior with all his hippie nonsense. You'll have to mind him, too, and his fanatical base. Don't forget, as I said at our last meeting, you've got resources available if you need any help sorting things out." Johnson paused to take a sip of his drink, raising his eyebrows at Brewster. "You'll have lots to keep you busy, my friend. I hope you're ready."

"Ready and willing," he answered, not entirely truthfully.

He'd done plenty of collaborating with Johnson before, but all of this felt different. More urgent somehow, and *bigger*... the deals, the amount of money to be made, the stakes if things went wrong. Brewster wasn't sure he liked this new way of doing business. Mostly, he wanted to net some cash for himself and then get out.

Johnson gave him a broad smile. "Excellent. In that case, let's eat."

For the rest of the lunch, Johnson rattled on about the various failings of his political opponents and his wide-ranging complaints about the state of things in Canberra, requiring little input from Brewster.

When their food had been cleared away, Johnson checked his watch.

"I've got to get back," he said with a frown. "Why don't you walk over with me? I've got a spare suite I can set you up in while we get this vote over with."

•

A few hours later, Brewster was in Johnson's expansive Parliamentary office, sitting on a large leather couch. He'd helped himself to a glass of Johnson's brandy. Over the top of the tumbler, Brewster's eyes followed the path of aides and secretaries scurrying back and forth across the room. The PM himself was on the phone. Brewster had no idea who was on the other line, but he did not envy them.

"What in the *bloody hell* happened to our margin in the House of Representatives, hmm? What happened to a quick single round of votes?" Johnson demanded, waving off an aide who was attempting to show him an intelligence briefing.

The vote had gone poorly. At the start of the legislative session, Susan Harrison had made an impassioned speech against the bill. Although he'd never dare say so to Johnson, Brewster was privately quite impressed with it. She'd spoken at length about the social ills of gambling... how its worst effects inevitably fell upon the poorest and most vulnerable of a society. As an ex-addict herself, Harrison's description of the damages wrought by addiction was moving, and, in the end, very effective. The first vote had resulted in a stalemate; the bill wasn't dead, but it didn't have enough support for passage. It would go to a second round.

Gradually, over the next two hours, the steady stream of aides in and out of the office slowed and then stopped as they all either went home or simply gave up trying to get Johnson's attention. By nightfall, Brewster and Johnson were the only ones left. Some of the lights had been turned off, and the room was dim and quiet.

Johnson gave himself a generous pour of brandy and sat heavily on the sofa beside Brewster. He stared into his drink, swirled it around a few times, and enunciated, "Fuck."

He shook his head and glanced up at Brewster, who tried to look sympathetic. "What did I tell you? That bloody woman Harrison. I've already rung my Chinese investors. They're getting nervous. I promised them this is just a little setback, but they expect to see results. Soon. I've given them my word that things will be taken care of." He shifted closer to Brewster on the couch. "You've got to do something about Harrison, Wayne. You've got to have this sorted out when you get back to Sydney."

"Of course," Brewster offered smoothly. "As soon as I'm back, I'll pull some strings…"

"Pull some strings?" Johnson repeated, sounding scandalised. "You'll have to do better than that. Do you understand the scope of the situation, Wayne? We are talking about the wellbeing of the entire Australian economy. We are talking about *billions* of dollars of investment that we could lose."

"I understand," Brewster said. "I'll do everything I can, I assure you." He paused. "There are just a few other things I have to sort out first. I've been looking at the books in Sydney, and it seems that some big city contracts have been given out improperly. Someone skimming off the top based on overpriced estimates, that sort of thing. I'll have to get the police involved. I'm not sure, but it seems to come down to an accountant in the Civil Boroughs office. He's got a connection to a Ukrainian company…"

Johnson cut him off with a wave of his hand. "Fine. Get that taken care of as quickly as you can, and then forget about it. We've got bigger problems to deal with." He sank back into the sofa and sulked for a few moments. Then, gesturing with his tumbler towards Brewster, he asked, "Whatever happened with those murders in Sydney, anyway?"

"Still unsolved. But mostly out of the headlines now."

"Still unsolved?" Johnson rubbed his jaw thoughtfully. "Who's heading that case?"

"A bloke called Ryan Campbell. He and I don't get on. I told you before, I used to have a good relationship with Sergeant MacDonald, but lately it seems like Campbell's got MacDonald working against me," Brewster explained, thinking back to his encounter with MacDonald at Palm Beach with a flicker of annoyance. Putting it out of his mind, he looked back up at Johnson and added, "You might want to be careful with Campbell. I hear he's been sniffing around the Leadman case again."

"That architect in Pittwater?" Johnson said in disbelief. "Jesus, that was years ago. We don't need anyone digging that back up now. I'll have to have a talk with the Sydney police commissioner." He gave Brewster a scowl. "I thought you said you were going to meet with him."

"I am," Brewster said, a bit too quickly. "I have a meeting with him this week."

"Good. I'll call him tomorrow morning. Warm him up for you." Johnson took a sip of his brandy, his eyes far away. Something seemed to click into place as his gaze slid back to Brewster. "I'll tell him I'm concerned about the lack of progress on the murder investigations, and worried about whether the right people are in charge. That'll plant the seed for taking Campbell off the case. Then, when you meet with him, tell him you're looking for someone to head up the investigation into that dodgy Ukrainian company account. He'll be able to make both of us happy by moving Campbell onto that case."

Brewster frowned. "I'm not sure about getting Campbell involved with this city contracts investigation. As I said, we've never been on good terms and…"

"That doesn't matter," Johnson said impatiently. "What matters is that we get him away from the Leadman case and into a position where you can keep a leash on him."

Brewster was still reluctant, but there didn't seem to be much point in arguing. He could tell by the determined glint in Johnson's eye that the issue had been decided.

"Come on, Wayne, I shouldn't have to explain all this to you," Johnson chided. "This sort of thing is exactly why I have you around. To keep an eye on everything in Sydney for me." He gave Brewster a slick smile. "Or did you forget that's why I had you elected?"

"No," Brewster murmured, after several moments of silence. "I didn't forget."

CHAPTER 38:
SUSAN HARRISON

Pulling her suitcase behind her, Susan Harrison arrived at the front door of her flat in Sydney.

Her flight from Canberra had been delayed, and she was even more tired than she usually was coming back from the capital. After a few tries, she managed to wrestle the door open without dropping either her purse or her coffee. Yanking her keys from the doorknob, she called inside, "Robyn, babe! I'm home!"

She waited a few seconds, but no reply came.

That was odd. Robyn, Susan's girlfriend of four years, often worked long hours at her nonprofit's office, but she was normally home by now. Frowning, Susan lugged her suitcase over the threshold and closed the door behind her. "Robyn? Are you here?"

Still nothing.

She didn't even have a chance to put down her things before she caught sight of the envelope propped up on the coffee table. 'Dear Susan' was written across the envelope's front.

Susan's heart dropped to her stomach. As soon as she saw it, she knew what it was. Even so, she forced herself to carefully set down her purse and coffee, lean her suitcase against the sofa, and open the envelope.

The letter inside was short. Nothing she didn't already know. Robyn had stayed as long as she could, but she was tired of existing in the background of Susan's life while work was her sole focus. She knew that what Susan was doing was important. But she couldn't keep going on like this. She wished Susan all the best.

Susan sank down onto the couch while her eyes flickered over Robyn's familiar handwriting. She didn't know when she started crying, but by the time she'd finished reading, the paper was speckled with teardrops.

She let herself sit there in painful, disbelieving silence for a few minutes, but no more than that. Then she shook herself, dried her face with her sleeves, and straightened up.

Come on, Susan. There's more to do.

She set the letter aside and rose to her feet. Glancing around her apartment for something to do, she spotted the flashing light on her answering machine. She walked over and pressed play. There were a series of incongruously celebratory messages from friends and colleagues, congratulating her on the vote in the House. One was from The Addicts Society, inviting her to help organise a protest event next month. The last message was from a journalist at the *Sydney Telegraph*, Lisa Gordon. She was asking to arrange an interview whenever Susan was available.

"That'll be nice," she said absently to herself, and resolved to call everyone back tomorrow. For tonight, though, they would have to wait. She wheeled her suitcase into the bedroom and began to unpack.

CHAPTER 39:
THE CORONER'S REPORT

"So this is what it looks like outside the morgue, huh?"

Ryan looked up from his computer to find Pearl standing at his office door. "Dr Tabard," he said, waving her in. "Don't usually see you out and about. To what do I owe the pleasure?"

She held up a packet of papers. "Melbourne just sent this over. Thought you'd want to take a look."

He frowned. "What is it?"

"Coroner's report on one Alfred Kilkenny."

"Ah. Big Al."

She raised a brow. "Must be."

"What does the report say? Any similarities to the Pittwater murders?"

"As far as I can tell? Not many." She paged through the report, pulling out one of the sheets and handing it over to him.

Ryan accepted it and looked over several dense paragraphs of medical vocabulary that refused to coalesce into meaningful information. He glanced back up at Pearl. "Care to interpret?"

"Your Big Al had multiple stab wounds, three around the abdomen and one in the throat. All seem strategically placed for maximum effect. He would've bled out very quickly. But there's no evidence of strangulation, or any other injuries except those very efficient stab wounds. That's the first big difference. The blade wasn't the same type as was used in the Pittwater killings, either. That was a stiletto blade, probably around seven inches. This blade was shorter, just two to three inches, with a needlepoint tip. And, obviously, Big Al doesn't fit the profile of the other victims."

Ryan nodded slowly. "So… you're saying you don't think it's the same killer."

She shrugged. "Hard to be certain. What I *am* saying is this murder doesn't follow the pattern of the others. That's what I can tell you for sure."

"All right. Thanks, Pearl."

"No worries. Word from Melbourne is that their office decided this guy was likely killed by one of his criminal friends. So now that the autopsy is done, they're more or less shelving the case. Sounded like it was pretty low priority for them, so I don't expect to hear anything more about it. But if I do, I'll let you know." Pearl handed him the rest of the packet. "Keep this copy. I've got another one in the lab." She regarded him with a touch of worry in her expression. "Anything new on the Pittwater cases?"

"Nothing," he said, regretfully. "It's like looking for a needle in a haystack. And a bloody big haystack, at that."

"Well…" she sighed. "Just have to keep looking and hope you get lucky, I guess."

CHAPTER 40:
OFF THE CASE

Ryan's supervisor was a man named Peter Alford. He was in his late fifties, with salt-and-pepper hair and a permanent crease between his brows. Alford's office was not Ryan's favourite place to be first thing on a Monday morning. Not that he had much of a choice at the moment.

"You've had the Pittwater case for more than two months now," Alford said, staring down at Ryan. He was standing with his arms folded, leaning back against the edge of his desk while Ryan sat in an office chair in front of him.

"Yes, sir. I know it's been a bit slow going, but we have started to see some movement. As I said in my last report, the passport that was used at the Sydney SuperDome…"

But Alford didn't let him finish. "The higher-ups are not happy with your results. All these trips to Brisbane and Melbourne… and for what? You've wasted a huge amount of time and resources, Campbell. Do you realise that?"

Ryan fought a scowl off his face. "I was following up on leads, sir. There was very little to go off of here in Sydney, so we had to extend our search…"

"Yet you've still got nothing to show for it, even after running around half of Australia. And what's all this I've been hearing about you wasting time while you re-investigate some old case that's been closed for years?"

Shit. "With all due respect, I wasn't re-investigating," Ryan protested. "I thought that there may be a connection between that case and the Pittwater killings."

"Well, you've had your chance to find it. Time's up. It's been decided that you're being taken off the Pittwater case."

Ryan sat in stunned silence for several moments. Finally, he managed, "Decided, sir? By who?"

"Direct orders from the police commissioner."

"*What?*"

It would be one thing if Alford had made the decision, or a local superintendent. But for it to come straight from the commissioner… that was unusual. Maybe more than unusual. Immediately, a suspicion started to coalesce in the back of Ryan's mind: something was going on behind the scenes here, something bigger than Alford was telling him.

"But, sir," he said, struggling to recover himself, "I've been the head of this investigation since it began. I know it better than anyone. There has to be some mistake."

Alford gave him a look of warning. "The decision is final, Campbell. The Pittwater case will be reassigned to Ann Nguyen. You're being placed on a new case that's just been opened." He turned, picked up a file folder from his desk, and handed it to Ryan. "Here are the documents that have been collected so far. Looks like a profiteering scheme at the city boroughs office."

Ryan accepted the folder disbelievingly. "You're putting me on a fraud case?" He glanced up at Alford, trying not to look as angry as he felt. "I'm a homicide detective. I'm not a financial investigator."

Alford shrugged. "As of today, that's exactly what you are. Now get to work."

Ryan rose slowly to his feet. He could barely wrap his head around what had just happened. All those days and weeks, all those countless hours he'd poured into this case… now he was being booted off of it. And to add insult to injury, they were assigning him to a job that wasn't even his department.

He left Alford's office, narrowly managing not to slam the door behind him. Ignoring the sidelong glances of his colleagues in the hallway, he headed straight for his own office. Once there, he stared blankly at the folder Alford had given him, unable to bring himself to look inside.

Slowly, after a few minutes had passed, his anger started to ebb. It was replaced with a weary resignation. There was no getting around the fact that it was infuriating beyond words that he'd been reassigned. But what could he do about it? Orders were orders.

With a long sigh, he opened the folder and began to go over the new case.

CHAPTER 41:
A CLOSED-DOOR MEETING

The Masson Hotel, just a few blocks from Canberra Central, was one of Johnson's favourite places for conversations of a particularly sensitive nature. The reason was simple: the hotel featured a suite of meeting rooms, all of them very nicely appointed, fully soundproofed, and small enough to be quickly and efficiently searched by his security team for possible bugs. It was in one of these meeting rooms that the Prime Minister sat with Chan.

"Protests have already started against the Pacific Highway Act," he said. "Mostly that greenie Peter Duncan, as expected. But Harrison's gone and made herself a problem, too. She's been in the press every day, campaigning against that and the Gambling Act. I hear she's helping to organise a march in Sydney next week."

"Do you still believe that you'll be able to get both bills passed?" Chan asked, his neutral tone belying the weight of the question.

"Yes," Johnson said, with all the confidence he could muster, which was quite a lot. "No reason to think that these whingers will get their way. I've already assured my investors that the bills *will* be made law. We've got Brewster out there doing a lot of the heavy lifting. He's been on TV and in the papers, pushing the message that we're fighting for a stable future for Australia, for new growth in the economy. All that sort of thing. He's not bad at it, actually." His voice fell slightly, as if not to be overheard, although there was, of course, no one else to hear him. "Now, all that being said. It couldn't hurt to have you… prod things along in the right direction. I would like your help in making sure that our opponents are taken care of, at all costs. Be discreet, of course. I'm sure I can trust you with that."

Chan allowed a slow smile. "Of course, Prime Minister. Say no more."

CHAPTER 42:
PROTEST MARCH

The Saturday of the protest dawned grey and windy. A steady drizzle spattered the deck of the ferry as Lisa made her way across the harbour towards Fleet Park, where the march would begin.

She arrived about a half hour early. A row of white stalls had been set up at the starting point. Most of the people in the booths were soliciting signatures for petitions or hawking Liberal merchandise, but Lisa managed to find one stall that was selling food. She paid for a bagel and a cup of coffee, then sat down on a bench to have breakfast and watch the crowd gather.

She'd wanted Paul to come along and take some photos of the event, but by the time she was ready to leave, he was still in bed with some new girlfriend, or maybe it was the same one from before; Lisa had given up trying to keep track. She'd had to settle for borrowing one of his cameras, and her editor would just have to make do with whatever shots she could get.

Once she'd wiped the cream cheese off her fingers, she took the camera out of its case and snapped a few photos of the march organisers, who were busy handing out leaflets and unfurling banners. Several hundred people had congregated in the park by the time Lisa finally spotted Susan Harrison.

She was talking with a small knot of rally-goers and press members huddled around her. Lisa hurried over to get some quotes and photos for her article. She'd interviewed Susan a number of times before, and Harrison, spotting her in the ring of faces, greeted her warmly. They had a friendly chat about what the Addicts Society hoped to accomplish with the event before Harrison was pulled up to the front to lead the march.

At last, decked in blue ponchos that volunteers had handed out, the crowd set off down George Street. Almost immediately, the rain started to pick up. Before long, the poster board signs carried by protesters grew soggy, and marker ink streaked through slogans about protecting Sydney's communities from the Gambling Act. But the group was cheerful anyway, participating in chants led by the marshals and sometimes spontaneously breaking out into protest songs. They got a few cheers from passersby on the street. Lisa was towards the back of the pack, but every once in a while she caught a glimpse of the police officers at the front who were halting traffic at each intersection. Everything seemed to be going very smoothly, until, abruptly, it wasn't.

The march became a standstill. The attendees surrounding Lisa murmured amongst themselves, speculating about what was causing the holdup. Lisa tried to see what was going on, but even with the heeled boots she was wearing, she wasn't tall enough to see what had halted their progress. Then, gradually, the sounds of a commotion began to swell and filter backwards to where Lisa was standing. She heard yelling, beeping car horns, and then the roar of motorbikes.

Spouting rapidfire apologies, Lisa shoved her way to the front of the group. By the time she got there, the scene had broken into chaos.

For a few seconds, Lisa was too stunned to react… but only for a few seconds. Then her journalistic instincts kicked in and she raised the camera to her eye, firing off shots as quickly as she could.

A convoy of leather-clad bikers had just come tearing off the highway. The police officers gestured frantically for them to stop, but the bikers streaked past them and into the crowd. Protesters dived out of the way as the bikes circled and wove through the mass of people, shouting and jeering at everyone they passed. They were clearly determined to antagonise the participants of the march, although Lisa couldn't fathom why. The initial frightened screams quickly became yells of outrage, demanding that the bikers leave. Lisa didn't see who did it first, but one by one, protesters began to grab the bikers off their motorcycles. Scuffles quickly escalated into all-out brawls as more and more people joined the fray.

This was *not* what Lisa had expected to come out of a dreary Saturday morning.

The officers at the front must have radioed in for backup, because squad cars arrived within a few minutes. As soon as they began to appear, the bikers got back on their motorcycles and roared off again. The police managed to restore order quickly, but by then, more than a few people had badly bloodied faces and knuckles. Some of them were being escorted to the fringes of the crowd to have their injuries treated by a medic.

Eventually, the march got underway again. But the mood had soured. There were no more songs, and only half-hearted responses to the organisers' attempts to re-energise the atmosphere. The rain grew worse. Over the next several blocks, many of the protesters drifted away from the group. By the time they reached Hyde Park, where the march was slated to end, the size of the congregation had diminished considerably.

A small stage had been set up in the park. On it, several community organisers gave speeches to the remaining attendees, all focused on the shortcomings and dangers of the proposed Gambling Act.

Susan Harrison gave the final speech. As usual, she was the strongest speaker by far. She gave a confident, energetic performance that managed to draw cheers and applause from the subdued audience. Lisa huddled under a tree to take notes without getting her steno pad wet. Afterward, she ventured out into the rain to take a few more photos.

And then, as quickly as she could, she stowed the camera in its case, packed her notepad into her purse, and headed back towards the ferry. Despite the success of Harrison's speech, the incident with the bikers had cast a lingering cloud over the whole event. It had been a harrowing day, and Lisa was eager to get home and put it behind her.

CHAPTER 43:
SATURDAY NIGHT ROUTINE

Susan Harrison stepped off the stage. One of the march organisers, a woman named Nicole, handed over an umbrella, which Susan gratefully opened up.

"Your speech was phenomenal!" Nicole chirped, wrapping Susan in a one-armed hug.

"Oh, thanks. You all did a great job setting this up. Not to mention getting things back on track after those bikers showed up," Susan replied.

"God, that was crazy, wasn't it?"

"Absolutely crazy," Susan agreed. "But at least everyone was okay."

"Yeah, thank God for that. Are you sticking around? A few of us are going to get dinner later."

"Ah, no, I'd better get home." Susan managed an apologetic smile. "Thanks for the invite, though. You have fun."

They said their goodbyes, and Susan walked back to her car alone in the rain.

By the time she got to her flat, she was shivering from her wet clothes. She took a long, hot shower to ease the chill and wash off the strangeness of the day. Then she brushed out her short, sandy blonde hair, which always had more grey in it than she remembered, and got ready for her typical Saturday night routine: dinner at her favourite local Chinese restaurant.

She called to arrange a taxi, and it dropped her off at the door. The hostess smiled as Susan walked in, greeting her fondly as she took her coat and showed her to her usual table.

Susan settled into a small, cosy booth near the rain-streaked window. A few moments later, she was approached by a smiling waiter who asked how she was doing.

"Oh, hello," she said, peering up at the unfamiliar face. "I don't think I've seen you here before. Usually Lian is working at this time."

"Lian has the night off," the waiter explained, in the same melodically lilting accent as the rest of the restaurant staff. He pulled a notepad from the pocket of his black jacket. "But I'll be happy to serve you this evening. Can I get you started with something to drink?"

"Just water, please. And I'm ready to put in my food order as well."

While she was waiting for her meal to arrive, she took a call from one of the march's organisers who wanted her feedback on the day's event. She was still chatting with him when the waiter reappeared, carrying steaming plates of bao and potstickers.

She covered her mobile's speaker with her hand and thanked him.

"Is there anything else I can get for you?" he replied, setting the dishes in front of her.

"No, I think I'm all set."

"Are you certain, madam? Something to drink?"

"Oh… well, all right. I'll take some mango juice, please."

"Of course. I won't be a moment."

By the time the waiter returned with the glass, Susan was finally extricating herself from her conversation with the organiser. She assured him she'd check in with him in the next few days, hung up, and happily tucked into her meal.

CHAPTER 44:
ALL ACCORDING TO PLAN

Things had been a bit tense when Harrison declined a beverage. Under normal circumstances, Chan would've offered a glass of wine on the house. But of course ex-addict Harrison didn't drink, so that plan was no good. It was a shame, because alcohol was ideal for this sort of thing… it was strong enough to easily cover up the taste of the sedative. But mango juice would work just as well.

The kitchen was shrouded in billows of steam. Chan stood behind a stainless steel shelf and from a small, unmarked vial, poured a white powder into the glass of juice. He gave it a stir and within seconds, the powder had dissolved without a trace.

On the whole, he reflected as he watched the orange liquid swirl, everything was going quite smoothly. Arranging this stint at the restaurant had been simple enough. All it took was a couple of well-placed phone calls with some of his Chinese contacts until he found someone who was owed a favour by the restaurant owner. Chan assured the owner that his hands would be entirely clean. All he had to do was let Chan work one shift on one night, and he would be handsomely rewarded.

Once he'd delivered the juice to Harrison's table, he positioned himself near the door to the kitchen so that he had an unobstructed view of her. He watched as she took several gulps of the mango juice.

Chan waited until he saw her blinking rapidly, trying to clear the blurriness that, he knew, was creeping into her vision. With her elbow on the table, she cradled her head in one hand. He swept over to her booth.

"How is your meal so far, madam?" he asked.

She looked up at him, visibly struggling to focus her eyes. "I'm… I'm feeling a little sick," she managed thickly, her words seeming to crowd together in her mouth.

Chan feigned concern. "I'm very sorry to hear that, madam. You don't look well at all. May I call you a cab to take you home?"

"Yes, please," Harrison slurred. "I think that'd be best."

With Chan on one side of her and the restaurant manager on the other, Harrison stumbled to the taxi waiting at the curb. On their way out, the hostess handed Harrison her coat and softly wished for her to feel better.

They loaded her into the back of the taxi and sent it on its way. The manager watched with a scowl as its brake lights receded. "Glad to get her out of there. It's packed tonight," he said, and shot Chan an annoyed glance. "You didn't say anything about having a sick person in my restaurant."

"It was only for a minute," Chan responded impassively. He slipped off the waiter's jacket that he'd borrowed from Lian and handed it to the manager. "But now she's gone. And my shift is over."

•

After retrieving a small black duffel bag from the kitchen, Chan took his time navigating to Harrison's apartment. This was partially to give the drug a chance to take effect and partially to avoid CCTV cameras, which meant he had to follow a circuitous route to reach her apartment building. Once there, he took the staircase to her floor and slid on a pair of black gloves. Then he picked the lock on her front door so efficiently that even if the neighbours had thought to look out at the hallway, they barely would've had time to see him.

The apartment was still and silent. A light was on in the living room. As he took a few steps inside, he saw that the scene had been set perfectly... he could hardly have done better himself. Harrison was sprawled out on her couch, with an empty glass in her hand and a puddle of water on the floor where it had spilled.

Chan took a quick tour through the flat. First, he found the letter from Robyn on the bedside stand and placed it on the coffee table near Harrison's limp hand. Then he checked the medicine cabinet in the bathroom, where he was pleased to find a mostly full bottle of antidepressants. He knew from his research that she'd been prescribed them in the past, but had stopped taking them some time ago. He'd brought along a spare bottle, just in case she'd thrown these out, but clearly she'd forgotten them here on this dusty shelf. He took the bottle and returned to the living room, where Harrison was still unconscious.

She did not stir as Chan knelt beside her. With gloved hands, he turned her face upright, took a small handful of capsules from the bottle, gently pulled her jaw open and tapped the pills onto her tongue. From the duffel bag on his shoulder, he took a bottle of vodka, unscrewed the cap, and poured the liquor slowly into her mouth.

She sputtered, a sliver of white rolling beneath her eyelids. Chan tilted her chin back until she reflexively swallowed. He paused a few moments, waiting until her breathing settled again. Once he was sure she wouldn't wake up, he repeated the process with another handful of capsules, then did it once more for good measure. He set the pill bottle, with the cap still off, and the now nearly empty bottle of vodka on the table beside Robyn's note.

When everything had been arranged, Chan stepped back to admire the overall effect. The conclusion would be inescapable. Harrison was an addict whose girlfriend had just left her, a politician facing constant criticism along with waning popularity. People would say her suicide was sad, of course, but really, was it much of a surprise?

He allowed himself a smile. The bikers at the rally had been quite a nice touch, he thought; they'd effectively stolen the headlines and distracted the public from the event's purpose. And everything afterward had gone just as he'd hoped. Looking down at the pale, pained face of Susan Harrison, Chan felt the satisfaction of a job well done.

CHAPTER 45:
SAD NEWS

In between yawns and sips of coffee, Lisa tapped out a steady rhythm on her keyboard. It was Monday morning, and she was hoping to finish up her latest piece in the next few hours.

While she was wrestling with an awkward phrase, her concentration was broken by a knock on the wall of her cubicle. She glanced up to find her editor's face looking down at her. He wore a grim expression.

"Hi, Brian," she said, surprised. "Everything all right?"

He nodded towards her laptop. "Is that the article on Harrison's protest?"

"Yeah, it is. I should be done with it around lunch…"

"You're going to have to change it."

Lisa frowned. "What do you mean? You haven't even seen it yet."

"Harrison's cleaner found her dead in her apartment this morning. Suicide, apparently."

"*What?*" She stared at him in horror. "How is that possible? I just talked to her on Saturday. Her speech was amazing. She was looking forward to more protests…"

"I don't know, Lisa." She'd rarely seen Brian display real emotion, but even he looked a little shaken. "That's all we've heard so far. You better go and try to get some details. Whatever you can find out, fold it into your current article and we'll try to get it into the late edition."

Lisa nodded numbly as she stood and grabbed the jacket off the back of her chair.

The police were still at Susan's apartment, and they'd cordoned off her front door. At first, they tried to brush off Lisa's questions. When she mentioned that she'd spoken to Susan two days ago, though, their interest was piqued.

"We'd like to get a statement from you," said the detective at the scene, a woman Lisa didn't recognise. "Is it all right if we contact you in a day or two as part of our inquiry?"

"Yes, of course. Here's my card." Lisa fished one out of her wallet and handed it to the detective. "Since there will be an inquiry, does that mean that the cause of death is still under investigation…?"

"We'll have a press conference later. You'll be able to ask questions then."

"I was just wondering if you could confirm whether…"

"There will be more details at the press conference. We'll reach out to you to get your statement within the next forty-eight hours."

Lisa watched with a scowl as the detective ducked under the police tape and disappeared into the apartment. "Almost as rude as Ryan," she observed in an undertone.

Not long after, she returned to her office. There, she revised her draft to reflect Susan's death. In the version that was printed, the article focused on Susan's impact on the Sydney community, her passionate advocacy and fierce activism, and all that she had accomplished while fighting her own demons. Lisa was glad to have the chance to write that tribute, even though it made her feel the tragedy of Susan's death all the more keenly.

Whatever your politics, no one could doubt the devotion that Harrison brought to her work, Lisa's article read. *She was profoundly committed to making this city and this country a better place, and she will be deeply missed.*

CHAPTER 46:
CLIMBING IN THE
BLUE MOUNTAINS

Two months had passed since Susan Harrison was found dead in her apartment.

Peter Duncan, darling of the Eco and Environment Party and expert-level rock climber, was on a trip in the Blue Mountains west of Sydney.

Chan Jianjun was also on the trip.

He was not there as Chan Jianjun. He was there as Yeung Mingli, a Chinese tourist. Unlike many of Chan's aliases, Yeung was a real person. He was due to fly back to China in a few days. After calling around his network, including an old acquaintance at the Chinese embassy, Chan had been put into contact with Yeung. They'd agreed to a mutually beneficial arrangement. Chan borrowed his documents and asked him to lay low in a hotel in Sydney. Yeung, assuming he cooperated, would return home from Australia with a significantly healthier bank account than when he'd arrived.

All six climbers, plus the instructor, were staying in the same hostel. On the first night, they ate dinner and had drinks together. Chan remained quiet, making polite small talk when it was required of him and otherwise observing the dynamic of the group. Climbing started on the second day, which gave Chan an opportunity to note when the ropes and harnesses were checked for safety.

That night, Chan sat next to Duncan at dinner. He feigned an interest in Duncan's enthusiastic descriptions of the region's geology, invited him to tell stories from his previous climbing trips. That was all it took for Duncan to act as if they were long time friends.

By the third day, Chan had all the groundwork he needed.

They left the hostel early that morning, heading deeper into Blue Mountains National Park than they had the day before. Around the middle of the day, after all the gear had already been examined, Chan found an opportunity to discreetly swap out Peter Duncan's climbing rope with one that he'd brought in his own rucksack. The new one was identical to the original, except for a particular spot where the fibres on the replacement rope had been nearly worn through.

On the last route of the afternoon, Chan was the lead climber. Peter Duncan was immediately below him. They were ascending the face of a massive sandstone cliff, and their climb brought them steadily higher above the eucalyptus-blanketed valley floor. It was a truly beautiful view. But Chan didn't have time to linger.

They had come up alongside an overhang on the rock face. Chan would need to pass over it to continue on the route. He halted briefly to fix Duncan's quickdraw and rope to a bolt hanger, then turned and shouted down, "All right, Peter! Start climbing!"

He waited until the moment that Peter shifted his weight. Then Chan launched himself horizontally towards the lip of the overhang, his fingers easily finding a handhold in the rock. He steadied himself and looked down.

When Chan jumped, Peter Duncan's rope had gone slack. Without the tension holding him up, he lost his grip and fell backwards. The rope—the one that Chan had replaced just a few hours before—reeled all the way out to its maximum length.

For a few breathless moments, Peter Duncan dangled in mid air. His eyes were huge, and his mouth formed a silent 'O', as if the sudden drop had stolen the breath from his lungs and left him nothing with which to scream.

Then the rope snapped.

Duncan plummeted down... how many feet, Chan wasn't sure exactly, but he'd made a point of waiting until they reached a height that was likely to be fatal. One of the climbers shrieked as Duncan fell straight past her, and then his body was swallowed up by the trees below. The others began to panic, even as the instructor called for calm. They retreated back down the rock face as quickly as they could, and the instructor radioed in for emergency services.

The climbing party stood at a safe distance and watched as a stretcher bearing Duncan's body was winched up into a helicopter waiting above the treetops. Then, as a group, they slowly, numbly made their way back to the hostel.

As they entered the makeshift lounge on the hostel's ground floor, they were met by the police, who requested to speak with each of them individually. Chan mimicked the shock and dismay of the other climbers convincingly enough that the police officer interviewing him barely looked up as he took Chan's statement. From the next table over, Chan heard someone ask if there would be a full investigation, and the officer assured him that there would be.

After the police left, some of the other climbers huddled together around a table, their hands clutching mugs of tea. Rather than sit with them in their tedious grief, Chan excused himself and went back to his own room.

The group had a shuttle bus scheduled to take them back into Sydney the next day, but Chan decided not to wait for it. He woke very early and caught the first train back into the city. Just as the train rolled out of the station, a news alert chimed on his phone. He opened the notification and read that Peter Duncan had died on the helicopter before it reached the hospital.

CHAPTER 47:
A NEW FRIEND

For the first time in a long while, the killer had settled into a comfortable routine.

During his first several weeks in Melbourne, he'd worked his way through most of the city's biggest cultural attractions. The drawer in his bedside table quickly filled with pamphlets and brochures from art galleries and museums. Once he was satisfied that he'd taken enough time to see the sights, he set about getting a job.

He called a few different places to ask about openings: a restaurant, a men's clothing store, a movie theatre. None of them particularly inspired him. But then, as he skimmed through the newspaper one morning, he saw a 'help wanted' ad for a book shop. It was located right in the heart of the city, and it looked perfect.

He put on his favourite blue shirt and his most agreeable smile. When he walked in and inquired about the ad, the owner, who was behind the sales counter, asked if he was free for an interview now. Half an hour later, he was hired.

The work was pleasant. He often used his employee discount to buy books on all kinds of subjects, and spent most evenings reading his latest purchase. His co-workers treated him kindly enough, although he could tell that some of them thought he was a bit odd. That suited him all right, though. Mostly, he kept his head down, did his work well, and enjoyed becoming an accepted, inconspicuous part of the shop's daily rituals.

One day, after he'd been working there for a few weeks, a new temporary sales assistant was hired onto the staff. The owner introduced her as Hanna.

"Lovely to meet you," she beamed at him. She had waist-length gold hair, bright eyes and a seemingly permanent rosy glow to her cheeks.

"You too," he said. He smiled back at her, slowly. "You remind me of someone."

"Do I? Who's that?"

"Oh… no one. Someone from home."

Her first week at the shop, all of their shifts overlapped. With her constant upbeat chatter and his preference for listening rather than speaking, the two of them made a good pair. She told him she was from Sweden, travelling the world on a gap year. Next fall she would begin her studies at the University of London. When he heard where she was headed, he was quick to tell her all of the best places to visit… famous landmarks she couldn't miss and hidden gems that were some of his personal favourites. She listened raptly to his descriptions and even asked him to write down the names of some of the places he mentioned.

Hanna was eager to explore Melbourne while she was here. When she lamented hardly knowing where to begin with all the different galleries and museums, he offered, in a quiet voice, to show her around. She gleefully accepted.

CHAPTER 48:
THE THIRD JOB

Chan knew from the start that Jenkins would be trickier than the other two. He'd need to find out the rhythm of Jenkins' life… not just the public appearances and workplace routines, but also the comings and goings of his home life. Unfortunately, after the leak about his affair, Jenkins had all but placed himself on lockdown. He was clearly going out of his way to avoid being observed, and Chan had to be very careful not to arouse any suspicion. It took a long time for Chan to gather the right information. When he finally had everything he needed, he enlisted the help of an old friend.

Olav was a paunchy, balding man with two prominent gold teeth and several rings to match. He ran a series of illicit enterprises… under-the-table betting shops, poker syndicates, illegal money lending and the like. His clients did not like him and he did not like his clients. He and Chan, however, had an excellent working relationship. Chan found it very useful to have access to a roster of people who owed money they couldn't pay back. All he had to do was agree to settle their account, on the condition that they did a favour for him in return. If they were desperate enough, they almost always accepted the terms. The debts, as insurmountable as they seemed to the debtor, were usually a paltry sum compared to Chan's seven-figure contracts. He always kicked back a little to Olav, too, to keep himself on Olav's good side. It had often proved to be a very worthwhile investment.

He arranged to meet Olav in the back room of a travel agency, which was in fact a front for money laundering for Olav's various schemes. They sat down in creaky office chairs under a buzzing fluorescent light.

"What can I do for you, my friend?" Olav asked through a thick Russian accent.

Chan smiled. "So quick to get down to business."

"I know you only come to see old Olav when you need something. But that is okay. I live to serve."

"Well, you're right. I do need something. I'm hoping one of your clients might be able to help me with a job."

"Tell me what you are looking for. I find right person for you."

"Do you know who Colin Jenkins is?"

Olav's bushy eyebrows shot up. "The politician?"

"Yes. Once a month, Jenkins drives north to a place called Saint Albans to visit his mother. He makes this trip alone, without his wife or his children. The road to Saint Albans is mountainous and winding, and it can be dangerous. I need someone to ensure that it becomes very dangerous for Colin Jenkins, specifically."

"Ah. Say no more, my friend. One moment. I find you what you need."

Olav rose laboriously from his seat and went to the rusted metal desk in a corner of the room. He opened a drawer, which squealed in protest, and pulled out a notebook.

Chan waited patiently as Olav sat back down and flipped through the greasy spiral-bound journal. He skimmed the pages for several moments, like a scholar seeking a lost passage, and finally jabbed the paper with a triumphant, "Ha!"

"Well?" Chan prompted, when Olav didn't elaborate.

"Here. I have client. Owes lot of money on his gambling debts. He is Vietnamese, three years past his visa. Only matter of time until he is caught and sent back."

Chan arched a brow. "And?"

"And, he is tow truck driver. You pay to cover his debt, throw in little extra for him to get home to Vietnam with his pride. I think he will be happy to help you with this favour."

"You never fail to impress, Olav."

"It is my pleasure."

Chan was quiet for a moment, turning over the plan in his mind. A tow truck driver would be perfect, but there was one piece still missing. "I'll need someone else too," he said. "Someone with a family, to stage a breakdown on the side of the road."

Olav's tuneless humming filled the room as he once again paged through the notebook. "Okay. Here you go. Australian. Business owner, close to bankruptcy. He has been making stupid bets, so I know he is badly in need of money. I try to talk him into this. Should be easy." He looked back up at Chan. "Of course, you will include the usual finder's fee for your friend Olav."

"Of course."

"Very good." Olav snapped the notebook shut decisively. "Now, is there anything else I can help you with? I have some Vietnamese girls, just come in this week. You want to spend some time with a pretty Vietnamese girl?"

"No, thank you," Chan replied, and glanced across the room to the glass bottle sitting atop the desk. He nodded towards it. "I wouldn't say no to some of that Russian vodka, though."

Olav roared his approval, snatched up two grimy glasses and began to pour.

CHAPTER 49:
JOHNSON'S DEAL

Brewster had always liked a party, perhaps more than the average person. But Johnson *loved* parties. Lavish ones, with all the trimmings… high-end catering, expensive wine, sophisticated venues and guest lists that featured every celebrity and wealthy executive that he could find. It was something of a pastime of Johnson's. He hardly needed a reason to throw one of these galas, but the passage of the Gambling Act, after a gruelling second round of votes, was certainly as good an excuse as any. He'd invited Brewster down to Canberra for the occasion.

"And so, to all my supporters, all my constituents, all my colleagues and friends," Johnson proclaimed. He was standing three steps up the grand staircase of the Hotel Azure's lobby, holding a champagne flute aloft. "I want to say thank you. It is because of your hard work and dedication that we are able to take this huge step forward in securing a prosperous future for our country." His gaze panned across the crowd, and Brewster was startled when Johnson's eyes locked on his. "I want to give a *particularly* warm thank you to my friend, Wayne Brewster, who was absolutely instrumental in reaching this goal. Cheers to you, Wayne."

A chorus of "hear, hears" echoed through the high-ceilinged lobby. Brewster raised his own glass, forcing a smile for the suddenly overwhelming number of faces turned towards him. While everyone took a drink of their champagne, Brewster glanced up at Johnson. Johnson winked at him.

•

"Now, with all that nonsense in Parliament settled, we can get on with the real work. Eh, Brewster?"

They were in a private lounge of the Hotel Azure, relaxing in brocade armchairs, each holding a snifter of brandy.

"Absolutely," Brewster answered.

"We've got the finances lined up. Land lots are being purchased. Our investors are ready to sink money into this country like you can't imagine." Johnson took a pull of his drink. "And so much of it is thanks to you. I meant what I said out there, you know. You rallied the troops, got the members of the other parties to fall in line. Very impressive work."

"It helped that three of the strongest objectors died," Brewster said, flatly. "That rather took the wind out of the opposition's sails."

Johnson pulled a face. "Ah, well. That was a terrible thing, wasn't it? But…" He shrugged his shoulders theatrically, the brandy sloshing nearly to the rim of the glass. "What can you do? Some people have the worst luck."

"I suppose so," Brewster said, his voice thin.

The press coverage had treated the three deaths as straightforward, open-and-shut cases. All except for one paper: the *Sydney Telegraph*. Specifically, that bloody woman who could never mind her own business: Lisa Gordon. Her articles implied that there may have been something suspicious about the timing and manner of the deaths. Brewster hardly expected that he'd be agreeing with her, of all people. But he couldn't shake the feeling that there was a connection between the three events… Harrison's apparent suicide, Duncan's climbing accident, and the most recent occurrence, a car crash on a rural highway that killed Colin Jenkins. More than likely, Brewster suspected, the connection revolved around Chan, that *freelance agent*, as Johnson had referred to him.

But there seemed little point in mentioning any of these concerns to Johnson. Either he would deny it or he would make Brewster an accessory after the fact.

"We've already got contracts pending with the construction companies for the casinos on the Gold Coast," Johnson went on, sounding smug.

"I see," Brewster said, glad for the change of topic. "So when do my building companies start to make some money?"

Johnson shot him a look with his eyebrows raised, but he seemed more impressed by Wayne's ambition than angry. "Not to worry," he said. "You'll get your share. We just have to be careful. Remember last time, when we converted those Sydney warehouses into penthouses? People will be on the lookout for that sort of thing now. But…" He held up his hand in a placating gesture as Brewster made to protest. "I saw that you're still a major shareholder in LeMay Building Supplies. As it so happens, LeMay will be awarded the contract for supplying the Pacific Highway's construction. Sand, gravel, concrete, tarmac, ballast, all of it. Not as flashy as casinos, I know. But in the long run, if you play it right, you'll make *quite* a profit."

Brewster frowned. Skimming off the top from local building projects was one thing, but this was quite another. There were a lot of variables at work here. The supply prices were dictated by the international market. The value of stocks was erratic at best, and he'd only make money if he timed the sale of his shares just right. This, frankly, sounded like a young man's game… suited for someone who had time to wait out economic downturns and recover from miscalculations. Brewster was no spring chicken. He wanted to go enjoy his retirement, not gamble on the price of materials and the state of the stock market.

"That's an idea," he allowed. "I'll have to do a little thinking on how to handle it."

If Johnson noticed his lack of enthusiasm, he was unbothered by it. "You think on it," he said, with his usual showy smile. "And once you realise how rich you can be, you can thank me then."

CHAPTER 50:
THE PARAGON HOTEL

After the deaths of the first two Sydney politicians, Lisa had begun to harbour a suspicion that these were more than senseless tragedies. Then, when Colin Jenkins died in a car accident just a few months later, she'd become utterly convinced of it.

Brian had been quick to tell her to lay off the conspiracy theories. On some level, she knew that he might be right. Whenever she tried to explain the deaths as anything other than oddly timed coincidences, she did start to sound like a basketcase, even to herself. But her instincts had been right before. So she decided to dig a little deeper, even if she didn't have her editor's blessing.

She dialled Ryan's number from her office phone so that he wouldn't have a chance to screen her call. It took a good ten minutes of cajoling, but he finally agreed to meet with her.

It was a Tuesday afternoon when Lisa left her office and headed for the Paragon Hotel. She'd chosen this spot because it was next to Circular Quay Wharf. She hoped that being so close to her ferry back home would remove any possible temptation to go back to Ryan's place. At the moment, though, she wasn't feeling especially tempted. What she felt, more than anything, was eager, eager for the chance to talk to someone about her misgivings, someone who had a real shot of finding out if she was right.

The day was hot and humid. The plaza in front of the hotel was crowded with people who'd just gotten off work, enjoying cold drinks in the shade. Lisa flicked an impatient glance at her cell phone to check the time. Ryan was late, by twenty minutes and counting.

She decided she'd give him another ten minutes and then go home. With some dissatisfaction, she recalled that he hadn't sounded especially enthusiastic on the phone. Maybe he'd changed his mind about the whole thing.

Finally, as she stared out over the groups and pairs of people sitting at outdoor tables, she heard from beside her, "Sorry I'm late."

She turned to see Ryan, flushed and out of breath as if he'd been running. "Got here as soon as I could," he added, pushing his hair back from where it had fallen into his face. "I got stuck late at the office."

"No worries. I haven't been here long." This was decidedly not true, but he really did look apologetic, and she didn't want to make him feel worse. "It's chockablock here. Do you want to try and find a spot outside, or go in?"

"Better go in," he said, peering over her shoulder at the crowded plaza. He held the door for her as they stepped into a spacious indoor seating area, lined with high tables and lit by sleek, modern chandeliers.

It wasn't much emptier inside than out, but Lisa spotted an open table towards the back.

"I'll grab that," she said, already heading towards it.

Ryan started for the bar. "Light beer okay?" he called to her.

"Perfect."

She sat down at a two-person table in the corner and draped the strap of her purse across the back of her chair. Ryan returned a few moments later with a pitcher of beer in one hand and two glasses in the other. "Dunno about you," he said as he started to pour their drinks, "but I have had a long day in a very hot office."

She allowed a smile. "So have I," she admitted.

"Then we could both use this." He slid a glass over to her and sat down.

Lisa reached into her purse and pulled out her steno pad. He glanced at it, concern clouding his expression.

"Easy, tiger," she told him. "We're off the record. I just want to be able to take notes."

He nodded, relaxing a bit, and took a few swallows of his beer.

"I did want to say," he said abruptly, "that I'm sorry for how things turned out between us."

Lisa froze midway through opening her notepad. She thought he'd want to avoid talking about anything personal, in fact she'd rather hoped so. Trying to recover, she managed a nonchalant shrug. "It's fine. Nothing to apologise for."

"I meant to call a few times. I was just... well, I was pretty tied up with the Pittwater case."

"Believe me, I understand. Actually, I meant to call too. Well, I did call, once. But I rang off before I left a message."

Something seemed to click into place behind Ryan's eyes. "Ah," he said. "I thought I recognised that missed call."

Lisa gave him a *guilty as charged* smile.

"I don't get many," he went on mildly, arranging a coaster under his beer glass. "People calling, I mean. Other than people from work or my daughter."

She nodded and took a sip of her own drink, not quite sure what to say, suddenly wishing she'd had the nerve to leave a message all those weeks ago. "How's everything been with you?" she finally asked.

"Oh, all right. Nothing much new." He paused. "Except that I got booted off the Pittwater case."

"I thought I heard that Ann Nguyen was taking over," she said carefully. "Can I ask what happened?"

"Well, for one thing, they didn't like that I was looking into a different case. This one was from years ago, but it was related. I was sure of it. But they thought I was just wasting department resources." Ryan shrugged. "I'm still not convinced they were right. Nothing much I can do about it now, though." He fell silent, his gaze drifting out over the restaurant. "It's a shame," he said, brusquely. "I told

Lindsay Brook's parents that I would do everything I could to catch the person who killed their daughter."

"You did do everything you could," Lisa said softly.

He shrugged and didn't answer.

After a few moments, she prompted, "So what are you working on now?"

"I'm looking into a financial fraud case down in the city offices."

She raised an eyebrow, surprised she hadn't already heard about it. "Oh?" she said, trying not to betray her interest.

"Yes. Working for Brewster." His tone of distaste told Lisa everything she needed to know about Ryan's opinion of the Sydney governor. "Apparently, there's a Ukrainian family who's been paying bribes for years to get the council's garbage and street cleaning contracts. That's why I was late. I had to finish filling out a report on it."

From their previous conversations, Lisa hadn't expected him to be so forthcoming with the details of his work. He must have read the expression of surprise on her face. "I don't mind telling you about the financial cases," he explained. "They're not the same as murders, where there's a grieving family involved. Besides, I'm sure once everything's said and done, Brewster will stand up in front of the press and take all the credit for my work. So someone might as well know that I was involved."

She covered her mouth, trying not to laugh before she swallowed her mouthful of beer. "That certainly sounds like Brewster."

Ryan shook his head. "Now that I've been spending more time around him, I can confidently say that I am not a fan of his."

"I know exactly what you mean. I've interviewed him loads of times. He *loves* throwing his weight around and soaking up the media's attention. More than anyone except Johnson, maybe." She rolled her eyes and then let her smile fade. "Speaking of politicians…"

He gave her a sideways look over the top of his schooner. "You want to talk about Susan Harrison," he said, somewhat reluctantly.

"And Peter Duncan. And Colin Jenkins. Look, I've been on this beat for a long time. I *know* when something is off. And something is off about those three deaths."

"What makes you so certain?" he challenged.

"Just think about it, Ryan." Without realising it, Lisa had put her elbows on the table and leaned in towards him. "All three of them were political opponents of Howard Johnson. All three were going to cause huge problems for the legislation that he was so hellbent on pushing through Parliament. And then all three of them turned up dead within a few months. You've got to admit, that doesn't seem like something that just… happens."

"I read your articles, you know."

"And? What did you think?"

"You said it yourself in the latest one. There's no proof. There was an inquiry into each death, and none of those investigations found anything suspicious." Ryan refilled both of their glasses and gave her a slight frown that was either concerned or scolding, or both. "You've got to be careful, making unfounded accusations like that. You'll make a lot of enemies that way."

She accepted her glass when he slid it back over to her and sipped the foam off the top. "I interviewed Susan Harrison two days before she was found dead. She was thrilled that the vote in the House had halted the Gambling Act, and she was so motivated to stop it for good." Lisa shook her head, thinking back to that rainy grey Saturday. "At the protest march, there were these bikers…"

Ryan suppressed a roll of his eyes. "I heard about the fight with the bikers. Now you've got them involved in your conspiracy theory, too?"

"No!" she snapped, then lapsed into a short silence, chewing her lip. "I don't think they're involved with Harrison's death. But I *do* think someone put them up to it. They're part of the whole thing, somehow."

"Put them up to what, exactly?"

"Driving into the protesters. Causing a diversion so that the media would focus on them instead of the purpose of the march."

"And who would've hired them to do that?"

"Well, you're the detective."

"To be honest, I don't find it all that suspicious that bikers would cause problems at a protest march. Not exactly known for their progressive political views, are they? And as for Harrison…" He gave an apologetic shrug. "She was an alcoholic. It's sad, but alcoholics fall off the wagon all the time. Especially when their girlfriends walk out on them. She had a history of depression, too."

"I know she did. You know how I know? Because she talked about it openly. We spoke about it that Saturday, in fact. And she said she was in a good place. Why would she start lying now, after all this time?"

"I don't know, Lisa. People lie."

Lisa took a deep breath, trying not to let her frustration get the better of her. "Okay," she said slowly. "What about Peter Duncan?"

"What about him?"

"Don't you think that freak accident on the climbing trip was suspicious?"

"I might, if there hadn't been a full investigation immediately afterward. But the police took statements from everyone on the trip and they all told the same story. It was just an old rope that snapped when it was placed under too much stress. Stress fibre failure. Plain and simple."

"No. No way." She shook her head vehemently. "I looked into that, too. There's no way a reputable climbing company would let that kind of thing happen. They check the ropes after the last climb of every day and again at the beginning of the next day. Not to mention how bizarre the accident was that killed Colin Jenkins."

"Those mountain roads can be dangerous."

"Of course they can. But do you really believe that there just *happened* to be a tow truck with faulty brakes, at the exact same moment Jenkins just *happened* to stop to help a family broken down by the side of the road? Come on, Ryan."

He drummed his fingers on the side of his beer glass.

"All I'm saying," Lisa went on, in a more subdued tone, "is to think about all of them together. Individually, sure, accidents happen. But three high profile political deaths in a row like this? That's a pattern."

He let out a long breath and glanced around the restaurant, as if worried someone might overhear him. "All right. I'll admit, taken altogether, there *might* be something a little weird about this. I'll take a look at those case files and see if I can spot anything."

Lisa's face lit up in a smile. For a moment, Ryan seemed unable to stop himself from smiling back at her, but he caught himself quickly.

"I'll have to be careful," he warned. "I'm not exactly flavour of the month right now. I can't have my supervisor seeing me get involved in other people's cases."

"Thank you so much, Ryan. I appreciate this." She flipped to an earlier sheet in her notebook and swivelled it around to show him a list of names. "I can get you a few places to start," she said, moving her finger down the page. "This is the name of the climbing company… I already talked to them and they swore blind it couldn't have been one of their ropes. Here's everyone who was on the trip with Duncan. I've also got the name of the garage that the tow truck came from, might be worth looking into them…"

"Hang on," Ryan interrupted, with a scowl forming on his features that reminded Lisa of the first time they'd met. "I said I'd have a look at the case files. I'm not about to launch my own personal investigation. Especially with Brewster breathing down my neck all the time. The last thing I need is to give the police commissioner a reason to demote me."

"I know, I know. Don't go losing your job over me." She offered a playful smile when he looked offended. "Seriously. Just… do whatever you can. Anything you can find out would be amazing."

Ryan nodded slowly, looking a little embarrassed by her sincere gratitude. He nodded towards the empty pitcher. "Did you want any more, or are you heading out?"

"Oh. Well…" She paused to consider it, peering down at the last sip of beer still in her glass. "I don't have anything else planned for tonight. I could stay for a bit. I'd better have something to eat, though."

"I could eat, too," he agreed, rising from his seat. "I'll grab another pitcher and some menus, yeah?"

"Thanks," she said.

Now that they'd wrapped up the business portion of the conversation, Lisa was a little worried that things might be awkward between them. But when Ryan returned to the table, she was surprised to find that it wasn't awkward at all. They seemed to pick up right where they'd left off last time, falling into easy, relaxed conversation, as if they ate together all the time.

When they finished their meals and the second pitcher of beer, he told her that as soon as this fraud case was squared away, he was planning to take some time off work. "I'm going to New Zealand, to visit my daughter Madison," he said with a smile.

"I'm sure that'll be lovely," she answered, studying the expression on his face. It was quite endearing, how excited he was to see her.

"Yes," he said warmly. "It will be."

Lisa glanced across the restaurant, which had begun to empty out. She checked her cell phone for the time. "Oh, I should be getting on if I don't want to miss the next ferry," she said, frowning.

"Yeah, I should get home as well," Ryan replied. They stood, gathered up their things, and left the restaurant to the few couples and families who remained.

Once they were outside, they lingered under the awning. The oppressive heat of the day had given way to a pleasant evening with a warm, gentle breeze.

"My ferry's that way," she said, hooking a thumb in the direction of Circular Quay.

"Yes. I'm getting a cab, so I'll be going that way." He nodded towards the street behind them. "Well…"

The moment stretched on and on. Finally, Ryan was the first to move. He leaned forward, and Lisa leaned forward too. She realised that he'd meant to kiss her on the cheek at the exact moment that she pressed her lips to his.

They broke apart quickly, both of them hurrying to apologise for the misunderstanding. Their words tangled awkwardly over one another's until they trailed back into silence, their faces glowing pink.

"Okay," Ryan said, clearing his throat. "I'll find out what I can about those cases and give you a call soon."

"All right. I'll look forward to that," she said, and smiled. "It was good to see you."

"Yes. You, too." He returned her smile, seemingly relieved. "Goodbye."

"Goodbye."

They went their separate ways. As she began the short walk to the quay, just before she went around the corner, Lisa glanced back. She had to laugh… she caught Ryan turning to look back at her, too. They exchanged a little wave, and then he was out of sight.

CHAPTER 51:
THE KILLER'S MOOD CHANGE

"Yes, I'm sure you would like her. She's fun to talk to, and very kind, and pretty, too. Not as pretty as you, of course. No one's as pretty as you."

The killer was alone in his apartment. He often spoke aloud to the empty living room, but these days the talks were generally pleasant and mild. Things were going well for him. He'd settled into his job at the book shop, and he liked everything about it. Almost.

The only trouble was the university students who sometimes came in. They tended to be brash and loud and so confident in their stupidity. They were one of the few things that still made the crueller voices in his head start to whisper. So he avoided the students as best as he could, and often pretended to be busy with reshelving or fixing the displays when they walked through the door. Better to let his co-workers handle them, since they didn't seem to mind.

But the other customers were all right. Many of them had begun to seek out his recommendations for their next purchase. His knowledge of the store's offerings had quickly become encyclopaedic; he regularly devoured whole books in a day or two. He read nonfiction on a wide range of topics, as well as every conceivable genre of fiction. Mystery, fantasy, science fiction, thriller… he enjoyed all of it. The crime fiction often made him laugh, though, with all its inaccuracies and silly mistakes.

He found himself drawn to the classics, and he'd developed a particular liking for novels written in the Georgian era. To him, the stories from centuries past represented a better, more ordered time than the one to which he was confined. He liked to imagine himself in those bygone days, when the world made more sense and people still knew their place.

Sometimes, while he was on the couch in the living room, he would look up from the book in his lap and smile. "You would have loved to live in those times," he told the silent flat. "Ladies were so elegant back then. So well-mannered. You would look beautiful in those old evening gowns. You would walk into any room and light it up like sunshine."

One evening, after his usual routine of cooking himself dinner and having a glass of wine, he realised that he had finished the last remaining unread book in the apartment. He resolved to pick up a new one from work tomorrow. For tonight, though, he'd have to find something else to occupy his time.

He felt restless, although he couldn't have said why. He cast around for something to do. Television wasn't an option. Lately he refused to even turn it on, regarding it as nothing but a conduit to pump rubbish into people's minds. And he could only spend so long in the apartment without anything to distract him before he started to hear the more unpleasant voices again.

It would be best, he decided, to go out. He showered and changed, then made his way into the city centre.

He wandered for a while with no particular destination in mind, trying to decide if he wanted a drink and where he ought to get one. As he surfaced from his thoughts, he found that he'd ended up back on the row of loud, trendy restaurants and bars that he'd hated so much when he first happened upon them. His lip curled in disgust. This was no place for him. He was about to turn around and go back home when he caught sight of a familiar face.

It was Hanna, his co-worker and friend, with her blonde hair and her permanent effervescent smile. She was just walking into one of the neon-soaked bars.

He decided to follow her in.

As soon as he stepped inside the door, he cringed. The music was loud, and blue lights were pulsing rhythmically to the thump of the bass from the speaker system. Crowds of people were dancing or milling around, drinks in hand. He pushed through them and finally spotted Hanna.

She was waving to someone. He followed her gaze and saw another girl, this one with a mass of loose brunette curls swept up into a ponytail. She beckoned Hanna over to a long, high table with a row of seats on either side. The other girl moved her coat and purse off a tall chair – the only one vacant in the whole place – so that Hanna could sit down.

The killer felt a surge of jealousy crash through him. His bones suddenly seemed to vibrate in time to the blaring music. Who was this girl? He had seen Hanna at work today, and she hadn't mentioned that she was going out.

He stepped away from the crush of people on the main floor of the club and positioned himself in a corner near the bar, where he had a clear view of the two of them. He ordered a drink to get the bartender to stop staring at him, then went back to watching the girls.

They chatted for a few minutes. Several times, the brunette leaned forward and touched Hanna's arm or leg while she laughed. Then the girl stood up and crossed over to the bar, walking directly past the killer in the process. She ordered a bottle of white wine and two glasses. His eyes followed her as she took them from the bartender, thanked him with a flirty smile, and then returned to her seat beside Hanna. He caught a breath of her sweet perfume as she passed by him again. In the strobing light, he noticed two tattoos, a peacock on her shoulder, clearly visible with her sleeveless dress, and a butterfly on the back of her neck beneath her swaying ponytail.

I thought you said your new friend was a nice girl, said a voice in his head, sounding wounded. *But she hangs around with people like this tattooed whore?*

He wanted to protest that Hanna *was* a nice girl, but he, too, felt a niggling doubt.

The brunette put down the bottle and two glasses on the table in front of Hanna. Then, just before swinging up onto her seat, she cupped Hanna's cheek in her hand and gave her a long kiss on the lips.

He threw back the rest of his vodka tonic in a single gulp and then before he realised found that he was standing directly in front of them.

"Leave her alone," he heard himself snarl at the brunette. "Get *away* from her."

He grabbed Hanna's arm, intending to pull her away from the tattooed whore. Hanna let out a yelp and recoiled, trying with all her strength to yank her arm free. She succeeded, and her leftover momentum carried her off the tall chair. She fell to the floor, hard.

Everyone within a ten-foot radius of them turned around and stared. The brunette girl shot to her feet and stood between him and Hanna. "What the fuck is your problem, freak?" she spat.

In one fluid motion, the killer picked up the wine bottle and smashed it into the girl's face.

The onlookers erupted into pandemonium. A chorus of angry shouts welled up, almost loud enough to drown out the music, as blood began to pour from the girl's nose like a faucet. She let out a stifled scream and stumbled back. He was watching with satisfaction as her face went ghostly pale under the spatter of bright red blood when a man's hand grabbed his shoulder. The man spun him around and then landed his fist full-force into the killer's face.

One second the killer was cradling his jaw while waves of pain radiated across his skull. The next, he found himself wrestled down to the ground, face pressed against the cold grey tile.

He struggled, but he was being pinned by two muscle-bound men. "Stay down," they growled at him each time he tried to get free.

Above the din, he heard Hanna's voice. *"What the hell is wrong with you?"* she demanded through tears.

A group of women surrounded Hanna protectively, and another group had formed around the brunette, who was being whisked to the exit. Other people were standing with their phones held in front of them, panning between the killer on the ground and the brunette's bleeding face.

"What a head case," one of the bystanders observed. "Did you see that? He just attacked them for no reason. Bloody lunatic."

Get up, said the voice in his head, urgently. *You have to get out of here. Now.*

"Let me go," he said, his voice muffled against the floor. But the man with his knee on the killer's back didn't relent. "Listen, I'm sorry," he said. "Please. I can't breathe."

After a moment of hesitation, the pressure on his back finally eased. He waited until he was certain that the man no longer had him pinned. Then he gathered up all his strength an in a sudden burst of movement, shoved off both men who were restraining him and launched towards the doors. He managed to evade the various hands grasping at him as he pushed indiscriminately through the panicked crowd. When he finally stumbled out the doors onto the street, he broke into a flat-out sprint. He ran for blocks, for what felt like miles, until the sound of Hanna's frightened crying finally faded from his ears.

CHAPTER 52:
BREWSTER'S BUSINESS MEETING

After Canberra, Brewster flew straight back to his villa in Pittwater. He had some personal affairs to sort out.

He sat in his study with his laptop open in front of him. The French doors out to the veranda were open and a pleasant, cool breeze came in off the bay below. He was carefully reviewing a folder on his computer. Password-protected and buried in a misleading labyrinth of subdirectories, it contained all of the recordings he'd made of his conversations with Johnson. It was all here… audio and video, with dates that ranged over the past several months. For this last trip to Canberra, he'd even invested in a microphone that sat under his lapel, no bigger than the tip of a ballpoint pen. Of course, he hadn't dared to wear it when he was meeting Johnson in his Parliament office, since he'd inevitably be swept for electronics before being allowed to enter. But there were a few occasions, at the Hotel Azure, for example, where he'd been willing to risk it. And the reward was here: a series of MP3 files that encapsulated Johnson's scheming, lying and corruption.

The Prime Minister's increasingly brazen behaviour meant more danger for Brewster. Knowing full well that Johnson wasn't the type to stop until he was caught, Brewster was taking the opportunity to get his insurance in order. No mistakes this time. No room for error.

With the concentration of a heart surgeon, Brewster copied each file onto a data disc. When the first disc filled up, he used a second, then a third. He repeated the process a second time with another set of discs, bringing the total to six. Six slim silver discs that represented all the protection he had.

Then, after he triple-checked that all the files had been safely copied over, he erased all of them from his hard drive. He couldn't afford any loose ends.

Once everything was in order, he tucked the discs into individual cases and put the first set of three in one padded envelope, and the second set in another. He slid both envelopes into a desk drawer to keep them out of sight. He would put them in a more secure location shortly. But at the moment, he needed to make a phone call.

•

Charles Pearce, CEO of LeMay Building Supplies, was a very old friend of Brewster's, going back to his days before politics. He'd stayed in construction while Brewster went into public service, as it were. He'd been happy enough to meet Brewster in Sydney in a few days, and happier still when Brewster explained that he would cover the expense.

Brewster's assistant – his personal one, not the ever-attentive Ms Atwell at the governor's office – had made all the arrangements: the flight for Charles and his wife Linda, the hotel stay, and the lunch reservation at a restaurant on the water, with a lovely view of Lavender Bay and the Sydney Harbour Bridge. Brewster was sitting at their table, gazing out over still, sparkling expanse of blue, when he heard the scrape of a chair being pulled out across from him.

"Wayne, it's good to see you," Charles proclaimed with a broad grin.

Brewster rose from his seat to shake the other man's hand.

"Thanks for coming out to meet me," Brewster said, as they sank into their chairs.

"Oh, my pleasure. Thank *you* for inviting us out here. Your assistant did a phenomenal job with the bookings."

"Everything go all right with your trip so far?"

"It's been marvellous."

"Glad to hear it."

The waitress approached to hand them their menus and take their drink orders. Brewster conferred briefly with Charles, then ordered a bottle of Chardonnay. As the waitress retreated, he asked Charles, "And how is Linda? I hope she's enjoying Sydney."

"Oh, Linda's great. Our daughter is getting married in a few months, so she's off shopping for an outfit to wear to the wedding."

"How lovely. Congratulations." Brewster picked up the menu and glanced it over. "Well, let's choose lunch first, and then we can get down to business, eh?"

A few minutes later, after they'd received a plate of lobster risotto and Cape Grim beef tenderloin, respectively, Brewster refilled both Pearce's wine glass and his own.

"Now, Charles," Brewster said. "I'm sure you've heard about Prime Minister Johnson's latest round of legislation."

"Yes, me and everyone else with a telly," he chortled. "It's been all over the news for weeks? Johnson's hardly stopped talking about the Pacific Highway Act since it was passed." Charles sawed off a chunk of tenderloin and popped it into his mouth. "I'm surprised, though. Thought there would be more opposition to denationalising the heritage sites and nature reserves."

"There was plenty of opposition," Brewster admitted. "Johnson just didn't let any of it slow him down. He's very… determined, when it comes to his political goals."

An understatement if there ever was one, he thought, and took a sip of his wine.

"Anyway, I've got some good news on that front. Construction on the eastern portion of the highway is due to begin very soon, and Johnson is going to award the contract to LeMay Building Supplies for all the raw materials."

"What? Are you sure?"

"Quite sure. Well, as sure as you can ever be of anything with Johnson."

Charles let out a disbelieving laugh. "Hell, that *is* good news. Best news I've heard in a while."

"I might have a way to make it even better."

"Oh?"

Brewster nodded, and then chose his words carefully. He and Charles were old friends, but it had been a long time since they had worked together. "You see, I was hoping that we would get the contract for the hotels and casinos on the Gold Coast," he said. "But Johnson, unfortunately, is working with other investors on those projects."

"Shame," Charles said, using a forkful of tenderloin to swipe some gravy off his plate. "Company's been hit pretty badly by the price of materials. They're through the roof lately. We really could've used some of those bigger projects."

"I know. But we do have an opportunity to make a little extra on the side."

Charles arched a brow at him wordlessly.

Brewster leaned forward with his elbows on the table. "I've been working with Johnson a lot. He's the one who suggested that I run for governor again, because he wanted my help ramming his policies through Parliament. I agreed, because I knew he could get me elected. But I don't trust him, Charles. If you ask me, he's gone mad with power."

"Doesn't surprise me," Charles said, waving his fork dismissively. "Never liked the bloke all that much. I dunno if you heard, but the two of us had a falling out a few years back. He came to Perth when he was campaigning for election. Wanted some help from the local CEOs. Making TV appearances, giving statements in his support, that kind of thing. And I swear, nothing anyone did ever made that man happy. He always found something to complain about. Told us that we still had lots to learn in Perth and the west coast, like we were all a bunch of idiots. After we'd agreed to campaign for him! I mean, frankly, what an asshole." Charles took a long swallow of his wine. "So, anyway. No love lost between the Prime Minister and I."

Brewster allowed a slight smile. This would be easier than he thought.

"Then it seems we're on the same page," he said smoothly. "I have a proposition for you. A way to make some extra cash off Johnson."

"I'm all ears."

"Remember way back when we were first starting out? We sold short measures to those land management agencies…"

"…so that we were essentially raising the price on every unit of material," Charles finished. "Sure, I remember. Those were good days."

"Yes. Exactly. So, with this raw materials contract, we could do the same thing. Bigger scale. Bigger profits."

Charles was silent for a few moments, apparently deep in thought, while he used his tongue to try and extract a bit of tenderloin from between his teeth. "I like the way you think, Brewster. Always knew you were one of the smart ones. I think I have a way I can make it happen."

"Go on, then."

Charles opened his mouth and fell immediately silent as the waitress reappeared.

"How was everything, gentleman?" she asked brightly.

"Superb," Charles said with a broad smile and a wink.

"Glad to hear it. I'll get these out of your way," she said, clearing away the plates.

With their empty dishes balanced on her tray, she vanished through the patio door into the restaurant to the kitchen. Charles leaned forward again and lowered his voice slightly.

"We're just about to open a depot, not far from here," he said in an undertone. "It'll be used as a processing plant and distribution centre for all types of materials. In a few days, we'll have a company coming in to calibrate the weighing stations for measuring out orders. Now, suppose that company made a mistake when they were setting the parameters, so that the orders all came out a bit underweight."

Brewster smiled. "I suppose mistakes like that must happen all the time, Mr Pearce," he said levelly.

"Oh, they do. And then, of course, clients end up needing to purchase more material from us if they don't want a half-finished job."

"It's a shame for the client, but you know, these things happen to the best of us."

Charles let out a hearty laugh. "That's right, Brewster."

Brewster nodded slowly, seeing the pieces come together. "LeMay's stock prices will go up when we post the increased profits," he said slowly. "If you want to make some extra cash, you can sell your shares as soon as Johnson's people find out about the short-selling, and you'll earn good money there, too."

"Outstanding," Charles declared, and raised his wine glass in a toast. "You've thought of everything. Cheers to you, sir."

"Cheers, Charles." Brewster clinked his glass to Charles's, and they both drank. "And," he added, as he finished off his wine, "as a goodwill gesture, I've brought a little present for you. Something you can wear to your daughter's wedding, perhaps." He picked up an unmarked, brown paper bag that he'd kept by his feet and held it out to Charles. "It's a pair of designer brogue shoes. I remember how keen you were on them. You might take a quick look, to see if they're the right size and colour."

Charles accepted the bag with one eyebrow raised. Brewster gestured at him to go ahead.

He took the shoebox out of the bag, glanced over his shoulder, and lifted the lid very slightly. Inside were several neat stacks of crisp hundred dollar bills. With a smile, he slipped the lid back on and returned the shoebox to the bag.

"They're perfect, Wayne," he said. "Just what I was looking for."

CHAPTER 53:
THE FRAUD CASE

In the end, the fraud case arrived at a quick and thorough resolution. Ryan had orchestrated simultaneous dawn raids at the houses of the major players, and they'd all been summarily arrested. After an analysis of the paperwork and electronic devices that were seized in the raids, the police had been able to charge five additional Ukrainian profiteers who were connected to the plot. Ryan may not have been a financial fraud investigator by training, but he had to admit he made a pretty damn good one.

Still, it was far from what he wanted to be doing. He would much rather be working to keep Sydney safe from murderers, specifically, from the murderer of Lindsay Brook and Paula Thorn. The sting of being taken off the case had never fully faded. He resisted the temptation to follow every minor development, knowing it probably wasn't good for him to remain too invested where he wasn't wanted. But he had caught up with Ann about a week ago and what he heard was not encouraging. Apparently there had been no significant breakthroughs and the department had begun scaling back the staff and resources dedicated to the case. He sensed Ann's frustration, and shared it. The writing was on the wall: the top brass had all but given up.

There was nothing Ryan could do about that now, though. Frankly, he was exhausted and burned out, and he couldn't wait to wrap up this fraud investigation. As soon as the court case was done, he'd be able to fly to New Zealand and spend a few weeks with Madison.

Finally, after a blessedly swift trial, Ryan found himself outside the courthouse in front of a bank of microphones. They were not pointed at him. Instead, they were pointed at Wayne Brewster, who was standing at a podium. A small crowd of reporters faced him, and the flashes on their cameras popped like tiny fireworks.

"We are all glad to see justice delivered today," he declared. "It is vital to the wellbeing of our city that we are able to track down and stamp out corruption. We must hold fraudsters accountable, particularly those fraudsters who would take advantage of the hospitality Australia has offered them."

The reporters launched into a barrage of questions, but Brewster held up his hand for silence.

"My office and I, with the full support of my good friend and colleague Prime Minister Johnson, have been working hard to ensure that this kind of double dealing is not allowed to continue. By removing these bad actors from city offices, we open the doors to focus on our primary goals: improving our infrastructure, bolstering our economy, and building a brighter future for Sydney and for Australia."

Ryan, standing off to the side, rolled his eyes at the exact same moment Brewster threw out his arm to point at him. He managed to provide a straight face as the cameras swung towards him. "And of course, I want to thank Detective Ryan Campbell and all of the other officers who lent their time and talents to the investigation. It was truly a collaborative effort to bring these criminals to justice."

Yes, everyone else collaborated and you showed up at the end to take credit, Ryan thought to himself, raising a hand to acknowledge the smattering of applause from the crowd.

"Now, I would be more than happy to take any questions…"

The reporters immediately began to shout over one another. Ryan didn't bother listening to them, much less Brewster's responses. He was busy mentally packing his suitcase.

The press conference ended and Brewster took off in a black government car without so much as a goodbye to Ryan. Under other circumstances this might've annoyed him, but in this case, he was happy to be spared any more of Brewster's dishonest gratitude. Ryan got into his own car and made his way back to the office to finish up a few last forms. With that done, he turned off the light in his office and closed the door behind him. He was now officially on a month-long leave.

The next morning, sipping coffee at his kitchen table, he read the *Telegraph's* front-page article about Wayne Brewster, who, according to a journalist who was not Lisa, was quickly establishing a reputation as a no-nonsense protector of the public's interests. Some of the more sensationalist papers were even billing him as 'the saviour of Sydney', cleaning up the city after years of unchecked corruption and crime. *Some saviour,* Ryan mused bitterly. *Too bad Brewster couldn't catch the killer of those schoolgirls.*

He drained the last of his coffee and went to start getting everything ready for his flight to Wellington.

CHAPTER 54:
LUNCH DATE

Before Ryan's flight, he had one more thing to take care of. Lisa wanted to meet with him to go over what he'd been able to find out about the deaths of the three Sydney politicians.

He'd been very clear in their phone conversation that he didn't have any especially hot tips, but she said that at this point, she'd take anything she could get. So, they agreed to meet at a place called Victoria's in Woolloomooloo Bay the day before Ryan's departure.

He got there before she did, and found a table on the patio overlooking the wharf. He sat out in the sun, watching the weekday crowds meander along the jetty, sipping a cold beer and reflecting that he could probably get used to this.

Ryan's phone rang. He picked it up after making sure it wasn't the office. "Hello?"

"Hi, Ryan, it's Lisa. I'm sorry, I'm running a bit late. I need to finish up this article so it can go out with the late edition tonight."

"No worries," Ryan said, swirling his drink. "You can take your time. I'm not in a hurry."

She laughed. "Listen to you, Mr Vacation," she said. "All right. If you're enjoying yourself, I won't rush too much. See you in a bit."

"Ok."

By the time Lisa finally turned up, it was over an hour after they'd originally planned to meet. Ryan had polished off a few beers. He spotted her as she stepped onto the restaurant's deck and scanned the tables, looking for him. He put up a hand to wave her over.

"Lisa!" he called.

Her head turned towards his voice, and she navigated through the other tables and took the seat opposite him. "Sorry to keep you waiting."

It's, no problem. This is a nice place."

She looked at him and tilted her head. "You look different."

"I got a haircut."

"I don't think it's the haircut."

He shrugged. "More relaxed, maybe," he said, leaning back in his chair and interlocking his fingers behind his head. "I'm finally on leave after that bloody fraud case."

"Oh, yes. I just did a feature on Eastern European crime families in Sydney. I wrote about your case."

A waiter appeared, holding a couple of menus. "Can I get you some drinks? Something to eat, maybe?"

Lisa and Ryan glanced at each other. "I skipped breakfast, as usual," she admitted. "Could do with lunch."

"Sure. I haven't eaten yet either."

The waiter handed them each a menu. They ordered food, and Ryan asked for another beer.

"I'll take one too, please," Lisa said.

He arched an eyebrow at her as the waiter went back into the restaurant. "Drinking on the job now, are you, Gordon?"

She rolled her eyes, smiling. "For your information, I finished up for the day before I got here. I don't have to go back to the office."

"Oh, good."

She flashed him a brief look. Ryan couldn't quite tell whether she was confused or pleased by his comment, but either way, it was gone in an instant.

"When's your flight, then?" she asked.

"Tomorrow afternoon. I'll be gone three and a half weeks."

"Wow, you really *are* different," she observed. "What happened to workaholic Ryan?"

"He went and worked himself out. Between having to answer to Brewster and writing up all those reports for the fraud case, it was past time for a break."

"Oh, poor you, having to do a little writing. I can't imagine," she said, her voice full of mock pity.

They both laughed as the waiter arrived with their drinks.

"Food will be just a minute," he said, laying out the silverware and napkins.

They thanked him and then, as he walked away, lapsed into a somewhat uncomfortable silence.

"How've you been?" Ryan ventured. "I've caught some of your recent articles. They've been very good."

"Well, isn't that kind," she said, and he wondered for a moment if he'd sounded patronising, but she pressed on before he could figure it out. "Yes, there's been loads going on. I thought it would slow down after the governor's election but it never really did. On that note... what have you got for me?"

Ryan took a breath, trying to put everything in order in his mind, which was not as easy as it had been three beers ago. "Well, like I said on the phone, I didn't find all that much. Nothing concrete. But there were a couple things that seemed... strange. Remember, though, that I'm not supposed to know about any of these things, and neither are you. We've got to be careful."

"Of course," Lisa said. "I know how to keep a secret, Ryan. Don't worry. No one will find out where the information came from."

He nodded, finding it surprisingly easy to trust her. "First, I managed to read the records from Susan Harrison's psychiatrist. He was interviewed after her death. According to him, Harrison had been doing relatively well. The best she'd been in years, in fact. Her addictions were under control. Over the last few years, she was still experiencing occasional bouts of depression, but not in the months leading up to her death. She'd expressed to him that she was looking forward to revitalising her political career and taking on her opponents."

"See?" Lisa exclaimed. "I told you. When I interviewed her, she was so eager to get back to work."

"Hold on. It's not that simple. He *also* said that she was still struggling with relationship issues and had felt uncertain about her future with her partner for a long time, well before she walked out. So it's possible that the partner's leaving is what sent her over the edge."

Lisa frowned, but before she could reply, the waiter showed up with their food. As he set the plates down in front of them, he asked if they would like another round of drinks.

"Oh, go on then," Ryan said.

"All right," Lisa said. "I'll have one too, please."

The waiter smiled, glancing between them with a look that was perhaps a little too knowing, and told them to enjoy.

"Well, I'm still not convinced about Susan Harrison," Lisa said between bites of her tortellini. "She'd *just* gotten back from Canberra, where she'd helped strike a huge blow to the Gambling Act. She was at a high point."

Ryan shrugged as he cut into his Barramundi. "Sometimes that's how it is with depression. High one minute and down the next."

Lisa nodded reluctantly. "I suppose so," she said, although she still didn't sound convinced. "What about the others?"

"Nothing much you didn't already know about the climbing trip with Peter Duncan. The investigation couldn't find anything off about the climbing company's safety practices. But they do run a lot of trips. Dozens of climbs per month. So the conclusion was that something must have slipped through the cracks."

"And that something happened to be the rope that was holding up Peter Duncan?" Lisa shook her head. "I don't buy that."

"Dunno what else to tell you. The only new information I found was that the officers had a few follow up questions for the other climbers. They tracked down all of them but one. He was a Chinese tourist, a backpacker who flew home right after the trip ended. The police went through the Chinese embassy to try and set up a video call with the guy, but the embassy declined."

"What?" She looked taken aback. "So much for international cooperation. And after our government climbed into bed with all those Chinese investors."

"I know. But the trail ends there. Couldn't find out anything more about the backpacker, and there weren't any other loose ends."

"And Colin Jenkins?"

"I followed up with the name of the garage you gave me, where the tow truck came from. Belongs to a bloke named John Harvey. He sends tow trucks to collect broken-down vehicles pretty regularly and strips them for parts. Nothing strange about that. Driver of the truck was a Vietnamese immigrant on an expired visa.

The garage had been raided for employing illegal immigrants before, so nothing strange about that, either. But I didn't find out anything new about the crash itself. Just the same stuff that was in all the papers."

"Yes, it was pretty well reported," Lisa said with a frown. "But maybe I'll do a little more research on the garage. Just to be sure."

Ryan finished off the last few bites of his fish. "You really are dedicated to your work," he said. "But it doesn't always make you too popular, digging into all these things people don't want dug up."

"The public needs to know the truth. If we didn't have that, where would we be?"

Ryan smiled. "Yes, I suppose. Don't run into many truth-tellers in my line of work. None, in fact."

"Then you know how important it is," Lisa chuckled. She set down her fork and leaned back from the table. "So what are you doing with your afternoon? Or what's left of it?"

"Probably just going home and getting packed for the trip. I hate packing. Not a man's thing, you know?"

"Oh, you chauvinist. Tell me you're joking."

"I am."

Lisa breathed a laugh and finished the last of her drink.

"I really do have to get packed, though. Haven't even started."

"I see. Well…" Lisa seemed to think it over for a moment. "Since I don't have to go back to the office, I suppose I could go with you and give you a hand. If you like."

Ryan felt a smile tugging at his mouth. His vacation was turning out to be even better than he'd hoped. "I suppose you could."

•

Ryan's alarm sounded shrilly into the silence. He hit snooze.

Beside him, Lisa stirred and rolled over to face him. "What time is it?" she asked, her voice drowsy and soft.

"Nine-thirty," he answered.

She blinked the sleep from her eyes and looked around his bedroom. "Bloody hell," she murmured. "So much for your packing."

He laughed. "That's all right. I'll get to it. Coffee?"

"Yes, please. But it'll have to be quick. I'm late."

"I'll make it while you have a shower. I can order a taxi for you."

Lisa smiled. "Cheers," she said, and tossed back the covers. He stayed in bed and let his eyes follow her as she crossed to the washroom, her bare skin lit by the midmorning sun. Then he got up, threw on some clothes, and went to the kitchen to make the coffee.

The taxi arrived a half hour later. Ryan walked Lisa to the door.

"I am sorry about the packing," Lisa said on the front step. "Will you have enough time before your flight?"

"Yes, don't worry. I'll just toss some things in the suitcase."

"Okay. Ring me when you get back."

"I will," he promised. "And in the meanwhile, be careful what you write in those articles. You'll end up having more enemies than friends."

"I think I already do," Lisa laughed. She leaned in to give him a kiss. "Have a good trip. Bring me back something from New Zealand."

"Of course," he smiled. "Take care. See you when I get back."

They kissed once more, and then Lisa hurried to the waiting taxi.

CHAPTER 55:
THE KILLER'S NEXT JOB

The killer hadn't been to work since the incident at the bar. He'd mostly been shut up in his apartment, enduring the tirade of the voices who told him he had to leave now.

"Not yet," he answered. "I have some things I have to sort out first. Then we'll go home."

You know what you have to do, she told him.

He'd stopped shaving, and he'd nearly stopped sleeping too, allowing dark circles to surface under his eyes. He was worried that the book shop may come looking for him, or worse, that Hannah may have reported the incident to the police. So he dyed his hair a different colour and let his neat haircut grow shaggy. Between that and the scruff on his cheeks, he once again looked like a new person. But he didn't like this one as much.

He only went out for two reasons: to buy necessary supplies and to follow the two whores, finding out where they went and learning their habits. He often drove behind them, slowly, leaving enough space to ensure he wouldn't be noticed. Patiently, he waited for the right moment to strike.

But as the days dragged on, his patience began to wane. The apartment fell into disarray. Unwashed dishes piled up in the sink and dirty clothes lay scattered around the floor. He'd lost interest in his books, and most of them had been tossed irreverently into a corner and promptly forgotten.

He opened his laptop one day to find a new email from Barbara Stevenson, the woman who owned the flat. She told him that she'd gotten into some fight with her sister's husband and that she was cutting her trip to England short. She was going to be home in three weeks and would reimburse him for what was left of their twelve-month agreement. He would have to leave the apartment.

Another bitch who doesn't keep her promises.

"Don't worry, Barbara," he said with the email still open on the screen in front of him. "I'll leave your apartment nice and clean. I'll even add a few new ornaments for you. I think you'll like them."

That night, he drove to the now familiar downtown district that was home to the most popular bars and nightclubs. He circled the streets until he spotted them. It wasn't especially hard. He had grown very adept at picking Hanna's face out of a crowd.

They were both drunk. He could tell by the way they walked, stumbling along and propping each other up. At an inconspicuous distance, he followed behind them as they turned from the main street onto a dimly lit side road. Having followed them down this road before, he was familiar with its geography, and knew it would offer an ideal opportunity to carry out his plan. It was still risky, though.

Now or never. Get it over with. I'm sick of these stupid fucking whores. I want to go home.

"Okay," he said. "We'll go home in a few days. I just have to take care of my patients first."

He waited until the girls were on a sidewalk alongside an abandoned warehouse. Then he jammed his foot down on the accelerator. The car jolted forward, bounced over the curb, and swerved hard towards the two figures. He hit the brakes just before the car's bonnet could make contact with the warehouse. They were both pinned between the car and the wall.

The killer paused to look carefully up and down the street. No one else was in sight. He reached over to the glove compartment and pulled out a needle, a syringe and a small vial. He filled the syringe, tapped out the air bubbles with practiced efficiency, and stepped out of the car.

The brunette had been knocked unconscious when she collided with the wall. Hanna was awake, though. He was vaguely aware that she was trying to plead with him as he approached, but he couldn't seem to hear her. He pushed up her sleeve and pressed the needle into her arm. After a few moments, her whimpers subsided and her head lolled on her neck like a rag doll's.

He injected the remaining sedative into the other girl's arm, then backed up the car a few inches so that he could pick up each unmoving body and load them into the trunk. With another surreptitious glance around the silent neighbourhood, he drove back to his apartment building.

Once he was inside the flat, he immediately began to scrub the place from top to bottom. It had to be spotless for his next job… and for Barbara's return, of course. He shaved, showered and washed his clothes, almost feeling himself again. It was nearly time to go home.

Nothing left to chance, he repeated to himself as he painstakingly sterilised his instruments. How many times had he been told that by his professors? He remembered their lessons well. He'd been an excellent pupil, and a great surgeon. His professors hadn't seen that. But he knew that with these scalpels and syringes and a canvas of skin – this was his art, and he'd always known he had a gift for it.

CHAPTER 56:
LISA'S ARTICLES

Lisa sat down in her editor Brian's office for her weekly check-in. She didn't bother with small talk.

"I want to do follow-ups on the deaths of those three politicians."

He raised his brows. "You seem… eager."

"I am. I think those stories need to be revisited."

Brian frowned. "Your first articles on the accidents were already pretty good. They covered a lot. Are you sure you have anything new to say on this?"

"Yes. I've been looking into them and I've got some information that hasn't been reported before."

He thought it over for a few moments, flipping through the folio-sized editorial calendar on his desk. "All right. If you're sure it's worth your time." He glanced up at her. "But no unsubstantiated conspiracy theories. I don't want to deal with a libel lawsuit."

"I'll do my best. No guarantees." When he scowled at her, she added, "I'm only kidding, Brian. Of course. Nothing but the facts, as always."

He nodded. "While you're at it, write something nice about Wayne Brewster. His approval ratings as governor are really climbing after he won that corruption case against the Ukrainian fraudsters. And voters are excited about the Pacific Highway Act." Lisa must have pulled a face. "People like him, Lisa," he said. "No sense in alienating our readers, or our advertisers. Don't go round making enemies."

"What, me? Never." She laughed at Brian's sour expression. "You know, you're the second person to tell me that this week."

"Good. Clearly you need to be reminded." He closed the calendar and looked back up at her. "Get to work on those follow-ups. Best of luck."

•

The paper published three of Lisa's articles over the next few weeks, one about Susan Harrison's death, one about Peter Duncan's, and one about Colin Jenkins'. In each article, Lisa walked through the official story as given by the police and then enumerated the holes in it. Her argument in all of them was, essentially, the same: too many questions had been left unanswered for these cases to be considered closed.

The articles gathered momentum, and by the time the third one ran, they had become one of the most controversial and widely discussed series that the paper had printed in years. Many people dismissed Lisa's theories altogether – and a whole host of them wrote nasty letters to tell her how wrong she was – but a small number of readers began to publicly demand that the police reopen their investigations. And that number was only growing.

If she was honest, Lisa was amazed at the traction her articles had gotten. But she was pleased, too. Maybe something would really happen because of them.

As busy as she was with her investigative reporting, she still often found herself missing Ryan. He'd decided at the last minute to extend his trip, so she wasn't sure when he would be back. It had already been over a month since their lunch at Victoria's. In that time, she'd received a handful of texts from him, most of them accompanied by pictures of him and his daughter at various landmarks around Wellington. He looked so different from when they'd met. Tanned, for one thing. Relaxed. Happy.

Lisa herself was considerably less relaxed, and the primary reason was her unreliable lodger, Paul. She'd finally lost her patience and told him he needed to find a new place. She didn't relish having to kick him out. In fact, she'd have been happy to let him stay, if he would just pay the damn rent. But he was months behind now, and she was worried about going into arrears with her mortgage company. So she gave him a month to clear out and braced herself for the hassle of finding a new tenant.

As long as she was rethinking her living situation, it seemed like a good time to re-evaluate some other aspects of her life, too. Outside of these latest developments at the paper, she couldn't help but feel that she'd fallen into a bit of a rut. When she was at home by herself after work, she found herself wondering where she was headed exactly. She wasn't getting any younger, and she had a nagging feeling that she hadn't accomplished whatever she was meant to have done with her life. Sure, she was a good journalist, but there had to be more to it than that.

Although her fiercely independent twenty-year-old self would never have admitted it, what she really wanted out of life were more people to share it with. More real friends who weren't just casual acquaintances from the office. And who knew? Maybe even a husband. Maybe even kids, someday. She wasn't too old to have kids, was she?

Lisa told herself to pull it together.

She did miss Ryan, but she tried not to get too hung up on the romance front. After all, there were plenty of other things she wanted to do, too… learn a language, read the classics, travel internationally. She would love to visit Tokyo, see the Acropolis in Greece.

Maybe I'll write a book, she thought to herself. She'd always wanted to do that.

CHAPTER 57:
PRESS CONFERENCE

Midnight had come and gone, and Brewster was still working in his study in Pittwater. To his complete surprise, the phone rang.

He stared at it for a few moments, trying to think of all the people who could possibly be calling him at this hour. It was a short list.

Finally, he picked it up on the last ring. "Hello?"

"Brewster. It's Johnson." Of course it was. "We've got a problem, a big one. We have to get a lid on it before it causes any damage. I need your help."

He sounded agitated. "All right," Brewster said, already uneasy. "What do you need?"

"We're going to do a press conference and a set of interviews, and you're going to be there. There's a lot riding on this, so I need you at your best. I've already sent a helicopter out to you. It'll be there in a few minutes. Make sure you're ready. And don't say a word to anybody before you leave."

"Where are we going at this time of night?"

"Newcastle."

The line went dead.

Brewster slowly set the phone back in its cradle. Whatever this was, he sensed it wasn't something he wanted to be a part of. It was past time, he decided, to start stepping back from his involvement with Johnson.

For now, though, he was going to Newcastle. Apparently.

Brewster was waiting by the jetty when the lights of the landing pad suddenly flooded through the darkness. He heard the helicopter before he saw it, and the sound seemed to be louder than normal. As it touched down, he realised that it wasn't the helicopter Johnson typically used for personal transportation. It was huge, military grade by the looks of it.

The moment the helicopter touched the ground, two special forces personnel dressed all in black jumped out of it. They were holding semi-automatic machine guns, and they beckoned to Brewster.

"Get in! Quick!" they yelled over the thunder of the rotors.

Shit, Brewster thought, staring at them, *are we going to war?*

Reluctantly, he clambered into the cabin, followed by the two commandos. Johnson and Chan were in the seats opposite him, flanked by two more armed soldiers. The helicopter rose into the air, and Brewster watched Pittwater fall away beneath them.

Brewster tried to ask what was going on, but it was almost impossible to communicate over the noise of the helicopter. Johnson, who was clearly in a foul mood, shouted that he would explain everything as soon as they got to the hotel.

For most of the ride, Chan's eyes were fixed on Brewster. At some point, Chan leaned over and said something in Johnson's ear, but Brewster couldn't have guessed what it was.

The helicopter landed outside a government building in Newcastle. It was pouring rain, and occasional spasms of lightning forked through the sky. They all disembarked, including the soldiers. Two black vans, both with heavily tinted windows, were waiting for them at the curb. Chan, along with two of the armed guards, immediately headed for one of them.

Johnson pointed to the other van. "That one's for you," he said, still shouting over the muted roar of the rain. "We'll meet you at the River West Hotel. You've got a room booked there. It's already been secured. I'll catch up with you soon. Chan and I just need to speak with some people first."

"What is this all about?" Brewster asked, shielding his eyes with his hand from the sheets of rain that threatened to blind him. "Has there been a terrorist attack or something?"

"Oh god, no. Just some international procedures that need sorting out. Some... diplomatic agreements to be reached."

With that, he hurried over to the first van, which pulled off into the night the moment Johnson was inside. Brewster turned to the second van, where one of the special forces operatives was holding a door open for him.

"This way, sir," he said.

It was clearly not up for negotiation. Brewster nodded and climbed in.

The van dropped Brewster off at the hotel a few minutes later. The black-clad guards escorted him as far as the front door to the lobby, and then Brewster was on his own.

He gave his name at the concierge desk and was shown to an immaculate suite, furnished entirely in various shades of minimalist grey. Once he was alone, he helped himself to some brandy from the suite's minibar, took a seat in an armchair, and settled in to wait.

Hours ticked by. It was past two am, and Brewster was starting to nod off. He couldn't imagine what was keeping Johnson. But then again, he couldn't imagine what any of this was about.

There was a knock at the door.

"Finally," he said. But when he rose to answer it, he found, not Johnson, but one of his tuxedoed agents.

"The Prime Minister will see you in the morning," he informed Brewster, without greeting him. "He'll be giving a press conference at ten am. You'll be briefed before then. That's all for tonight."

Brewster stifled a sigh. "All right. I'll arrange an early wake-up call. Good night."

The man turned and left without another word.

Confused, exhausted and apprehensive for what tomorrow would bring, Brewster went to get ready for bed.

By the next morning, the storm had broken and dawn arrived with golden sunshine. At eight thirty, Brewster was eating the last few bites of his breakfast when, at last, his phone rang. It was Johnson, informing Brewster that one of his men was on the way to bring him up to Johnson's suite on the seventh floor.

A few minutes later, Brewster was in an elevator beside yet another agent wearing sunglasses. He still had no idea what to expect from his meeting with Johnson, but he spared a moment to be grateful that no matter what was coming, at least he'd already made those backups of his recordings.

There was more security than usual posted outside the door to Johnson's suite. Before Brewster was allowed in, he was patted down by one guard and checked with a metal detector wand by another. Finally, an agent opened the door with a keycard and gestured him in.

Johnson was sitting on a sleek white sofa in a sunken lounge area in the middle of the suite. Chan was standing just behind him. What was it about Chan that it reminded Brewster so much of a Pekingese lap dog?

"Come on in," Johnson called. The tension and anger that had been in his face yesterday was gone. In fact, he was smiling. Which, frankly, was disconcerting. "I apologise about last night," he continued, waving Brewster over to sit beside him. "It was a delicate matter that needed to be taken care of right away." He let out a sigh. "Here's what happened, Wayne. A major drug operation was uncovered by the Maritime Border Command. I needed to do damage control. But, as it so happens, we can use this to our advantage. Do you want coffee?"

"No, thank you, just had some," Brewster said, uneasily. "Since when does the Prime Minister get involved with drug operations? Seems like something for the intelligence service."

Johnson smiled. "The Prime Minister must have his eyes on everything that affects the prosperity of our country. I've told you before, Wayne. It's a new world. The days of the old Italian mafia are long gone. Now the threat is from Russia and Eastern Europe. Those gangs are bad news. Wherever they go they bring weapons, murder, prostitution, human trafficking. It needs to be controlled. Of course, there will always be *some* crime. That hidden economy, under the surface… that brings in revenue and allows important relationships to be forged."

Brewster stared back at him. This was it, he realised. Johnson had really gone off the deep end.

"The Chinese have understood this for years. That's how the Communists keep things under control. They've got it all figured out. After all, in any society, there are always going to be the weak ones who…" He made a gesture with his hand as if to indicate falling snow. "…filter to the bottom. The ones that fall prey to drinking, drugs, gambling, sex, all the rest. It's unavoidable. But if the addicts and gamblers and their whole economy of minor crime can be managed, then it can be very beneficial. And how do we manage it? By letting someone else get their hands dirty while they keep everyone in line. As long as the people running the syndicates are allies of ours – like, say, the Chinese – then it's a mutually beneficial arrangement. They get to maintain their operations without interference, *and* they make sure that the Russians and the rest of the Eastern Europeans don't get a foothold in our country. Everyone's happy this way, you see. The wheels keep turning. The world remains in order."

The longer Johnson spoke, the more the reality of Brewster's situation set in. Johnson was talking about propping up Chinese crime syndicates as part of the national government's agenda. This wasn't what Brewster had signed up for.

All he wanted to do was serve one more term as governor. Make enough to retire on. Maybe even do a little bit of good while he was in office, if the opportunity presented itself. Now, it seemed like a very real possibility that his life might be in danger. He truly had no idea what Johnson was capable of.

"So," Brewster said, hoping to redirect the conversation, "how is a drug operation going to help us? It sounds like bad publicity for your administration."

"It would have been," Johnson agreed. "You see, last night our business partners were bringing in their stock from China. It was all part of the Gold Coast operations… getting everything set up for when the casinos and hotels open up. Not to mention that with the Pacific Highway, there'll be a whole new north-south supply chain for easy transportation of the product. Anyway, our partners would've been successful, except for a port pilot who just had to raise the alarm. He'll need pensioning off, at the least."

A flash of yesterday's anger resurfaced in Johnson's expression, but it was gone quickly as he went on.

"As you saw, there was quite the storm last night, and that didn't help things either. There were some issues offloading the cargo. Our investors lost money and needed to be reimbursed. That was why I had to move quickly when we got to Newcastle… to make sure all the remaining cargo was secure and the funds were in place. Now there's the matter of finding out who made the decision to offload in that storm. They'll have to be dealt with."

Johnson lapsed into a brief silence, apparently envisioning what that would entail. He shook himself and seemed to return to the present.

"But for now, Brewster, you and I need to get our story straight. The press conference will take place at this hotel, in one of the meeting halls. Here's what will be in the official press release. The Prime Minister and governor of Sydney were on their way to the Gold Coast to oversee the beginning of the new developments and to meet with our international investors. During their flight on the Prime Minister's helicopter, the pilot received a message from the intelligence service that the New South Wales Maritime Border Command had just foiled a massive drug haul. The operation is thought to be the work of a very large Eastern European crime syndicate. If it had not been for the diligence and hard work of John Fuller…"

"Who's John Fuller?" Brewster interrupted, frowning.

Johnson pointed a finger at him approvingly. "See, this is the sort of thing we need to clear up before we go in front of the cameras. John Fuller is the meddling port pilot who got us into this mess. Anyway, as I was saying. If it had not been for John Fuller's diligence and hard work, this dreadful crime may never have come to light. It is believed to be the biggest shipment of heroin ever captured in Australia's history."

"Jesus," Brewster muttered under his breath, but Johnson didn't seem to hear him.

"The Prime Minister and Sydney governor decided to land the helicopter in Newcastle to personally thank John Fuller and the rest of the Maritime Border Command. This reflects our government's commitment to eradicating organised crime wherever it is found. The culprits will be brought to justice, and our administration will continue to ensure that Australia is kept safe from these criminals." Johnson waved his hand in a motion that meant *et cetera, et cetera.* "So. How does all that sound?"

Brewster could hardly believe the sheer audacity of Johnson's hypocrisy. How could this man go on national television and lie to the entire country without an ounce of shame? Brewster knew that he himself was no saint... he'd taken the odd bribe, made his fair share of under-the-table deals. But those seemed like harmless schoolboy pranks compared to what Johnson was talking about. Doing deals with international drug lords and covering up for crime syndicates that destroyed people's lives... if he'd known what Johnson was up to, he never would have agreed to run for governor again.

He had to find a way out of this. But he would have to be very, very careful.

CHAPTER 58:
NICE AND TIDY

The killer woke early, just after dawn. He loaded the trunk of his car with the contaminated plastic sheets and the black garbage bags that held the girls' clothing, taking care not to be seen by the neighbours. Then all that was left to do was to tidy up the apartment for Barbara's arrival.

He wiped down the whole bathroom with bleach, studiously disinfecting every surface. Then he tackled the kitchen. All of the dishes were washed and put away neatly, and the sink and counters scrubbed to a shine. In the living room, he vacuumed the rug and even polished the furniture. As he stepped back to admire the cleanliness of the flat, he felt rather sad to be leaving. It had all gone so well at the beginning. They had liked it here.

All told, though, he was satisfied with the way things had turned out. His last night in Melbourne had been nothing short of spectacular. He was immensely pleased with his work, confident that it was a real showcase of his talent and skill. In fact, he was rather certain it was his best one so far.

The night before, he'd gone to the petrol station to fill up so that he wouldn't have to stop on his way out of town. While he was there, he'd noticed a display of flowers. He decided that it would be a nice gesture to buy them for Barbara.

Now that the rest of the cleaning was finished, he filled a vase with water, added the bouquet, and set it on the kitchen table, where they'd had their first conversation all those weeks ago. Alongside the flowers, he left the key to the apartment and a short letter.

He pulled up the handle of his suitcase. Everything else was already in the car.

"All right. We're going home now," he announced to the empty flat. Then he smiled. "Yes, I think so too. It's a nice day for a drive."

CHAPTER 59:
LUNCH IN NEWCASTLE

Everything went according to plan at the press conference. Brewster stood dutifully in the background as Johnson regaled reporters with the fabricated story of their arrival to Newcastle. His impassioned vow to protect Australians from the dangers of international crime was met with a standing ovation. Brewster clapped along with the rest, hoping his uncomfortable smile wasn't obvious to the cameras.

Afterward, Johnson invited Brewster to lunch with him and Chan.

"Come on, we've already had the location cleared by my security detail. You might as well tag along," Johnson said spiritedly. Ever since the press conference had ended, his mood was nothing short of buoyant.

Brewster agreed, somewhat reluctantly, and they took a limousine with blacked-out windows to a place called Restaurant Mason. After they finished their entrees, Johnson turned to Brewster, who instinctively tensed.

"Oh, Brewster, I nearly forgot. Chan mentioned that you had lunch in Sydney with a Mr Charles Pearce, the chief executive of LeMay Building Supplies."

Brewster was taken aback, but he tried to recover quickly. He aimed for a light-hearted chuckle. "Did he?" His eyes bounced between Chan and Johnson. "And what would you know about my lunch meetings, Chan?"

"Now, don't get defensive. And don't feel too special, either. Chan keeps me informed about lots of people."

I'll bet he does, Brewster thought with a thin smile. "Well, who I have lunch with is my own business, I'm afraid."

"Of course it is. I understand," Johnson said smoothly. "I just hope it wasn't anything I should know about. Considering I gave LeMay the contract for the Pacific Highway's raw materials."

"If you really must know, Charles is an old friend of mine," Brewster replied. "His daughter is getting married next month, and he and his wife were in Sydney so that she could do some shopping before the wedding. Since he was in town, he wanted to invite me to the wedding personally. I've known their daughter since she was born."

"How lovely," Johnson said, with a smile that didn't reach his eyes.

"Of course, I had to say no. I'll be too busy with events at the governor's office next month to attend the wedding. But it was nice to catch up with Charles, all the same." He managed to keep his tone mild and disinterested, although internally he was seething at the thought of Chan spying on him. He should have expected that. He would need to be more cautious.

"See, Chan?" Johnson said, turning to him. "I told you. Just an innocent visit with an old family friend."

"Of course," Chan concurred. "A visit with a friend."

Johnson looked back to Brewster. "Although I have to say, I'm not sure what you see in that Pearce. When I met him, in Perth he was not at all keen to support our goals for the future of this country. Seems the millionaires in Perth would prefer to fritter away their money on their own comforts rather than invest in Australia." He glanced down at his watch. "Ah. We'll need to get going." He flashed Brewster a quick grin. "Hope you've got good sea legs, Brewster."

Brewster frowned. "What for?"

"We're going on a little excursion down at the port."

CHAPTER 60:
WELCOME HOME

Barbara Stevenson had a very long and unpleasant journey back from London.

Between flight delays, crying babies, and a gentleman who'd fallen asleep on her shoulder smelling profusely of French onion soup, it had been a memorably awful return trip. Now that she was standing outside her own apartment door, she could not wait to get inside, drop all her bags, and climb into bed.

She turned the key and let herself in. The first thing she noticed was the flowers on the table.

"Oh, how nice," she murmured to herself. As she walked over to admire them, she spotted a notecard next to the vase. She picked it up, and a little smile appeared on her face as she read it. It was a lovely letter from her lodger, welcoming her back from London and thanking her for letting him stay in the flat. He said he'd had a wonderful time exploring Melbourne and was now on his way to Adelaide. The last line puzzled her somewhat: *I hope that you'll find the apartment cleaned to your satisfaction, and that you enjoy your presents.* With a shrug, she decided 'presents' must mean the flowers, as she didn't spot anything else that might qualify as a gift.

Leaving her bags in the kitchen, she wandered into the living room to see what kind of state the place was in. She was suitably impressed; everything looked spick-and-span, probably cleaner than when she'd left it.

The door to the bedroom was closed. Barbara walked over and pushed it open, then stopped unable to move rooted to the spot.

A scream tore from her throat, but she didn't hear it over the ringing in her ears. She stumbled backward, her legs threatening to crumple underneath her with every step. She barely stopped herself from tripping over the couch and continued to back away as her screams dissolved into gasping sobs.

She fled to the hall and staggered over to her neighbour's apartment. Over and over again, she banged on the door with the flat of her palm, but no answer came.

Finally a soft voice interrupted her. "Miss, are you okay? Do you need help?"

She spun and found herself face to face with the postman.

"The bedroom," she mouthed.

He frowned at her. "What?"

Barbara managed to summon her voice. "The bedroom," she rasped, pointing to the open door of her flat.

The postman gave her an uncertain glance. Then, cautiously, he set down his bag and walked inside.

•

An hour later, the Melbourne Homicide Police and a squad of forensics technicians had converged on the apartment. Barbara had been taken to the hospital, where she was being treated for shock.

Detective David Haines stood at the door to Barbara's bedroom.

"Never seen anything like it in my career," he said to the crime scene photographer has, she lowered her camera from her eye.

"What a fucking welcome home present?" she said grimly.

Haines shook his head. "What possesses a person to do something like this?" he muttered, more to himself than anyone else. It wasn't like somebody could have given him an answer.

Against the back wall of the bedroom was a full-length mirror. Scrawled in red lipstick across the glass were the words 'FUCKING LESBIAN WHORES'. Directly above the bed, there was more writing, underlined in dripping red: 'A BITC'. The detectives on the scene could only assume it was missing the letter 'H.' This message seemed to be written in blood.

On the bed itself lay the naked body of a young woman. She had brunette hair and a tattoo of a peacock on her shoulder. Her hands were tied above her head and fastened to the headboard. Her feet were also tied, one to each of the lower corners of the bed, so that her legs were spread open. Her torso was cratered with stab wounds. Both nipples had been cut from her breasts, and both eyelids had been removed. The letter 'C' had been sliced into the skin of her abdomen, a neat semicircle drawn with artistic precision. The most gruesome detail of all was her mouth: it had been sewn shut with thick black sutures, giving her a doll-like smile.

A second young woman, this one blonde, had been posed in an armchair near the bed. She, too, had been stabbed repeatedly in the torso, and her nipples and eyelids had been painstakingly removed. On her stomach was carved the letter 'T.' Her arms and legs had been bound to the chair, which had been turned towards the bed, as if she'd been forced to watch the torture of the other woman. Her face was frozen in an expression of horror, her lidless eyes huge and staring. She would have been unable to look away and unable to scream, as she, too, had her lips sewn together in a smile.

CHAPTER 61:
RYAN'S RETURN

Lisa was in her office, staring intently at her computer screen, when her cell phone rang. She was in the middle of the final edits on her latest article, and she was somewhat annoyed by the interruption until she caught sight of the name on the screen.

"Hello?"

"Hey, Lisa."

"Ryan," she said, as a smile bloomed across her face. "Hey. How are you?"

"I'm doing well." He sounded like it, too. "It's been great being in New Zealand and spending all this time with Madison. But I just wanted to let you know that I'll be back in Sydney next week."

"Eager to get back to work?"

"Hardly. I ran out of leave."

She laughed. "Fair enough."

"How are you? Hope you haven't been sticking your nose where it's not wanted."

"As if I would ever do that," she replied innocently, and listened to him chuckle. "No, you'll be glad to hear that I've been keeping out of trouble lately. Not too much going on at the moment. I did that series on the deaths of Harrison, Duncan and Jenkins, and those pieces have gotten a decent amount of attention. Some big names from the Democrats and the Eco and Environment Party have started putting pressure on the police commissioner to reopen the investigations, especially the one on Peter Duncan. Since Johnson won't shut up about his good relationship with China, they're saying he should be able to get that missing Chinese tourist to Australia for questioning." She leaned back, swivelling slightly in her office chair. "And they just had the ribbon cutting ceremony at the starting point of the Pacific Highway, north of Sydney. But other than that, not much to get excited about over here."

"I saw something on the news about a drug bust."

"Oh, that's right," Lisa said. "It only happened a day or so ago. I haven't seen the press release from the PM's office yet. There was a press conference up in Newcastle, but it was more of a publicity event for Johnson than anything else. Brewster was there, hovering in the background behind Johnson, as usual. Everybody's just waiting for more information to come out. It's all a bit vague so far. But supposedly it's the biggest shipment of heroin ever seized in Australia."

"Huh. Well, glad to hear law enforcement has been getting on fine without me," Ryan said. "Guess there's no need for me to rush back, since I haven't been missed."

"I've missed you," Lisa said. She felt a warm blush creep up into her cheeks, and was silently thankful Ryan couldn't see her.

"Oh, have you?" Ryan asked, with a note of affectionate teasing. "Well, it's a good job I got you a present then."

"What is it?"

"You'll just have to wait and see." She could hear the smile in his voice. Then, in the background, she thought she heard someone else, a young girl maybe.

Ryan answered the other person, although his words were muffled as if he'd covered the phone with his hand.

"Anyway, I have to go," Ryan told Lisa. "But I'll call you as soon as I'm back."

"All right. Have a safe trip."

"Yes. Take care, Lisa."

"Cheers."

CHAPTER 62:
THE DRIVE HOME

The weather was bright and clear, and traffic was light. The killer's car hummed smoothly over the asphalt, eating away at the miles between him and Sydney. It gave him a certain pride and satisfaction to think that he was, perhaps at this very moment, being looked for on the roads to Adelaide.

He heard her laugh at the idea, and it made him smile. "I feel like a weight's been lifted from my shoulders," he said. "I think… I think I've finished what I need to do."

No. You haven't.

His heart skipped a beat.

There's one more. Then the bitch will be gone forever.

He fidgeted, tapping his thumbs on the steering wheel. "Do I have to?"

Yes. She was the bitch that started it all. Don't you forget now.

"Okay," he conceded. "One more. For now, let's enjoy our trip."

He decided to stop at the same little town that he'd visited before. "What was the name of it?" he asked.

Goulburn.

"Goulburn," he repeated. "You're right. We'll have lunch at that Greek cafe. That was good, wasn't it?"

The killer spotted the exit for Goulburn and hooked off the highway. He navigated back to the fast-food restaurant that he'd found on his first stopover. Conveniently, the dumpster behind the place was once again near to overflowing, so it was easy to hide the plastic sheets and black garbage bags from his trunk among the grease-soaked paper sacks and rotting food scraps.

He got back into his car and drove down to the Greek cafe. It really was a beautiful day, he reflected to himself, and he asked for a table out on the patio to enjoy the sunshine. When he was done with his meal, he left the waitress a generous tip and then took a stroll around the block, popping into a few shops to browse the homewares and clothing. But he couldn't stay long.

We need to get going. I don't want to get home in the dark.

"Okay. I'll just stop and get some fuel before we go. Oh, and I need cigarettes."

He returned to the car and drove to the petrol station across the street. When he went inside to pay, there was an elderly woman in front of him at the counter. The radio behind the cash register was tuned to a news station, and the announcer was halfway through reading a bulletin.

"…the latest from the Melbourne police. Earlier today, two young women were found brutally murdered in a flat in central Melbourne. Our reporters tell us that the apartment's owner, returning from an extended overseas trip, arrived home to find the grisly scene. We'll have more details…"

"Oh, how awful," the woman at the counter said. As she spoke, she was counting out change from a coin purse at what felt like a glacial pace. "What is the world coming to nowadays? It was only a few months ago that there were those terrible murders up in Pittwater."

He shifted his weight from foot to foot, suddenly on edge and wishing he were already back on the highway.

"Let's hope they catch him," the cashier replied. "The last thing we need is some serial killer scaring off all the tourists."

"Yes, let's hope they do," the woman said, sadly. "Those poor families, can you imagine…"

"Hurry up and get out of the way, you old bag. I haven't got all day."

The woman's mouth fell open in shock. He pushed past her and slammed forty dollars on the counter.

"That's for the fuel," he snarled at the cashier, then turned and left without a backward glance.

He got into his car and swung out of the parking lot, narrowly avoiding a collision with a lorry that was just pulling in. The lorry honked at him, but he paid no attention, tyres screeching as he shot towards the highway slip road. As soon as he got back on the M31, he hit his fist against the steering wheel in frustration. "Shit. I forgot the cigarettes. *Shit.*"

His good mood had vanished, and with it his plans for a leisurely drive home. He jammed his foot on the accelerator and roared towards Sydney.

CHAPTER 63:
ABOARD THE
REGINA CAELORUM

"Are you going to tell me where we're going, or are you leaving it as a surprise?"

"I have told you," Johnson said amiably. "We're going on an *excursion*. Not to worry, we won't need to go beyond the harbour. It won't take long."

The black limousine dropped them off at the port. Brewster hung back slightly behind Johnson and Chan as they spoke with a port official, who then led them down the pier to a pilot boat. Glancing around, Brewster was almost certain that there were not normally this many armed guards present on the Newcastle docks.

As they arrived at the gangway, a bearded man emerged from the pilot boat to meet them. He was carrying two black shoulder bags. They looked heavy. He set them down in front of Chan, who opened one and peered into it, then nodded decisively and closed it again. Johnson seemed pleased.

Chan picked up both bags and slung one strap over each shoulder. The three of them were waved onto the boat.

Once they were out of the slip, Johnson pointed to a grungy, weather-beaten barge anchored on the still blue water. It was one among many cargo ships waiting to dock in the harbour.

"That's where we're going," he said to Brewster. "The *Regina Caelorum*."

The bows of the cargo ships loomed above them, great curved sheets of rivet-studded metal that slipped past soundlessly. The pilot boat navigated between their anchor chains. Brewster followed the huge steel links with his eyes as they met the water and quickly disappeared into the gloom.

"What do you know," Johnson said, rather abruptly, "about Lisa Gordon?"

Brewster turned to him in surprise. "That journalist from the *Telegraph?*"

"Yes, that's the one."

He shrugged. "Not much. I've met her a handful of times for interviews." He paused, sensing this was not the answer Johnson had been looking for. "Why?"

"She's causing trouble with this latest series of articles. People are asking questions. What is her reputation? Her background?"

"All I know about her reputation is that she's supposed to be one of the better political reporters. I think she's won a couple of journalism awards over the years. She can be very annoying, but she's rather good at her job, apparently. Couldn't tell you anything else."

Johnson looked out over the water, clearly unsatisfied with Brewster's input. He glanced at Chan. "We'll have to keep an eye on her," he said, in a tone that implied Brewster was no longer part of the conversation.

As the pilot boat pulled alongside the *Regina Caelorum*, a bulkhead door opened, and a set of metal steps was lowered down to them. Johnson gestured for Chan and Brewster to go ahead. "After you, gentlemen," he said with a showman's grin.

Trying not to think about what would happen if he slipped, Brewster followed Chan up the slick, narrow staircase. When Brewster arrived at the top, he found himself in a dimly lit corridor. Several Chinese men in dark suits were waiting for them. Chan handed off one of the black bags to them. As Johnson joined them, the door was closed with a resounding *clang*.

Johnson nodded a greeting to the men in suits. "Lead the way, then," he said.

Without speaking a word, the men turned and guided them deeper into the ship. The labyrinth of dingy hallways finally gave way to a staircase that descended steeply. It seemed to go on forever. Finally, they arrived in a dark, cavernous cargo hold.

The space was almost entirely empty, except for several battered wooden tables and chairs in the centre. Two of these chairs were occupied by people Brewster took to be Chinese businessmen. Around the tables, a few small lamps cast pools of sickly yellow light. Chan and the guards who had escorted them set down the two black bags in front of the businessmen.

"Wait here," Johnson told Brewster in an undertone, and glided over to catch up the others.

The businessmen rose to their feet at Johnson's approach. They shook hands with both Johnson and Chan before gesturing for them to take a seat. As soon as they did, all four of them began to converse in low, intense voices.

At this distance, Brewster couldn't hear most of the conversation. It seemed to take place mainly in Cantonese, with Chan translating for Johnson.

Then, suddenly, the Chinese businessmen called out to the guards. One of them crossed quickly to a bulkhead door, opened it, leaned in, and began shouting in Cantonese. Moments later, three scruffy men who appeared to be members of the ship's crew were shoved into the cargo hold. Their hands were bound behind their backs.

The second guard stepped forward and barked out a command to the crew members, then repeated it more harshly when they didn't move. The crewmen dropped to their knees. The guard pulled out a pistol and put it to the back of the nearest crewman's head.

Before he could stop himself, Brewster drew in a sharp breath. Swallowing hard, he prepared to turn away. Another quick, heated exchange took place between the businessmen and the guard. Chan intervened and seemed to smooth things over. The guard, looking resentful, put up his pistol and tucked it back into his belt. The crewmen rose to their feet and were led away before the door slammed shut behind them.

Both Johnson and Chan seemed unfazed. Johnson allowed enough time for the echo to die from the closing of the heavy metal door before resuming the conversation. Brewster caught the words, "Show them," and Chan reached over and opened one of the black bags. He held it out to the Chinese businessmen, who both offered what sounded like words of approval. They began to smile.

The four of them stood and went through another round of handshakes. Something had clearly been decided, although Brewster didn't quite know what. The businessmen collected both black bags and then disappeared through the same door where the crewmen had been led away. Chan, Johnson, and Brewster were left alone with the guards in the empty hold.

Johnson crossed over to Brewster. "Come on. We're leaving."

The guards brought them back up the staircase and through the maze of dim hallways to the exterior door where they'd begun. Chan, Johnson, and Brewster carefully descended the slippery steps to the pilot boat waiting below.

On the way back to the docks, no one spoke a word. Every time Brewster blinked, he saw the crewman knelt on the floor with the barrel of a pistol to the back of his skull. If Johnson was anywhere near as shaken as Brewster was, he didn't show it.

They disembarked and stood on the pier. "I've got to go up to the Gold Coast for some meetings, and then onto Brisbane for a conference," Johnson said, as if they were wrapping up a perfectly standard business meeting. "But the official helicopter will come round to take you back to Pittwater."

"All right," Brewster replied slowly. "Anything I ought to know before I leave?"

"Not really," Johnson said, sounding disinterested. "Oh, by the way, Chan will be going with you back to Sydney."

"What for?" Brewster asked with a frown.

"He just needs to look into some business for me. Nothing you need to worry about." He flashed an easy smile. "You take care, Wayne. I'm sure I'll see you again soon."

CHAPTER 64:
BACK TO WORK

Ryan couldn't say he'd been especially eager to return to the office. But he had to admit that once he sat down at his desk, it did feel good to be back.

He'd just started digging into the backlog of emails that had arrived in his absence when a knock sounded at his door. He looked up just as Ann stepped into his office.

"Well, well," she said. "Look who decided to grace us with his presence."

He smiled. "Good to see you again, Ann."

"Good to see you too, Campbell. How was New Zealand?"

"Fantastic. Madison and I had a great time."

"I'm happy to hear it. And *you'll* be happy to hear that I've got some good news for you."

He arched a brow. "That so?"

"Yes. You're back on the Pittwater case."

He sat up straighter at his desk. "What? What do you mean?"

"I mean what I said. There's been a new development. You've heard about the killings in Melbourne, haven't you?"

"No," he frowned. "I just got in last night."

"There were two murders there a few days ago, and it looks like our killer. It's just been a skeleton crew working on the Pittwater cases the last couple of weeks, but after these new victims, I phoned the commissioner and requested to have some personnel added back onto the investigation. And I asked for you specifically. He agreed. But I'm still in charge."

Ryan's face split into a grin. "That's great news. Cheers, boss." He leaned forward with his elbows on his desk, his expression immediately sobering. "So tell me about these new murders."

"We're flying down to Melbourne today. I'll bring you up to speed on the flight. Can you be ready in two hours?"

"Sure. No problem."

"Good. I've already got our tickets booked." She tapped the door frame for emphasis. "Two hours. Be ready."

She vanished down the hallway.

Ryan shook his head, still hardly able to believe it. Just like that, he was back on the case.

He finished going through his emails as quickly as he could, then picked up the phone to call Lisa.

"Hello?"

"Lisa, it's Ryan. But I've only got a moment. Listen, I'm back at the office today, and I just found out I've got to fly down to Melbourne. I'll let you know when I'm back."

"Melbourne? Because of the two murders?"

He fiddled with a pen on his desk. "It's probably better if I don't say much more. I'm sorry. Ongoing investigation and all that."

"Of course," Lisa replied. "Don't worry, I don't cover Melbourne anyway. Good luck, and be safe. Phone me when you're back in Sydney. We can try to find a time to meet up."

"Will do," he said, and he meant it. "Take care."

Ryan drove to his house and threw some clothes into an overnight bag, which was easy since he hadn't properly unpacked from New Zealand yet. Ann came to pick him up a few minutes later, and they made their way to the airport. As usual, by the time they were through security they didn't have much time to spare, but they did make their flight.

Once they were settled into their seats Ann, brought him up to speed on what he'd missed in the last few days. "Haines called me right away. Apparently, a woman called Barbara Stevenson was returning from a trip abroad and found the victims in her bedroom. Haines had seen the reports from the Pittwater killings and recognised that the mutilation of the bodies was similar. It's either the same murderer or a very close copycat."

"Are the forensics reports in yet?"

"Haines was still waiting on them when I talked to him. But the victims match the profiles of the Pittwater killings… they're both young women in their early twenties. They've got stab wounds to the abdomen and letters carved into their stomachs."

Ryan grimaced. He hadn't especially missed hearing sentences like that while he was on vacation. "Okay. Anything else I should know?"

"Just that they think the killer might be headed to Adelaide. Oh, and Stevenson said that she was renting the place out to an Englishman. The Melbourne team is still looking into that. They've contacted British police and Interpol."

Ryan was quiet for a few moments. "One of the bar staff at the SuperDome was English."

Ann nodded. "I remember that, too. I think there's more that the Melbourne folks haven't told us yet, but we'll have to wait until we get there to hear the rest of it."

"I guess all my theories were off the mark," he admitted. "Thinking that the Leadman case was somehow connected to this killer. It just goes to show, I suppose. You can't always trust a hunch."

"Case isn't solved yet," Ann reminded him. "Let's catch him first, before we decide what didn't work."

"Yes. You're right." He took a steadying breath. "Hopefully that'll be soon."

CHAPTER 65:
BACK HOME

It was late evening by the time the killer got back home. He was exhausted, and a crippling headache had set in sometime after Goulburn. The voices in his head had been relentless.

It's okay. We're home now, she told him soothingly. He was knocking things off a shelf as he rummaged around for his pills. He felt certain that he'd black out if he didn't take them soon. *Don't worry. We're back where we belong.*

At last, he found the bottle and swallowed a few tablets. Then, when the pounding in his head began to ease, he did his usual rounds, making sure everything was the way he had left it. As soon as he was convinced that the place had stayed secure in his absence, he sprawled out on his bed, fully clothed on top of the blankets, and fell into a deep sleep.

He woke with a start, hours later. By then it was dark. He lay there confused and disoriented, scrambling to figure out where he was, before he finally made sense of his surroundings.

See? Safe at home, she said.

As long as he was awake, he decided he could use a cigarette. After forgetting them in Goulburn, he'd stopped on the outskirts of Sydney to buy a pack. He picked up the box from where he'd left it beside his bed, then climbed the stairs, pushed open the door, navigated past the workbenches, and made his way out into the cool night air.

All was peaceful and still. He guessed it was around two am, still a few hours before dawn. The steady drone of crickets underscored the quiet of the warm, humid night. As he took the first drag on his cigarette, he gazed across the water, admiring the yachts in the silver moonlight. *It's good to be back*, he thought.

A few more pulls and the cigarette burned down to the filter. He flicked it to the ground and headed back inside for a little extra sleep.

The next morning, as soon as he woke up, he started unpacking. He dug out his newest Polaroids and pinned them on the large cork board in the centre of the wall. They fit in nicely alongside all the others. By now, his collection had grown quite impressive.

The next task was to transfer the trophies. He cleaned four jars, then filled each one with surgical spirit. From the zippered front compartment of his backpack, he extracted four polythene bags. Handling the bags with care, he removed the contents, two pairs and another two pairs again – and deposited them, delicately, into the jars. He sealed them and placed them up on the shelf next to a series of identically filled glass containers.

He paused for a few moments to survey the shelf proudly. Then he began the laborious process of sterilising and putting away the medical equipment he'd brought back from Melbourne, returning all of it to its proper place.

Looking over his stock, he realised that it was time to replenish his supplies. And besides, he needed to get rid of this car. He would have to go into the city.

He got himself ready and did up all the locks. Before he left, he looked out over the water and waved to the old man on his yacht. Then he climbed into the car and started the drive to Sydney.

CHAPTER 66:
BREWSTER WANTS OUT

Ever since his return from Newcastle, Brewster's schedule had been packed. Between meetings with the city planning department and a slew of public events to talk up the construction of a new social housing project in inner-city Redfern, he barely had a moment to spare. But whatever free moments he could find, he used them to start making preparations.

He'd always known Johnson to be ambitious to a fault, but lately he seemed nothing short of unhinged. The Prime Minister was dangerous and unstable, and if he went down, he'd drag Brewster right along with him.

Unless he got out. He had no intention of spending his retirement in prison, or worse. There was no chance that he would be able to extricate himself from Johnson without vanishing altogether. So that's what he would have to do.

He didn't know when the opportunity for his getaway would come, but he'd already begun getting ready for it. Very quietly, he started moving money to offshore accounts, untrackable by the Australian government. He scheduled a full maintenance check on his seaplane, to ensure that it would be in good condition in case he needed to make a quick escape. He had three international passports on hand… one from Australia, one from New Zealand courtesy of his father's side of the family, and one for America from his mother's side.

He would've had more choices, but he was limited to documentation he could obtain from personal connections, people he'd known for decades. He couldn't trust anyone else. Not with Chan watching him. Ever since Johnson mentioned Chan's report of the lunch meeting with Charles Pearce, Brewster had grown increasingly suspicious of… well, everything, frankly. He'd had his security detail sweep his government office for bugs, and he hired an investigator to do the same with his home office in Pittwater. He was satisfied that the physical spaces were clear of listening devices, but he was less certain of the security of the computer network. It seemed like the IT department was always doing updates to his official computer. His laptop had been pulled for security patches three times in the last month. Unfortunately, he didn't know the first thing about digital espionage, and so he had little choice but to trust that the tech team at the governor's office was doing what they claimed to be.

The discs with all the videos and recordings were still in a strongbox at his Pittwater villa. He needed to make arrangements to have the recordings go public if something happened to him. But he hadn't felt safe enough to take any action that might draw the attention of Chan. So that would have to wait a little longer.

It was about five pm, and Brewster was in the governor's office. He'd just finished up with his work for the evening. The day had been a long one, as they had all been lately, and he decided to pour himself a brandy. As he reclined in his office chair, sipping slowly, the intercom chimed.

The voice of the receptionist was piped in from her desk outside. "Excuse me, Governor Brewster. A Mr Chan is here to see you."

Brewster was quiet for so long that the secretary must've thought he hadn't heard her. "Governor Brewster?" she prompted uncertainly.

He hit the button on the intercom. "Yes, very good. Send him in, please."

The locked door to his office buzzed, and Chan strode in. He was in one of his usual finely tailored suits, this one a dark burgundy over a solid black shirt.

"Wayne," he said, with a smile that passed as polite. "Good to see you."

Brewster rose to his feet. "You as well," he replied, making a minimal effort to sound sincere. "What brings you here this evening?"

"Just a social visit. Prime Minister Johnson wanted me to check in with you. See how things are going."

Brewster gave a sceptical hum and walked around to the front of his desk. "Well, rest assured, everything is going well. We've been busy putting things in order for the new social housing project up in Redfern."

Chan nodded and didn't respond.

Brewster drew in a slow breath through his nose. "I've finished up with work for the day. Just poured myself a brandy. Would you like one?"

Languidly, Chan crossed over to an armchair and sat down, making himself comfortable before he answered. "That would be nice. Thank you."

He turned away to pour the second brandy, trying to decide if he was more nervous or irritated. By the time he turned back, he had managed to arrange his face into a mostly neutral expression.

"I have to say," he said, handing over the brandy, "I'm surprised to see you. I would've thought you and Johnson had more important things to do besides check up on me. I've been so busy lately with official duties that I haven't had time to do much of anything else." He leaned back against his desk.

Chan sipped the brandy and took a moment to savour it before responding. "That's what I told Johnson," he said. "It's a big job, running this city. I didn't think you had any time to be making mischief."

"And why would I be making mischief?"

Chan smiled slowly. "I'm only joking," he replied. "Actually, Johnson asked me to look into that journalist, Lisa Gordon. He wants to know if there's anything in her background we ought to be aware of."

Brewster frowned. "I don't think there's any need for that," he said. "Anyway, I can get it under control. I've arranged a meeting with her editor, Brian Palmer, down at his yacht club in Woolloomooloo Bay. I'm seeing him for lunch tomorrow."

"I see. And what would be the purpose of this meeting?"

"Nothing interesting. We'll talk about the press releases for some upcoming events, like the ground breaking ceremony for that social housing project."

"And you'll mention Lisa Gordon in this conversation."

"If Johnson's that worried about her, yes. I'll express concern about the unsubstantiated claims in her articles and encourage Palmer to curb Gordon's enthusiasm."

"You think that will be enough to put an end to her meddling?"

"I expect it will. So let's wait and see what happens after my meeting with Palmer before you do anything… untoward concerning Lisa Gordon."

Chan looked down at his remaining brandy while he swirled it in the tumbler. "All right. I'll tell Johnson you have the matter in hand." He glanced up at Brewster. "But make sure that you do. Johnson does not wish to read any more troublesome articles." He finished the last swallow of his drink and leaned forward to set the empty glass on Brewster's desk. Then he rose from the armchair and straightened his jacket. "I'm glad we were able to get on the same page. Thank you for the drink. Good night, Wayne."

He turned and left the office. The door closed behind him and the automatic lock buzzed as it reengaged.

Brewster sank heavily into his chair and shook his head as he refilled his own brandy. There was something so off-putting about that Chan fellow. He couldn't quite put his finger on what it was, but he was sure he'd never get used to him.

CHAPTER 67:
THE ENGLISH MAN

"Unfortunately, we don't have a lot to tell you. Our forensics team said they'd never seen a cleaner crime scene."

Ryan and Ann were seated in Haines's office. Haines and his team had given a press conference a few hours ago, and afterward he'd met the two Sydney detectives in the Melbourne police headquarters.

"You mentioned that on the phone," Ann said with a frown. "Nothing ever turned up?"

"Nothing so far. No fingerprints, no clothing fibres, no blood splatters. It was like the whole place was scrubbed top to bottom. But we're still working on it. We'll find something, sooner or later. There's always something the killer misses."

"Okay, so no forensic evidence," Ryan said slowly. "Anything unusual about the crime scene?"

"We haven't had a chance to talk with Barbara Stevenson yet… that's the owner of the flat. She's still at the hospital, being treated for psychological trauma. So we haven't been able to confirm with her if anything was missing or changed from the way she'd left it. We did find a couple of things under the kitchen sink that we bagged as potential evidence. Disposable white suits and latex gloves. Unopened. All medical grade."

"Doesn't sound like the kind of thing Barbara Stevenson would have lying around," Ann murmured.

"Right," Haines agreed. "So we think those must have been left behind by the killer."

"That fits with your theory, Ann," Ryan said to her, "about the murderer working in the medical field."

Haines nodded. "That's what we thought, too. Between those hospital supplies and the precision of the mutilation… seems a good bet that we're looking for someone who's taken some anatomy classes." He suppressed a shudder and tried to hide it by taking a sip of his coffee. "Anyway, we're still working on tracking down the English lodger who was staying in the apartment."

"You said you contacted British police," Ann said. "Did you hear anything from them?"

"No, nothing useful. And nothing from Interpol, either."

Ann's frown deepened. "They're not going to make it easy on us, are they?"

"Maybe it's time to get back in touch with Jan Weiler."

Haines looked at Ryan blankly. "Who?"

"Jan Weiler," Ryan repeated. "Do you remember the case a couple of months ago, where a man was stabbed outside a dive bar called The Last Schooner? Jan and her boyfriend Simon Catterick were some of the last people to see the victim alive. We interviewed her back then. Her boyfriend bought a stolen passport off an English bloke, and we thought he might've been connected to the Pittwater killings."

"Ah. I do remember that case, yes. And you think that English bloke is the same one who was renting Barbara Stevenson's apartment?"

Ryan shrugged. "Based on the evidence, I think it's worth checking into the possibility."

"Then I'll dig up Weiler's contact information," Haines said. "We'll give her a call and set up another interview."

"We need to check with the British embassy, too," Ann added. "Ask them for a record of passports that have been reported missing or stolen over the last six months. If it is the guy who sold the stolen passport, he could have other IDs or passports that he's been using."

"You're right. I'll have our team look into it and report to the Sydney office with the list once they have it." Haines took a long, thoughtful swig of his coffee. "Other than that, we've mostly got to sit and wait. The results of the post-mortem should be back soon. And with any luck, we'll have the surveillance footage from the wine bar in a day or two."

Ann looked at him quizzically. "The wine bar?"

"Didn't I tell you?" When Ryan and Ann shook their heads, Haines shuffled through several manila folders on his desk, picked one up, and handed it to them. Ryan looked over Ann's shoulder as she opened it.

"This is an incident report for an assault on a woman named…" Ann squinted at the poorly photocopied page. "Samantha Whelan."

"One of the murder victims. Our system flagged it as soon as we had positive identification of the two women found in the apartment."

Ryan glanced up at him. "So, Samantha Whelan was attacked in this bar two weeks before her death?"

"Looks like it. Hanna Lindgren, the other victim, was there as well. That's why we asked the bar to turn over their security tapes. Here's hoping they haven't erased them yet."

"Yes," Ryan muttered, letting his eyes fall back down to the incident report. "Here's hoping."

CHAPTER 68:
NEW MOTORBIKE

The killer's mood had improved significantly since his return from Melbourne. He'd had great success selling the car. The man at the dealership gave him a very fair price, in cash. He took the stack of bills and went directly to a different dealership, this one for motorbikes.

There, he found a second-hand motorcycle in beautiful condition, only a year old. The killer explained to the salesman that he was rather in a hurry, and asked if it might be possible for him to take the bike right away and let the dealership handle all the paperwork without him. The salesman spotted the envelope stuffed with cash and agreed.

Of course, all the personal information he'd given was fake… another one of his stolen identities that he'd been keeping in reserve. He had used up one for the bookstore, and now another for the bike. He would have to top up soon.

The identification he'd provided was from an American tourist who hadn't set foot in Australia for over a year. But by the time the salesman's computer system caught that, the killer would be long gone.

He took the bike to Pitt Street to do some shopping. With this new vehicle, he thought it would be only fitting to refresh his appearance, to transform again.

A few hours later, he got back on his motorbike, now wearing a black leather jacket, new jeans, and black boots. As he pulled into the street, he asked, "What do you think?"

I love it. She sounded pleased. *The new look suits you.*

He thought so, too. He liked the feeling of freedom that the motorbike gave him, the ease with which he weaved between the slower moving cars, the sensation of the sun and wind on his face. It was tempting to go roaring through the streets at full speed, but he made sure not to draw too much attention to himself. It would be such a shame, after all his work, to get pulled over by the police for speeding.

He considered going straight home, but then thought better of it. Instead, he made up his mind to cruise the city for a while, enjoying his new persona. It was quite a departure from the chinos and pressed shirts of his last personality. But he liked the difference. This change, he felt, was just what he needed.

CHAPTER 69:
A LEAD IN THE CASE

In a small, windowless room in the Melbourne police station, Ryan and Ann were just finishing up their interview with Jan Weiler.

They'd been speaking with her for close to an hour, and it hadn't been especially fruitful. Mostly, she'd repeated what she told them before; the man who sold Simon the passport spoke quietly, had an English accent, and wore clothes that marked him as out of place in a bar like The Last Schooner. They asked her again if she recalled any unusual features in his appearance, any scars or visible birthmarks, but she just apologised and told them she didn't remember anything like that.

There was one detail that came up for the first time in the course of their conversation, though.

"I'm not sure if me or Simon mentioned it before," she said, "but I do remember that sometimes it seemed like he was talking to himself."

"Talking to himself?" Ann repeated.

"Well... I guess it was more like he was talking to someone who wasn't there. I couldn't really hear what he was saying, but he would sort of... say something, and then pause, and then nod like he'd gotten an answer." She shrugged. "It was strange, but he wasn't causing any trouble, so I didn't think about it too much."

They questioned her for a while longer, trying to extract more useful information, but without much success. She started to grow frustrated with their seemingly circular questions. Ann and Ryan exchanged a glance that meant it was about time to wrap things up, but before they could, there was a knock at the door. It was Detective Haines.

"Sorry to interrupt," he said. "But I need to grab Detectives Nguyen and Campbell for a minute."

"Then can I go?" Jan asked tiredly.

"Not quite yet, Ms Weiler. Apologies. We'll ask you to hang around for a few more minutes."

She nodded, a little sullenly, and sunk down in her chair.

Ann and Ryan gave Haines a puzzled look as he beckoned them out into the hall. "What is it?" Ryan asked.

"I think we may have a lead. Come on."

He brought them into the incident room. The place was a flurry of activity as members of Haines's team wrote on whiteboards, tapped away at their laptops, and spoke into their phones in urgent voices. Ryan hadn't even had a chance to visit his own incident room in Sydney since he got back from New Zealand.

It was a strange sort of relief to be in one again after so much time away. There was something almost comforting about the familiar electricity in the air.

Haines led them over to a bulletin board, onto which had been pinned an eight by ten glossy photo of a young man. He removed the thumbtack and rolled it back and forth across his palm while he handed the photo over to them.

"This," Haines said, "is Benjamin Lovett."

"Okay," Ann replied as she accepted the photo. "And who's Benjamin Lovett?"

"Lovett studied at the University College London Medical School. Graduated with a first class honours degree. He was doing a two-year postgraduate residency at the Royal Free Hospital in London. Professors there say that he was an exceptional student who showed remarkable skill and knowledge. He took a summer holiday to Hong Kong, where he was staying with friends. Then he said he was going off to Thailand, and that was the last anyone heard from him. He's been missing for five months. His friends in Hong Kong reported that before he disappeared, he was showing signs of a mental breakdown. They thought it was because he couldn't cope with the pressures of his residency. The university therapist corroborated that theory. She said Lovett had been to see her several times, and he'd expressed that he often suffered from terrible nightmares where he was cutting up bodies. Here. I'll get you the full report."

Haines swiped a folder off his desk and offered it to Ryan while Ann continued to study the photo. "When did this come in?" Ryan asked.

"British authorities have been looking for him for months, but it was just forwarded to our office a few minutes ago. Apparently, Interpol thought that Lovett was a good fit for the profile we shared with them. English citizenship, a background in medical work, extensive anatomical knowledge, and a fragile mental state."

"That ticks a lot of the boxes," Ryan murmured as he gave the file to Ann.

"It does seem promising," she agreed as she flipped through the pages. She glanced up at the other two. "Guess we better run it by Jan."

Jan was staring at the wall when Ann opened the door to the interview room. She stirred and turned as the three of them filed inside. "You know, I was happy to try and help, but my shift at The Last Schooner is starting soon, and…"

"I understand, Ms Weiler. We just need to ask you one more thing." Ann slid the eight by ten photo across the table towards her. "Is this the man who sold Simon the passport?"

Jan picked up the picture and studied it for what felt like an eternity. Finally, she gave a slow shake of her head. "Honestly, I don't know. There's a resemblance. But the man we met had dark brown hair, or maybe black. Definitely not blond. He wasn't this pale, either. He had a dark tan. And he was a lot skinnier than this bloke, too." She set the photo back down with a shrug. "I'm sorry, but I can't say for sure whether it is or isn't him."

"That's all right," Ryan said, trying not to let his frustration show. He reached over to take the photo back. "We appreciate your help."

"If you think of anything else, you know how to reach us," Ann said with a smile. "Thanks again, Ms Weiler. You're free to go."

Jan nodded and rose to her feet, and Haines showed her out.

A few minutes later, the three detectives met back up in Haines's private office.

"So," Ryan said as Haines closed the door behind him, "what do you think?"

"This has gotta be him," Haines answered eagerly. "Interpol said Lovett has been missing for five months, right? That's plenty enough time to lose some weight, dye his hair and get a tan."

"That's true," Ann said, with more reserve. "But then again, there could be a lot of people who fit Jan's description. She only met him once, in a dark bar, months ago. Her memory won't be perfect. You could probably show her a dozen young, white, British men and she would say they all looked more or less like the person who sold the passport."

Ryan nodded. "Good point. So I guess our next step is to show the photo to someone who might've seen Lovett more recently."

Ann met his eyes and nodded. "Time for a chat with Barbara Stevenson."

CHAPTER 70:
BREWSTER'S WEEKEND PLANS

Brewster took some time to think on his predicament, and by the weekend, he'd finally come up with a plan that he was pleased with.

He made one more set of duplicates of the incriminating recordings of Johnson. That brought the total to three copies of three discs. One set of discs would come with him. The second set he would have sent by bonded courier to his lawyer. And the third set... well, he was still making arrangements for that one.

Although he'd deleted the files from his laptop, he had grown increasingly concerned that they might still be recoverable from somewhere within the depths of the hard drive. So he bought another laptop, the same model as his original one. He populated it with replicas of the files that he'd used for his personal work and correspondence, finance forms, articles he'd saved, the sort of digital debris that accumulates over extended periods of use. He even added some photos from a few years ago, to make it look as though he'd had this device for a long time. The old laptop, with the compromised hard drive, was packed in his suitcase. It would disappear along with him.

Next, he had to take care of the pinhole cameras and hidden microphones in his Pittwater office. He removed each of them from the vantage points he'd so carefully chosen before that first fateful meeting with Johnson: the flower vase, the small figurine of a man on horseback, the base of the antique brass lamp on the desk. He stashed all the recording equipment into a small cloth bag and tucked the bag into the strongbox, where it would be safe for the time being. As soon as he was out over the water in his seaplane, he would drop the bag in the ocean. God willing, he'd never be in a position where he needed to employ any of those devices again.

With the strongbox closed and locked, Brewster picked up his phone and called over to the dock. The man in the maintenance shed answered.

"Hi, Blake. It's me, Brewster. Just letting you know that I'll be down to the dock to check up on my plane in about an hour."

"No problem," Blake replied. "I'll make sure everything's in order for you."

"Great. Thanks."

Blake met him at the entrance to the jetty. They walked out to Brewster's seaplane, and started in on the usual litany of safety and equipment checks. It had been a while since Brewster had done any maintenance on his plane. He'd actually missed it quite a bit. There was something calming about the routine of it: changing the oil, starting the engine, checking the wing flaps, making sure the instruments were calibrated. Blake pointed out that the altitude gauge seemed to be sticking, but they would have to take it up in the air to be sure.

He paged through the maintenance logs on his clipboard. "There are a couple of mentions in here about that gauge playing up," Blake said with a frown. "So this might've been going on for a while."

"I'll call around and find a replacement," Brewster answered. "Wouldn't want to run into any problems."

"Good idea." Blake dropped the clipboard to his side. "Anything else you want checked out?"

"No, I think that's it. Just write up a report and put it in the logs. Thanks, Blake."

Blake nodded. Before he could respond, a third voice spoke over him.

"Hello, Wayne. You've got a beautiful old plane there. That model is quite a rarity nowadays, isn't it?"

Chan?

Brewster turned to see him standing just behind them on the dock. He was wearing a casual short-sleeve shirt and light-coloured pants. It was the first time Brewster had ever seen him in anything but a dark suit.

"What are you doing here?" Brewster asked, staring at him.

"Oh, I'm just here on a social visit. Nothing to worry about. I called your villa, and your staff told me that you were down at the dock."

"Yes. I have to do an annual maintenance check. The insurance company requires it."

"I see. And do you ever fly the plane? Or do you just do maintenance checks?"

"No," Brewster said, finding himself annoyed by Chan's tone. "I fly at least three or four times a year on my own. And I'm a patron of the Prince Albert Yacht Club, so I help with the annual Pittwater Regatta. I go up with the official photographer to track the progress of the yacht races out at sea." Brewster's scowl deepened. "Not that it's your business."

"Of course it's not," Chan said, without any change in expression. "I was just being friendly. I fly myself, as a matter of fact." His eyes trailed past Brewster to the plane resting on the water behind him. "Did you find any problems during the maintenance check?"

No point in admitting how close he was to leaving if he could help it. "Actually, yes, she needs some work before I can take her out again. For one thing, the altitude gauge is buggered. It'll take a bit of searching to find one for an old model like her."

"Ah. Well, I'm sure you'll find one. Persistent man that you are." Chan smiled. "I was hoping to have a word with you in private before I go. Perhaps we could have a drink at the clubhouse bar, if you don't mind."

"It will have to be quick," Brewster said stiffly. "This is supposed to be my weekend off."

"Not to worry. This won't take long," Chan assured him. "Then I'll let you get on with your weekend."

Brewster nodded unenthusiastically and said goodbye to Blake. Then he walked alongside Chan, down the jetty and into the clubhouse.

Most of the members who were sipping drinks or enjoying mid-afternoon snacks were sitting outside in the shade. The inside of the clubhouse was almost empty. Chan chose a quiet spot in the corner, out of earshot of any other tables. At the bar, Brewster asked for two servings of brandy from his preferred distillery and brought them over to Chan.

"Now, what is this about?" Brewster asked, taking a seat across from him. "Checking up on me again, are you?"

"No," Chan laughed, as if the suggestion were absurd. "It's a nice day. I decided to go for a drive. But since I happened to come up this way, there is something I wanted to tell you." He leaned in and folded his hands on the table. "I had a call with Johnson. He wants to know if you met with Lisa Gordon's editor."

"Brian Palmer? Yes, actually, I did. You'll have no more problems with Lisa Gordon or her articles. He's given me his word on that."

"Good. That's solved, then. Johnson also mentioned something about the building materials coming from LeMay."

Brewster paused with the brandy halfway to his mouth. "What about them?"

"It appears that the supplies delivered for the first section of the Pacific Highway must have been underweight. The completed length came up short of what was expected."

Brewster tried to look unperturbed. "Well, that's not terribly surprising. As Johnson well knows, I worked in construction for many years, and I can promise you that the first round of estimates is always off the mark. Things are different on the ground than they are on paper. It's not all as simple as the accountants want you to believe."

Chan sipped from his glass while Brewster spoke. He seemed to wait patiently until Brewster had finished speaking. There was a look in his eye that Brewster noticed but couldn't quite identify. Amusement, maybe.

"Well, if that's your professional opinion on the matter, then I trust your judgment," Chan said. "I'll let you get back to your weekend. Oh, but before I go… I was thinking of driving down to Palm Beach for the evening. Can you recommend any good restaurants there?"

"Not off the top of my head, I'm afraid," Brewster replied. "But I'm sure you'll find something you like."

Chan smiled again, that enigmatic smile that so annoyed and unnerved Brewster. "Yes. I'm sure that if I go looking, I'll find something."

CHAPTER 71:
LISA'S NEW PROJECT

It was a quiet, average Saturday, and Lisa was at home, doing laundry. Normally, she did some of Paul's too, if he had a few things to toss in. But she wasn't currently on speaking terms with him, so she left the jacket and shirt he'd spilled coffee on piled in the corner.

She was embarrassed to admit that they'd had a rather public row in the office. It happened on Friday, just after Lisa had walked out of a meeting with her editor. Brian had informed her that he was putting an end to her investigation of the deaths of the three Sydney politicians. When she asked why, Brian told her that the series had run its course, she'd had a chance to make her case, and now it was time to move on. Besides, Brewster had been busy enacting more of his popular policies, so there were plenty of other stories for her to cover. She was assigned an article on the social housing development going up in Redfern and dismissed from his office.

Already in a poor mood, Lisa was standing at the copier, gathering some reference materials for the new assignment. Then Paul walked up and said that he'd heard she was getting the Redfern story, and offered to send her some photos he'd taken of the lot where the housing project would be built. He also informed her that he would be going to a party in Manly later, and probably wouldn't be home all night. And then, after she'd already told him that she wouldn't put up with his overdue rent anymore, he had the gall to ask her for forty dollars so he could buy drinks for the party.

Something in her had finally snapped. She rounded on him, completely forgetting that she was in full view of her co-workers.

"Really, Paul? You want forty dollars? Well, *I* want all the money you already owe me. You know, I gave you a place to stay when you needed one. I was more than patient and understanding when you said you were having trouble coming up with the rent. Now, three months on, I've got the mortgage company after me for late payments because you won't pay your share. So no. I'm not giving you any money. I'm not giving you a month to find a new place, either. I want you moved out by next week. And I want *all* of the back rent paid by then. No more of your excuses."

As she stood there catching her breath, she gradually became aware that everyone in earshot had fallen silent and was staring at the two of them. She pushed past Paul, doing her best to ignore the shocked looks she was getting, and sat down at her desk in a huff. She dived into work and didn't leave her cubicle for the rest of the afternoon.

In that time, she'd managed to write up a draft of the Redfern article. That had been a fairly brief overview of the expected timeline for the project's construction and opening. But she already knew what she was working on next: a more in-depth report on the recent drug operation in Newcastle.

Once she'd folded and put away the last of the laundry, she decided she might as well get a headstart on that, and put on a pot of coffee.

A few minutes later, she settled into her usual seat at the kitchen table with a mug beside her and her laptop open in front of her. She began her research by replaying a video of Johnson's press conference at the River West Hotel. As she listened, she jotted down notes in her steno pad:

- *Port official = John Fuller*
- *Largest amount of heroin ever seized in Australia*
- *Chinese-registered ship = Regina Caelorum*
- *Operation conducted by Maritime Border Command*
- *Eastern European gangs??*

The video ended and for a while Lisa just stared down at her own handwriting, tapping her pen against the paper, trying to find the right angle for her story.

She recalled that another drug-related story had cropped up in the last few days. That one had taken place in Brisbane. According to the early reports, three men had been killed in a heroin deal gone wrong. The details were still very vague, but rumours had immediately begun to circulate that the murders were in some way tied to the drug bust in Newcastle. If they were, Lisa couldn't afford to leave them out of her Newcastle feature.

As it so happened, she had a connection in the Brisbane police department, an old friend from school. She glanced at the clock, saw that it wasn't too late yet, and decided to ring him.

"Hey, Jeremy," she said when he picked up. "It's Lisa Gordon."

"Ah, yeah, Lisa. I figured you would be calling."

Lisa was caught off guard. "You did?"

"Yes. Ever since we had those shootings here. After the articles you did on Harrison and the others, everybody knows you're the busybody journalist who gets into people's business whether they like it or not."

"I'm going to take that as a compliment. You caught me, Jeremy. I'm calling to see if you can tell me anything about those three men who were killed in Brisbane."

"Well, that depends. What have you heard already?"

"Just that the men all died of gunshot wounds, and there were a couple of others who were injured in the dispute. And that there might be a connection to the Newcastle drug haul."

"I can't tell you too much more than that. For one thing, it's not my department. I'm in the cyber crime division these days. Plus, they're keeping everything pretty hush-hush on that case. But you're right. It *is* connected to the Newcastle drug haul."

Surprised, she picked up her pen and held it poised over the paper. "How do you know that?"

"Those three blokes who were killed. They were crew members of a Chinese cargo ship. The *Regina Caelorum.*"

Lisa stared at the words already written on the steno pad. "That's the ship that got busted by Maritime Border Command."

"Yes. Exactly. The story I've heard from the police commissioner is that the crewmen were killed by some big Eastern European gang, because the Chinese are trying to muscle in on their turf." Jeremy fell silent briefly before he went on. "But that didn't quite make sense to me. It wasn't a big Eastern European gang. The people who had non-fatal gunshot wounds… they were part of a little Romanian crime family. Everyone knows them around here. Local criminals pushing marijuana, amphetamines, ecstasy. They own a couple of takeaway shops and a laundrette. No guns, just muscle. Baseball bats. Threats and intimidation. That kind of small-time stuff."

Lisa was quiet for several moments. "So someone is trying to blame an Eastern European gang when they had nothing to do with the shootings. Why would anyone want to cover for the Romanian crime family?"

"I'm not sure he was covering for the Romanians." Jeremy paused. "It did seem like he was covering for someone, though."

She frowned. "Who? Why would the commissioner do that?"

"I don't know. I've probably said more than I should have already." She heard Jeremy shift uncomfortably at the other end of the line. "Look, I told you, all the reports I've heard have been pretty sparse on details, and some of them are just flat-out contradictory. So maybe it's all just a misunderstanding. I'm sure things will clear up once the dust settles."

Or it'll all get buried and forgotten, Lisa thought, but she sensed it would be pointless to push Jeremy any further. "Yeah, you're probably right. Well, thanks a lot, Jeremy. That's all really helpful."

"Just don't go naming your sources."

"Of course. Cross my heart."

"Cheers."

Jeremy hung up.

Lisa leaned back in her chair and let out a long breath. Now she'd learned the connection between the shootings and the drug haul, but in the process she'd stumbled upon a whole nest of other questions that needed answering.

Clearly, there was more to all of this than anyone had seen… or at least more than anyone was admitting. Maybe she wouldn't be allowed to publish anything more about the deaths of Harrison, Duncan, and Jenkins, but she was determined to get to the bottom of this Newcastle story.

She stood up to pour herself a fresh cup of coffee and then got right back to work.

CHAPTER 72:
DAVID LEEDS

Around lunchtime on Saturday, David Leeds drove to the Prince Albert Yacht Club in Pittwater. He parked and made his way towards the entrance, past the chandlery, where sailors were purchasing supplies for their boats.

Leeds was dressed in a pair of deck shoes, expensive designer jeans and a bomber jacket, which he slipped off and hung over his shoulder. As he entered the reception area, he paused to sign the club guestbook, then walked up to the desk.

The redheaded receptionist looked up at him with a smile. "Well hello, Mr Leeds," she said. "We haven't seen you around here in a while."

He smiled back. "I've been up in Brisbane, visiting relatives," he explained. "Did I miss anything while I was gone?"

"Oh, nothing too exciting. What can I do for you?"

"Well, with the regatta coming up, I was wondering if Ian needs any part-time bartending staff."

"You know, I'm not sure if he's still hiring. Why don't you go in and ask him? He's in his office, I think. You remember where it is. Right down the corridor. Just knock before you go in. He'll be pleased to see you."

"Thanks, Lily," David said. "I'll catch you later."

He went down the hallway and knocked on the door to the manager's office.

"Come in," Ian called.

David stepped inside with a small wave. "Hello, Ian."

Ian glanced up from the clipboard balanced on his knee. "Hey, David! Good to see you. Give me a minute, would you? I'm just about done with this order sheet."

There was a chair in front of Ian's desk. David sat down in it while he waited for Ian to finish up with his order sheet. After a few moments, Ian pushed his reading glasses up onto his head and set the clipboard on his desk.

"Sorry about that," he said. "Now, what can I do for you?"

"I was wondering if you had any part-time work available at the bar."

"Ah, I'm sorry to say I've already filled all the open positions. The regatta is coming up so soon, we wanted to make sure we had everyone lined up by the time things got into gear." Ian leaned back in his chair and crossed his arms, looking at David thoughtfully. "But then again, the regatta *is* our busiest season. We could always use another hand in the chandlery. Someone to help out at the marina. Same pay as the bar staff. What would you think about that?"

"Oh, that'd be fine," David said. "I prefer to work outside anyway. Used to help out at the marina all the time as a kid on my summer holidays."

"Perfect. Can you start on Monday? We need to get the place all cleaned up for the big event."

"No problem. See you Monday, then."

CHAPTER 73:
TRACKING THE KILLER

Unfortunately, interviewing Barbara Stevenson proved to be more difficult than Ryan and Ann had anticipated.

It had been two days since she'd discovered the victims in her apartment, and she was still under a psychiatrist's care. The doctor refused to let Stevenson speak to the police, citing concerns about her patient's mental state. Haines tried to change the doctor's mind, but she wouldn't budge, insisting that being forced to relive the incident might be more than Stevenson could handle. Ryan was frustrated by the holdup, of course, but he couldn't blame the psychiatrist for being protective. Nor could he blame Stevenson for needing longer to recover. He'd seen plenty of terrible things in his work, but that's what he'd signed up for. To find something like that in one's own home, out of nowhere… he could hardly imagine it.

While they waited for Stevenson's psychiatrist to give the okay, they had no shortage of work to keep them busy. By then, they had gotten the security footage from the wine bar where Hanna and Samantha had been attacked. The cameras had captured an unimpeded view of the whole event: a man walking over to the long table where the two women were sitting, calmly picking up a wine bottle, smashing it into Samantha's face, and then being wrestled to the ground by some of the other patrons. But in the darkness of the bar's interior, there wasn't an especially clear image of the attacker's face. The best frame they could find was still grainy and indistinct. They had the Melbourne technicians clean up the image as best as they could, and took the result to the bookshop staff.

The employees generally agreed that it looked like a man they had worked with, but none of them knew him as Benjamin Lovett. They said their co-worker's name was Joshua Hart. When asked for a description, everyone said more or less the same thing: a soft-spoken Englishman who mostly kept to himself, he was a hard worker and good with the customers, except the uni students, whom he seemed to dislike. When Ryan and Ann told them he was being investigated for an assault, they all expressed surprise. All except for the shop owner.

She just stared at the photo in her hands for a few moments and then asked, "This is about Hanna, right?"

Ann and Ryan exchanged a glance. The names of the murder victims hadn't been released to the public yet, and Hanna wasn't visible in the cropped image they had given her.

"Yes, it is," Ann said. "How do you know that?"

The owner sighed and handed the photo back to Ryan. "I knew they got to be friends after Hanna started working here. Then one day, Hanna came in and asked to speak to me privately. I brought her into my office. She was clearly upset, and she looked like she'd been crying. She told me she was quitting, effective immediately. That wasn't like her at all. I always got the impression that she was really happy working here. So I asked her why the change of heart. All she would tell me was that something had happened with Joshua, and that she couldn't work with him anymore. But she needn't have worried."

"What do you mean?" Ryan asked, frowning.

"Joshua never showed up again after that. Never even called to say he quit."

Ryan nodded slowly. "I know this is going back a while now, but do you have any security footage that he might be in?"

The owner managed a thin smile. "Lucky for you, I haven't gotten round to erasing the drives lately. I'll see what I can do."

Eventually, she did find some footage of the man calling himself Joshua Hart, although none of the shots of his face were much better than the ones, gotten from the wine bar. Still, they gave a better sense of his height and gait. So, Ann and Ryan made sure to collect a copy and bring it back to the Melbourne office.

That afternoon, they rejoined Haines in the incident room. They had some frames from the bookshop owner's footage printed out, blown up, and added to the growing assemblage of images on the pinboard. The collection now included frames grabbed from witnesses' cell phone videos of the assault in the wine bar.

As the three of them stood shoulder to shoulder, staring at the series of blurry, pixelated photos, Haines said, "By the way, the post-mortem results came in while you were gone."

Ann pivoted towards him. "What did they say?"

"Just what you two predicted. The cause of death was strangulation for both victims. An extremely sharp instrument was used for the mutilation, apparently by someone with considerable surgical skill."

"Just like the victims in Pittwater," Ryan said.

"Yes. Exactly like them."

"Did forensics ever recover any other evidence from the scene?" Ann asked, after a brief silence.

Haines shook his head. "The killer was *extremely* thorough. Even the drains in the kitchen and bathroom were scrubbed clean. No clothing fibres. No fingerprints. There was one strand of hair that was found on the bouquet of flowers. But we're not sure it came from the killer— it'll have to be analysed against the florist and Barbara Stevenson."

Ryan let out a tense breath. "Let's hope it is from him. That'd be the only piece of concrete evidence we have."

"We certainly have a lot more than we started with," Ann pointed out, nodding towards the pinboard.

"More than we started with," Ryan allowed, "but still not much. We know the man who worked at the bookshop was the same one who committed the assault. We haven't proved that it was the same one who committed the murders.

We don't know for sure that it's the Benjamin Lovett from Interpol's files. And, most importantly, we don't know where he is now."

Just then, one of the officers in the incident room spoke up. "Detective Haines," he called, and all three of them turned.

"What is it?" Haines asked.

"I've got the Goulburn Refuse Department on the line." The officer held out a phone towards Haines. "I think you'll want to talk to them."

CHAPTER 74:
TURNING IN THE ARTICLE

On Monday morning, Lisa arrived in the office early. She'd finished her article over the weekend, but she wanted to tidy it up before she showed it to Brian. In the end, she was quite pleased with how it turned out. She thought it was probably one of the best pieces she'd ever written.

The story covered both the raid on the *Regina Caelorum* in Newcastle and the shooting of the three men in Brisbane. She made a point of noting that these incidents didn't just represent an uptick in drug-related offenses. They were both tied, specifically, to Chinese crime syndicates. At the same time, the Australian government was working extensively with Chinese investors on billion-dollar deals that the public knew almost nothing about.

Other countries had displayed more caution in giving contracts to Chinese companies, often conducting investigations and releasing information about potential conflicts of interest, but the Australian government had shown no such restraint. Lisa didn't make the claim that Australia should end its dealings with China. But she did raise the question of whether this partnership was really what the Australian people wanted, and whether it could have any unintended effects… such as the rise of Chinese drug trafficking within Australia's borders.

Once she'd finished her edits, she printed off a copy and brought it to Brian's office. She sat in silence while he read it, watching his expression as his eyes skimmed through the text. Then he set the papers on his desk and said, "Good work, Lisa. Really good work."

Lisa let out a breath and relaxed her grip on the arm of her chair. "Thank you."

"This'll get people talking. Excellent investigative reporting. Engaging and informative without being inflammatory. Well done. We'll put it on the front page tomorrow."

"The front page?" Lisa repeated, allowing a broad smile despite herself. She'd only made the front page a handful of times before. "That's brilliant. Thanks, Brian."

"Thank you for writing this."

Lisa gathered up the sheets of paper and went back to her own desk. Brian's reception of the article was surprising, considering how grumpy he had been in their last meeting. She hadn't pointed it out to him, but she'd deliberately written the article to serve as a sort of litmus test. The series on Harrison, Duncan, and Jenkins had been openly critical, borderline accusatory, of Prime Minister Johnson. For those stories, she'd earned a sharp reprimand from Brian, although he'd never said outright that it had anything to do with her portrayal of the PM.

In this new story, she deliberately avoided mentioning Johnson, and Brian had no complaints. She could do the maths.

Before she got to work on her next piece, Lisa decided to treat herself to a nice lunch. It was another beautiful day, and rather than taking a taxi, she walked down to Darling Harbour. The street was thronged with tourists, office workers on their lunch breaks, and buskers vying for the crowd's attention. The last time she was here, it had been with Ryan. She wondered how things were going in Melbourne, and whether he would be back soon.

She ate on an outdoor patio, enjoying the sun and the antics of the street performers. After she'd finished her meal and paid the bill, she ambled slowly back in the direction of her office.

Just before she turned the corner towards her building, she stopped short so abruptly that several people almost collided with her. They shot annoyed glances back at her as they continued on their way. But she remained in the same spot, the hairs on the back of her neck rising. She was struck by the sudden feeling that she was being watched, or followed.

Lisa looked around carefully, but she couldn't spot anything out of the ordinary on the busy street. Just the usual shoppers, diners, and sightseers going about their day, paying her no attention. She shook her head as if to clear it and started walking again.

On the way back up to her office, she stopped to get a large latte from the coffee shop on the ground floor. By the time she settled back into her desk, she'd managed to shrug off her unease. She successfully kept it out of her mind until she finished up her work for the afternoon and got on the ferry to go home.

As she was sitting on the deck, the feeling returned, just as strong as before. Surreptitiously, she glanced around at the other passengers, trying to catch someone looking at her. But no one seemed a likely candidate. This, she supposed, should have comforted her. But it only frayed her nerves more.

She was glad to get home. Out of habit, she almost called out to Paul, but he hadn't been to the house in days. Not since they had that argument at the office. To be honest, she wasn't sure if he was coming back at all. He'd taken most of his clothes to his girlfriend's apartment, but he'd left quite a few things lying around his bedroom.

That reminded her. She needed to get her finances in order. In a little notepad, she began to make a record of all the money that Paul owed her, both from the months of unpaid rent and all the small loans she'd given him here and there. Tallied up, it was a considerable sum.

Until now, she'd been putting off writing an ad to find a new tenant, half-hoping that Paul would just come up with the money and she wouldn't have to go through the hassle. But after seeing how much he actually owed her, the last of her goodwill towards him finally evaporated. She would be glad to be rid of him, and to have a new lodger who paid the rent on time.

CHAPTER 75: GOULBURN

Haines took the call from the Goulburn Refuse Department in his office. Ryan and Ann remained in the incident room, where they pored over all the paperwork Haines had left with them. When Haines returned, they both snapped their heads towards him.

"What did they say?" Ryan asked.

"Apparently, a few months ago, a local fast-food restaurant was fined for putting domestic waste and clothing in their food disposal containers. So the refuse department had been notified to check the restaurant's bins, in case they put anything other than food in them. Just today, they did find some non-food waste. Disposable sheets and medical gowns, all covered in blood. The people at the Refuse Department had heard about the killings in Melbourne, so they contacted us as well as the Goulburn police."

"Goulburn," Ann said slowly. "That's not on the way to Adelaide. That's towards Sydney."

Haines nodded grimly. "Looks like the killer might be heading back to where he started." He checked his watch. "The town is a bit of a drive from here, so we should head out as soon as possible."

"We're ready when you are," Ryan said.

"Okay. Let me put a forensics team together and we'll get on the road."

Haines took the first driving shift. As the landscape rolled by outside the window, Ryan felt like he was suspended somewhere between hope and a sense of foreboding. On one hand, if this new find really was connected to their killer, it could be the breakthrough they'd been waiting for. It would mean the killer had made a mistake, a major one. But on the other hand, it was clear that the killer had been playing games with them all along. They'd wasted time in Melbourne chasing down shadows. And every moment that passed could be bringing them closer to the next murder. The clock was ticking down, and Ryan had a terrible feeling about what would happen when it hit zero.

By the time Ryan, Ann, and Haines reached Goulburn, the local police had cordoned off the dumpsters behind the restaurant. The team of forensic technicians arrived a few minutes behind the detectives. As soon as the technicians got there, they donned their white suits and began bagging evidence.

Ryan and Ann asked to interview the staff of the restaurant, but the Goulburn police chief told them that had already been done.

"All of them swore blind they didn't know anything about the sheets or the gowns. Nobody seems to have any idea where they could've come from," she explained. "We got all the employees' names and contact details, in case you need to follow up with any of them later."

The franchise owner was hovering near the police tape, scowling at everyone who crossed his field of vision.

Ann nodded towards him. "What's wrong with him?"

The police chief rolled her eyes. "He's upset that the restaurant will be closed for a day or two while forensics goes over the place."

"I'm also upset about having to pay for something I had nothing to do with," the man called loudly, evidently having overheard her. "Last month it was some clothes in the bin that I'd never seen before. Now this."

"Oh, that's right… the clothes." Ann turned to the representative from the refuse department. "Where are the clothes that were recovered here last month?"

"Long gone, I'm afraid," he replied. "Any time we find salvageable clothing, it gets sorted and shipped off to developing countries. They weren't kept separate, so even if they were still in the country, we'd have no way of knowing which clothes they were."

"But you knew who to issue the fine to," the franchise owner shouted over to them.

Ann gave him an amused glance. Ryan ignored him and pulled out the image that had been taken from the nightclub's security footage. "Are the staff still here? We'd like to see if any of them recognise this man."

The police chief pointed to a small huddle of employees near the front door of the restaurant. Haines hung back to talk to the Goulburn cops while Ryan and Ann walked over to the employees. But it was a waste of time… all of them said that they'd never seen the man in the photo.

They started across the parking lot towards Haines. "Do you think we should release the photo to the public?" Ann asked in an undertone.

"I've been thinking about that," Ryan said, "and I don't think so. If we start posting his face around town, we might just push him into hiding, and then we'll never find him. Or worse, it might make him angry and cause him to strike again."

"I think you're right," she agreed. "No telling what that madman will do if we antagonise him. Better play it close to the chest, then."

They rejoined Haines just as he was finishing up a conversation with the police chief.

"There you are. We just got another call," he told Ryan and Ann. "This one's from a petrol station on the outskirts of town. The owner contacted the Goulburn police after she heard about the find here at the restaurant. Says we might be interested in hearing about a strange customer who came in recently."

CHAPTER 76:
CHAN MAKES PREPARATIONS

"I thought you said Brewster had taken care of it."

Johnson was pacing the length of his Canberra office with such intensity that it seemed he would wear a track in the plush crimson carpet.

"That is what he told me," Chan answered, his tone impassive.

"Did you see Gordon's latest article? Front page of the *Sydney Telegraph*, going on and on about how the public doesn't know enough about our dealings with China. This is *exactly* the sort of meddling Brewster was supposed to put a stop to." He shook his head and glared at Chan. "So what happened?"

"Brewster told me that he had a meeting with Brian Palmer, Gordon's editor at the *Telegraph*. He said he expressed his concerns about Gordon's recent work, and Palmer gave him his word that there would be no more issues."

"Brian Palmer." Johnson spat out the name. "His word isn't worth a damn. He's spineless, always has been. Our Chinese friends are not happy about the kind of attention she's drawing to them. They're threatening to pull out of our contracts if we can't rein in the news coverage. They want assurances that we can stick to our plans, without interference from political opponents or these pests in the papers." His voice became a snarl. "And meanwhile, Brewster's losing his nerve. I don't think we can trust him anymore."

Johnson came to a halt and cast a sideways glance at Chan. "I need you to sort out that Lisa Gordon, once and for all. And I need you to keep an eye on Brewster. Remind him that he is in this all the way. He's a squirmy character. He'll try to jump ship if he thinks he can get away with it. Now, I hired you because I was told that you were the best at making things like this disappear without any repercussions. So that's what I expect. Nothing less."

Chan gave Johnson a look that put a chill in his blood. Swallowing, Johnson forced himself to hold Chan's gaze. After all, he was the one in charge here. He was the Prime Minister, for God's sake. It wasn't as if he were in any real danger from Chan.

Still, at that moment, Johnson was silently glad to have a military-trained security detail whose sole job was to protect him from people who looked at him like that.

"You have had no problems with my work." Chan's voice was quiet but steely. "It has been professional and discreet. Between the two of us, Prime Minister, you are the one who should be more concerned about discretion. I can become someone else in an instant. Start a new life anywhere in the world. But you are tied here, with your plans and your responsibilities. You have everything to lose. So it's best if you concern yourself with running the country and leave the little problems to me. Lisa Gordon will not be a problem. I have a plan for her. As for Brewster, he'll come back around to our way of thinking with a little persuasion."

Johnson gave a stiff nod. "I'm glad to hear you're so confident."

"I am, yes. Remember what we said when we started this. We have a very bright future, the two of us, if we both concentrate our efforts where they matter most. So you focus on governing Australia, and I'll focus on my work." Chan rose to his feet. "I think it's time for me to be on my way. If you need anything else, you know how to reach me. Good night, Prime Minister."

Without waiting for a response, Chan walked out of the office, leaving Johnson staring at the door as it shut behind him.

CHAPTER 77:
TEST FLIGHT

At the entrance to the marina, a small van pulled up. It had a logo for SYDNEY AVIATION MAINTENANCE & SUPPLY emblazoned on the side. A moment later, Chan stepped down to the sidewalk.

He was wearing overalls and a T-shirt with a company logo to match the van. It was a pleasant morning, and the warm sun was tempered by an agreeable breeze off the water. Chan had chosen this day and time because there was virtually no chance of Brewster turning up. He'd phoned Brewster's personal assistant to ask if he would be around in the next few days. She'd told him that unfortunately, Governor Brewster was very busy with his official duties, and that he'd arranged to stay in Sydney until the end of the week to avoid the commute from Pittwater.

"What a shame," Chan had replied, already calculating how long he would need to get the vehicle and the overalls. "I was going to pay him a visit. Well, anyway, thank you very much."

From the back of the van, Chan grabbed a metal toolbox and a second smaller box. This one was cardboard, and it contained a new altitude gauge. With all of his supplies in hand, he started towards the dock manager's shed.

On the way, he passed several boaters loosening their mooring ropes as they prepared to take their yachts out. They waved at him, and he said hello as he walked by.

When Chan reached the small, sun-bleached hut, he took his place in line and waited while the manager made small talk with a couple of men buying a fishing license. After a few minutes, they headed off to their fishing vessel, and Chan stepped up to the counter.

The dock manager, a man named Gavin Blake according to his name tag, looked him over, his friendly smile fading to a look of puzzlement.

"Can I help you?" Blake asked.

Chan procured a business card from the pocket of his overalls and handed it through the open window. "I'm here to do some work on Wayne Brewster's seaplane. It needs a new altitude gauge, and some recalibration on the other instruments. He wants a test flight conducted as well."

Blake squinted at him. "You're not the usual maintenance man."

"Yeah, the regular guy is busy today. Doing a full refit on a boat plane on the Gold Coast. Lucky him, eh?"

"I see. All right, well, I'll just have to give Mr Brewster a ring to make sure he's signed off on everything."

"You can," Chan said smoothly, "if you want a roasting of his secretary. Brewster's down in Sydney, in official meetings all day. He wasn't even coming back to Pittwater for a few days because he had so much on his schedule. And he needs the seaplane up and running in time for the Pittwater Regatta."

A number of other people had formed a queue behind Chan, more fishermen waiting for licenses. Blake glanced at them with a slight frown, and then shrugged. "Okay, fine. Here." He ducked briefly out of sight and re-emerged with a set of keys, which he slid across the counter to Chan. "Just let me know when you want to take her up so I can clear the water."

"Sure. No problem," Chan agreed, and began to walk down the jetty.

When he had expressed admiration for the vintage model of Brewster's seaplane on his last visit, he was being entirely sincere. Chan had always liked flying, ever since he'd been trained as a fighter pilot in the Russian Secret Service. He had flown a boat plane not unlike Brewster's before, and he was very much looking forward to flying this one.

He got straight to work. With skilled efficiency, he replaced the faulty altitude meter with the one he had brought. This new one had a few modifications, namely, it had been wired to a small circuit board attached to a red-and-green diode. These electronic components fit snugly behind the dashboard, leaving no outward evidence of their existence. The circuit board could be operated remotely with Chan's mobile phone, if needed. But if everything went to plan, that wouldn't be necessary. As soon as the gauge hit a pre-programmed altitude, it would trigger the detonator of a small explosive device that Chan had hidden under the plane's fuselage. Should Brewster decide to cut and run, he wouldn't get very far.

Chan returned to the dock manager's shed and handed over the maintenance report to be filed into the logbook. "I'd like to take her up now," Chan said, as Blake checked over the report.

He stepped out of the shed and peered over the water. "There's a yacht coming in," he said, nodding towards the mouth of the harbour. "I'll need to help get her moored. Then I'll radio in and clear the marina for takeoff."

"Of course," Chan replied. "Have to make sure everyone is safe."

A few minutes later, the incoming yacht had docked, and Chan was settling into the cockpit as Blake gave him the radio channel and frequency to reach the marina control. Chan fired up the engine, letting it roar before bringing it down to a low growl.

He gave Blake the okay to release the mooring ropes. Then he gently manoeuvred the craft out into the open water for takeoff.

The plane shuddered as it gained speed and began to climb. The yachts in the marina shrank gradually into toy-like miniatures of themselves. Chan noted that the controls were a little tetchy at first, but once he got a sense of how to handle her, she flew beautifully. It would be a shame to see this old lady retired.

The sky was a perfect, cloudless blue, and the waters below sparkled like ripples of jewel-encrusted silk. As the plane skimmed through the air, Chan took note of the many luxurious villas of Pittwater's wealthy inhabitants tucked up into the rolling hills. Out on the water, dozens of sailing yachts and motor cruisers cut sleek white paths across the azure sea.

He descended slightly as he navigated inland, drifting low over the backwaters. These little inlets stretched for miles, folded in among the lush green slopes. Then he turned back towards the coast. He passed over Lion Island, which stood guard at the place where Pittwater's lagoons met the open water. Loosely following the curves of the shoreline, he came around the side of the Barrenjoey Lighthouse, stationed out on the headland to guide sailors into safe harbour. From there, he flew over the golden sands of Palm Beach, dotted with children making sandcastles, parents lounging on folding chairs with magazines, and surfers wading out into the waves. All in all, he thought to himself, he couldn't have asked for a more perfect day for a joyride.

Chan dialled to the radio frequency for the marina control and informed them that he was heading back. Through a crackle of static, they responded that they'd clear a space for him to come down.

As he circled around and returned to the marina, he guided the plane slowly and smoothly towards the surface of the water. He put down the flaps and made a clean landing.

The dock manager was waiting at the slip to secure the mooring ropes. Chan turned off the engine, reached beneath the dashboard, and flipped a concealed switch to activate the controls for the detonator. Unseen behind the console, a small red light began to blink. Everything was ready.

Chan stepped onto the jetty and handed the keys over to Blake.

"Everything go okay?" Blake asked, slipping the keys into the breast pocket of his vest.

"Oh, yes. Beautiful flight. She's a lovely old lady. I think Mr Brewster will be very happy. Everything's running smoothly now."

"Good," Blake said. "Well, if you're all done, I just need a signature from you on the log before you go."

"Of course." They walked back to the maintenance shed. As Chan picked up the pen to sign the log, he said, "I gave you my card, didn't I? That's right, I did. So you have our phone number. If there's any trouble, just give us a ring."

CHAPTER 78:
LISA'S ADVERTISEMENT

The *Sydney Telegraph's* Classifieds section ran the following ad:

Seeking a lodger for an extra room in a two-bedroom bungalow in Mossman. Must be a mature professional. The let will start at three months and if all goes well, we can move to a six-month agreement. Serious inquiries only, please.

Lisa had hardly seen Paul since the incident in the office. The one time they'd spoken, he had, rather sheepishly, given her a small amount of money, but nowhere close to what he owed. Meanwhile, many of his belongings were still scattered around what used to be his bedroom. She'd given him a final warning: he had until next week to pick up the rest of his things, or she would take them to the rubbish dump.

The late fees from the mortgage company were still piling up. So she was quite pleased when her ad attracted several promising candidates within just a few days. One of them, a man with a light British accent who sounded like he might've been in his thirties, said that he would be interested in stopping by that evening at seven thirty.

Lisa arrived home from work a little early so that she'd have time to neaten up the place. Off and on for the past week, she had continued to experience that strange feeling of being watched while she was in public. She had the same feeling now, as she stood on her front step and unlocked the door. But since nothing had happened to justify her unease so far, she'd more or less convinced herself that it must've all been her imagination.

After changing out of her work clothes, she spent a few minutes tidying. She washed the dishes stacked in the sink and put away the various photocopied pages and notebooks she'd strewn across the kitchen table while working on her latest article.

Then, at around seven twenty pm, there was a knock at the door. Lisa frowned. He was early.

She opened the door to find a tall, smiling man on the step. He wore jeans and a T-shirt, with black hair mussed by the wind.

"Hi," the man said. "My name is Thomas Wang. I phoned earlier, about the ad for the spare bedroom."

"Yes, of course," Lisa said, stepping out of the doorway. "I'm Lisa Gordon, the owner. Please come in."

CHAPTER 79:
AN INSIDE LOOK

Chan could hardly believe his good luck when he saw Lisa's advertisement in the newspaper. Under normal circumstances, he'd have to rely on publicly available blueprints and covert surveillance to get a sense of the interior of her home. But here she was, inviting him inside with a gracious smile.

He followed her into the bungalow and set about committing the layout to memory. Directly inside the front door was a hallway, with a cloakroom on the left-hand side. The corridor opened out into an L-shaped living room with a bay window overlooking the street at the front and patio doors that led to a small yard in the back. On one side of the living room was a galley kitchen. Just to the left of the stove, there was a small door with a key sticking out of the doorknob. When he asked about it, Lisa waved her hand dismissively and told him it was just a utility room.

Through the kitchen was another hallway. This one brought them to the bedrooms. As Lisa opened the door to the second room, she apologised for the mess inside.

"My old lodger left some of his stuff lying around, unfortunately," she said, "but it'll all be cleared out by the end of the week."

He made a show of looking over the room thoughtfully before turning back to her. "Well, everything seems great to me. You've got a very nice place," he said.

"Yes. It is quite nice. I like it." Lisa looked at him curiously. "Sorry, remind me what you do?"

"I'm in software development," Chan replied. "I live in Hong Kong but I've been transferred to the Sydney office for six months. Here…" He pulled out a business card and handed it to her. "The phone number on the back is my supervisor. You're welcome to ring him, if you'd like a reference." In fact, that number had long since been disconnected, but it didn't matter. She wouldn't get a chance to call it.

"That's perfect. Thanks." Lisa accepted the card and pocketed it, then led him back towards the living room. "Let's see… what else. The rent payment will cover electricity, water, and internet. You'll just need to pay for your own food. That's about it, really." They stood opposite each other in a square of sunlight streaming in through the front window. "Any other questions for me?"

"No, I don't think so."

"All right, well, I've got two more people coming in tomorrow. I'll have a chat with everyone and check their references and probably get back to you by the end of the week."

"Wonderful," Chan said as she showed him to the door. "I'll look forward to your call. Nice meeting you, Lisa."

"You, too, Thomas. Have a good night."

"Take care."

CHAPTER 80:
THE INTRUDER

Chan sat in his car, watching the light in Lisa Gordon's living room window.

It was almost midnight, and the street was quiet. A man walking his dog passed by, then disappeared into a house at the end of the block. There was no other movement. A few streetlamps and a handful of solar lights in the neighbours' front gardens provided the only illumination, leaving plenty of shadows in which to hide.

Chan was dressed in a black jogging suit with black gloves. A black mask was at the ready on the middle console.

About fifteen minutes later, the warm gold glow behind the living room curtains vanished, and the light in the primary bedroom came on. Ten minutes after that, the bedroom light went out, too.

Still Chan waited. Nearly an hour passed. By then, almost all of the windows on the street were dark. Every house was silent. The neighbourhood was asleep.

Finally, he slipped the mask over his head, got out of the car, and crossed the road to Lisa's front door. Within a few seconds, he had soundlessly picked the lock and let himself in.

He only made it a few steps into the living room when the sound of a car approaching made him freeze. Headlights suddenly washed into the room through the front window. Someone had pulled up in front of the house.

From outside, Chan heard muffled voices. Two of them. It sounded like a brief, expletive-riddled argument. Then a car door slammed, and tyres screeched off into the distance.

Chan stood perfectly still. He strained his ears, but he heard nothing else.

He decided it must have been one of the neighbours coming back from a late night at the pub. Letting out a breath, he started towards Lisa's bedroom. But he'd hardly moved before there was another sound: the creak of hinges.

The front door started to swing open.

A memory from earlier that day sparked into Chan's mind. The door in the kitchen with the key in the handle. He darted towards it, planning to hide in the utility room until this unwelcome visitor was gone. But when he grabbed the doorknob, he found that the key was gone. With a hiss of frustration, he tried to turn the handle.

Locked.

By then, the interloper had stumbled into the dark kitchen. Before Chan could find somewhere else to hide, an overhead light blazed into life.

The man stared at Chan, his eyes widening and his mouth falling open in a theatrical display of shock. He looked to be in his twenties, very drunk, and dishevelled, as if he'd been bodily tossed out of whatever bar or party he'd just come from. *Gordon's previous lodger*, Chan realised. This must have been the photographer, Paul.

Finally, Paul drew in a long breath to fill his lungs and shouted, "What the fuck?"

Chan reached for him but Paul ducked away, falling into the kitchen counter and sending an avalanche of pots, plates, and glasses to the ground with an ear-splitting crash.

He dived after Paul, seizing a handful of his shirt, and they both fell hard to the tiled floor. Paul fought viciously, flailing and kicking as Chan struggled to pin him. From somewhere within the house, another door slammed open, and panicked footsteps raced towards them. Next time Chan got his head up, he saw Lisa Gordon standing over them, dressed in her pyjamas.

A metal saucepan had clattered to the edge of the kitchen when Paul knocked into the counter. Lisa snatched it up and then backed away again, holding the pan high and looking for a clear shot to bring it down on Chan's head.

In the brief moment that Chan was distracted, Paul managed to get to his feet. He staggered towards Lisa, and Chan lunged after him. Paul tumbled into Lisa with the full force of Chan's momentum. All three of them crashed to the floor. On the way down, Lisa's skull caught the corner of the kitchen wall with a distinct *crack*.

Paul turned to stare in horror at Lisa, now unconscious and bleeding from the back of the head on the tiles beside him. While Paul's attention was diverted, Chan shot to his feet. He spotted a large kitchen knife on the counter and grabbed hold of it. Paul let out a scream as he saw the weapon in Chan's hand and dragged himself to his hands and knees, trying desperately to crawl away. But Chan caught him by the shoulder, roughly spun him around, and buried the blade in Paul's chest.

Paul fell backwards, collapsing across Lisa's motionless body. A sickening gurgle emerged from his throat and blood bubbled up from his mouth before he went completely still.

Chan stood there panting as he looked down at the two bodies at his feet.

This had not at all gone to plan.

He knelt and pressed two fingers to Lisa's neck, finding a clear, strong pulse. She was definitely alive… just unconscious. And she could wake up at any second.

He looked hurriedly around the kitchen, then the living room, searching for something he could use as a way out of this. At last, in the bedroom, he found something useful: a pile of bills from Lisa's mortgage company, with increasingly urgent demands for payment and mounting late fees. Beside it was a notebook, folded open to what looked like a ledger of dollar amounts. After a few moments, Chan puzzled out what the numbers meant: it was a tally of how much money Paul owed Lisa. That would do nicely.

Chan returned to the kitchen and dragged Paul's body off of Lisa's onto the floor opposite her. He set the notebook, still open to the page detailing Paul's unpaid debts, on the kitchen counter, and scattered the bills from the mortgage company around the room, as if they'd been knocked over along with the pots and pans. Then he wrenched the knife from Paul's chest, held it over Lisa, and flicked the blade a few times. Once her face and clothes were sprinkled with Paul's blood, Chan carefully tucked the knife into her limp hand.

Then he walked down the hall and opened the front door a crack, listening closely for any noise. But all was once again silent.

Chan slipped across the street to his car. He got in, opened the glove compartment, dug out a pay-as-you-go burner phone, and dialled the police. In an Australian accent, he told the dispatcher that he had heard a disturbance coming from a house on his street. "A lot of shouting and banging, and then some screaming." He gave Lisa's address and hung up.

As he shifted into gear and started to drive, he used one hand to pry open the back of the phone. He plucked out the SIM card and then dropped it out the window of the moving vehicle.

He rolled the window back up and the car sped off into the night.

CHAPTER 81:
CLOSING IN ON THE KILLER

After months of false starts and dead ends, the pieces had finally started to come together.

At the petrol station in Goulburn, Ann and Ryan interviewed the cashier and took a copy of the store's security footage, which captured the odd interaction the cashier had described. In the video, a man abruptly shoved past an older woman, slammed his money on the counter, and stormed out. There was no audio, but the cashier said that the incident had taken place while she and the other customer were discussing a news report about the murders in Melbourne.

The disposable sheets and medical gown, plus a surgical cap that was recovered later, were being analysed in the forensics lab. Ryan and Ann were waiting on the results to verify whether the blood matched the Melbourne victims.

Meanwhile, a report had come in from Thailand. It turned out that Benjamin Lovett had been arrested in Chiang Mai for selling marijuana in backpacker bars. He'd been held in a local jail for several months, mainly because he had no personal identification to prove who he was. According to his statement, Lovett had come to Thailand with an old friend who was part of the same class at his medical residency in London. But a few weeks before the arrest, the friend had run off on him, and taken Lovett's passport with him.

For the next several days after their return from Goulburn, Ryan, Ann and Haines coordinated between the Sydney and Melbourne offices, compiling an ever-growing pool of information about the killer. Interviews, security tapes, forensic reports… slowly but surely, it was beginning to form a portrait of the man they were searching for.

One morning, after they had been in Melbourne nearly a week, Ryan and Ann were in Haines's incident room, going over a new report that had just come in from forensics. They'd hoped it would be the results of the testing on the bloodstained sheets and gown, but that was still a work in progress. It turned out to be something just as tantalising, though. The DNA analysis from the strand of hair found on the flowers in Barbara Stevenson's apartment. The hair wasn't a match for the florist, nor Stevenson, nor either of the victims… which meant they had a DNA sample from an unknown person, almost certainly the killer.

While they stood at Haines's desk, discussing what this latest breakthrough could mean, Ann's cell phone rang. She glanced at the screen, told them, "Hold that thought," and stepped over to a quieter corner before answering the call. Over the ambient noise of the incident room, Ryan couldn't hear what she said, but he caught her giving him an odd look as she spoke.

A few moments later, Ann hung up and crossed back over to Ryan. Her expression was uncharacteristically solemn.

"That was Sydney headquarters," she said. "Lisa Gordon has been arrested for manslaughter."

CHAPTER 82:
BREWSTER AND
THE TAXI DRIVER

Brewster was sitting on the sofa in his living room, leaning over the coffee table. He had the evening news on in the background as he sorted through some personal papers, looking for anything he ought to burn before he left. He paused as he heard a familiar name on the television.

"In breaking news tonight, we've just learned that award-winning political journalist Lisa Gordon has been arrested. She is currently being held on suspicion of manslaughter. The bond hearing is scheduled for tomorrow morning. We'll bring you more details on this developing story…"

But Brewster didn't need to hear anymore. He already had a pretty good idea of what might've happened to Lisa Gordon. It seemed that Chan had caught up to her after all.

"Mr Brewster?"

Brewster turned at the sound of his maid's voice. Her name was Allison, and she had worked for him for years. She was a sharp girl, one who rarely needed to be told anything twice. And, importantly, she was discreet. Which was why he had asked to have a word with her before she went home for the day.

"You wanted to see me?" she said, standing in the doorway to the living room.

"Yes, I did. Does your brother still pick you up after work?"

"Yes, sir. My brother Joe."

"Joe, right. He's a taxi driver, isn't he?"

Allison frowned at him, clearly unsure where this was going. "He is, sir."

"Good. I have a little favour to ask of him. It's all above board, of course, but it is a delicate matter. Strictly confidential. If you can help me, you'll both be compensated for your efforts."

She was silent for a few moments, regarding Brewster warily. "What's the favour," she finally asked, "and how much?"

•

Joe Carrington watched as his sister Allison disappeared into her apartment building. On the drive there, she had relayed to him a series of instructions, and he repeated them to himself under his breath as he pulled back onto the road.

The instructions were rather complicated, and he did not intend to make a mistake. The amount of money Allison had quoted him was worth a week of driving the cab. He was not about to let it slip through his fingers.

When Allison had gotten out of the car, she'd left behind two parcels, a sheet of paper with unfamiliar handwriting, an envelope with a letter in it, and a keycard. All of them were still sitting on the passenger's seat. He glanced at them occasionally as he made his way towards his first destination.

Half an hour later, he arrived at a large industrial park, nearly abandoned in the long shadows of late evening. Among a row of nondescript concrete warehouses, he finally spotted a building with a sign on the front that read Malloch Property. He parked, picked up the keycard, the envelope, and one of the parcels, and got out of the car.

He used the keycard to let himself in through the glass double doors. Inside, he was greeted by a long, empty corridor. If there was anyone else in the building, Joe never saw them.

The right side of the hallway was lined floor to ceiling with individually numbered postal boxes. Joe walked along the rows of grey metal cubes, his footsteps echoing in the silent hall, eyes skimming over the neat black labels until he finally stopped in front of number 142.

He opened the box, set the parcel inside, and took the key off the hook from inside the door. Then he closed and locked the compartment. Immediately, he dropped the key inside the envelope and sealed it.

He went outside, climbed back into his car, and started driving again.

His next visit was to a law firm. Feeling somewhat out of place in the ornately decorated lobby, he held the second parcel and asked the receptionist to please tell John Elvey's secretary to come down.

"Is that package for Mr Elvey?" she asked, nodding to the parcel under his arm. "I can take it to him." She held out her hand expectantly.

But Joe shook his head. "I'm sorry, miss, but I was told not to give this to anyone except John Elvey's secretary."

The receptionist frowned. "Who is it from?" she asked, rather rudely.

"It's from Bully." When the receptionist raised her pencilled-in eyebrows, Joe added, "She'll know who it is."

The woman appeared sceptical, but she picked up the phone and spoke into it briefly, then hung up and looked back at Joe. "Marcella will be down shortly."

Joe nodded his thanks and wandered away from the desk. Not long after, an elevator at the other end of the lobby dinged. A well-dressed woman who looked to be in her sixties stepped out and crossed over to the receptionist. The two of them exchanged a few words. Then she walked over to Joe, who unconsciously straightened up as she approached.

"I'm Marcella, John Elvey's secretary. I believe you have something for me."

Joe nodded and held out the parcel.

Marcella took it from him with a curt nod. "Mr Elvey will receive this promptly. Thank you very much for your time." She turned and vanished back into the elevator. The receptionist stared openly at Joe as he walked back across the lobby and out of the door.

He had just one errand left, and he suspected it might be the trickiest. He needed to deliver the sealed envelope with the key in it to the office of the *Sydney Telegraph*.

There was a line at the front desk in the lobby, and he had to wait for some time before he could speak to this receptionist. When it was finally his turn, he said, "I need to see the paper's editor."

She gave him an amused little smile. "I'm afraid that's not possible, sir, unless you have an appointment."

"I don't have an appointment. But it's very important that I see him."

"May I ask why? Perhaps there's something I can do to help."

"I need to give him something. If I can't see him, could you possibly call the editor's secretary and ask them to please give him this message?" He slid the handwritten piece of paper across the desk towards the receptionist.

She took the paper and read it. Then she looked back up at him with a frown and wordlessly picked up the phone, cradling it to her ear with her shoulder.

Someone answered, and the receptionist explained the situation. Joe didn't quite catch what the other person said, but the receptionist responded, "Well, he's adamant that it should go to Mr Palmer, personally. He's given me a note…" The receptionist cleared her throat and, with a last uncertain glance at Joe, read the paper aloud: "To Pammy. Here's a love letter from an old friend. Most sincerely, Bully."

A long pause followed. The receptionist lowered her voice, although Joe could still hear her plainly, and asked in an undertone, "Do you want me to call security?"

The person on the other line gave a reply that sounded like, "No. That's all right. Let me talk to Brian."

A few minutes later, a man in a suit jacket appeared from the elevator and strode across the lobby to stand in front of Joe. "Did Bully send you personally?" he asked, by way of a greeting.

"Yes, sir."

"Did he say anything else?"

"He just told me to give you this." Joe held out the envelope. "And he said that he hopes you and your family are well."

The editor accepted the envelope slowly. "Very good. Thank you. Tell Bully we are well and hope that he's in good health."

"I will, sir. Have a good night."

The man pivoted on his heel and returned to the elevator.

Joe left in a hurry, eager to be back in the familiar interior of his car. The money for this little assignment was good, but it was all too much secrecy and mystery for his taste. He would be glad to go back to driving his boring old taxi.

•

That evening, after Allison left with Joe, Brewster sat at his desk in his study, picked up the phone, and dialled.

"Charles Pearce speaking."

"It's me, Brewster."

"Wayne! What a surprise. Always good to hear…"

"Listen, Charles. I'm calling because I want you to know that Johnson has gotten suspicious about the building supplies. His accountants and surveyors have been looking at their estimates and they've caught on to the short measures."

"Oh, relax. I know all about Johnson's suspicions. His people contacted me. But not to worry. I've sent six cargo ships to Newcastle, and a convoy of lorries, with accurate deliveries. That will smooth things over. They'll forget their suspicions and we can pick back up on the short measures in a few weeks."

Brewster let out a breath and leaned back in his office chair. "All right. Glad to hear that. I knew it was all in good hands."

"Of course," Charles said airily. "No need to fret."

"Well, here's hoping we can get together sometime soon."

"Absolutely. Take a trip out to Perth sometime, Wayne. You know you're always welcome. And my family sends their love."

CHAPTER 83:
BACK TO SYDNEY

The developments in the investigation were suddenly moving at a breakneck pace. Although their time in Melbourne had been more than worthwhile, Ryan and Ann decided that it was time to get back to Sydney.

They bid farewell to Haines and his team, and booked the first available flight out of Tullamarine Airport. As they got settled into their seats – Ryan by the window, Ann on the aisle, as usual – they discussed the latest news of the case.

While Ryan and Ann were still in Melbourne, the Sydney office had faxed over a document. It was an order form, dated six months ago, from a place called Vital Medical Supplies. The name on the order was one Benjamin Lovett. The form indicated that the purchase was for North Sydney General Practice. But when the detectives followed up with the hospital, the staff members had no record of that purchase, nor of any employees named Benjamin Lovett.

Shortly after that, the forensics report on the Goulburn findings had finally come in. It proved conclusively that the blood splashed on the medical gown and spilled on the disposable plastic sheets belonged to Hanna Lindgren and Samantha Whelan. That wasn't all… the last piece of evidence that had been recovered, the surgical cap, contained a few hairs that matched the one found on the bouquet in Stevenson's apartment. Now they had all but incontrovertible DNA evidence of the killer at the scene of the crime and in the town of Goulburn on the way back to Sydney. And, thanks to the security footage from the petrol station, they also had the number plate, make and model of the car the killer was using.

Ann had told their supervisor, Peter Alford, about these new updates. He'd responded by immediately deploying additional resources to the case. More officers, more technicians doing lab work… it was all hands on deck. After months with next to nothing to go on, they were almost overwhelmed by all the puzzle pieces they now had to fit together.

Time was not on their side. After the last two victims, the killer still needed an 'H' to finish spelling out his message. No one was saying it outright, but they all knew it was a matter of when, not if, he would strike again.

The stewardess came by to take their orders for in-flight drinks. In the brief silence that followed, Ryan finally broached the topic he'd been studiously avoiding.

"So," he said, as the stewardess handed over two glasses of chardonnay, "have you heard anything more about Lisa Gordon's arrest?"

"Nothing much," Ann replied. "The name of the victim was Paul Seidel. Apparently he was Lisa's lodger. He'd moved out, but he owed her quite a lot of money. Seems like he came back to her house late one night, there was an argument, and things got physical."

"Has Lisa said anything?"

"So far, she's denied the whole thing. Insists there was a third person there, a masked intruder. She says it was him and Paul who were fighting. When she tried to intervene, she ended up getting shoved into the wall and the impact knocked her out. Supposedly."

"Who called it in?"

"A concerned neighbour, saying that they heard a commotion coming from a house on their street. When the police arrived, the front door was unlocked, and Lisa Gordon was unconscious on the floor with the bloody knife in her hand. There were overdue bills and letters from her mortgage company scattered around the room. Paul had been stabbed in the chest and was declared dead at the scene. No sign of forced entry, or any masked intruder. She was taken to the station as soon as she woke up, and ever since she's been telling anyone who would listen that she didn't do it. But the prosecutors are looking to charge her with manslaughter in self-defence, at minimum."

Ryan shook his head. "I've seen all kinds of killings in this job, and self-defence is the most common motivation. So I can't say it's impossible." He frowned into his wine. "But it does seem strange that she was reporting on the suspicious deaths of those Sydney politicians just before this happened."

"What do you mean?"

"I'm just not sure if it's all as straightforward as it looks."

Ann raised her brows. "The evidence against her is pretty damning. Are you getting soft, Campbell? You know, you never really said how your dinner date went with her."

He scowled. "Stop it. All I'm saying is, there are two sides to every story. We can't know yet whether she's guilty or not."

Ann shrugged. "I suppose you're right," she said. "We'll just have to wait and see."

CHAPTER 84:
LISA'S BAIL

Lisa was acutely aware that her situation was not good.

As soon as she was arrested, she'd been interrogated, photographed, and fingerprinted. That was two days ago. Since then, she'd been held in a cold, cramped cell, and every officer and detective she'd spoken to had dismissed her increasingly frantic protests. No one believed her about the man in the mask. And the bloody knife that had been found in her hand wasn't helping matters.

"Besides, we already talked to your co-workers," one of the detectives told her exasperatedly during one of these exchanges.

"Yes? And did they tell you I would never, ever do something like this?" she demanded.

"No. They told us that not two weeks ago, you had a heated argument with Paul in front of the whole office about the money he owed you."

Lisa slumped against the bars of her cell.

Considering the hopelessness of her situation, she was rather astonished when a guard arrived, unlocked the door, and gestured her out into the dingy corridor. "Your bail's been paid," he said, in response to her look of disbelief.

"By whom?"

"Guess you'll have to go and see."

The guard led her to the front of the station. There, Brian Palmer, her editor, was hunched over the police sergeant's desk, filling out paperwork.

"Brian?" she said, equal parts pleased and surprised to see him. "You paid my bail?"

"Not quite," he said, signing one last form before clicking the pen and looking up at her with a frown. "The paper did."

CHAPTER 85:
BRIAN'S STORY

A few hours later, Lisa and Brian sat in his office while he poured a glass of whisky for each of them. He'd barely said a word from the time they left the police station until they arrived at the *Sydney Telegraph* building. Lisa sensed a tempestuous mood beneath his stony silence, so she waited for him to speak first.

Finally, after a long draft of his whisky, Brian said, "I had to pull some strings to get the paper's owners to pay the bail. It wasn't easy."

"I appreciate it, Brian. Honestly. Thank you. But I'm innocent. I swear there was a third person in my kitchen. He must have been the one who stabbed Paul, not me. I know it sounds ridiculous but I've had the feeling that someone's been following me for weeks, and…"

"It's okay. I believe you."

Lisa's voice died in her throat. She stared at him in surprise. "You do?"

"I do. There's more going on here than either of us know. But there are some things I should tell you." He stood up from the chair behind his desk and gestured to a series of framed photos on the wall, most of them taken from the decks of yachts. "You know that I used to sail."

"Yes. You've told me that you were quite good," said Lisa, who could not begin to guess where this was going.

"That's right. For years I was on a racing team. We used to race every Thursday night in Sydney Harbour. We won a lot of trophies over the years. The three main members of the team were Wayne Brewster, Sergeant Jack MacDonald and myself, along with a couple of younger crewmembers. The three of us had nicknames for ourselves… Bully, Scotty and Pammy. We sailed and drank our way all over the Sydney coast. This was all a long time ago, of course, before I was married. Anyway, after a couple of years racing in the harbour, we decided to enter the 1998 Sydney to Hobart Race. The trouble was that none of us had our Yachtmaster certificate. Every team who wanted to enter needed at least one person on their crew with that certificate. But Bully – Brewster – said that he knew someone he could ask to join us. That person turned out to be Howard Johnson."

"The Prime Minister?" Lisa said, dubiously.

"This was long before he was Prime Minister. But yes, him. And straight from the start, Scotty and I were not keen on him. Johnson thought he knew better than everyone, never showed any respect to the rest of us. He was always barking commands and snapping at the younger crewmembers. None of us were fond of him, but Bully had already entered us into the race, and we were determined to make a good showing."

Lisa had just started to put something together in her head. "Wait. You said the 1998 Sydney to Hobart," she said slowly. "That was…"

Brian nodded. "The worst disaster in yacht racing history. We knew from the start that the weather forecast was bad, but we had no idea how ugly it would turn out by the end of the race. Johnson was at the helm, shouting out orders. We could barely hear him over the wind. By midway through the course, I was terrified. Massive waves were crashing over the bow. Some of the ropes holding the foresail snapped. I thought the sail would be torn clean off by the wind. The young crewmembers on the deck could hardly stand up. Johnson had too much sail out, and we could see that it was going to drag us over. Bully and I were shouting at Johnson to reef down the mainsail, but he just kept saying, 'No, we can ride it out.' And then, out of nowhere, the biggest wave I'd ever seen in my life hit us broadside. Next thing I knew I was underwater. When I came up, the yacht had capsized."

Brian fell silent for several moments. By the time he spoke again, his gaze had left Lisa and shifted to the window, where he seemed to be looking towards the harbour in the distance. "We floated there for hours, being tossed around by the waves. In the end, fifty-five sailors had to be rescued. Bully, Scotty, Johnson and I were among them. But not everyone was so lucky. Six people died that day. One of them was a crewmember on our yacht. Andrew Barker. He drowned when the boat overturned. Seventeen years old. Telling his parents what happened was the hardest thing I've ever done." Brian let out a slow breath. "The three of us never sailed together again after that. We all drifted apart over the years. These days I only sail with my wife and kids."

Lisa didn't answer right away, caught between surprise and sympathy for the haunted expression in his eyes. Quietly, she said, "I never knew any of this."

"Nobody does," Brian answered bluntly before finishing the rest of his drink in one swallow. "It's not something I like to talk about."

"So why are you telling me now?"

"Because the night before your bail hearing, I got a letter from Wayne Brewster. Lisa, I believe your life is in danger."

She stared at him. "What do you mean?"

"Your articles have upset a lot of powerful people. Those stories you wrote on the deaths of the Sydney politicians… I think you were onto something. They were more than just accidents."

"Do you have any proof?"

"No. But I know you didn't kill Paul. I think this whole thing was a setup to get you out of the way, because you'd gotten too close to the truth. That's why I believe you about the intruder. My guess is that he was there to kill you. If I'm right, then he'll try again."

Fear began to twist into Lisa's stomach as the reality of Brian's words set in. "I can't believe someone would want me dead," she said numbly.

Brian offered a mirthless smile. "You always were a bit too good at your job."

She took a deep breath, trying to force herself to think rationally despite the buzzing of panic that had surfaced in her brain. "I wish Detective Campbell was back in Sydney," she murmured. "I could really use his advice about what to do. I'd spoken with him about those three allegedly accidental deaths."

He gave her a quizzical look. "I didn't realise you two were close," he said. "I thought you disliked him."

Utterly against her will, Lisa's face pinkened enough for Brian to get his answer. "Ah," he said. "I see."

"Anyway, he can't help me now," she said. "He's down in Melbourne on a case."

"Well, I'm not Ryan, but if you want my advice, I think we need to get you out of the way for a while."

"Hold on. What exactly did Brewster say that made you think all this?"

Brian settled back into his chair before he responded. When he did speak, he seemed to choose his words carefully. "Brewster's letter said that there are things going on that are beyond his control. He said that when he ran for Sydney governor, he had no idea that Prime Minister Johnson was out of his mind with power and ambition, but he knows better now. He saw that you had been arrested, and he felt that he needed to do something."

"Brewster said he needed to do something for me?" Lisa repeated, torn between disbelief and dread.

"Yes. He believes his own life is in danger, and so he made arrangements for certain information to reach the press through Lisa Gordon of the *Sydney Telegraph*."

"*What?*" she spluttered. "Why me? I thought Brewster hated me."

"I don't know. But frankly, I don't want to be a part of any of this, so I'm going to tell you what he told me and then wash my hands of it. He's given you a key to a postal box. He says that there's evidence inside it. He did everything he could to make sure it's secure and that no one else knows about it, but he can't be sure of that."

"Fuck me." Lisa shook her head. "If someone is already trying to kill me, I don't know if I want to get involved with Brewster's postal box full of evidence. Can't we go to the police?"

"Brewster doesn't think so. He wrote that Howard Johnson's corruption has reached every level of government office, including the police commissioners. He says they can't be trusted."

"You have to print that letter," Lisa said firmly, meeting Brian's eyes. "You have to tell the world what's going on."

"I can't do that."

"What? Why not?"

"A letter addressed to Pammy and signed Bully? The paper would have my head if I printed that with my name on it. Besides, we have three politicians and one photographer dead. I don't want to add an editor and a journalist to that list."

Brian rubbed his temples. "Like I said, I'd prefer to just stay out of the whole affair. But I'm worried about your safety."

Lisa managed a choked laugh. "You're not the only one."

"I've talked it over with my wife, and we may have a plan to keep you safe. At least until we figure out what's happening and see what Brewster's next move is."

"Go on, then."

"I remember you said you knew how to sail."

"I've done some sailing round Sydney Harbour, but that's all. I'm just a novice, really. Why?"

"Well, we have a small yacht that we sail out of Woolloomooloo Yacht Club. Last month, a couple – old friends of ours – borrowed it and took it up to Palm Beach. They were moored at the Prince Albert Yacht Club in Pittwater when one of them got a call that he was urgently needed back at work, so they both took a cab back to Sydney. My wife and I were planning to go up and sail the yacht back to Woolloomooloo, but we haven't gotten round to it yet. If you go to the Prince Albert Yacht Club, you can take the boat and hide out in the backwaters for a while. Pittwater has loads of little inlets and lagoons. It would be easy for you to find a place out of the way somewhere and hide out until it's safe for you to come back."

She gave him a sceptical look. "I told you, I'm really not much of a sailor. And even if I could handle your yacht, what would I do for food and supplies? Besides, I'd be breaking my bail conditions. Not a great look for someone claiming to be innocent."

"It's up to you. Your other option is to go home and wait to get attacked by another intruder, or get hit by a car, or mysteriously fall overboard on the ferry."

"Okay, I get it," she said, wincing, and then let out a long sigh. "Guess I don't really have much of a choice."

"Agreed. Now listen. My wife is waiting for me to call her. She's in a rental car, just in case anyone is keeping tabs on our own cars. I packed a bag for you. You've got your laptop, clothes, and a few other things I picked up from your house. Plus food and some basic supplies. It's all in the boot. There's also a piece of paper with the call sign for our yacht club and the radio frequency to use in an emergency. If anything happens, just call and say you need to speak to me. I suggest that you leave straight from here and not go to your house, since it's likely being watched."

"Wow," Lisa said, impressed despite herself. "You've really thought of everything."

"Look, Lisa, I don't know how deep any of this goes," Brian said seriously. "And I've got a family to protect. As long as you're in danger, so am I, and so are they." He shook his head, suddenly looking older and more tired than Lisa could ever remember him. "Let's all just try to get to the other side of this. Are you ready to go?"

She squared her shoulders and nodded. "I'm ready. There's just one thing. If Ryan Campbell contacts you, tell him what's happening. You can trust him."

"All right. I will." He picked up his phone. "I'll tell my wife to meet us in the basement car park. She'll take you to Pittwater."

After a terse conversation, Brian hung up and turned back to Lisa. "She'll be here in a few minutes. We can head down there now. But first…" He reached over, unlocked a drawer in his desk and extracted an envelope. He held it out to her, his expression grim. "Take this."

She stared at it without moving. "What is it?"

"Brewster's letter. And the key to the postal box. It's yours."

Reluctantly, Lisa leaned forward and accepted the envelope. "Why is Brewster doing this?" she asked softly.

"If I know Brewster? To save his own skin," Brian said. "Now let's go."

They took the elevator down to the car park. Before long, a nondescript black car pulled up and a woman rolled down the driver's side window.

"Lisa," Brian said, "I'd like to introduce my wife, Debbie Palmer."

Debbie gave a little wave. "Nice to meet you, dear," she said. "I'm only sorry it's not under better circumstances. But let's get you somewhere safe, shall we?"

"That sounds great," Lisa said, managing a weak smile. She turned to Brian. "Thank you for arranging all of this."

"Of course. There's one more thing." He took out a prepaid burner phone from an inside pocket of his jacket. "Take this. I've got one too. The number for mine is already programmed into yours. Keep your regular mobile off. It could be used to track you."

"Got it." Swallowing hard, Lisa started to get into the passenger's seat, but Debbie stopped her.

"Better not, dear," she said. "If I were you, I'd lay down in the back until we're out of the city. Just in case the *Telegraph* building is under surveillance."

"Of course," Lisa said in a slightly strangled voice, as if she'd committed a breach of well-known etiquette. "Silly me."

She climbed in the back and lay down across the two seats, then looked up at Brian through the window.

"Be safe, both of you," he said. "Lisa, I'll be in touch as soon as I find out anything more off Brewster."

Lisa nodded. "Thanks again, Brian."

"Good luck."

Debbie put the car in drive, and they set off for Pittwater.

CHAPTER 86:
BREWSTER'S NEXT MOVE

Standing at the French doors in his study, Brewster looked out absently over Pittwater as he held his phone to his ear. After a few rings, Blake, the dock manager, answered.

"Blake, it's Brewster. Has the maintenance appointment for my boat plane been scheduled yet?"

"Oh, it's all taken care of already, Mr Brewster. Altitude gauge replaced, instruments recalibrated. You should be all set."

It was a welcome surprise. Brewster had been worried that he would have to wait quite a while for the altitude gauge he'd ordered, but he was pleased with how quickly it had all been sorted out.

Earlier that day, Johnson had called to say that he was visiting Sydney this week and that he would be coming to see Brewster. He hadn't been specific about the purpose of his visit, but Brewster knew it wasn't likely to be a friendly check-in.

Before Johnson showed up, Brewster wanted to make sure that the boat plane was ready to go. He drove down to the marina and went straight to the dock manager's hut, carrying a couple of overnight bags with him.

"Morning, Mr Brewster," Blake greeted him.

"Morning. I was wondering if I could take a look at the maintenance report from a few days ago. Just to see what was done."

"Of course. Here you are." Blake pulled out the thick binder from the shelves under the counter, flipped through it, and then spun it around towards Brewster.

He skimmed over the page, finding nothing unexpected. It seemed like all of the issues he'd spotted during his own inspection had been addressed. As he closed the binder and handed it back, Blake noted, "It wasn't the normal maintenance guy who came out."

Brewster frowned slightly. "Oh?"

"No, this was someone I'd never seen before. Said the regular guy was up on the Gold Coast doing a refit on an old model." Blake seemed to notice the concern in Brewster's face. "This bloke seemed to really know his stuff, though," he added. "Did a thorough job, from what I could tell. He took her on a test flight and said everything was working smooth as you would expect. He really appreciated the old bird, by the sound of it."

Brewster nodded, somewhat reassured. He'd been using Sydney Aviation Maintenance & Supply for many years now, and he had great confidence in their engineers. Not that he had much of a choice at this point, anyway.

"Will you be taking the plane up for a flight today, Mr Brewster?"

"No, unfortunately. I've a lot to do today. I just wanted to stop by and check her over. Oh, and I want to get her fuelled up for the regatta."

"Of course." Blake held out the keys to Brewster. "All right if we wait until Monday on that last? The fuel pontoon is packed today, it being such a nice weekend and all."

"That would be fine." Brewster took the keys, picked up his bags, and headed down the jetty towards his plane.

The sun was glistening off of her wings. She really was a beauty. He found himself looking forward to taking her up for the regatta, and then wondered whether he would be able to attend this year, or if he would be gone by then.

He opened the door to the cockpit and hoisted up the bags. There were a couple of watertight lockers behind the backseats of the cabin. Working quickly, he emptied the contents of the bags into the lockers… cash, clothes, passports, the compromised hard drive from his original laptop. Everything ought to be safe there until he needed it.

Then he climbed out onto the plane's large floats, ducking underneath the fuselage to check the wing flaps and tail flaps. All of it looked to be in good working order. He returned to the cockpit and sat in the pilot's seat, looking over the instrument panel. With satisfaction, he noted that the dashboard had been cleaned.

He put the key in the ignition, pulled out the choke, and turned over the engine. It started up straightaway. He revved it a few times and let the engine tick over into neutral until all the gauges read out at the correct levels. As far as he could tell, everything had been perfectly calibrated. Brewster was pleased. The boat plane was primed and ready for a quick getaway.

"Everything okay with the old bird?" Blake asked as Brewster handed the keys back over to him at the dock manager's shed.

"Oh, yes, seems they did an excellent job. Those folks at Sydney Aviation haven't let me down yet. Listen, Blake, don't forget to have her fuelled on Monday, all right?"

"Not to worry, Mr Brewster, I've already got it here in the log."

Brewster nodded. He returned to his car and started the drive back to his villa.

CHAPTER 87:
LISA GETS SET TO SAIL

By the time Lisa and Debbie arrived at the Prince Albert Yacht Club, clouds had rolled in, and the sky had turned to a moody, overcast grey. They avoided the car park, which was quite crowded, and instead pulled into a space in front of the marina's chandlery.

They got out of the car and Debbie opened the trunk. As she started to unload the bags, Lisa stared uneasily around at the groups of people coming out of the chandlery, eating at tables out in front of the restaurant, and clustered out on the jetties. The last few hours had put her on edge, and she found herself startled by every shout or loud noise.

"Awfully crowded, isn't it?" she mentioned to Debbie.

"It's all the crews getting ready for the Pittwater Regatta. They're doing trials for their starting positions, or competing in smaller day races here, for the smaller clubs and younger crewmembers showing off for their girlfriends." Debbie handed over one of the duffel bags to Lisa. "Don't worry, Lisa. I think the crowds will work to our advantage. With all this going on, no one is going to take any notice of us."

Lisa wasn't prepared for the weight of the bag Debbie handed to her. It was so heavy she nearly dropped it. "Brian's packed me enough provisions to start a new life out at sea," she muttered.

"Well, better to have it and not need it, and all that," Debbie said. She lifted one bag out of the trunk and hooked the strap on her shoulder, then did the same with another. "Do you think you can get the last one?"

Lisa managed to haul the last bag from out of the trunk, and the one she was already holding promptly fell to the asphalt.

"I think we'll have to make a second trip," she panted.

"Do you need some help with those?"

They both turned at the sound of a young man's voice. He nodded to the bag now sitting at Lisa's feet. "I'm one of the marina hands. I can help you carry your bags, if you like."

"That'd be lovely, dear. Thank you," Debbie answered. She handed one of her bags over to him. He took it and then picked up the one on the ground, so that he had two and Lisa and Debbie each had one.

The marina hand gestured politely to Debbie. "Lead the way."

She slammed the trunk shut and guided them down the Jetty. "We're going to mooring 158 the yacht's called the *Paper Chase,*" she said, as they passed a series of small posts numbering each mooring.

Finally, they arrived in front of a mid-sized yacht. The marina hand jumped on board, set the bags down, then returned to the rail.

"Here, give those to me," he said, extending his hands down so that he could haul up the two remaining bags to the deck. Then he jumped back down on to the jetty.

"Thanks so much," Lisa told him.

"Happy to help. If you need anything else, just let me know. I'll be around the marina or up in the chandlery. Catch you later." With a brief smile, he turned and headed back towards the crowded grounds of the yacht club.

Lisa and Debbie climbed aboard the *Paper Chase* and brought the bags into the cabin. The two of them put away the food in the fridge and freezer, and then Debbie gave Lisa a quick tour.

"I'm glad to see it's electric," Lisa said as Debbie pointed out the head and the shower. "Can't say I'm sorry that I won't have to hand-pump the head."

"Oh, no. This thing is kitted out with all the latest appliances. Fridge, coffeemaker, telly, the lot. You've got a little satellite out on the stern that will let you pick up radio, mobile and TV signal, as long as you're not too far out at sea. Now come on, let me show you around the controls."

Debbie led Lisa over to the navigation table. She pointed out on the charts where Lisa might have some luck finding a safe place in the out-of-the-way inlets of Pittwater. In the cockpit, Debbie offered a rundown on all the instruments and gauges… wind speed and direction, depth sounder, speedometer, compass. She pointed out the radio, the throttle and the gear levers. Back up on the deck, she did a quick demonstration to show Lisa how to raise and lower the sails, and how to operate the electric anchor. Thankfully, it was all more or less the same as the yacht that Lisa had learned to sail.

Lisa made a point of asking where to find the lifejackets, the controls for the lifeboat, and the emergency flares, all of which, Debbie was quick to reassure her, were easily accessible and in good working order.

"I'll let you get acquainted with the place while I go make a pot of coffee, hmm?" Debbie said, patting Lisa's shoulder.

While Debbie went to the galley, Lisa took the rucksack with her clothes, laptop, sleeping bag and other personal belongings to the small berth. Then she went back to the cockpit to go over the controls again. She was reasonably confident that she knew what she was doing. But at the same time, she'd never sailed alone, and she'd certainly never sailed alone while breaking her bail and evading an assassin's attempts to kill her. *First time for everything*, she thought darkly.

Lisa returned to the tiny dining table and accepted the cup of coffee Debbie offered to her. "Brian's only told me a little of what's going on," Debbie said, sipping at her own mug. "It all sounds very dangerous. But you seem like you've got a good head on your shoulders. I'm sure you'll make it out all right."

"I hope so," Lisa agreed with a faint smile.

"Brian thought it would be best if you left the marina as soon as possible," she said. "I'll settle up the mooring fees and tell them we're sailing back to Sydney, just in case anyone comes asking after you. You probably want to be on your way."

Lisa shifted uneasily. "I'd rather spend the night here, and then get an early start in the morning."

"Don't worry, there are some mooring buoys not far from here. You can just motor on the engine. No need to put the sails up tonight."

She nodded, trying to soothe her jangling nerves. "Thanks, Debbie," she said. "I really appreciate all your help."

Debbie seemed to sense her lingering apprehension and gave her a reassuring smile. "It'll be all right, Lisa. Don't think about it too much. Take everything in your stride and you'll be just fine." With that, Debbie rose to her feet, setting down her empty mug. "Come on, then. I'll help you cast off."

Lisa fastened her life jacket as Debbie climbed back down on to the jetty and released the mooring ropes. Taking her place at the helm, Lisa drew a deep breath and experimentally revved the engine a few times. Then she reversed out of the mooring and began to manoeuvre slowly out of the marina.

When she glanced back, Debbie gave her a wave, then turned and walked down the jetty.

Lisa turned to face forward, now alone as her eyes fixed on the horizon.

CHAPTER 88:
RYAN'S BACK IN SYDNEY

When they arrived at the Sydney Airport, Ryan let Ann take the first taxi. As he waited for the next one, he found himself staring tiredly into the middle distance, his eyes and mind unfocused. He was more worn out than he'd realised.

He got home and dropped his bag off in his bedroom, then went to check his voicemail. There were two messages, both from his daughter. In the first one, she told him that she'd won first place at a swimming competition at her school. The excitement in her voice made him smile despite his exhaustion. The second one was simply asking if she would be able to talk to him soon. He checked the clock… it was too late to call her now, but he resolved to check in with her as soon as he could.

There was nothing from Lisa. He'd heard that someone had paid her bail, so he tried to call her cell phone. But she didn't answer.

Trying to put her out of his mind, Ryan took a quick shower and fell into bed. Within moments, he'd fallen fast asleep.

He slept straight through to the next morning. Luckily he'd thought to set an alarm, or else he probably would've dozed until noon. But he managed to wake up early enough to have breakfast and coffee at home before arriving at the office around nine am.

At ten, Ann called a meeting in the incident room. She briefed the team on everything she and Ryan had learned in Melbourne and then asked if anyone had any updates to share.

"We just had a report come in from Redfern," offered Detective Julie Ross. "Someone bought a car from a second-hand lot and when they tried to register it, it was flagged as having been stolen. The plates didn't match the registration. From the vehicle description, I think it may be the same car that the killer was seen driving in Goulburn."

"Good find," Ann replied with an approving nod. "We'll need to get up there and do some interviews. Find out who sold the car and when. If it turns out to be the vehicle we're looking for, then we'll have a forensics team do a full sweep on it. Any other updates?" She glanced around the room, but no one volunteered. "In that case, we should have somebody follow up with North Sydney General Practice about the person who placed the medical purchase order under Benjamin Lovett's name."

Ann's eyes travelled around the ring of faces looking back at her with a fiercely determined expression. "We've got descriptions from witnesses, DNA samples, and photo evidence. We're getting close, people. Don't let up now."

After the meeting, Ryan went back to his desk in the incident room to start on the reports for their time in Melbourne. But a few minutes later, Ann appeared at his side.

"Julie and I are going to go up to Redfern to interview the person who bought the car," she told him. "What are you doing right now?"

"Just filling out the paperwork for last week."

"That can wait. For now, could you check out the North Sydney Medical Practice? I think that's one of our best leads, and I want someone who knows what they're doing."

"Sure. I'm on it."

"Thanks, Campbell. See you later."

Ryan leaned back in his chair as he watched her leave the station with Ross. He certainly wouldn't complain about putting off the paperwork, especially when there was far more interesting work to be done.

There was something weighing on his mind besides the case, though. He knew he shouldn't be letting himself get distracted at this critical moment, but he couldn't help wondering just what the hell was going on with Lisa Gordon.

CHAPTER 89:
A SAFE PLACE

That first night, Lisa didn't venture far from the Prince Albert Yacht Club. Shortly after she left the relative safety of the marina, it began to rain, and the wind picked up rapidly. She didn't want to bother with the sails in the poor weather, so as soon as she had reached what seemed like a safe distance from the marina, she hooked the first mooring buoy she could find.

It took her four tries. After the third attempt, she was so exhausted that she nearly lost her balance and fell overboard. She paused for a few moments, staring into the dark waters, and mused ironically that she'd been right to worry about being able to handle the *Paper Chase* on her own. But she cornered her resolve and tried again. This time she managed to snag the pick-up line.

She let out a sigh of relief and silently congratulated herself. One hurdle cleared.

After that, she settled into her sleeping bag in the bunk. Despite the rain and the wind, it was actually quite cosy inside. Between her exhaustion and the steady motion of the waves rocking the yacht, she dozed off quickly. It was the best night's sleep she'd had in a long time.

Lisa woke to a bright, clear dawn. She made herself a cup of coffee and went out on the deck to drink it. The air felt so fresh out here, with the morning dew still gleaming on the rails and the rigging. She could hear the morning chorus of birds in the shore side trees, and their song mingled with the sound of water lapping against the side of the yacht. Under other circumstances, it would have been a perfectly serene, relaxing morning.

She made herself a quick breakfast, which she ate while looking over the navigational charts. She needed to find somewhere that didn't require any difficult sailing, somewhere within range of a signal for the sat nav and her burner phone, but remote enough that she wouldn't be easily found. Unfortunately, many of Pittwater's hillsides were dotted with houses and villas. She would have to find a bay or creek in an unpopulated area… she didn't want anyone watching her from their living room window.

Night Bay looked promising. She traced a potential route with her finger; she'd have to sail north, up past Scotland Island. But the bay had a shallow draft, and she wasn't sure if the *Paper Chase's* keel would clear it. So she kept looking.

Just south of Night Bay was another passage, this one with a deeper draft. Lisa followed the thick blue line of the inlet with her eyes until she found the name marked on the map: McCarrs Creek. It twisted inland for a long way, bounded by steep hills that seemed to be almost entirely undeveloped. And it was closer than Night Bay, too. Perfect.

She put the coordinates into the chartplotter and then went to release the bow line from the mooring buoy. Back in the cockpit, she started up the engine and motored out into open waters, turning the yacht into the wind. Then she winched up the sails.

It was nerve-wracking at first, handling the boom and the ropes by herself. But she had a good, steady wind at her back, and as she stood at the helm, getting a feel for the ship's controls, her confidence began to grow. Soon, she had relaxed enough to enjoy the salt-tinged breeze and the warm sun on her face. She even managed a friendly smile and a wave as she passed a few other boaters.

As she drew closer to her destination, she turned the helm so that she passed along the landward edge of Scotland Island. Almost immediately afterward, the mouth of the creek opened to her port side.

With one eye on the depth sounder, she kept the helm steady as she passed into the creek. Though it was wide at the mouth, it quickly began to narrow, with the land on either side rising into heavily wooded hills.

From the charts, she knew that she was getting close to the place where the draft would become too shallow for a yacht this size. She winched down the mainsail to slow her speed as she approached the last navigable stretches of the creek.

Compared to the bustle of the crowded marina, it was almost eerily quiet here. The water was still and calm. The trees on the hillsides seemed to dampen every sound.

She came upon a couple of mooring buoys with three yachts tied up to them. The yachts looked old, maybe even abandoned, at first glance. But as her eyes adjusted to the deep shadows of the creek after the dazzling brightness of the open water, she saw that there was someone on one of the boats. He was in the process of dropping several fishing rods into a small dinghy tied alongside the yacht.

Lisa watched him for a few moments, then shook herself and refocused on the task at hand. She needed to hook one of these buoys. She steadied the helm and let the yacht drift towards the nearest pick-up line. When it got close enough, she lay down on the bow and reached out with the boat hook. To her own surprise, she managed to grab the line on the first try.

But her feeling of triumph was short-lived. The boat was drifting too fast. The hook slipped from her grasp and tumbled into the water.

"*Shit!*" she cried, her voice echoing off the hills. With a groan, she rolled onto her back and stared up at the sky, cursing her clumsiness.

While she lay there, gathering the will to go after the fallen hook, she heard the whir of an approaching outboard motor. A voice cut over it. "All right up there?"

Lisa stood and peered over the rail of the yacht. Disconcertingly, she found herself looking into the concerned face of the marina hand from the Prince Albert Yacht Club. He was the one she'd seen loading the fishing rods into the dinghy.

"Er… not exactly," she called down. "I've dropped my boat hook."

He brought the dinghy alongside the *Paper Chase*, scooping the hook up out of the water as he went by. "Put down the anchor," he told her, "before you drift any further."

Lisa hurriedly opened the lid of the anchor unit and pressed the drop button. The anchor hit the water with a splash. The boat continued to drift out to the end of the chain, which, unfortunately, brought it out of range of the buoy she'd chosen. But the next one wasn't too far away in the other direction.

"I think I've overshot," she said sheepishly, leaning over the rail.

"That's okay. Here." He tossed a rope up from his dinghy. "Tie me on."

"Thank you."

"My name's David," he told her as she knotted the rope around a cleat on the bow. "That's my yacht, over there next to Old Jack's. The one past mine is Bob and Mary's, but they hardly come here anymore."

"I'm Lisa," she said. "I think we've met before, actually. You work at the Prince Albert Yacht Club, right? You helped me load my bags."

"So I did," the man agreed. "Funny running into you again. It's my day off from the marina. I'm just heading out to go fishing." Lisa finished tying the rope and straightened up. "But first let's get you moored."

David handed up the boat hook, and she exchanged it for her bow line. He motored off towards the nearest buoy and skilfully secured the *Paper Chase's* rope. He checked to make sure it was tied safely and told her that she was all set.

Lisa untied his rope and tossed it back down to him. "Thanks again," she said.

"No worries. Well, I guess I'll be off."

"Hope the fishing's good."

He flashed a smile, and the dinghy began to putter towards the mouth of the creek.

Once he was gone, the almost oppressive silence returned. There didn't seem to be a single house in sight… or so she thought. She looked more closely in the shadows of the trees and saw that there was a house on the shore, but it was so overgrown with vegetation that it was hard to make out any details. A small jetty extended outward from the house's rotting deck. Beside the jetty, she spotted a boathouse, also thoroughly camouflaged under a thick layer of vines. It seemed safe to assume that the place was abandoned.

Lisa turned in a slow circle, her eyes tracing the steep hills that surrounded her. The only sounds were the birdsong and the gentle jangling of the yacht's rigging in the breeze. She let out a slow breath. She would be safe here, she decided. At least for now.

She went to the stern and switched on the satellite unit. Somewhat doubtfully, she tried the TV, expecting nothing but snow. But she was pleased to discover that she had a very serviceable signal. She flipped through the channels, watching a few minutes of the local news and then the national news. It seemed that there hadn't been any critical developments in the last few days. There was a brief mention of the investigation into the Pittwater killings, which was once again in full swing because of some new evidence that had been uncovered. But the details were vague. With a pang, Lisa wondered where Ryan was and what he was doing.

After a quick lunch, she decided to lay down in her bunk and rest her eyes for a few minutes. It had been a busy morning, and who knew what the evening would bring. But the rocking motion of the yacht, even gentler here than out on the ocean, soon lulled her into a deep sleep.

Hours later, she woke to the sound of someone shouting her name.

She sat up, momentarily at a loss for where she was and who was calling her. Then it all came back; she was on McCarrs Creek, and the voice belonged to David.

Smoothing a hand over her hair, she clambered out of the bunk and made her way up to the deck. David had brought the dinghy alongside the *Paper Chase*, and he was looking up at her with a hand shading his eyes from the sun.

"Hi there," he said. "I had a good day fishing. I was just wondering if you wanted some of the catch."

"Oh, well…" She tried to think of a diplomatic way to say this. "That's nice of you. I love fish, but I've never prepared anything that fresh."

"Don't worry. I'll gut it for you."

She gave a relieved smile. "That sounds great, then. What kind of fish?"

"Barramundi. I'll come back around six for dinner. Do you think you could prepare a salad?"

"Er… I'm not sure I have the ingredients." Lisa frowned, trying to remember what had been in the bag of groceries Brian packed for her. She brightened as she recalled one staple she did have on hand. "I've got wine."

David laughed. "That'll do. I'll bring the fish and salad, you bring the wine. See you later, then."

Lisa watched him motor over to Old Jack's yacht. A man with white hair and a white beard appeared on the deck… Old Jack himself, Lisa assumed. David chatted with him for a few minutes and handed up some fish, then returned to his own yacht.

Stifling a yawn, Lisa checked her watch. It was almost four thirty now. While she waited for six o'clock to roll around, she opened her laptop and scrolled through some of her old articles, hunting around for the particular detail that could've landed her in this mess. But an hour and a half later, she still had no idea why an assassin was after her. Or why Wayne Brewster would ever want to help her.

A few minutes before six, Lisa heard the sound of the outboard motor that signalled David's return. She grabbed the bottle of wine that she'd stuck in the refrigerator and went up to the deck.

David was tying up his dinghy to the side of the *Paper Chase*.

"Hello, Lisa," he called. "Here. I'll hand these up to you." She leaned over the rail to take two bowls covered in clingwrap. "That's the salad and the fish."

"Thanks so much, David. This is really kind of you."

"My pleasure." He climbed up onto the deck. "Well, shall I start cooking?"

"Sure, the kitchen's this way." She led him to the galley and showed him the stove.

"Perfect. You'll just need to turn the gas on so I can roast the fish. Should only take fifteen or twenty minutes."

"Okay, I'll go turn it on. I was thinking we'd eat in the cockpit, since it's so nice out. That all right with you?"

"Sounds great."

Lisa headed up to the small locker beside the helm, opened it, and shouted, "Gas on!" as she twisted the valve on the top of the canister. Then she got napkins, plates and silverware to set the table.

A few minutes later, David emerged from the cabin carrying a steaming plate of fish. He set it down on the table in front of her.

"Oh, that smells marvellous," she said. "Do you want a glass of wine?"

"Yes, please."

She poured a glass for him and freshened her own. They dug in.

"It's lovely out here, isn't it?" she said, gesturing with her fork to the peaceful hills surrounding them. "I really need to get out of the city more."

"Is that where you live?" David asked.

"Yes. I'm a…" She'd started the sentence before she remembered that she was actively breaking her bail conditions, and very possibly had a warrant out for her arrest by now. She changed course. "…an executive assistant. I haven't taken a vacation in ages. So my friend offered to let me use his yacht for a while. Not that I'm much of a sailor."

"Yes, I could tell," David said, and they both laughed.

In the brief silence that followed, Lisa prompted, "What about you? Tell me about yourself."

He looked at her quietly for a few moments, long enough that Lisa worried she'd said something wrong. Finally, he replied, "Well, I'm an orphan. My parents died in a car crash in England last year."

"Oh, I'm so sorry."

"That's all right. We weren't close. I'm from here, Australia, but I was sent away to boarding school young, so I did most of my growing up in England. As a boy, before I left Sydney, I used to work at the Prince Albert Yacht Club on summer holidays. Anyway, I've been living in London the last few years, but I decided to come back here for a while. Travel a bit, do some sailing. I have an auntie on the Gold Coast. She used to sail but doesn't do it much anymore, so she let me borrow her yacht and bring it down here. But I'll probably move on after the Pittwater Regatta is over."

"Well, I hope you enjoy your travels," Lisa said. Noticing his empty glass, she offered, "Would you like some more wine?"

"No. I need to get back. I have an early start in the morning." He stood, rather abruptly. "I'll clean up before I go."

Lisa was taken aback. "That's okay. I'll clean up," she said, wondering if she'd offended him.

"No, I'll do it. I like to clean. You can just put away the table and turn off the gas."

"All right. If you're sure," she said uncertainly, but he was already halfway down to the cabin.

Lisa rose from her seat and crossed over to the gas canister. "Gas off!" she called as she closed the valve. She cleared the folding table and packed it away, leaving one chair for her to sit out on the deck. Then she walked over to the stairs down to the cabin, but she hesitated as she heard David speaking. She listened for a few seconds, but he didn't seem to be talking to her, just muttering to himself.

He glanced at her as he came back up to the deck. "I'm sorry," he said. "I didn't mean to be rude. It was just that talking about my parents upset me."

"Oh, I'm sorry, David. I understand. Listen, thank you again for the meal. The fish was delicious."

David gave a thin smile and brushed past her. He started to climb back into his dinghy, then paused and looked up at her. "If you're going to be here for a while, I'll see you around. Cheers, Lisa." He cast off and coasted across the still water back to his yacht.

Slowly, Lisa returned to the galley, where she retrieved the half-finished bottle of wine and her glass before bringing them both up to her chair on the deck. As she sipped her Chardonnay, she reflected that David seemed like an awfully nice young man, if a bit sensitive.

She poured herself another glass to finish the bottle. By the time that one was gone, dusk had started to settle over the creek. The depth of the quiet, interrupted only by the very slight sound of the water and the drone of the crickets, had started to unnerve her. So, as the sky faded into a darkening mauve, she returned to the cabin and got ready for bed.

CHAPTER 90:
RYAN'S INVESTIGATION

Ryan tried calling Lisa a few more times, but now her mobile didn't even ring. His calls went straight to voicemail, as if the phone had been turned off. He asked a friend working on Lisa's case if she'd heard about any new developments, but nothing had changed since Ann filled him in on the plane ride back from Melbourne. All the evidence pointed to one conclusion: Lisa killed Paul Seidel. But Ryan still had a hard time believing it. He was worried about her. Something didn't feel right.

But there wasn't much he could do. The whole department, Ryan included, was still working at full throttle to solve the Pittwater case. His next task was to drive out to North Sydney General Practice, armed with photographs of the suspect. They had photos from quite a few different angles now… from the security footage of the Melbourne wine bar, the bookstore, and the petrol station in Goulburn. He brought along a copy of the order sheet, too, hoping it would jog someone's memory.

When he spoke to the receptionist, he was directed to the office manager, a petite brunette woman wearing a cheerful, multi-coloured scarf atop her oversize sweater. The receptionist introduced her as Leanne Martin.

"Thanks for taking some time to talk with me, Ms Martin," Ryan said as she brought him into her office. "Here's the purchase I wanted to ask about." He handed her the order sheet as they sat down on opposite sides of a wooden desk. "These supplies came here, to your hospital. Is that right?"

She studied the piece of paper. "Oh, yes," she said, tapping the date in the corner of the page. "This'll be the one that caused all the confusion."

"Confusion?"

"Well, the suppliers phoned us to ask if we were happy with all the equipment we ordered. But we hadn't ordered any equipment. Not from them, anyway. I asked all of our doctors, and no one knew anything about this. I called the suppliers back to tell them there must have been some mix-up, and they insisted that someone from our practice had come to pick up the order from their warehouse. They said it was our intern doctor."

"I see. And…" Ryan pulled out the photos of the suspect and slid them over to Leanne. "This wouldn't happen to be your intern doctor, would it?"

Leanne glanced at the photos and shook her head. "No, it's not. This guy is white and our Dr Zhao is Chinese, for one thing." She started to hand the pictures back, but then she stopped short and squinted at them more closely. "I *have* seen this person before, though."

"You have?"

"Yes. At least I think so."

"Where?"

"Well, he's not our intern doctor, but I believe he interviewed for the position. If it's the guy I'm thinking of, he made it through several rounds of interviews, so I spoke to him more than once. Here. We keep photos on file for our candidates so we can remember them all, in case we have another opening. Let me check."

She swivelled her chair over to her computer, her fingers clattering efficiently over the keyboard. After a few moments, she swung the monitor around towards Ryan. "Yes. That's him, don't you think?"

Ryan leaned forward eagerly. Sure enough, staring back at him from the computer screen was the same man he'd been chasing down in frozen frames of grainy security footage.

"Yes," Ryan said, his eyes glued to the screen. "I think you're absolutely right."

The man had on a jacket and tie. He looked respectable enough, with a clean-shaven face and short-cropped hair. "You said he made it through the first few rounds. Do you happen to remember why he didn't get the position?" Ryan asked.

"He had a very good resume. Too good, in fact. That's why we didn't hire him. He said he'd been practising surgery in a major metropolitan hospital. He was far more qualified than we needed for an intern at a local general practice like this." She clicked around on her screen, and the photo was replaced with a text file. "This is it, right here. His resume. Says he trained in London and practiced in America."

Jackpot, Ryan thought. "This is extremely helpful, Ms Martin. Could you print out the photo and resume for me?"

"Of course."

"Thank you very much."

A few minutes later, Ryan had added Leanne's contributions to his file folder. After he left the clinic, he sat in his car and called Ann.

"Detective Nguyen speaking."

"Hey, Ann, it's me. Any luck at the garage?"

"Yes, actually. Looks like we've got the right vehicle. Forensics is on the way to collect it. Julie and I are heading back to the office. How'd it go at the medical clinic?"

"I've got a good lead. Let's meet back up at the office and I'll tell you more."

"Okay. See you soon."

CHAPTER 91:
JOHNSON WANTS
A SHOWDOWN

Chan stood at the edge of the landing pad, his hair and jacket blown back by the wind from the helicopter rotors.

It was late afternoon, and the grounds of the Admiralty House in Sydney were flooded with sunshine. Johnson had phoned the night before to tell Chan that the two of them would be paying a visit to Brewster. He had sounded furious on the call, and as he disembarked from the helicopter and strode towards Chan, it was clear that his temper had not improved.

"Good. You're here," Johnson said. "Let's go find that son of a bitch."

Chan sensed that this might finally be the day that his services were required to resolve the Brewster situation. But he wasn't worried about that. He had come prepared.

Brewster was waiting for them as they stepped into his office. By his ramrod posture and the look of resolve on his face, he seemed to already know what kind of meeting this would be.

"Welcome, gentlemen," he said. "Is this an official conversation or an unofficial one? I'd like to know if I should keep records."

"Cut the bullshit, Brewster," Johnson snapped. He slipped his jacket off his shoulders and threw it onto the large leather couch. "Chan, pour some drinks."

"Please, help yourself," Brewster said to Chan, gesturing towards a decanter and a set of tumblers on a bar cart against the wall. He sat down at the chair behind his desk. Through the window behind him, Sydney Harbour lay in the distance, speckled with white sails and glimmers of sun off the water.

Chan poured two drinks, one for Brewster and one for Johnson, and then made a tonic water with lemon and ice for himself. He handed one of the brandys to Johnson, who accepted it wordlessly and took a seat on the sofa. After distributing the other brandy to Brewster and picking up his own tonic water, Chan stationed himself near the window, his eyes on the harbour below.

"You are very privileged to have such a wonderful view," Chan said to the governor. "But I suppose that comes with the job."

Despite Brewster's obvious efforts to appear impassive, he seemed a little unsettled to have Chan standing so close to him.

Johnson took a long swallow of his brandy. "Where the hell is Lisa Gordon, Wayne?"

"Last I heard, the owners of the *Telegraph* bailed her out. The bail conditions required her not to leave Sydney, so I assume that's where she is."

"Then it seems I know more about what's going on in this city than the governor does," Johnson replied coldly. "Gordon has gone missing. She has not been seen for several days, according to our surveillance."

"I didn't realise she was under surveillance," Brewster answered. "Which is odd, considering that the governor is supposed to be informed of any surveillance operations conducted here."

"Of course she's under surveillance," Johnson hit out. "One of us had to do something, since your so-called intervention came to nothing. And another thing, Brewster. Are you planning some sort of trip without informing your official staff? Chan tells me you've been preparing for a journey in that boat plane of yours."

"Your henchman is not always right," he said flatly, without looking at Chan. "I know he's been watching my every move, but I'm afraid he's off the mark. There's no secret trip. I've been preparing my boat plane for the Pittwater Regatta, which is coming up in a few days. I'm on the board for the Prince Albert Yacht Club, you see. Every year I help monitor the race and then present the trophies at the banquet."

"Enough about your social life," Johnson said. "I want to know what's really going on with you. I know you and your friend Charles have been delivering short loads for the Pacific Highway. As soon as I mentioned it, the measurements magically started to line up with the estimates. If Pearce was trying to cover up for your scam, he did a pretty sloppy job. I can't believe you would try and double-cross me. After all the opportunities I've given you. You could've had so much more than your petty little LeMay scheme. But you just couldn't see the bigger vision of it all. Our international investors…"

Brewster interrupted him with a low, dark chuckle. "Don't play the saint with me, Johnson. Acting like your *investments* are for the good of the country. Your deals with corrupt billionaires aren't intended to benefit anyone but yourself. Look at everything you've done. Getting involved with international crime syndicates. Killing off your political opponents, and anyone else who happens to get in the way. You're not fit to be Prime Minister. If only the public could get a glimpse behind all your PR events and pretty speeches. I could show them who you really are."

Johnson's eyes flickered to Chan for just long enough for Chan to know that he was worried. But when he answered, his voice was cold and hard. "And how would you propose to do that?"

"Right from the start, when you asked me to run for Sydney governor, I didn't trust you. Not this time. I never forgot that you made me take the fall for you. When the story broke about that architect and the corruption in the city's building contracts, you left me out to dry."

"I saved you from prison," Johnson replied harshly. "Thanks to me and Chan, that architect didn't survive to take the witness stand. If he had, we both would've gone to jail."

"A little girl died in that explosion, Johnson. Don't you have any shame?"

"There is always collateral. That's the world we live in," Johnson said impatiently. "You should be grateful for what I've done for you. Taking care of that architect, getting you re-elected as governor, giving you a chance to be a part of my vision for this country's future."

"I don't want to be a part of your vision for the future," Brewster spat. "I don't want to be involved with criminal gangs that ruin people's lives. I don't want to have people murdered as a sacrifice to your ambition."

"And what do you want, Brewster?" Johnson asked, in a voice that dripped disdain.

"I want a thirty million dollar payoff to stay quiet about all the crimes you've committed. Give me that and I'll walk away. I'll give up the governor's job and say that it's due to poor health. Surely you can have one of your lackeys take over the post."

Johnson was silent for a few moments. Then, slowly, his face split into a smile. "And why in God's name," he asked, amused, "would I do that? I already have you right where I want you. If you try to damage my reputation, I could destroy you."

"Not this time," Brewster said softly. "This time, I've got an insurance policy."

Throughout their exchange, Chan had been at the window, listening as he looked out over the harbour. At Brewster's words, however, he turned to face the room. "Gentlemen, it seems this is going to be a long meeting," he said. "I think we'll need more drinks."

Chan collected Johnson's and Brewster's glasses and brought them to the bar cart. He sensed that Brewster was watching his every move. Until Johnson spoke.

"What do you mean? Insurance policy?" Johnson asked, his tone guarded.

Brewster turned to face the Prime Minister. The moment he looked away, Chan crushed the capsule he'd been hiding in his hand ever since he fixed the first round of drinks. Then, with one quick movement, he poured the powder from his cupped palm into one of the brandies.

By the time Brewster glanced back at him, Chan was busy slicing a lemon for his second tonic water.

"As your henchman here will know, it's very simple to set up hidden surveillance equipment these days," Brewster said, pausing to give Chan a nasty look as he set the brandy on Brewster's desk. "So that's what I did. And now I've put plans into motion to ensure that if anything happens to me, everything I have on you will be revealed to the public."

Johnson looked stunned for a few moments. Then he took a bracing swig of his brandy and reclaimed his resolve. "You're bluffing."

"I thought you would say that," Brewster said, and took a pull of his own drink. "That's why I brought a little sample to show you."

He lifted the lid of his laptop and turned it around so that it rested on the edge of the desk. A triangular 'Play' icon hovered in the middle of a black screen. Brewster clicked on it.

An image of his home office in Pittwater appeared. Through the laptop speakers, Johnson's voice began to speak:

"If you become governor, that's a mutually beneficial arrangement, isn't it? I happened to check and see that you still own those building supplies companies. You could stand to gain from some new construction projects."

Brewster paused the video and leaned back. "This is just a taste, Johnson. Just to show you how long I've been building up the evidence against you. Think about everything you've ever admitted to, starting the day you asked me to run for governor again. I've got all of that on tape." He took another deep draft of his brandy.

Johnson stood up. He walked towards Brewster's desk slowly, his gaze fixed on the laptop. When he finally raised his eyes to Brewster, his expression was livid. "You bloody fool," he snarled. "This could destroy all of us."

Brewster opened his mouth to respond, but he didn't get the chance. His expression morphed into one of terror, and he seemed to struggle to force his voice out of his throat, with no success. His face turned a slowly deepening shade of red as he began to gasp for air. He fell back into his seat, pulling desperately at the collar of his shirt as if tugging at a noose around his neck. And then, with puce-coloured veins standing out on his forehead, he slumped over in his chair.

Johnson stared at Brewster's unconscious form. "What the fuck is this?"

"Don't worry," Chan said calmly as he reached past Brewster towards the phone on his desk. "He'll be fine in a few hours. The doctors won't be able to trace the drug because of the alcohol. This will give us enough time to decide on our next move and track down those recordings." He buzzed Brewster's secretary. When she picked up, Chan said with affected concern, "Please, we need an ambulance right away. The governor is unconscious. We think he's had a heart attack. He's... he's not responsive. Tell them to hurry."

CHAPTER 92:
INSURANCE CLAIM

The forensics team was going over the killer's car inch by inch. Ann communicated daily with the Melbourne team, coordinating between the two offices as they sorted through the evidence that they had each acquired.

Meanwhile, Ryan kept a close watch on the new case files for crimes around Sydney, checking for any possible resemblance to the killer's MO. It had already been over two weeks since the Melbourne killings. He was growing more and more worried that the next attack was just around the corner.

While Ryan sat in the incident room, combing through the most recent batch of crime reports, Detective Everly shouted over to him that he had a phone call.

With the constant buzz of other conversations, it was difficult to hear in the incident room.

"Transfer it to my office," he said. "I'll take it in there."

Once he was seated in the quiet of his office, he picked up the phone from the desk. "This is Detective Ryan Campbell. Who am I speaking to?"

"Hello, Detective Campbell. This is Dean Rogers from Queensland Insurance. We received a request from your office to look into a very old insurance claim."

Ryan leaned his elbows on the desk. "Yes, that was me. Did you find it in your records?"

"Took a bit of digging, but yes, I tracked it down."

"What can you tell me about it?"

"Well, the claim was about a yacht explosion in Pittwater. There were two deaths, Mr Leadman and his young daughter, Suzie Leadman. After a thorough investigation, our company determined that the explosion was the result of a faulty gas canister. We didn't find any suggestion of foul play, unless you have new evidence for us."

"I'm afraid not," Ryan answered. "But I was wondering if you could tell me what the settlement was."

"Well, we paid out life insurance policies for both Mr Leadman and his daughter. *Sweet Janet* was a different matter."

"*Sweet Janet?*"

"The yacht."

"What happened with the yacht?"

"The widow, Mrs Leadman, wanted a payout for it. But it was over five years old, so the policy only covered a replacement yacht of a similar age and condition. She wasn't having any of it. Insisted that she didn't need a boat and that she wanted a cash settlement to live on. We told her that we couldn't give her cash, but that she could sell the new yacht as soon as it was registered. It seems she was living with her sister in Brisbane at the time. So, we arranged for a comparable vessel to be delivered to her yacht's moorings."

"What happened then? Did she sell the replacement?"

"Our records say she registered it under the same name, but I don't have a way of knowing if she ever got round to selling it. The claim was closed as soon as the replacement yacht was legally hers."

"That's great. Thanks very much, Mr Rogers," Ryan said. "Could you send a copy of that claim over to the Sydney Police Department?"

"Right away, Detective. If I can do anything else, you just let me know."

CHAPTER 93:
LISA'S EDITOR GETS A VISIT

Brian Palmer was at his desk on the fifth floor of the *Sydney Telegraph* building, reading a press release from Wayne Brewster's office. It stated that the governor had suffered a minor heart attack. He had already been released from Sydney Hospital, but would need to take some time off from his official duties to recover. The deputy governor would be taking over Brewster's role, effective immediately.

This concerned Brian. He considered ringing Lisa on his burner phone, currently located in an inside pocket of the jacket slung over the back of his chair. But before he could make up his mind about whether or not to do so, there was a knock at the door.

His secretary poked her head in and said, "Excuse me, Mr Palmer. There are some people here from the government. Should I show them in?"

Before he could answer, two men pushed past her into his office. He stood up and glanced them over. They both wore tailored suits and expensive-looking earpieces. Brian didn't like where this was going at all.

"Can I help you?" he asked.

"Mr Palmer, we're from the Australian Secret Intelligence Service. We have orders to search this building and seize any documents or electronics belonging to Lisa Gordon or yourself."

"On what grounds?" Brian demanded. "You may do nothing of the sort until I speak with our legal department."

"You're welcome to contact your legal representative. But you must not leave the building. Be advised that we have agents posted at the exits. We will need to take you in for questioning after our search."

"This is an outrage," he muttered as he grabbed the landline phone from his desk and dialled the extension for the legal department. As soon as someone picked up, he said, "Please send June to my office immediately."

Within a few moments, the head of the legal department, June Morgan, an older woman with dark brown eyes and sleek black hair who habitually wore a sanguine shade of lipstick, strode into Brian's office.

"What is this all about?" she asked the agents in a clipped voice. "On whose authority are you here?"

"I'm sorry, ma'am, but I can't say. You can take a look at our documents. You'll see that everything is in compliance with legal guidelines."

One of the men held out a sheaf of papers. She took it and thumbed through it rapidly.

"We have freedom of the press in this country, you know," she said brusquely. "Tell whoever you're working for that we'll be lodging a complaint."

June handed the papers back to the agent, visibly disgruntled that she hadn't been able to find anything wrong with them. She stepped to the side of the room to stand next to Brian, and they watched as the agents began to scour his desk and file cabinets.

"Can I have a word outside?" Brian asked in an undertone.

"Don't forget, you're not to leave the building…"

"Yes, he knows," June snapped. "We'll just be outside the door."

He went to pick up his jacket, but the nearest agent intercepted him. "Before you go, we'll need your mobile phone," he said.

Brian scowled at him. "Some search team you are. It's on my desk right in front of you."

"Thank you," the agent said, impassively. He took Brian's jacket off the back of the chair and handed it to him.

Brian stepped out into the hall with June.

"What's going on, Brian?" she asked, her eyes piercing through him. "The owners are not going to like this. They already weren't happy about posting Gordon's bail. Now you've got federal agents crawling all over the office?"

"I think this has to do with Lisa, and the articles she wrote about the government's involvement with China. I'm sorry to have to tell you that Lisa violated the conditions of her bail."

"What?" June said, a frown line steadily deepening in her forehead. "How do you know?"

"Because I helped her."

June closed her eyes for a moment in exasperation. When she opened them, she looked furious, but managed to keep her voice to a whisper. "You do understand my job is to keep you out of jail, right?"

"There are things going on here that the public needs to know about. Lisa was set up." Brian took June by the elbow and started to guide her farther away from the door to his office, but she seemed so scandalised that he immediately released her arm. "Listen, June, we don't have much time." He reached into his jacket, pulled the burner phone from the inner pocket and held it out to her.

"What's this?"

"It's a pay-as-you-go phone. Lisa Gordon has one too. Her number is the only saved contact. I need you to call her and tell her what's going on. Tell her not to pick up the package. It's too dangerous now."

"What package?" June asked, and then shook her head as if she didn't want to know the answer. "Brian, I can't get involved in this."

"I'm sorry, but you have to. Lisa's life is in danger."

June still looked reluctant. But before she could reply, they heard the voices of the two agents inside Brian's office. It sounded like they were approaching the door.

She grabbed the burner phone and slipped it into her pocket. "I'm not promising anything," she murmured, just before the door opened and the two agents stepped out.

"We'll need to know where Lisa Gordon's desk is," one of them said.

"Brian can help you with that. I'm headed back down to legal. Brian, I'll arrange for a representative to go with you for your questioning. Don't speak until you've got a lawyer with you." She gave the agents a last, cold look. "Good day, gentlemen," she said, and swept back to the elevator.

CHAPTER 94:
BAD VIBES IN
PITTWATER

Lisa was getting nervous. She'd been in the creek for several days now, and she hadn't heard anything from Brian. She had tried to call him a few times, but there was never an answer. Worried that someone else might have gotten hold of his phone, she always hung up rather than leave a message. She especially wanted to call Ryan, but she knew she couldn't risk it.

She'd seen the reports on the news about Wayne Brewster, who, allegedly, had suffered a heart attack and stepped down from his post until further notice. Maybe, she thought, it was just a case of especially strange timing. Or then again, maybe it wasn't.

Lisa had spent the better part of the last few days trying to figure out how to get to the postal box now that she was camped out in this remote corner of Pittwater. The logistics of it seemed to grow more complicated and perilous the longer she considered it.

She was starting to run low on supplies, too. Pretty soon, she was either going to have to venture out of the creek or recruit someone else to do it for her.

While she was up on the deck, staring out over the water and giving herself a headache trying to come up with a plan, the burner phone finally rang.

The sound seemed to crack open the day's muggy stillness. She dived into the cabin to retrieve the phone and managed to pick it up on the last ring.

"Brian. Thank God you called."

"Lisa, it's June Morgan from the legal department."

"June? I…"

"Just listen. I don't want to know where you are or what's going on. Brian asked me to call you. The Australian Secret Intelligence Service has taken him in for questioning. They confiscated your laptop as well as Brian's. He wanted me to give you a message: don't pick up the package. It's too dangerous now. Whatever that means. But I don't want to implicate myself more than I already have, so I can't say anything more. Take care, Lisa."

The line went dead.

"No! Shit…" Lisa scrambled to call her back, but it went straight to voicemail, as if the other phone had already been powered down.

She let out a long breath, feeling distinctly alone.

She couldn't contact Ryan without putting them both in danger. Brian was in the custody of ASIS. June didn't want anything more to do with her.

So what now? she thought, staring blankly at the useless phone in her hand.

"Lisa!"

Startled by the intrusion, she went up to the deck and found David waving up at her.

"Hi, David," she said, doing her best to hide her anxiety behind a friendly smile. She quickly tied his dinghy to the yacht. "Haven't seen you in a bit."

Once he'd climbed aboard, he took a grocery bag from under his arm and held it out to her. "Brought you some bread and milk, in case you were running low on provisions."

"Oh, thank you," she said, accepting the bag. "I am running low, actually. Is there somewhere nearby where I could stock up on the basics?"

"Closest would be Holmeport Marina, near the mouth of the creek. It's got a little restaurant, if you want to stretch your legs a bit, and a decent store with food and supplies."

"Holmeport Marina. I remember seeing it on my way in. I'll try there. Thanks."

David leaned comfortably against the railing. "How are things here? Are you planning to stay a while?"

"Probably just a few more days. Then I'll head back to the Prince Albert Yacht Club."

"Well, I'll be sorry to see you go. Might as well wait for the Pittwater Regatta to be over, though. That place will be a zoo until after the race."

"You're right. I'd forgotten all about that." Lisa scolded herself. She'd only been away for a few days and already she'd completely lost track of time. She needed to keep her head on straight. "So you'll be working this weekend, I suppose."

"No, I'm going to Sydney for the weekend," he said. "I've got to pick up some supplies. And Old Jack over there wants me to get him a new water pump. He says his old one is playing up."

Lisa cocked her head. "You're going into Sydney?" she repeated slowly.

"Yeah, that's right. Did you need me to pick anything up while I'm there? I already have a few stops to make, so it's no problem."

"Well…"

Lisa hesitated. Brian's message had warned her that picking up the package would be too dangerous… for her. But if anyone was watching the place, they would be looking for a woman in her thirties, not this young man. He could probably go get it without anyone noticing him at all.

"There is one thing," she admitted. "There's a package for me. A… family member sent it, and it's got some time-sensitive documents in it, so it's important that I get it right away. It's in a postal box in Double Bay. Will you be anywhere near there?"

"Sure," David said casually. "I have to stop by Paddington, right next to Double Bay. I can pick up your package then. Just give me the address. I won't be back here until Sunday, though. That all right?"

"That's no problem. Let me get you the address." Lisa went down into the cabin to grab a piece of paper. She found Brewster's envelope, took out the key, scribbled down the address that was mentioned in his letter, and then stuffed the envelope back under the mattress where she'd been hiding it.

She re-emerged onto the deck and handed the key and the piece of paper over to David. "That's to get into the postal box. Thanks so much."

"Happy to help." He gave her an easy smile and tucked the paper and key into his pocket. "Anything else you need while I'm in town?"

"Oh, no. That's it."

"Okay." David climbed back into his dinghy and gave Lisa a cheerful wave. "See you Sunday," he called. "Have a nice weekend!"

"You, too."

She watched him until he reached his yacht at the far end of the creek. Then she returned to the cabin, trying to calm her nerves and convince herself that this would all work out for the best.

CHAPTER 95:
RYAN GETS ANSWERS

Sunday morning found Ann and Ryan at the police headquarters, where they had been every day since their return from Melbourne. They were in Ryan's office, going over the incident reports from the last twenty-four hours. So far, it seemed like a typical Saturday night… a few drunken fights, some car jackings, at least one armed assault. Nothing that caught their attention. But they weren't willing to risk letting anything fall through the cracks. Not when they were this close.

While they were looking at the details of the assault, Ryan's phone rang. He answered it absently, only half listening until he heard who was on the other end. Then he straightened up and said, "Detective Haines. Good to hear from you. What've you got?"

Ann watched Ryan's face as he nodded, his expression growing gradually more animated. "Excellent work. Send the report over right away. This is great news, Haines. I had a feeling all along."

He set the phone back in its cradle and stood up, eyes gleaming.

"What is it?" Ann asked with a frown.

"Haines just got a report from the British police. He'd been researching the students who were in the same class as Benjamin Lovett at his medical college in London. Something finally turned up."

Another question started to form on her face, but before she could ask it, his phone rang again.

"Haines is going to fax the report straight to your desk," he told her. "As soon as it comes through, we can start calling the team in."

Ann nodded and disappeared down the hall towards her office.

Ryan answered the phone.

"Ryan Campbell speaking."

"Detective Campbell, this is Brian Palmer, the editor at the *Sydney Telegraph*."

Ryan tried to imagine why Palmer would be calling him and came up with nothing. "How can I help you, Mr Palmer?"

"I'm assuming you already know that Lisa Gordon was arrested for murder."

He frowned. "Yes, I'm aware."

"I've just been released by ASIS. I believe that Lisa has been framed because of the articles she wrote about the Australian government. Someone wants to silence her. I can't prove it, but I think Prime Minister Johnson is behind all of this."

Slowly, Ryan said, "That's an interesting theory, Mr Palmer, but I'm not involved in Lisa Gordon's case."

"I know that. I'm contacting you because Lisa thought you could be trusted."

Palmer took a deep breath, and then he told Ryan about his connection to Brewster and Johnson, the letter Brewster had written, the key he'd left for Lisa Gordon. He described how he'd helped Lisa escape to Pittwater on a yacht called the *Paper Chase*.

"The agents who interrogated me, they… they told me that I would never work again. That my family would suffer the consequences if I didn't cooperate," he explained, with remorse in his voice. "So I told them about the evidence Brewster had left for Lisa to find. I'm sorry. I hope I haven't put Lisa in more danger. But I called you because the last thing Lisa said to me before she left was that I could tell you the truth. You need to find her, Ryan. Her life is in danger."

Ryan was stunned into silence for a few moments. Then, he managed, "Thank you, Mr Palmer. I'll do everything I can."

"Good luck, Detective."

Palmer hung up.

Ryan stared at the phone in his hand, his mind reeling from everything Brian had said. The whole story sounded almost too outlandish to be true. And yet it all made too much sense not to be.

Now he had to find the killer and Lisa before it was too late.

He would have to move fast.

CHAPTER 96:
THE BOATHOUSE

After a quick sojourn to the Holmeport Marina to buy some supplies, Lisa was on her way back to the *Paper Chase*. As she piloted the dinghy up the creek, she spotted Old Jack crossing the wooden deck behind the abandoned house. He cast furtive glances around him while he walked, as though he was expecting someone to try and stop him.

With surprising speed for a man his age, he hurried over to the decrepit boathouse at the side of the property. He took something out of his pocket, looked over his shoulder once more, and then fiddled with the handle. The door swung open, and Old Jack disappeared inside.

Lisa was more than a little curious about what he was doing. But that old house gave her the creeps, and she wasn't sure she wanted to tangle with it. Besides, it really wasn't any of her business.

Then again, that had never stopped her before.

She diverted her course towards the jetty. After mooring her dinghy, she followed in Old Jack's footsteps to the boathouse.

Like the rest of the property, it was in bad shape. Under the mottled sunlight, she could see that the old house appeared rotten, and the plywood boarding up the windows had started to fall off.

She approached the door. From inside, she could hear Old Jack swearing to himself under his breath, accompanied by some scuffling and banging. She listened for a few moments, then pushed the door open and went in.

He straightened up and spun around with a hammer clutched in his hand. As he registered Lisa's face, he dropped the hammer to his side.

"Oh," he said, letting out a sigh of relief. "It's just you."

"Are you all right in here?" Lisa asked. She peered around the dark interior of the boathouse. It was crowded with workbenches and shelves full of old sails and supplies. Old Jack seemed to be tinkering with something on one of the benches.

"Yes, I'm fine. I'm trying to mend this old water pump."

Lisa frowned. "I thought David was getting you a new water pump in Sydney."

"I can't afford a new one. I told him I had a spare with my other supplies, but he wouldn't let me in here to get at it."

"Wait… you mean all this stuff…" Lisa gestured to the densely packed shelves. "…is yours?"

"Damn right, it's mine." Old Jack looked indignant. "When I moved here, this place had already been boarded up for years. The property management company had been trying to find a tenant, but nobody wanted to live way the hell out here. So I asked if I could use the boathouse, seeing as it was just sitting here empty anyway. But nobody ever got back to me, so I broke the lock and put on a new one. I used it for storage and as a place to do repairs. Then David turns up out of nowhere, claiming that this is all his private property. I don't believe a word he says. One minute he's nice as pie, and the next he's shouting and cursing like he's lost his mind."

Lisa was taken aback. That didn't sound like the David she knew... he'd never been anything but friendly to her. But before she could protest, Old Jack continued.

"Anyway, he demanded that I turn over my keys. I gave him one and kept a spare, but he doesn't know that. He seemed to live here in the boathouse for a while. I saw him coming and going at all hours. I asked him a few times if I could get my supplies, but he said I'd be trespassing if I came in here. Couple months ago, he vanished. Didn't see him for weeks and weeks. Then all of a sudden he showed up again and started living on the yacht *Sweet Janet*. And ever since then he's acting as sweet as you please, always bringing me fish he caught and offering to help with the maintenance on my."

"That's odd," Lisa murmured. "I suppose he was probably grieving his parents when he first got here. Maybe that's why he was acting so strangely."

Old Jack was sceptical. "Maybe," he said with a shrug, and turned back to the workbench. "I just want to finish fixing this spare pump and get out of here. You should do the same."

Lisa nodded. But instead of leaving, she took a few steps deeper into the boathouse, and then a few more.

All the way at the back, Lisa found a stack of mouldering boxes, a couple of children's bikes, and a few lifejackets. A tattered child's duvet was hanging loosely from a rafter. The pattern was badly faded, but Lisa could make out rainbows, stars, and unicorns.

There were footprints on the dusty floor that led behind the duvet. Curiously, she pushed the quilt aside and found a door with a new padlock on it. The padlock hadn't been snapped shut.

She glanced behind her and saw that Old Jack was still busy at the workbench. She dropped the duvet so that she was hidden behind it, then removed the padlock and stepped through the door.

CHAPTER 97:
THE MISSING PIECES

Ann got the report that Haines sent from Melbourne. He'd tracked down the names of all the students who were part of Benjamin Lovett's residency class. Then he'd checked them against crime databases in Thailand, the United Kingdom, Australia, and America. One of the names finally got a hit. That name was Robert David Leadman.

According to the report, Mrs Janet Greenburg, Robert's mother and David Leadman's widow, had moved to America a little over ten years ago and married a Dr John Solomon Greenburg of Los Angeles. Robert was wanted by American police for the murder of Mrs Greenburg.

Before her death, Janet was involved in a drunk driving accident in which she hit and killed a six-year-old girl. She had been charged with vehicular manslaughter while intoxicated. Shortly after she posted bail and returned home, security footage revealed Robert breaking into her house. Janet Greenburg suffered multiple stab wounds in a frenzied, vicious attack, and she bled to death on her living room floor.

Haines also sent a psychological evaluation from Robert's university counsellor, dated several years back. It explained everything: Robert's unresolved trauma from the yachting accident that had killed his father and younger sister; his overwhelming hatred of his mother, whom he blamed for their deaths; his inability to form relationships and predisposition towards violence against women.

After the accident and a brief stint at his aunt's house in Brisbane, he had been sent away to a series of boarding schools, where he struggled socially with his peers. He rarely interacted with his mother or stepfather except to receive financial support while he trained as a surgeon. He was intelligent, with an above-average IQ, but had been plagued by manic depression and schizophrenia throughout most of his adolescence and adulthood. He indicated that he knew his conditions could be managed with medications and therapy, but he didn't like to take his prescriptions and rarely did so for any sustained length of time. The counsellor believed him to be unstable. She concluded the report with a recommendation for further intervention, *"before the patient causes harm to himself or others."*

That evaluation had occurred well before Janet Greenburg's murder. But Ryan didn't need Dr Brannan to spell it out for him: the little girl who died in the crash had triggered Robert's long-held rage over the death of his beloved younger sister. He had killed his mother and then fled to Australia. And that was where Ryan first encountered Robert's handiwork on an abandoned lot in Pittwater.

Ryan felt a sense of grim vindication. He had been right about the connection to the Leadman case after all. He just hadn't been able to put everything together until now.

Finally, they knew the real name of the killer.

Now they just had to track him down.

Thinking back to his visit to the Leadman house, Ryan remembered the well-trodden tracks in the undergrowth and the footprints in the dusty kitchen. Could Robert have returned to his childhood home when he arrived back in Australia?

He and Ann rounded up four additional officers and prepared to head out to Pittwater. He knew they would need more than just the six of them on the ground, so he decided to call MacDonald. He would ask the sergeant to deploy a helicopter crew and to take a police boat up to McCarrs Creek as soon as possible, so that they could search by water and air as well as by land.

And somehow, in all this, Ryan needed to find Lisa Gordon.

CHAPTER 98:
THE KILLER'S LAIR

On the other side of the door, it was pitch-dark. Lisa's fingers fumbled along the wall for a switch. After a few moments, she found one and flicked it on. She winced against the sudden flood of light until her eyes adjusted.

She was standing at the top of a staircase. The steps went down into what appeared to be a sizable room running under the main house. The space was dominated by a large desk with a computer and a phone on it. The electronics appeared to be about ten years out of date, although there wasn't a speck of dust to be seen down here.

As she descended the stairs, she saw that the walls were hung with a combination of hand-drawn architectural plans and computer-generated blueprints. Some of the exterior drawings seemed familiar. When she looked closer, she realised that she recognised them from her commute to work. They were penthouses and high-end hotels in downtown Sydney.

She ventured a little farther into the room. Past the desk there was a sofa, which backed up against a black-and-white room divider. Cautiously, she passed through the gap between the wall and the divider and found herself in someone's bedroom.

There was a twin bed on a low frame, and next to it a sideboard. Papers covered the walls here, too, but they were different from the ones in the office. These were mostly old newspaper clippings. After skimming over a few, she noted that they were all about the same thing: a terrible yachting accident that had taken place on McCarrs Creek, causing the deaths of a father and his young daughter. The articles mentioned a son, Robert David Leadman, twelve years old at the time, who had survived the accident.

Lisa stepped back from the wall, her mind churning. Robert Leadman. The little boy who lived through the explosion. Could that be David?

Growing more and more unsettled, she walked over to the sideboard. On it sat a record player, a stack of 45s, and several framed photographs. She studied each picture. One was of a boy sitting on a man's shoulders, both of them grinning. Another showed the same boy and a younger girl playing on the beach. In the last one, both children stood in front of a sign for the Taronga Zoo while the girl clutched a stuffed toy koala.

Lisa spotted another door on the far side of the room. She walked over and tried the handle, but it didn't budge. Stepping back, she could see that the lock was old and damaged. She backed up one more pace, then turned her shoulder and threw all of her weight into the door. The lock gave way with a squawk of rusted metal.

Once again, she found herself standing in darkness. The smell was different, though; it smelled of dampness and chemical cleaners, and something that reminded her of a doctor's office.

She located the switch and flipped it. The overhead lamp buzzed, flickered, and finally turned on, washing the small space in dull yellow light.

It was a cramped, windowless bathroom. There was a toilet and a shower cubicle, and opposite that, a large pinboard affixed to the wall. On it was a neatly arranged assortment of glossy Polaroids, depicting pale shapes on dark backgrounds. She stepped closer, trying to make sense of the photographs. Finally, she understood what she was looking at: the bodies of naked women, twisted and mutilated into inhuman contortions. In some of the photos, the subjects seemed to still be alive. In others they were dead... but not just dead. Tortured. Put on display.

"Oh god," Lisa breathed.

She turned away from the grisly images and caught herself on the sink, her ears ringing. After a few moments, she realised that she was standing in front of a series of shelves mounted above the sink. Hesitantly, she raised her eyes and saw that the bottom shelf was filled with scalpels and other medical instruments, all polished to a mirror shine. The shelves above were lined with glass jars. She took one look at them and then dropped her head to throw up into the sink.

The jars were filled with clear liquid – surgical spirit, by the smell – and they all held small pieces of preserved flesh. Some contained nipples, each one a neat circle that had been meticulously carved away from the body it belonged to. Others contained eyelids. The eyelashes were still attached.

Lisa wiped the sick from her mouth and staggered back to the bedroom, then out to the office. Her heart was pounding so loudly in her ears that she thought she would pass out. She had just set her foot on the first stair when she heard a noise from upstairs.

Two male voices, shouting. Then a heavy thud.

The next instant, the door at the top of the landing flew open.

David stood there with a rucksack in one hand and a paddle in the other. He looked different than Lisa had ever seen him. There was a bloody graze on his cheek, and his face was distorted with rage.

For a few moments, both of them were still as stone.

Then David asked, "What are you doing in Father's office?"

"Wh... what?" she managed. "I'm sorry, I didn't mean to..."

"He told you that he doesn't like you in here, you bitch. You never listen. Do you, Mother?"

He started to come down the stairs.

Lisa stumbled back, trying instinctively to keep the distance between them. "David, it's me." She fought to keep her voice level. "It's Lisa, from the yacht."

"Yes. The yacht. And you promised you would come with us, and we would have a day out as a family. But you never keep your promises." He continued to advance towards her. "Suzie says *you're* the bitch who started it all. Father and Suzie and I were happy. But you did something to the yacht, didn't you?"

"Who are you talking to?" Lisa said, fear trapping her voice in a whisper. "David, I'm not your mother."

"You're coming out on the yacht with us. Suzie, Father, me, and you. We're going to the beach to cook the fish we caught, just like we were supposed to."

Without warning, he darted towards her. Lisa dodged out of the way and stumbled into the room divider, which crashed to the floor.

"I'm not going with you," she shouted.

He dropped the rucksack and gripped the paddle with both hands, cocking it back like a bat.

Lisa vaulted over the sofa and made a break for the staircase. At the same moment, he swung the paddle towards her and the edge of it caught her temple. She sprawled to the ground as her vision went hazy.

The next thing she knew, a strong grip had closed around her upper arm and she was hauled to her feet. David shoved her ahead of him as they made their way up the staircase.

Once they were at the top, he released his grasp on her arm, and she collapsed dizzily to the ground. She heard him digging around on the musty shelves. A moment later, her hands were yanked sharply behind her back and bound with rope before she was pulled back to a standing position.

As they left the boathouse, they had to step over an odd, dark lump. Through the black dots still crowding her vision, Lisa could just make out that the shape was a man, and that he was bleeding.

"Is that Old Jack?" she asked hoarsely, but David ignored her.

He pushed her out into the sunshine. The harsh light caused the pain in Lisa's head to redouble, and she cringed and shrank back, barely keeping herself upright.

David's dinghy was on the shore. He forced her into it roughly and she fell onto the cold metal floor of the boat. Then he climbed in after her and started the outboard motor.

"Come on, Mother," he snarled. "We're going sailing."

CHAPTER 99:
AT BREWSTER'S VILLA

Citing concerns about the governor's health and need for privacy, Johnson arranged for Brewster to be returned to his villa as soon as he was released from the hospital. Brewster had effectively been under house arrest ever since.

Johnson left him in Chan's care. He had been explicit in his instructions: Chan was to find out the location of Brewster's recordings, using any and all means necessary.

Chan was pleased to have finally been given carte blanche in dealing with the governor. Brewster had been trouble from the start. It had taken Johnson a long time to see it, but now that he had, Chan had his blessing to deal with Brewster accordingly.

When he first heard that ASIS would be handling Palmer's interrogation, Chan had been a little sceptical about their effectiveness, bound as they were by some semblance of civilian law. But he was pleasantly surprised to hear that it had all gone smoothly. The agents reported that the editor had cracked as soon as his family was mentioned.

From Palmer, they had gleaned that one copy of the recordings had been entrusted to Lisa Gordon. But Johnson still needed Chan to find out whether there were more copies, and, if so, how they could be destroyed. After that, they would deal with Gordon.

He'd had two days to work Brewster over. Drugs, threats, old-fashioned physical violence… Chan had deployed his full suite of methods. Brewster was looking the worse for wear, but he'd proved unexpectedly resilient. Chan had learned that there was at least one more set of recordings, but much to his irritation, he didn't know where they were. Not yet, anyway.

Around noon, Chan got a call from Johnson. He said that he was in the helicopter on the way to Brewster's villa, and he wanted to see how things were coming along. Chan changed into a clean shirt and washed the blood off his knuckles before the Prime Minister arrived.

Some thirty minutes later, he and Johnson were seated in Brewster's living room, enjoying some of the governor's cognac. Brewster himself was locked up inside a guest bedroom with guards posted outside the door.

They only had a few minutes to chat before one of Johnson's agents appeared in the doorway. "Excuse me, sir," the agent said, "but Sergeant Jack MacDonald is here. He says he wants to see Brewster. And he mentioned the missing journalist. Would you like to speak to him?"

A slow smile spread across Johnson's face. "I certainly would," he said. "Send him in."

Moments later, a visibly annoyed MacDonald was led into the living room. Chan rose to his feet and took his usual place behind Johnson.

"MacDonald. Good to see you," Johnson said warmly. "It's been a while, hasn't it? How are you?"

"I'm sorry, Prime Minister, but I can't stay and socialise," MacDonald said. "I just got a call from the station as I was pulling into the drive. I'm needed to organise a search party, so I have to head back. I was just hoping to say hello to Brewster while I'm here."

"I'm afraid Governor Brewster is indisposed."

A look of suspicion went fleetingly across MacDonald's face. "Fine. Then I'll just be on my…"

"I hear you have some information on Lisa Gordon," Johnson interrupted. "Where is she, and how do you know?"

MacDonald shifted uneasily on his feet. "The call was from Detective Ryan Campbell, from the Sydney homicide division. He says he has a lead on the Pittwater serial killer."

Impatience sparked in Johnson's expression. "And what does this have to do with Gordon? Did he mention that she has violated the conditions of her bail and is currently a person of interest in an ongoing federal investigation?"

"I don't know anything about that," MacDonald replied.

"Where is she?" Johnson said again. "I can end your career right now if you don't tell me."

Reluctantly MacDonald added, "All he said was that she may be on a yacht that was moored at the Prince Albert Yacht Club."

Johnson's eyes narrowed. "Did he tell you the name of this yacht?"

"The *Paper Chase*. Listen, I need to organise a helicopter search, and then I've got to get on a police boat to the old Leadman house. This is urgent, all right? I have to go."

"The Leadman house?" Johnson repeated, with raised brows. His eyes cut to Chan.

Chan gave Johnson a brief nod to tell him that he remembered the name, too. Although he hadn't the faintest idea why Campbell would be going there now.

"I don't know anything else," MacDonald said. "Now can I get on with my job?"

Johnson smiled, relenting. "Yes, of course. If there's anything we can do to help, let me know."

"I'll keep that in mind," the sergeant answered. He turned on his heel, brushing off the agents beside him, and made his way back to his car.

CHAPTER 100:
BACK TO THE
LEADMAN HOUSE

Ann and Ryan were in one squad car, leading two more cars with the other four officers. With any luck, MacDonald was already on the way with the helicopter and police boat.

When the convoy pulled up in front of the dilapidated property, Ryan and the other officers gathered around Ann.

"The killer could be here right now," she told them grimly. "Stay sharp and be careful. Don't forget, this man is dangerous and unpredictable. Ryan, you've been here before, so you lead the way."

With the others close behind him, Ryan took the decaying staircase to the deck around the back of the house. As the creek came into view, Ryan's eyes skimmed over the water. He spotted three yachts… no, four altogether. One was sailing downriver at a good speed, and it seemed to have two people onboard.

It was already too far away to get a clear view of the passengers. Within a few moments, it had disappeared around a bend in the creek.

As Ryan stared after the yacht, something in the corner of his eye caught his attention. He turned and saw that the door to the boathouse was flung wide open.

"That was padlocked last time I was here," he murmured to Ann.

He approached the boathouse cautiously with Ann at his side. When they saw what was propping the door open, they both rushed forward and dropped to a crouch.

It was a man, barely conscious, his white hair plastered to his head with a sheen of blood. He seemed to be struggling to stay awake. His eyes rolled up to look at them.

"Don't worry," Ann told him, already wadding up her jacket to apply to the wound on his head. "We're going to help you."

Finally, the man managed to wheeze out a few words. "Stop him," he rasped. "He took the woman on his yacht. Hurry."

The woman?

The old man's head lolled back and he fell unconscious.

Ryan straightened up and turned to the officers who had gathered behind him. "Get him in your car and take him to the nearest hospital," he barked. Then, to the next pair of officers, he added, "We need a forensics team immediately. Call in to headquarters and get them out here." He took a few steps back onto the deck. "Where the hell is MacDonald with that police boat?"

One of the two remaining yachts had drifted slowly with the current, and the vessel's name was now visible. It was the *Paper Chase*.

"Bloody hell," Ryan said. "That really was her. He's got Lisa."

CHAPTER 101:
THE START OF
THE RACE

The *Sweet Janet* sailed from the calm waters of the creek into the rolling waves of Pittwater.

Lisa was tied to the rail behind the helm. As David steered, his movements were twitchy and erratic. Although she was still muzzy-headed from the blow to her temple, she could hear him talking to himself in a steady, uninterrupted monologue.

"Yes, Father, I've trimmed the sails. I can handle her, don't worry. Suzie is here as well. Yes, I know, Suzie. She will be the last one. Mother can't hurt us now. That bitch."

With effort, Lisa raised her head to get a better look at her surroundings. In the distance, she could see a flotilla of sailing yachts and rigid-hull inflatable boats. That must've been the entrants and racing stewards in the Regatta, heading for the starting line.

As Lion Island passed by on the port side, Lisa noted that the other yachts were gaining on them rapidly. Before long, the *Sweet Janet* would be in the midst of dozens of other craft.

David left the helm to adjust the sails for the strong headwind coming off the sea. While he was gone, Lisa tugged experimentally on the knots binding her hands. But they held fast, and all she managed to do was scrape her skin raw against the rough rope.

She let out a groan and turned to face the approaching yachts, wondering if she could scream loud enough to get anyone's attention. But if she did, there would be nothing stopping David from killing her right then and there.

Lisa tried to push away the thought. Panic would get her nowhere. Instead, she told herself the same thing she always did when she found herself caught in a political-rally-turned-riot, or facing the vitriolic attacks of public officials whose misdeeds she had exposed, or any of the other thorny situations she'd ended up in: *stay calm and pay attention.*

There was still a way out of this, even if she couldn't see it yet.

There had to be.

CHAPTER 102:
THE SEARCH IS ON

Ryan was standing on the jetty when MacDonald finally arrived. Another officer was piloting the motorboat, and two more officers were in the back.

"About time!" Ryan called as the pilot cut the engine and tossed a rope to Ann so that she could keep the boat from drifting. "Did you get the helicopter lined up as well?"

Before MacDonald could answer, a low whine emerged from the treetops and a blue and white police helicopter crested over the nearest hill. MacDonald held up a radio set. "They'll keep us updated on everything they see from the sky."

"Perfect," Ryan said as he climbed into the boat. "Did you notice a yacht coming out of the creek?"

MacDonald looked surprised. "Yes. But it was way ahead of us. I just caught a glimpse of it."

"I think that's the *Sweet Janet*, with our killer, Robert Leadman, on board. And I think he's taken Lisa Gordon hostage."

"Blimey. Let's get after it, then."

Ryan looked up at Ann, who was still on the dock. "You staying here?"

She gave a clipped nod. "I'll lead the forensics team when they get here and keep an eye on things in case Leadman comes back to the house. You go after the yacht. Be safe."

"You too." Ryan caught the rope as Ann tossed it back to him, and they set off.

As the wooded hills began to roll by on either side, the sound of helicopter rotors once again swept over the creek. Ryan glanced up, expecting to find the police helicopter again. But instead he saw a different aircraft, this one huge and black. It hovered briefly over the Leadman house, then flew low over the police boat and continued down the creek towards the sea.

"That's Howard Johnson's helicopter," MacDonald told Ryan. "He's the reason I took so long getting here. I went to Brewster's house to see how he was doing, now that he's home from the hospital. You called me just when I got to his place. I was about to turn around, but one of those secret service blokes stopped me. He asked what I was doing. I told him I was trying to leave, and explained about your call. He wouldn't let me go until I went in and talked to Johnson."

Ryan glanced at him in surprise. "Johnson was at Brewster's house?"

"Yes. Him and… someone I didn't recognise. Chinese guy. A bodyguard, maybe. I just wanted to get out of there. The place was crawling with agents. Unmarked black cars all over the grounds. And Johnson never let me see Brewster at all. There's something going on, Ryan."

"What did Johnson want to know?"

"Mostly he kept asking about Lisa Gordon."

"So what did you tell him?"

"Just what you'd told me. About the Prince Albert Yacht Club, and the *Paper Chase.*"

Ryan turned to face forward, where the creek was already starting to open up into wider waters. "What the hell does the Prime Minister want with Lisa?" he muttered. But he already knew that whatever it was, it couldn't be good. He shook his head. "We need to find her before he does."

CHAPTER 103:
BREWSTER'S ESCAPE

"Our first priority is Lisa Gordon," Johnson said curtly. "I'll take the helicopter, and you…" He turned to Chan. "…take a couple of agents to the Prince Albert Yacht Club. I'll have a secret service powerboat meet you there. When you get to the marina, see what you can find out about the *Paper Chase*. Bring Brewster with you."

Brewster, who had been half listening to all this, stirred slightly at the sound of his name. Chan and Johnson had come to collect him from the guest bedroom where he'd been locked up all morning. It had been a welcome break from Chan's interrogation.

He was in bad shape after the last few days. He had been drugged several times, and his thoughts were still sluggish and jumbled. He'd also taken quite a number of blows, mostly to the chest and abdomen… places that wouldn't be outwardly visible or hinder his ability to walk. That didn't mean they weren't painful, though.

"I'll radio you from the helicopter," Johnson said briskly to Chan. "Keep in touch if you find anything out."

Prodded along by the two agents, Brewster followed behind Chan as they left the house and walked down to the black van waiting in the driveway.

With his forehead pressed against the cool glass of the van's window, Brewster tried to come up with a plan. They were going to the marina. To the place where his boat plane was moored, with a full tank of fuel and all of his belongings already packed. He would only need to get away for a few moments to be able to reach it.

When they arrived at the yacht club, the agents went to speak with marina control while Chan waited in the van with Brewster. A few minutes later, the agents returned and reported to Chan that the *Paper Chase* had been docked here, but it had left about a week ago. The crew hadn't put in a voyage report, nor had they radioed to any of the coast guard stations about their planned route. "By now, it could be anywhere," one of the agents said with a shrug.

Chan breathed what Brewster assumed to be a curse in Cantonese. He picked up the small radio set he had with him and pressed the call button to reach Johnson. "The *Paper Chase* isn't here. It left a week ago. No indication of where it's gone."

A crackle of static preceded Johnson's acerbic response. "Get in the launch and start looking."

The two agents resumed their posts on either side of Brewster as he got out of the van. They walked in step beside him, staying close enough to imply a threat.

The docks were buzzing with activity as boats set off towards the starting line of the Pittwater Regatta. Marina hands and stewards rushed around them, finishing last-minute preparations for the race. No one took any notice of them.

Chan led the way down the jetty to a launch emblazoned with the Commonwealth Coat of Arms, marking it as an official government craft. He climbed in and started the engine, then called up to the agents to release the mooring ropes.

Brewster's attention sharpened. The drug-induced haze in his mind cleared just enough for him to realise that this was precisely the moment he'd been waiting for.

One of the agents left Brewster's side to untie the mooring ropes. That left only one, standing shoulder to shoulder with Brewster. He cast a casual glance towards the dock manager's shed. It was maybe ninety meters away. He could make it.

Brewster gathered all of his remaining strength, then turned and shoved the agent beside him as hard as he could. With a yelp, the agent stumbled and fell into the water. Brewster was already on his way towards the shed.

He risked a glance behind him and saw that the second agent had dropped the mooring ropes and started to go after him.

"Leave him," Chan shouted. "Just get in the launch. He's not going anywhere fast."

Well, he was wrong about that. Brewster would be out at sea in a few minutes. And then he would finally be able to untangle himself from Johnson and Chan and all their godforsaken schemes and lies. He would be free.

Brewster limped the last few steps to the manager's shed. "I need my keys," he said to Blake, trying not to gasp, although the bruises spangled across his ribs ached with every breath.

Blake frowned. "Are you all right, Mr Brewster?"

"Yes. Fine. I just need my keys."

"I thought you weren't doing the Regatta this year."

"I'm not, but I need to take the plane up. Is she ready?"

"Well, yeah. She's ready. Got a full tank. You sure about this, though? You're looking a little rough."

"Just give me the keys, Blake. Please. And then help me cast off."

CHAPTER 104:
THE PITTWATER REGATTA

With Brewster out of the way, Chan opted to leave the two secret service agents behind and pilot the launch himself. Johnson had radioed him to say that he'd spotted the *Paper Chase* from the helicopter. It was indeed at the Leadman house, but Lisa Gordon wasn't on it. Johnson suspected that Gordon had taken another yacht and planned to hide out among the swarm of boats participating in the Regatta.

"They're near Lion Island now," Johnson said. "I'll keep looking for her from up here."

"Copy that. I'll catch up to them soon."

A few minutes later, as the launch cleared Stokes Point, Chan noted that there was a strong wind coming in off the sea, and it was giving the yacht crews a difficult time. He saw that many of them were floundering with their booms, scrambling to turn the mainsails in the unrelenting wind. The stewards' rigid-hull inflatable boats were crashing over the crests of large swells and then plummeting back down the other side. The water seemed to be getting rougher by the minute.

A familiar mechanical buzz from above drew Chan's attention. He looked up to see Johnson's helicopter gliding overhead. A moment later, Johnson's surprised voice came through the radio. "I see her. She's tied to the rail of one of the yachts. It's called the *Sweet Janet*."

The name sparked something in Chan's memory. It took him a few moments to pin down what it was: the name of the yacht he had disposed of twelve years ago, right here in Pittwater. Is that why Campbell had been at the Leadman house?

"Sink that goddamned boat," Johnson continued harshly. "And get rid of Lisa Gordon."

Chan grabbed a pair of binoculars and glassed the horizon as the launch weaved easily between the struggling yachts. He spotted the *Sweet Janet*, and right away he saw that it was in poor shape. Its sails were rippling out dangerously in the wind. As the captain fought to regain control, he narrowly avoided hitting another yacht, earning a chorus of shouted insults from the other crew.

The near miss also drew a reaction from the crowds of spectators that had gathered on the shore. They lined the beaches, many of them carrying binoculars so they could follow the progress of their team. The clamour of the crowd surged once again as the helicopter swooped low over the water. It was clear from their response that they thought it was all part of the Regatta. From the sound of their exuberant cheers, today had the makings of a great race.

CHAPTER 105:
OUT OF CONTROL

The ringing in Lisa's ears that had persisted since David struck her on the head finally subsided. Her vision cleared and she found herself able to think clearly, just in time to realise that David had lost control of the yacht.

An intense gust caught the mainsail. The yacht was steadily gaining speed, and despite David's best efforts to wrangle the boom, he couldn't seem to change course. *Sweet Janet* was at the mercy of the winds.

They were headed straight towards another yacht. After a number of close calls, the *Sweet Janet* finally collided with another vessel, their bow to the *Janet's* starboard side. The impact jolted Lisa, who yelped as the ropes bit into her wrists. David was thrown against the outer railing and barely managed to keep from falling overboard.

One of the crewmembers on the other boat was not so lucky. She tumbled into the water, to the horrified shouts of her crewmates. Two more yachts had to swing out to avoid hitting the *Sweet Janet*, causing others to change course to avoid them in turn. The water was getting more and more crowded as the channel narrowed towards the headland where the Barrenjoey Lighthouse stood. Meanwhile, the waves were only growing bigger.

"This is all your fault, Mother!" David shouted at Lisa over the sound of the airhorns that the race stewards were blowing in an effort to restore order. "You never let us be happy. You and your rich friends. I hate them all."

As he spoke, the boat pitched wildly with another fierce wave, and Lisa heard a sound that made her heart jump to her throat: sloshing water. She craned her head to try and get a look down into the cabin. Sure enough, she caught the glimmer of water rushing back and forth with the rolling motion of the ship. The collision with the other yacht must have cracked the fiberglass hull. They were taking on water.

She redoubled her efforts to wrest her hands free of the rope binding them. David had done the knots in a hurry, and they were starting to come loose. But she'd have to work fast. If she didn't, she would drown when the boat sank.

"David, you have to untie me!" she called, but he took no notice of her.

Before she could make another attempt to get his attention, the yacht was struck by another violent collision. With a gasp, Lisa twisted around and saw that a launch with a government seal had struck the starboard side in almost exactly the same spot as the other yacht. The sound of water pouring into the cabin grew louder.

A man leapt from the launch and grabbed hold of the *Sweet Janet's* railing. Then he hauled himself up over the side and began to stalk towards Lisa.

CHAPTER 106:
CHAN GETS ONBOARD

Chan's directive was clear: get Gordon to tell him where Brewster's tapes were, and then kill her. But the *Sweet Janet's* captain had other plans.

"Who the fuck are you?" he roared. He snatched up a winch from the deck and held it like a weapon. "Get off our yacht!"

He swung the winch full force at Chan, who ducked. Still unbalanced from his attack, the man lurched forward as the yacht was tossed by a monstrous wave. He ended up pinning Chan against the handrail.

Chan looked into his face as they both struggled to regain their footing. "You bastard," he panted. "It's you. Robert Leadman. I know you from the newspaper articles, after the explosion. You should have died with your father and your sister."

"I'll kill you," Robert yelled, and tried to close his hands around Chan's throat.

The two of them fell to the deck, locked in a grapple as the ship sank lower and lower into the water. Chan managed to land a sharp blow to Robert's face, which sent him tumbling backwards as blood flowed like a spigot from his nose.

Chan stood up and spun towards Lisa. "Where are Brewster's tapes?" he demanded.

"We're sinking!" Lisa snapped. "If you want to know where the tapes are, untie me and I'll tell you."

Robert had scrambled back to his feet. With all his strength, he swung the boom directly at Chan. Chan managed to catch it before it hit him, but staggered backwards.

A third boat had drawn up alongside the *Sweet Janet*. As Robert turned to look at the newly arrived craft, Chan swung the boom back towards him as hard as he could. Robert never even saw it. The boom cracked into the side of his skull while his head was still turned. He was thrown backwards against the rail and then dropped heavily to the deck, unconscious.

Chan drew his gun from the concealed holster around his waist and levelled it at Lisa. He had hoped not to use this – guns attracted so much attention compared to his preferred methods – but time was running short. Soon the waves would be over the bow.

He stepped towards Lisa, who had paled at the sight of the gun. "Brian Palmer told us that Brewster's recordings were in box 142 in Double Bay. Our agents checked the box, and it's empty. So we know you have them. Tell me where they are. Now."

CHAPTER 107:
THE FINAL FIGHT

By the time the police boat reached the *Sweet Janet,* the deck was almost level with the sea. Ryan steadied himself on the front lip of the boat and then threw himself onto the side of the yacht. His jump was a little short and his legs splashed into the water, but he managed to grab hold of the railing and cling on.

With his back turned to the police boat, Chan hadn't noticed Ryan's arrival. As he clawed his way up over the handrail and onto the deck, Ryan heard Lisa say, "I don't know where the recordings are. David said he was going to pick them up. Maybe they're in the cabin. Untie me and I can look for them."

Chan hesitated for a few moments with his weapon still raised. Then, keeping the gun aimed at her head, Chan used his free hand to loosen the ropes holding Lisa to the railing.

Ryan inched closer to Chan, waiting for the right moment to knock the gun out of his hand. But before he had a chance…

BOOM.

A colossal explosion directly above them rocked the frame of the yacht. Ryan looked up and saw a boat plane suspended in the air, fully engulfed in a bubble of flame.

It wasn't suspended for long. The plane began to disintegrate, and blackened pieces of metal rained down on the bay. Several smoking chunks of debris landed on the deck of the *Sweet Janet,* fizzling as they hit the water.

Chan paused for a moment too long to watch the explosion. Ryan saw his opportunity and seized it. He gathered his strength and launched onto Chan's back. They both tumbled to the deck, and the gun clattered out of Chan's hand. It landed beyond his reach, not far from Lisa. Ryan swiftly delivered three bone-splitting blows to Chan's face.

The ropes around Lisa's wrists had only been slightly loosened, but it was enough. She managed to tear herself free just as Ryan clambered to his feet and landed a sharp kick to Chan's jaw. The moment she'd gotten herself untied, she flung herself after the gun. Chan saw her and scrambled towards it on his hands and knees, but she was faster. He sprawled out on the deck, his fingers closing on empty air as she swiped the gun out from under him.

She turned and hurled the gun as hard as she could, and it disappeared into the sea.

"Ryan, we're going to drown if we stay here," she shouted. "We've got to get out of here, *now.*"

Chan was still struggling to get to his feet as Ryan raced over to Lisa and took her hand. The stern of the yacht had sunk faster than the bow, tipping the boat's nose upward. As they climbed onto the prow, a massive black helicopter buzzed by and hovered briefly overhead. Ryan glanced at Chan and saw that he was watching the helicopter too, as if he was expecting a rescue. But the helicopter just turned away towards the south, roaring off at full speed until it became a speck in the distance.

Lisa tugged Ryan's hand. "Let's go!"

He nodded and steeled himself, and they both plunged into the water.

A moment later they came up, coughing and spluttering as they pushed the wet hair out of their eyes. They looked back and saw that the *Sweet Janet* was now all but underwater, with only her sails still visible above the waves. Chan had already disappeared.

They treaded water for a minute or two, watching the last vestiges of the yacht vanish into the sea. Then a race steward's boat appeared alongside them. The two crewmembers leaned over the side, reaching out so that Lisa and Ryan could grab their hands. They did, gratefully, and let themselves be hauled up out of the water.

EPILOGUE

Lisa Gordon was lounging in the sunshine in the picturesque garden of a bed and breakfast. She had arrived in New Zealand yesterday, and she was already quite enjoying her trip.

It was, technically, a working vacation. She had her laptop open on the bistro table in front of her. But this was one article she was more than happy to write: a detailed, in-depth feature of Prime Minister Johnson's crimes. Brewster's lawyers had released all of his recordings to her, honouring the late governor's request that she be the one to tell the truth about Johnson.

Three months had passed since the Pittwater Regatta. A few days after the race, some flotsam from Brewster's boat plane had washed up on the rocks around Barrenjoey Lighthouse. But that was as much as could be recovered. His body was never found.

It turned out that his will had been changed just a couple of weeks before his death. According to the new version, his estate, along with a large sum of money, went to his maid, a very grateful woman named Allison Carrington. The rest of his financial assets were split up among a number of charities and distant relatives.

The body of Robert Leadman eventually turned up on Palm Beach. The autopsy confirmed that the cause of death was drowning. The coroner, Dr Pearl Tabard, concluded that he'd likely never regained consciousness after the blow to the head from the mainsail boom.

DNA samples from Leadman proved a perfect match for the hair found at the crime scenes. That, along with all the evidence recovered from the boathouse on McCarrs Creek, was enough to close the case of the Pittwater killings.

The former Prime Minister was currently in jail awaiting trial. An interim administration had stepped in after Johnson was removed from office. Investigators expected that it would take months to sift through the depths of Johnson's corruption.

Meanwhile, Johnson's favoured freelancer, Chan Jianjun, had been picked up by MacDonald and his team on the day of the Regatta. He'd been sent to a high-security detention centre. To avoid drawing interference from any of Chan's criminal associates, his case had been kept tightly under wraps. Lisa had heard a rumour that he'd escaped custody and was once again at large. Personally, Lisa doubted it. But stranger things had happened.

"Hi, Lisa."

Lisa glanced up from her laptop to find Ryan standing beside her.

"Ryan!" She rose to her feet and gave him a long kiss. "There you are."

"Sorry I'm late. I just got off the phone with Ann. Have you heard the latest about the Leadman house?"

Lisa looked back at him with a touch of wariness. "No, why?"

"Sounds like someone finally bought the place. They're going to tear the whole thing down and build one of those million-dollar penthouses."

Lisa raised her brows and shrugged. "No accounting for taste, I guess."

He laughed. "Well, anyway, I thought you'd want to hear the latest. But onto more important things. There's someone I want to introduce you to." He turned and called over his shoulder, "Madison!"

The door of the bed and breakfast opened, and a young girl ran over to greet them. Ryan wrapped an arm around the girl's shoulder as she reached his side. "Lisa, this is my daughter, Madison."

Madison looked up at her with a bright smile. "It's nice to finally meet you, Lisa."

•

On the other side of the world, in an affluent suburb of Paris, Chan opened the door of his luxury apartment and greeted his guests.

"Welcome, gentlemen," he said to the two government officials standing before him. "I understand you have a need for my services. Please, come in. We have much to discuss."

The Lady of the Sea

The Great Big Deep Blue calls us once again down to her shores,
she breaks so many men's hearts and takes their souls.

She can be so calm and gentle, so alluring but in an instant, she can turn so
aggressive into a raging storm. The only remaining true lady of nature, that men
cannot control. At night her silky soft blanket glistening into the moonlight,
tantalising us with her soft white breaking waves.

Her sound so sweet she can send a baby to sleep, but she can bring so much
destruction, that we turn our backs on her once again.

Knowing too well that we will return like the great love of our life
we cannot resist, addicted to her love and the taste of her salty kiss.

By Kevin E M Clark

Printed in Great Britain
by Amazon